Reasonable Doubts

REASONABLE DOUBTS

DONALD DEWEY

ST. MARTIN'S PRESS · NEW YORK

Design by N.S.G. Design

Library of Congress Cataloging-in-Publication Data

Dewey, Donald (Donald J.)
        Reasonable doubts.
        p. ; cm.
        "A Thomas Dunne book."
        ISBN 0-312-06447-0
        I. Title.
    PS3554.E9293R43   1991   813'.54—dc20   91-19030

First Edition: October 1991

10 9 8 7 6 5 4 3 2 1

For Marta

Reasonable Doubts

The First Day

1

Hobie Morgan reached the top of the subway stairs, threw back his chest, and inhaled deeply. As he waited for his lungs to come back to him, he watched two speckled pigeons pecking back and forth on the sidewalk. He would have bet a buck they were the same two birds he had watched doing the same thing yesterday. He liked the idea that they were on the same schedule as he was.

His breath back, Hobie let go of the staircase banister and started down the block and a half to the courthouse. The morning was still dark gray in the sky and only the fancy luncheonette and corner candy store were open, but he kept an eye out for Ed Mercer or one of the other building custodians. He wouldn't have put it past them to get up a pool to see if one of them could beat him to work. They would have loved nothing better than to get on him about ruining his record.

He saw nobody.

Passing the candy store, he glanced through the door. The Indian was stacking cigarettes in the slots behind the counter. Even if he smoked, Hobie thought, he would have no sooner gotten his butts from the Indian than he would have gotten into a cab with a Russian Jew. Since when did an Indian smoke in his own country or a Russian Jew have enough scratch to buy a medallion in Moscow? It was only in the U.S. of A. that they did those things. Once in the U.S. of A., everybody became an expert in something new overnight. Why did anybody bother getting born in another place to start with?

Hobie shook his head and crossed over to the courthouse block. He felt better immediately, standing before the silence of the locked gates. In another hour or so, all the fancy dans with their attaché cases would be rushing through the gates and up the steps like ants descending on sugar. But that was still to come. Now the building had its dignity; no lawyers, no sleazeball junk dealers, no jackass guards. In the morning twilight the building was just clean stone, like an American History monument, like something you could put on a stamp and know your letter would arrive. It was the one and only hour of the day when the place seemed worth anything.

Hobie took one last look at the entrance, then moved on down the street and around to the employees door. He saw no sign of Mercer or anybody else. Once again he had beaten them all.

2

Charles Allison felt comfortable in the jury assembly room. The fact of the matter was, he had almost always felt comfortable in government offices that others decried as abusive, impersonal, or dehumanizing. Aside from some initial embarrassment when he had gone for his army physical and a brief irritation with an unemployment office clerk, both episodes decades in the past, Allison had never had much trouble getting along with the civil servant of the moment. Before they had banned smoking, he had even looked forward to the stench of chilled cigar smoke that seemed to have been an ingrained part of government buildings. It was an odor that had reminded him of his father's bedroom on St. Mark's Place in Brooklyn, all brown and dark except for the figure of the white owl on the cigar box on the night table next to the bed. It was the odor, Allison had decided a long time ago, of a man making do.

Now, camped in the next to last row in the big green barn of an assembly room, Allison himself had to make do with a misleading analysis of twentieth-century foreign involvement in Southeast Asia. He was sorry that he'd been so hasty about grabbing the book at the candy store across the street. The thing was so bad, he thought, that if he had still been teaching, he would have used it as a countertext, to show his class how history should *not* be presented. According to the book, it wasn't the Vietnamese who had repulsed the French in the fifties, it had been France's lackluster commitment and Eisenhower's refusal to lend an A-Bomb. According to the book, it wasn't the Vietnamese who had driven out the United States in the seventies, it had been the United States's divided commitment and coolness toward using nuclear arms. According to the book, nobody had won, the losers had just beaten themselves. Warming to the possibilities of extending this theory, Allison told himself that if he still had students, he would ask them to write an essay on their favorite sports team, explaining why the team hadn't won a single game all season but had only, in the best of cases, come upon adversaries determined to beat themselves. Yes, he decided, wiggling in his chair with a flash of excitement, he would have gotten back some fascinating papers from such an assignment. Then, in recognition of their efforts, he could have exempted the worthiest workers from an exam. . . .

Allison sighed, and too loudly, but he seemed to be the only one aware of it. The fat black woman in the row in front of him didn't drop her gaze from the high window on the other side of the room. The two men three and four seats to his left in his row continued with their newspaper reading, both of them working on the same entertainment page of the *Post* and both of them with glazed eyes that said they didn't care about what they were reading. It wasn't that he minded people knowing that he often thought about his teaching days, Allison told himself; after the number of years he had put in, he would have had to be a robot not to entertain a reverie once in a while. But what he had become more and more aware of recently was people's impatience with—almost fear of—another's dissatisfaction. A sigh meant something amiss, implied a yearning for something out of reach, and that left him open to criticism. Allison had run out of time for criticizing and being criticized.

He put the paperback into his jacket pocket and straightened up to get a better look at the company he was keeping. The last two juror candidates were handing in their notices to the gray-haired clerk behind the long table at the front of the room; another five or six candidates stood off to the side, where they were filling out the address forms they had neglected to fill out before presenting themselves to the woman. In all, Allison figured, there must have been two or three hundred people spread out across the room, most of them seated as he was in a kind of green plastic saucer. In contrast to those seated, who were either reading or carrying on monosyllabic conversations with their neighbors, a couple dozen standees in the back seemed loose and amused with each other, like a group that had been meeting regularly in the room for years. For a moment he was on the verge of getting up and going to join them, but then he saw two elderly black men, one in a Mets cap and the other in a beret, winking behind the back of a young Latino who had just said something to them. The Latino, a little high on whatever his wisecrack had been and now looking for more applause from somebody, had also apparently taken it for granted that it was easy to fit in. Allison decided to stay where he was.

The gray-haired clerk finished collecting all the completed notices and dropped them into a big bowl. Allison warned himself against being too impressed; the serious waiting, he recalled from his last jury experience, twenty years ago, was only now about to begin. It was possible that he would get no further than the assembly room for the next week or so, that they wouldn't call him even for preliminary elimination. Partly as a hedge against this, knowing that he might have to rely on every misleading page of the book in his pocket to see him through the day, he paid attention to the clerk's introductory remarks. He was surprised that she could still speak so civilly, even humorously. How many times had she responded to queries about commuting reimbursements and daily fees? He thought of how often he had been asked how a teacher could stand repeating himself over and over, year after year, without going mad. What the questioner had actually been asking, of course, was whether Allison regarded himself as a hack for going over the same ground repeatedly. But he had never let on that he had been wise to that accusation, as he supposed the clerk would never let on if someone threw a similar question at her. Her answer, he was positive, would have been the one he had always given: as long as the people were different, it was never the same ground. He smiled to think of her as a colleague.

When she had dealt with the last raised hand, the clerk turned to the bowl that contained all the notices. Allison bet with himself that his name would be the 136th to be picked.

The gray-haired woman reached into the bowl. "The first name I have," she said, "is Charles Allison."

Allison couldn't fathom the reason for that at all.

3

The police wagon swayed around a corner, rattling all its springs and making even Dunne bounce up and down at the end of the bench. Manuel Torres laughed. It was like he was living his dream last night. He smelled water and rubber, imagined the sirens, pictured a bunch of old Anglos stomping their feet into their boots and trying to throw their big coats around their shoulders without falling off the sides of the engine. They were on the way, on the way. Manuel Torres laughed. Keep burning, flames. Coming to get you.

"Like Coney Island, huh?"

Manuel stopped laughing. He didn't know who the loser in the white shirt and tie across from him was, he hadn't seen him around the rec room or any other place before. He knew the guy was a loser, though. Only losers wanted to be friendly *before* their trials, like they knew they were going to be around for a while.

"First day?" the guy insisted.

Manuel looked over to Dunne for help. The guard was still holding on to the chicken wire on the back window, trying to keep his balance, but he seemed to understand. "Keep the chatter for your lawyers," the guard told the shirt-and-tie. "No talking during the commute."

The loser immediately dropped his eyes to the floor of the wagon in embarrassment. Manuel was right: the guy was a pussycat. He'd probably never done anything but go to church and write a bad check. Didn't even have someone to post his bail.

"That goes for you too, Torres."

Manuel felt stung. Why had Dunne thrown that in? He hadn't said a word. The stupid prick didn't know who was on his side and who wasn't.

"Got a problem with that, Torres?"

"No problem, Dunne. No problem."

Manuel knew that was as good as it was going to get. The shirt-and-tie admired him for saying Dunne's name. Dunne himself looked away like he was satisfied. He had retrieved some ground with both of them. Even the driver congratulated him by taking another corner on three wheels. He shut his eyes and sank deeper into the vibrations of the wheel under him. After a couple of seconds he couldn't smell the wagon's aroma of stale puke or the loser's sweat anymore. He was back to the excitement of his dream again. When he was on nobody's side but his own, he smelled only clean water and rubber. He was going to the biggest fire of his life, Manuel thought. Twenty, thirty alarms. Nobody would ever forget it.

4

John King didn't know who to ask. He had never needed any serious advice before. Judges, arbiters, attorneys—he knew them all, had sometimes used first names with them, but not once in eleven years had he gone to any of them with a professional question in which he had a personal stake.

Now though, as he reached into his locker for the cloth covering his service weapon, King needed a name. He was past telling himself that he was making up the problem, that it was just a coincidence, that the bank was perfectly within its rights, that he didn't have a foot to stand on. He was past all the excuses he had been letting distract him. He needed advice and he needed it today. Coming to work this morning had been the last straw.

King unwrapped his weapon and slipped it into his holster. Normally he despised even the feel of the damn thing and immediately buckled it over like some kind of growth on his hip best not seen. But now he lingered over the grip, felt a trickling thrill as he pictured himself fast-drawing and shooting down the two jerks he had passed outside the bank. The older one's big white teeth cracked and crumbled all over the sidewalk. The tall one with the pencil mustache looked down, shocked to discover a big hole in his chest, then crashed through the bank window to his death. The bank alarm went off. All the advertising posters in the window tumbled down. Two of them rubbed up against each other like sticks, causing enough friction to cause a fire. The whole bank started to burn. Before the fire engines arrived, the bank was reduced to a smoking ruin. There was nothing left to save. He felt better.

No, he didn't.

John King tossed the oily rag back in the locker and buckled his holster. He had an urge to slam the locker door closed, decided it would be an idiotic thing to do, and then slammed it as hard as he could anyway. He was disappointed again: although the lock caught, the bang wasn't nearly as loud as the clatter he had produced at least once a day with his high school locker. Nothing was the same as it had been. The changers had even gotten their hands on the old tin lockers. The fact that he couldn't hold on to his own name, that banks thought it was theirs to use however they decided, was just par for the course.

He still needed a lawyer.

Going to the elevator, King wondered whether his best bet was one of the public defenders or one of the Gold Row boys from Westchester or Long Island. The problem with PDs like Alvarez and Cunningham was that they were stiffer about initial consultation fees, counted pennies like their survival depended on it. The Gold Rowers like Steinwitz and Pacella, on the other hand, might bankrupt a client over the long haul, but they were softer on initial consultations. Maybe the smart thing to do, King thought, was to get an opinion from somebody like Steinwitz to be sure there was a case to begin with, and then if there was, to turn everything over to a PD. Even if he couldn't get Steinwitz to volunteer an opinion for old times' sake, why couldn't he get away with some vague promise to pay the thief when his ship came in?

King pressed the button for the elevator. He didn't believe it possible, as Edith contended, that another person would have been flattered by what the bank had done. How could anyone be flattered by having his name stolen in the interests of pushing a bank card? He hadn't been flattered that first morning when he had passed the enlarged card in the bank window and he hadn't been flattered any morning or afternoon passing it since then. If some bank wanted to promote a cash machine card with the name JOHN KING, it was either going to get John King's permission to do it or it was going to pay John King for the privilege. Maybe then, as the two laughing jerks had been cracking this morning in front of the bank, it wouldn't matter if he couldn't "squeeze the blowup into a wallet."

Hobie was on the elevator. The old black gave his usual grunt over having to pick up a court officer in the basement. "Must be new

8

around here," he said. "Staircase over there, half a flight up to the lobby."

King got into the car without saying anything; he wasn't in the mood for the spook's grouches this morning.

"They're callin' the names now," Hobie said. "Guess that's why you're in such a hurry, huh?"

King stared ahead as Hobie rattled the elevator gate closed. He wouldn't mind blasting the old coot through the bank window while he was at it.

5

Allison had been in similar courtrooms a hundred times before—at the movies, on television, in mystery novels. At first glance it was exactly the same as it had looked in *The Defenders, Perry Mason, Anatomy of a Murder, Slaughter on Tenth Avenue,* and a zillion other TV shows and movies—the same burnished wood walls, tables, chairs, and judge's bench. But what the movies hadn't at all prepared him for was the space. In height, width, and depth, the room was monstrous, closer to a chamber in a European palace than in a New York office building. He wondered whether so much size hadn't been a calculation, a constant physical reminder to the judge, jury, defense, and prosecution that space was the real issue up for debate, specifically, how much of it was the accused going to be allowed to have over the next few years?

Allison looked over at the defense table where a young Latino, his hands in his pants pockets, was slouching in a chair. He had a full, neatly combed beard and wore a blue cardigan and pressed white chinos. He seemed to be watching his lawyer, who was seated to his left, going through a dossier, but didn't blink when the woman flipped over a page. Allison decided that the kid—he couldn't have been more than twenty-one—was staring at a stain on the surface of the defense table. He also decided that the chinos and the sweater on the brisk morning were not a good sign, that the absence of a jacket suggested that the kid had arrived at the courthouse from the city jail rather than from home. Why? Because he was poor and couldn't afford bail? Or because some criminal record had made it too risky to release him on bail?

Allison began to feel queasy about being a juror.

It was hard to tell if he had company. Behind the pretext of smoothing a lump in the shoulder of his jacket, he turned around in his seat to get a glimpse of the juror candidates behind him. Only a young, pallid woman with tiers of colored beads around her neck returned his glance. Everyone else—an elderly Italian, two middle-aged housewives, a pimpled young man, a large blond in his forties who looked like a basketball player gone to seed—all either stared off at the front of the room or studied their nails. He had seen identical expressions every time he had entered a classroom at Sterling High with an exam under his arm.

"First time you been called?"

The man next to him had his eyes locked on the wall behind the judge's bench. "Yes and no," Allison said. "I was called a good many years ago but never got out of the assembly room."

The man nodded. He smelled of liniment and had the kind of stiff jaw that seemed proud of its immobility. "Spic," he muttered.

"Excuse me?"

The man nodded over to the defense table. "Spic," he said tightly. "Hope I get picked. Get one animal off the street anyway."

Allison groaned to himself. Suddenly he had a responsibility: if the defense somehow failed to eliminate the redneck, it would be up to him to inform the judge of the man's remark. He hadn't bargained on getting so deeply involved so fast.

"You know what I mean?"

Allison ignored the question. He tried to assure himself that the defense lawyer looked like someone who knew what she was doing. Like her client, she was a Hispanic. A large woman with straight black hair cut short. A somber expression. Not a ring or a bracelet anywhere. She was perfect, he told himself; he would leave the redneck to her.

"All rise! Superior Court of New York now in session. Judge Abraham Raymond presiding."

Allison stood up before the redneck could. He hadn't ex-

10

pected to see the judge hobbling up to his bench on a single crutch. He couldn't recall that in any old movie.

6

King pretended not to notice the way Barbarella was forking at the skin under his eyes with two fingers. He could make up his own mind about how many jurors would get through without help from a douche like Tony Barbarella. The crew in front of him wasn't even an especially hard one to read, and he marked four, not the two Barbarella indicated with his mongoloid hand signals, for survival.

King was sure of it. First there was the scrawny guy with the pus pimples all over his face; the public defender, Alvarez, liked the fact that he was some kind of writer—and probably a liberal—and the prosecutor, Foy, liked the fact that the guy had once been mugged. Then there was the Johnny Carson twin, the maintenance manager from the Port Authority; he would make it because he supervised twenty-five or thirty people, meaning that he was used to making decisions and probably dealt with minorities every day of the week. Number three was the pale nurse with the dime store's worth of beads around her neck; she had to make it because she looked and sounded like somebody who had dedicated her life to not being bulldozed by anybody for anything. And number four was the gloomy-looking woman who rented videos; Foy would figure she was sensible and Alvarez would hope that she had taken the time to see a couple of pictures where the defendant who has all the odds stacked against him still manages to win out in the last reel. All solids, King told himself, but the douche Barbarella probably saw only the writer and the Port Authority guy.

He forgot about Tony Barbarella and glanced over at Manuel Torres. He had to laugh at the idea of Manuel Torres getting off in the last reel. The best the punk could expect from one of the gloomy woman's videotapes was to have it wound around his neck—and

11

he, John King, would have been happy to do the winding. It wasn't just that Torres was up for his third or fourth burglary felony; what really bothered him was that, even caught red-handed this last time, Torres had turned down a deal from Foy's office and had insisted on a full-dress trial, gambling that a seven-to-fifteen conviction wouldn't be all that much worse than a four-to-seven compromise for a chance of an acquittal. It was all a game to the bastard, a little-to-lose shot in the dark. To hell with the fact that he had been nabbed at the scene, to hell with the fact that time and money had to be spent trying him, to hell with the fact that more urgent cases had to be put off because of him. Manuel Torres had decided to roll the dice, and the city of New York had to get down on its knees to cover the bet.

King shook his head at the unfairness of it all. Plea bargaining was bad enough, he thought, but sometimes the alternative could be worse. What was at stake in a Manuel Torres trial was the immortal question of whether someone had the right to go into a stranger's house and make off with whatever he put his hands on; what would have been in the pot for a John King suit, on the other hand, was the question of whether a bank had the right to break into someone's privacy and make off with his name. Even a douche like Tony Barbarella had to figure out *that* wasn't fair.

King made a decision: as soon as Raymond dismissed the jurors, he was going to corner Alvarez in the hall and explain his problem. She might have been a PD on the lookout for an initial consultation fee, but she was also a woman who owed him. He recalled it now so vividly that he got warm in the stomach. It had been two years ago in the parking lot outside the courthouse. The two of them had been walking to their cars in the late afternoon, he dawdling a few yards behind so he could watch her big, active ass moving up and down inside her blue suede skirt. She had been so busy reading a circular that she hadn't noticed the two black kids coming at her from across the street with rolled-up newspapers in their hands. By the time she had looked up, it had been too late: James and Larry Winters seemed to have started their swings eight or nine feet away from her, the blows landing on Alvarez's back and shoulders as the end of lunging follow-throughs. He had hesitated only long enough to take in that the younger boy, Larry, was sobbing, yelling that Alvarez had failed his father by losing his case, and that Alvarez, while instinctively covering her head with her

12

arms and shoulder bag, remained absolutely quiet, as though she had somehow anticipated the attack and had rehearsed her reaction to it. It had been such a peculiar reaction that, even as he had charged directly at James Winters, King had had to shake off the sensation that he was an intruder, that he was about to ruin some prearranged scene. But shake it off he had, grabbing James Winters by the neck and swinging the skinny, jelly body around so hard that the kid had slipped from his grasp again, lurching back against his brother so that both of them had ended up in a tangle of scuffed sneakers and old jeans on the parking lot gravel. The younger kid had clung to his newspaper all the way down, but James Winters had let go of his, unfurling some *Newsday* headline about politicians on the take.

King squirmed in his seat and then coughed to cover his movement. He saw that the cold-eyed man with the iron jaw in the front row of the jury box disapproved of him for some reason. King had marked down the guy as a loser when his name—Conboy? Conroy?—had been called and he had marched, all straight back and solemn as a priest, from the spectator seats to the jury box. Every single inch of him said that he didn't *habla español* and didn't think much of anybody who did. If he knew Alvarez, she wasn't even going to bother to put a question to the donkey.

And John King *did* know Elena Alvarez. Remembering the *Newsday* front page about the politicians on the take so clearly after two years was the least of it. He could still get the beginnings of an erection thinking about how Alvarez had grabbed his arm and moved between him and the Winters brothers. "It's all right, it's all right, Officer," she had said, finally opening her mouth and looking down at the kids as if they had needed the reassurance more than she had. "Let me take care of this." And it was then that he had made his big mistake: instead of standing quietly with her and enjoying the feel of her hand on his arm, he had made some crack about how she hadn't been handling things until he had come along, breaking contact with her to reach down and pull James Winters to his feet. Not once since that moment had he felt her touch again.

Foy finally threw the jury box the last of his weasel smiles and returned to his seat at the prosecution table. Alvarez got to her feet slowly, playing with her pencil as usual. As she approached the jury box, King boiled once again at the memory of that brief con-

13

nection with her big body. Who was to say that, once they got talking about his legal problem, they couldn't also talk about other things? Neither of the Winters kids had been carrying that day in the parking lot, but he hadn't known that when he had gone to her rescue. She owed him. Any jury in the country would have said so. The scrawny writer with the pimples would have said so. The nurse with the beads would have said so. The silver-haired guy sitting in the spectator seats and waiting his turn to be called for a screening, that guy would have said so too.

The only thing King wasn't sure about was why the silver-haired guy was smiling at him.

7

For the third straight time Allison answered yes to the prosecutor— and for the third straight time he was surprised by his decisiveness. When had he become so sure? It hadn't been when he had received the jury duty notice and had entertained defiant plans to throw it away. It hadn't been at Munson's office when the doctor had sat a sleeve's touch away from the notepad he could use to give Allison the best of all medical excuses for getting out of service. Even coming over on the bus this morning he had hardly been enthusiastic about staring at some absolute stranger for a week or more, listening to, at the very least, an account of his compromising doings, and then proclaiming some binding verdict. Allison didn't put much stock in binding verdicts: sometimes they had a way of causing students who might be hiding grave personal problems to fail and allowing others who might have cheated their way through to pass. And yet here he was now, suddenly very clear about wanting to answer the questions of the assistant district attorney in some right way—*their* way—so he wouldn't be dismissed by the judge and shunted back downstairs to the assembly room to await another dip in the fishbowl.

"You wouldn't have any trouble with that, would you, Mr. Allison?"

"No, I wouldn't."

The prosecutor Foy smiled. At the defense table the Alvarez woman wrote down something on her yellow pad. "And would you, Mr. Allison, have any difficulty making a decision that some might consider . . . "

As he answered again, Allison caught a glimpse of the big, mustached guard sitting near the side door. In his mid thirties, six three or six four, easily two hundred fifty pounds, an ample part of which bulged out over his belt buckle and holster, the man identified by his name tag as KING overflowed his chair like some kind of organic thing that hadn't finished growing. It was as though the guard had hardly begun to fill up the courtroom space around him and would eventually make everything become more KING.

Allison grinned nervously, timing it perfectly to some witticism of Foy's. The fact was, he realized, his decisiveness about serving on the jury had coincided with his first look at King. The guard was frighteningly indifferent in his posture; whatever took place during the trial, his expression announced, didn't matter in the least. Courtroom procedure, judges and lawyers, seating the jury—all of it was irrelevant, might as well not even be happening, for as soon as the court had been adjourned for the day, he, the one called KING, he with his dead eyes was going to turn to the defendant Manuel Torres and say *now you belong to me again.*

Allison had rarely felt so self-righteous, and with so little to go on. Even if his fancifulness contained some truth, what could he have done about it? He couldn't have gone to the judge about the guard, as he would have had to go to Raymond if the redneck James Conboy hadn't been dismissed immediately by the defense attorney. Even serving on the jury wouldn't prevent King from taking Torres into custody at the end of each day. Sometimes, Allison thought, he was such a feeble excuse for a fifty-six-year-old man.

"Thank you, Mr. Allison," Foy said.

"No questions," Alvarez seconded immediately.

And sometimes, Allison thought, he was just biding his time until his old strength returned to him. Which was why he wasn't going to let King dismiss him as meaningless and why he felt immediately more confident, giving the guard a smile every time their eyes crossed.

15

8

Elena Alvarez had her fourteen jurors and knew that she could have given the list to Foy and won his ready agreement. But she couldn't do it, not without further fueling Foy's barely contained show of tolerance about the trial. Especially in front of a judge like Abe Raymond, she didn't need any more grand gestures from Foy.

Sitting now in front of Raymond's desk and pretending to check her list of names with the same scrupulousness that Foy, a few feet away, was feigning over his, Elena had to remind herself that the key to her whole defense might turn out to be an arthritic hipbone, that as long as she could prevent Foy from convincing Raymond that they were all wasting their time and that the judge was being a superhero by limping on his crutch to the bench, she might win in law what she was certainly going to lose in evidence. The trick, she told herself, was in somehow simultaneously letting Raymond know that she sympathized with him in his affliction but that she also assumed he was too much the professional to allow pain to influence his judgment.

"Sometime before midnight, maybe?"

Foy instantly came up with a smile. Elena hesitated deliberately before responding. Raymond eyed the two of them from behind a veil of smoke; he was amused. "Who's gonna cut the crap first?"

Elena laughed, a little too heartily. "Innocent until demonstrated guilty is the way it goes, I think."

Raymond nodded and shifted his glance to Foy. Even that slight, almost infinitesimal move seemed to cause pain in the leg he had propped up on a chair behind his desk. "Counselor?"

"Our so-called 'domestic engineer' from Corona," Foy said. "I think we can do without her."

Raymond grunted a laugh, taking another drag on his cigarette.

"Too independent for you, Bernie?" Alvarez teased.

"Too behind in her magazine reading, I'd say," Raymond put in. "Anyone else?"

"The real estate agent," Foy said.

Elena was surprised, and realized too late that she looked it. Bernie Foy's grin told her that she had stumbled into his trap. "I just figured I would save Elena one of her challenges," he said smoothly. "I won't be using half her number, so I can afford the agent."

She looked back at Raymond; she imagined a huge package lying between them on the desk, and scrawled all over the package were the words WASTING TIME. "If the assistant district attorney has no more challenges of his own to make, maybe we're at the end," she said, hearing both her stiffness and her failed attempt to relax it.

"No more," Foy said promptly.

Raymond tilted his head as though he couldn't believe his luck. "Two in the first round and twelve in the second?" he asked, reaching out for the lists of names. "You're making an old man happy, lady and gentleman. What accounts for so much harmony?"

"We just agree that we should get on with it," Foy said.

Raymond perused the two lists. "You don't say."

Elena seemed to be talking even before the thought had fully formed in her mind. "I believe the other reason, Your Honor, is that neither of us wants to aggravate you too much in your condition."

Raymond suspended his cigarette in front of his mouth for a long moment before finally recovering his growl. "As long as we've admitted that much, let's clear some more air in here," he said. "I think this is a farce. Either the defense is working with a certifiably stupid client or the prosecution has a great deal of ambiguous evidence. Be that as it may, we're all here for the duration. What I would remind both of you, however, is that I don't savor approximate law. I'm not going to tolerate Morse code to the jury about the defendant's past record, and I'm not going to listen to the defendant being compared to Captain Dreyfus. Good law, hard evidence, all possible speed. The two of you manage that, and you won't have to worry about my hip or protracting my agony. Understood?"

It amounted more to a win than a loss, and Elena was glad to take it out to the courtroom with her. There hadn't been too many other victories on the day. From the moment that she had stopped off in her office to learn that Earl Winters, one of her first B&E clients two years ago, had hanged himself in his Attica cell, she had been operating on automatic pilot. Still numbly asking herself what she thought she'd accomplished with calls to the prison doctor and the prosecutor's office, she had arrived at the courthouse to discover that Manuel Torres's father hadn't brought a suit or sports jacket for his son as she asked but only a cardigan. To top it off, Santiago Torres had then insisted on settling his despondent presence in the courtroom during jury selection, practically trumpeting to one and all that he was beyond being amazed by accusations leveled against Manuel. Grouping her jury notes together now, Elena really did sympathize with Raymond: she didn't want to be where she was either.

She was grateful that Raymond made short work of explaining to the jurors which of them had made the final cut and what would be expected of them the following morning. She might have left her headache in the building altogether, she thought, if, after adjournment, she hadn't had to linger to fill in Manuel Torres. He seemed barely aware of what she was saying to him, needing her abrupt silences to cue him when to nod or shake his head. Glancing past him to Santiago Torres, still sitting alone in his leather jacket in the third row of spectator seats, Elena had to wonder again whether she had made a mistake in not pressing for a psychiatric workup. There was something just too umbilical between the gloom in the cardigan and the gloom in the leather jacket. But there was nothing she could do about that now, she scolded herself; in rejecting all deals with Foy, Manuel Torres had known he was getting an overworked lawyer, and she had known she was getting a client interested only in playing out the string.

Her headache seemed to open on two new fronts as she hurried out of the courtroom. The fat court officer, King, was dismissing the jurors in the corridor. As usual, he threw her one of his puppy dog looks. He seemed on the verge of saying something to her when one of the jurors distracted him with a question. She silently thanked the juror and kept going.

18

In the parking lot she was sorry that she hadn't taken a taxi from the office. The lot seemed like an unnecessary reminder of Earl Winters. As she pulled out of her space and rolled up to the exit, she felt a tremor at the memory of how the two Winters boys had attacked her after the trial two years ago. Sitting behind the wheel, waiting for a bus to get out of her way, she could have cried all over again for them. Thanks to the asshole guard King, who had pulled them off her as if he had been St. George slaying the Dragon, the boys could have ended up in almost as much trouble as their father had been in. She could still see the brick lying on the ground a foot away from where James Winters had been knocked down by King. Just one throw, and James Winters would have had an entirely different life. How could it all be so precarious?

Elena pushed open the glove compartment, searching for aspirin. She found what she had expected to find: nothing.

She wanted to scream.

The bus finally got out of her way.

9

As usual, Sofia was waiting for Allison right inside the door. Key in one hand and groceries in the other, he slid his loafer carefully under the cat's stomach and, anticipating her forward bound, quickly managed one of his most satisfying lifts to get her out of harm's way.

In the kitchen he told Sofia and Sofia's erect tail about how to pick a jury. She was more interested in the Amore cans he pulled out of the grocery bag and ignored him altogether once he had opened a Seafood Supreme and emptied it into her bowl next to the stove. Watching the black animal chomp into her food, Allison felt a sudden pang for the ten years that had elapsed since he had taken her home from the pet shop. He hadn't even wanted her as a cat, but merely as a thing that would have helped him forget having to pick Vienna's dead carcass out of the bathtub the day before. In a

19

way, he thought now, he had never been there for the kitten Sofia that had once pounced after floating threads and swatted at his pants leg. Allison hoped that Sofia didn't know that.

He took the mail out of the grocery bag. There was the usual statement from the bank celebrating numbers that he had never felt part of; he put it aside. The last people to find out that he was no longer a teacher, it seemed, were the publishers and professional bodies that he had been so keen to forget; he tossed all their invitations into the garbage. The only telephone message on the machine in the study was from his brother. He knew what that was about: it was time for their Other Holiday—the Saturday or Sunday midway between Christmases that Jerry and Peggy insisted he come out to Long Island for drinks, dinner, and more drinks. Sometimes it seemed like the Other Holiday had grown into more of a ritual than Christmas, since it sprang from no calendar obligation but from the personally initiated idea that brothers get together to ask how each other was. Allison didn't like the prospect of having to be even more evasive than usual this year.

He opened the study window to air out some of the odors from Sofia's box, letting in those of the cats that had taken over the back yard. The late afternoon hung over the warren of fences and splintered trees as heavily as the quilts on Mrs. Ellenman's clothesline next door. It had always been the worst time of day to look out the window—an hour of tormenting metamorphosis when he knew he couldn't retrieve the sunlight and dreaded that he had already somehow squandered the evening as well. Would he have felt different in another apartment? Allison had no taste for such conjecture at this point. He had never planned to spend every one of his fifty-six years in the same apartment, but now that he had he wasn't about to dwell on might-have-beens.

Allison changed into his corduroys and slippers, poured himself a sherry, and set to work. Since he had broken off the night before at 1968, he fished around in his bookcase for the 1969 register, found it squeezed between 1977 and 1978 for some reason, and brought it over to his desk. At the sight of ACKER DAVID, he pictured the class. It had been a relatively inconspicuous group: about equally divided between the sexes, twenty-five or so altogether, no geniuses. The bunching to the back of the room had been the varsity basketball team—Constantino, DeSapio, Magruder—the loner under his nose in the front had been Diane Ventura. Allison remem-

20

bered her as having big breasts and a penchant for black sweaters and tartan skirts. She had worn contacts until a boyfriend, he couldn't remember who, had persuaded her that glasses gave her broad face more of an edge. He had liked her; her politeness had never been forced or with an ulterior purpose.

But that wasn't enough to qualify her.

Allison found his candidate in Paul Harper. Harper had once corrected his pronunciation of the name of the French statesman Clemenceau, and had done so even though he had been majoring in German rather than French. Allison remembered the boy as brash, enamored of his image as the class provocateur. Paul Harper hadn't been quite as well-read as he wanted to appear, but neither had he read just newspapers.

He found three Paul Harpers in Queens, three in Manhattan, and two in both Brooklyn and the Bronx. None of the three in Queens answered. The first one in Manhattan no longer lived at the listed number, the second one was a dentist. The third sounded familiar, even allowing for all the years.

"Paul Harper who went to Sterling High?"

"Yes?"

"This is Charles Allison. You were once in my class."

"Mr. Allison??"

It was the moment that Allison prized the most—and also feared the most. On the one hand, he felt like a wizard who had flashed through barriers of time and space to catch up with people who had assumed he had been deposited in their pasts; on the other, once he had identified himself, he felt the marvel receding, felt himself slipping instantly into the routine of the person on the other end of the line. "I'm having a little party on the fourteenth of next month, Paul," he said quickly. "Sort of an informal reunion, but without the songs and speeches. I'd like to send you an invitation."

The surprise was still there, but not much else. "Well, thanks. But I don't really go in for that kind—"

"Exactly why I thought of you, Paul. You have my promise there will be no professional reunion types invited."

Harper laughed, dryly but spontaneously. He might have been a timid philosopher, he might have been a mass murderer; he didn't volunteer the information one way or the other. The important thing was that, leery as he sounded, Paul Harper would almost certainly be coming on the fourteenth.

Allison put down the telephone and decided against a backup for 1969. In 1969, he mused, his mother had still been alive, Vienna had been little more than a kitten, and astronauts had walked on the moon. All of it had seemed so natural, so much part of what had happened the day before. Paul Harper, on the other hand, had mostly been an irritant; bright, but still an irritant. Allison had never counted on leaving his money to Paul Harper.

He sipped his sherry, closed the 1969 register, and stood up and went over to the bookcase in search of 1970.

The Second Day

1

John King could count on Edith's rituals. At exactly 6:45 by the clock radio she threw off the bedcovers, got up, and tramped into the bathroom. No more than seven or eight minutes later she was back, finishing off some quick strokes to her hair with her blue brush and wearing the underwear she had left on the toilet tank the night before. As soon as she threw on a dress or skirt and sweater, she tapped him on the leg, told him it was seven o'clock, and went off to buy bagels and the *News* from the Korean's all-purpose grocery across the street. When she got back, she boiled just enough water for two cups of instant coffee, laid out plates, butter, and jelly on the table, and rewound the tape in the VCR to see the programs she had taped during the night. By the time King had finished dressing and appeared in the dining room alcove, Edith had filled the coffee cups, listened to Johnny Carson's opening monologue, given her hair a more elaborate stroking with the brush, glimpsed at the page-3 stories in the *News,* and finished buttering her first bagel.

It was a routine that, after thirteen years, comforted King, gave him some grip on the rest of the day. Its only drawback, he was reminded once more this morning, was that Edith also insisted on talking.

"I don't see what the big secret is. You're not on the jury."

"I'm not supposed to talk about it, Edith, that's all."

"What sense does that make?"

"It's the law, that's what sense."

King wolfed down half the top part of his bagel. It was too mealy and didn't have the burned ends that he liked, but he wasn't going to complain about that again. Even he was tired of listening to himself go on about how Koreans didn't know how to make bagels. Some things changed by the changers just had to be accepted.

"Then you might as well never talk about anything."

"What?"

Edith gave him one of her best offended shrugs; they always bothered him more when she was wearing a sundress. "You're always going to be on some case or other," she said. "We might as well not talk about your job at all."

He thought about correcting her, about telling her that it was merely J duty that was sensitive, but just went on chewing. If she was going to give him a reason for not having to talk, he was going to make the most of it.

"Well, isn't that true?"

"What's that?"

She was on the verge of sulking when the TV distracted her. It was some kind of bulletin about the Japanese yen. "Oh, that's terrible," she said.

"It's not a bulletin anymore, Edith."

She admitted she was watching a tape, but still seemed to have some doubt. "It was only a few hours ago. It must still be news."

"Yeah, probably. When I finish here, I'll go check how many yen we've got stashed in the bank."

As soon as he said it, King felt a pressure in his chest. It squeezed him so suddenly that he didn't care if Edith saw him putting aside his bagel and taking a deep breath. Until he got Elena Alvarez to help him with his lawsuit, he was just going to have to stop mentioning banks.

"John?"

"Goddamn bagels. Don't make 'em thin and burny like they should."

Edith said nothing, just stared at him across the table with some dark concern. King hated it when she did that. He had told her a million times that she could be a lot more help to him by *not* looking worried, by not making *him* worry about her reaction on top of everything else.

"Maybe we should stick to muffins in the morning," she said.

"The Koreans have probably screwed them up, too."

Edith dropped her big, sad eyes to her plate and sighed like someone who had had her last and best offer rejected. He suddenly wanted to reach across the table and reassure her, tell her that it wasn't her fault, that he just couldn't help being nervous when people started worrying about him.

The feeling passed immediately. In spades.

"I was talking to Mother last night. She agrees with me that you've let this bank card thing upset you for no reason. She says you should be glad about it, there might even be a way for us to make some money off it."

King felt another squeeze; now even if he won a suit with Alvarez, Edith was going to give the credit to Grace Chandler for having thought of it first.

"Mother says you should write a letter to the *News*. They'd print one of those pictures of you standing outside the bank. I'm sure they'd pay you something for it. I could call today and ask."

"Edith—"

"Mother says everybody's entitled to be famous for a day and this might be your day."

"Good. When's hers?"

"Oh, I told you a hundred times. . . ."

King couldn't believe his own stupidity. Once again it was the story of Grace Chandler being interviewed by the channel 5 news, telling the world how Billy Carter should have been arrested for being friends with Khadafy, and this time he was the one who'd prompted her to tell it. He grabbed the *News* and opened it.

25

"Seems so long ago, but I don't think Mother will ever get over it. . . ."

King couldn't believe his eyes. The headline on page 5 read CONVICT DEAD IN CELL; the caption identified Earl Winters. He read the story quickly, bewilderedly, unwilling to believe that there could be something in the paper having to do with him so personally. Here he was trying to get a favor out of Alvarez, here was Alvarez trying to pretend all these months that she didn't know him, here was the suicide Earl Winters—and somewhere out there were the two Winters kids, sure to be planning how to get even with Elena Alvarez for being responsible for their father's hanging. Elena Alvarez not only owed him, she damn well *needed* him.

"Laugh if you want, John, but a lot of people think this Khadafy ought to be assassinated. Mother was the first to say it on television."

"Yeah, I guess she was." He put aside the paper. He was too excited to eat. He wanted to get down to the courthouse as fast as he could.

"But you'll be famished," Edith said, following him into the bedroom as he grabbed his wallet and car keys off the bureau. "It's so early."

"Forgot something I had to do." He kissed her on the lips. He had meant it for getting her out of the way, but she kissed him back and held him for a second extra.

She smiled. "Well, if we're going to start changing routines."

King kissed her again on the forehead, scooped his jacket off the foot of the bed, and hurried out. He hoped Alvarez hadn't already gone into the protective custody she was going to need.

2

"You been thinkin'? What we talked about?"

"We talk about somethin' else, Manuel."

26

"We talk about that."

"You're crazy. What's the matter with you? The guards hear you."

"Forget them. They're too far away."

"You're the expert, huh? Think they don't have microphones in a place like this?"

"They have shit. I know."

"Yeah, you know."

"Alvarez knows, then. Okay? She told me they can't bug this place."

"She say that?"

"Yeah, the Madonna said it."

"She's tryin' to help you."

"You can do more."

"You listen to her. She's smart."

"Yeah, like you'd listen to her."

"I don't need any Mrs. Alvarez. That's the difference, Manuel. Sixty-one years, I never need any Mrs. Alvarez."

"Great. But I do. That what you want to hear? Okay, I need her. But I also need you."

"Not for what you ask."

"It's what I need!"

"To get yourself killed? That's what you need?"

"I don't get killed."

"Right. Because I don't help you be crazy."

"You mean you don't want dirty hands."

"I don't help kill my own son."

"Fast."

"What?"

"You don't help kill your own son fast. Slow, that's okay. You'd be able to live with it."

"Where do you get these demons?"

"My mistake."

"Right. That's what it is."

"No—my mistake in tellin' you the truth. I should've told you it was for somebody in my cell. But no, I gotta come right out and ask you."

"Mrs. Alvarez is right. There's somethin' wrong in your head, Manuel."

27

"I be out of your way. Ever think of that?"

"What are you sayin'?"

"The worst that can happen, I be out of your way. No more calls from the precinct. No more runnin' down here in the morning. The worst that can happen, you have a funeral, you have a cry, it's over. You go on runnin' a hundred errands for Victor. You stop worryin' about me."

"You should not say these things."

"Because they might happen?"

"You taunt them, they could."

"You really believe this superstitious shit, don't you?"

"I've seen more than you have."

"The worst thing that happens, I give you new things to do. Instead of hangin' around Victor's all day drinkin' coffee and playin' taca-taca, you can come to the funeral. Even Victor would understand that. He might even throw in a subway token and some flowers."

"You're no good, Manuel."

"I do it anyway. With or without your help."

"Yeah?"

"If I have to, I run at the cops with my head down."

"And they knock you on your ass."

"I do it over and over until they kill me or I'm out."

"They don't give you that chance. They put you in a strait-jacket. They're not stupid."

"You admire them so much, huh?"

"You're talkin' crazy."

"I don't sit there all those years, old man. They don't put me away like an animal."

"*Now* you think of that."

"Even if I have to kill myself. Like the one in the paper today."

"You don't have the courage."

"Courage!"

"You think it's not important?"

"That is what you call courage? Hangin' yourself?"

"It is late. They will be callin' you to get ready."

"I'm talkin' about something important, old man. I'm talkin' about givin' myself a chance to live."

"To get killed."

"The chance, old man! Not a guarantee, the chance! You don't understand, do you? You've been takin' handouts so long you don't know what's up and what's down anymore. The pigs are great because they can bust your head and put you in a straitjacket. That guy in Attica's great because he hanged himself. Alvarez is great because she's so smart. Everybody's great except me. And I'm offerin' you the chance to stop worryin' about me."

"By killin' you?"

"By not lettin' others kill me!"

"You make no sense, Manuel. Now, I have to go over to the courtroom. You just do what Alvarez tells you."

"I'm tellin' you, old man, I'll kill her, too. Just to show you she's no fuckin' Madonna."

"She's your lawyer. Listen to her. You can't afford anybody else."

3

Elena slipped her bank card into the cash machine slot. She had never used this particular branch before and decided to give it her goodwill examination by making her requests in Spanish. The instructions came back at once, flashing out at her correctly, exactly as at the branch back in her own neighborhood, not a single grammatical mistake or lazy Englishism in the procedure. She was disappointed. She wasn't in the mood for having the same central computer service all of the bank's branches; what she was in the mood for was a slight that would cast her as an unsullied victim up against Powerful Social Forces.

She removed the hundred dollars in twenties from the metal chamber and folded the money into her pocket as she stepped away down the boulevard. Too late, she realized how careless she was being; if not careless, whatever not careful was. How unlike her to go marching up to a sidewalk machine and to wave her money around without the slightest regard for whoever might have been hovering nearby for a snatch-and-run job! That there was in fact nobody relieved her without reassuring her. She had been a jangle of stupidity all night and all morning, thinking about Earl Winters and Manuel Torres and Santiago Torres, and even with a pill, she hadn't managed more than three hours of sleep. If it hadn't been for Raymond's arthritis and the agreement to move things along as fast as possible, she might have asked for the day off altogether.

Entering the court building, she thought again of the opening remarks she would be making to the jury. Wasn't it some kind of tasteless joke that her appeal on behalf of Manuel Torres could have been lifted verbatim from the opening remarks she had made for Earl Winters two years ago? The emphasis once again would be on how it was up to the prosecution to prove the defendant's guilt, not up to the defendant to establish his own innocence; on how the jury was not to draw any prejudicial conclusions from the fact that the defendant did not take the witness stand; on how the jury had to be convinced beyond all reasonable doubt of every individual factor that defined the felony indictment. It was, in short, what Alan Green liked to describe as "your basic PD-makes-an-effort" defense, with her main task being that of arguing it as though for the first time in the history of the American legal system.

The trouble was, that was precisely what she wasn't sure she could—even wanted to—pull off for Manuel Torres.

Walking over to the elevators, Elena kept her eyes on the old marble floor to discourage polite hellos. In somebody else's place, she told herself, she wouldn't have had even a polite hello for Elena Alvarez on this particular morning. If she, a somebody else, had spared any thought for Elena Alvarez this morning, it would have been merely to pity her. Not only had she spent a good many years perfecting an efficient, humorless persona, but now, the record revealed, she could still be inefficient to the point of murderousness. Where did that leave all the time, tuition money, dreary weekends, and other sacrifices that had gone into her vocation? More or less in the same hole as Earl Winters, that was where.

She took the elevator run by the grumpy operator named Hobie. Hobie always made riders feel like he was doing them a favor, and he was precisely the operator she needed this morning; on the way up to the top floor, she felt like burrowing down inside his misanthropy and matching him spit gob for spit gob. The only person on the courtroom floor was the cute guard, Myers, at the reception desk, and she didn't mind nodding to him. Walking into the courtroom from the rear door, she was surprised that even this morning it could immediately calm her. Earl Winters hadn't tied a bed sheet around his neck *here.*

She went through the railing and dropped her attaché case on the table. Only with her hands unencumbered and the edge of the table pressing into her thigh did she realize why she had come there so early. Now she was standing as she had stood two years ago, dressed that day in a blue cotton suit rather than the suede combination she wore today, but the same table nudging her body to take off, to pull away from her nook and meander over to the jury, where the real danger lay. Let the words be about the law, she had ordered herself, but let your voice and intonation be of people. Make those twelve human beings and two alternates understand that the issue isn't that of an impersonal jury interpreting bloodless laws, but of individuals coming to terms with Mr. Earl Winters. Do everything possible to make each one of them feel the weight of a personal responsibility for determining Earl Winters's future. Without saying it explicitly, dissolve their bonds as a group and hand them, one at a time, levers for opening the floor and dropping Earl Winters into the darkness below. *Make them all afraid!*

Elena could still quiver at the memory of that day. Stepping away from the table, alone in the middle of the floor in her black heels and with the top button on the back of her dress undone, knowing that not only was the jury watching her approach but that Judge Rubin, the bailiff Phil Drouet, and the Winters family were watching her from different angles and with different expressions, she had done what instinct had always told her to do when she was surrounded or overwhelmed—aim for the fear. It had seemed so easy, such a natural act. On her initial pass at the jury box she had painted a bull's-eye on each and every juror—they had brains, ears, and constitutional perogatives. Once she had done that, the actual target practice had been ridiculously simple.

They feared Earl Winters because he didn't share their social or ethnic or economic background?

Objection!

They feared Earl Winters because they lived in fear that their own homes might be broken into one night?

Objection! Impugning the motives of the jury!

31

They feared Earl Winters because he was sitting only a few feet away from them and had gotten a good look at them?

Objection! Your Honor, are we sowing the grounds for a mistrial here?

They feared Earl Winters with reason—because perhaps one day one of them would find himself or herself sitting at a defense table, accused of a criminal act that the prosecution lacked sufficient evidence to demonstrate. . . .

We the jury find the defendant Earl Winters guilty on all counts.

Elena rubbed her hand along the jury box. She could have rubbed it until her skin burned, but there had already been too much senseless physical self-abuse over Earl Winters, hadn't there? Still, she knew she had to do something to mark his death, and not just call up Kim Freisner for another round of therapy. Suppressed or confronted, her guilt settled nothing, added not a single slice of bread to the Winters table. And, as she had reminded herself over and over again in bed the previous night, it wasn't just what she had done, it was also what she had been allowed to get away with. The DA's office had been happy with the conviction, Judge Rubin had detected no slights from a legal point of view, her own office hadn't had the nerve or interest to come to her and ask about the grounds for an appeal. In the case of Earl Winters, her personal guilt had been about as effectual as an umbrella in a monsoon.

So, what then? Where could there be any satisfaction stronger than that provided by James and Lawrence Winters two years ago in the parking lot, when they and they alone had recognized her responsibility in a concrete way?

Looking back at her attaché case, Elena knew there was only one answer, one that she had already prepared the foundations for with her opening address to the jury. If nobody else was going to give Earl Winters another trial and prevent his suicide, she would. There was no way that she was going to allow a jury to murder him twice.

She went back to the defense table and sat down. It was her private nook, she thought, pressing her feet against the floor, but now she had no qualms about leaving it when necessary to beard the jurors. Manuel Torres had no idea how lucky he was. She wasn't even going to bow to the lesser charge of breaking and entering at the top. It was there, but that didn't mean she had to concede it.

Elena unzipped her attaché case.

4

Manuel Torres took a puff of his Merit and looked over to where Gwynn was staring through the barred window and Barbarella was sitting in a rickety chair, slowly turning the pages of the newspaper over his knee. The two guards were still pretending not to be having a fight, but Manuel had smelled the tension from the moment they had picked him up downstairs in the courtyard to escort him up to the detention room. All the way up, they had kept their eyes forward like military cadets, saying nothing they didn't have to say, Barbarella clearing his throat too much and Gwynn showing red patches of anger under his jaw. Manuel still had the feeling they were going to take it out on him in some way, if only to give his cuffs an extra yank when it came time to go into the courtroom.

He tried not to think about it; there wasn't much he could do about it anyway. He had a more serious problem with the *viejo*. The meter was going *tick-tick-tick* and Santiago was still looking at him like he was crazy whenever they talked about the escape. Who was to say that the old man hadn't already gone to Alvarez and told her the whole story?

Manuel took another drag and flicked ash into the rusty ashtray on the floor between his legs. It cleared his head. Santiago Torres might have been nothing more than Victor Diaz's oldest *sanguijuela,* he reassured himself, but he wasn't somebody who told stories out of school, either. The last person the old man would have trusted was Miss Madrid. She might have been smart in his eyes, but she was still cunt. No way the old man would have told her about the jacket.

He brushed ash off the front of his sweater. Both Gwynn and

Barbarella looked over at him. He dropped his eyes immediately to his cigarette. He didn't want a whisper of thought between them, especially about the sweater.

"Getting antsy, Manny?" Barbarella asked.

"Yeah. Antsy."

Barbarella crackled his newspaper and went back to reading. Gwynn, something tight and hateful in the air around him, took an extra second, then he returned to gazing out the window. Neither seemed to have heard what he had been thinking about. It wasn't something he could take for granted, not after Waxman. If there was one reason he was in the detention room to begin with, Manuel was convinced, it was because the cop named Waxman had been able to read his thoughts in the basement where he had been hiding. If only he had been able to block out all thoughts of the cops looking around for him in the house, he could have waited them out in his hiding place and slipped away after they'd left. But he hadn't been able to do it. For one stupid, panicky rush he had practically *felt* Waxman in the basement with him, had practically cried out for the cop to move away the cartons he had been lying behind. When Waxman had called out to him and cocked his gun at the cartons, Manuel had had the crazy impression, if only for a second, that he was going to be decorated for making his own collar.

Manuel took his last drag on the cigarette and leaned forward to twist it out in the ashtray. He didn't want to think about Waxman and he didn't want to think about Gwynn and Barbarella. He was better off thinking about Joey Edison's white socks. Edison's white socks had been in front of him over the edge of the upper bunk all night. They hadn't stunk, they had just been there, on Joey Edison's hanging feet, because Joey Edison was too tall for a city jail bunk and nobody was going to make special accommodations for someone like him. But those socks had reminded him of Eddie Robinson, the fireman. Robinson had always worn white socks, too; not the heavy kind that Edison had on, more like see-throughs, but they had been white all the same. All of the old firemen in the old neighborhood seemed to have worn white socks, but particularly Robinson in the Hook&Ladder.

Manuel suddenly laughed happily at the thought of Eddie Robinson. Both Gwynn and Barbarella shot him suspicious looks. Before they could tell him to shut up, though, there was a sharp knock on the door. "All set for you," said a muffled voice.

5

The jury room was small. Allison laughed readily when, after King had left them to tell the judge that they were all accounted for, the man who looked like an ex–basketball player cracked that they seemed to have been sentenced rather than impaneled. In fact, Allison estimated, the room was no more than half the size of the smallest of his classrooms. The only pieces of furniture were a long Formica table and wooden folding chairs in the center of the room, an open coatrack in one corner, and two trash cans in another corner. Two doors led to bathrooms, and the single floor-to-ceiling window overlooked the entrance to the courthouse and the shabby stores across the street. Taking deliberate inventory of it all, Allison had a feeling that he was going to become only too familiar with the dry goods shops and real estate office directly below.

"Did I hear them say your name was Allison?"

He turned back to the writer with the pimples on his face. "Have to plead guilty."

"You look like Jerry Allison, the TV newsman."

"My brother."

It was an opening, and Allison walked through it. First with the writer, then with the woman who rented videos, then with the others, he plunged happily into cabbages and kings. After a few moments he felt like he usually had in the first session of a new class, having to accept that no one really knew who he was, really knew how he felt about things. And so to the white-haired maintenance manager from the Port Authority he mentioned that his classroom subject had been world history. To the former basketball player he got across that he had made only one trip out of the

35

United States, that to Europe twenty years ago. Chatting with the pale nurse and the bookkeeper, both of whom had settled down with their knitting needles to wait, he slipped in some of the usual bachelor jokes, ignoring the deeper question flickering in their eyes about homosexuality. One morsel per person, what he felt he owed these strangers on their first real day together.

When King finally returned and lined up everybody according to the seating arrangement in the jury box, Allison felt ready, less anonymous even in his own eyes. Trooping down staircases and through a maze of dusty back halls, he even felt armed enough to take on the security guard.

"John," King said gruffly. "You like, you can always call me Mr. King." He rolled his eyes back for a laugh.

"Doing this long?"

"Eleven years. Watch your step, ladies. The last juror that fell in one of these halls, we had to leave him and send back help."

King's eyes lit up with the titters he received, but his mouth remained unsmiling. "Somebody said you were a history teacher. I was good at history. Almost won the history ring in grammar school. Never had any trouble with all those dates, the way most kids did. I had a system for remembering them."

"What was that?"

King looked wary. "My birthdays," he announced. "Working backwards. I was a hundred seventy-seven when there was the Declaration of Independence, ninety-two for the Civil War, four hundred sixty-one when Columbus discovered America. I just used to think of them in that way. What presents people got for me, where I had my party, what kind of cake there was." The hard challenge in his eyes couldn't disguise a deeper sheepishness. "Think that's nuts, Mr. Allison?"

Allison felt the same heat that he had felt in the jury box yesterday. "Not if it worked," he heard himself say. "They should have given you the history ring."

King grunted. "The rings went to the brownnosers. Isn't that how it always is?"

"No, I wouldn't say so."

"Good to hear it. That's something else that's changed." He suddenly realized that the Port Authority manager was going to reach the courtroom door before he was, and hurried up to the front of the line. "Okay, everyone, no more talking now," he said, grabbing the doorknob before the Port Authority man could even think of reaching for it. "Showtime!"

There were some more titters behind him, but Allison wasn't tempted to join in.

6

Elena stood up. She passed behind Bernie Foy's back, seeing the dandruff flakes. No doubt that was why he always wore light brown checked jackets. She picked out the distinguished silver-haired gentleman with the red cheeks and troubled eyes—Allison?—for her first pass. Her voice came back to her scratchy, the way it had sounded every morning when she had been doing a pack a day. She wished that there was an explanation for the scratchiness today.

The first time down the jury box she didn't turn the pencil a single time to poke the eraser into her palm. She was running ahead of her words and ahead of her gestures, able to double back and use both more slowly if she desired. She decided against it. A much better idea was to speak rapidly at the beginning, for after Foy's bantamlike pacing and hectoring tone, she needed a smoother bridge to her arguments than the standard explicative monotony. She had to expropriate Foy's cadences as her own, *then* move on to a rhythm more singularly hers. First lesson for the jury: the defense had more beats than the prosecution.

She settled back against the guardrail that separated the court from Santiago Torres, an old woman, and a hundred fifty empty seats. She didn't have to say too much about Manuel Torres and she was just as glad. Rarely had she experienced so little communication with one of her clients, at least, with one who hadn't been dropped on her already catatonic from a drug habit or a beating at the local precinct. Again this morning, he had barely acknowledged either her or his father as he had entered the courtroom between Gwynn and Barbarella. He was "Okay," his evening had been "Okay," and "Okay," he knew she was going to address the jury. And once he had slumped down in his chair and had settled his gaze on the middle of the judge's bench, even that minimal response had been too much for him. She couldn't believe that his behavior was just pessimism about the outcome of the trial. Even a street cynic like Manuel Torres entertained hopes once in a while; why else would he have insisted on the trial in the first place? She was sure the reason lay elsewhere, with some fear even more enervating than his dread of going upstate for seven years. Whatever that could be.

She spoke again to Allison. She knew that she didn't have to caption her illustrations of the law for him—he was a teacher of some kind—but she also sensed that he didn't mind having her deliver her message through him to everybody. Allison, she decided, sat like a man *predisposed*. To listen. To learn. To be helpful. To examine all sides of the question. She could speak to him today as she never could again during the trial. Should she ever linger over him again in the next few days, she knew, he would interpret it as a presumptuous appeal to his sympathy and reject her out of hand. Those were the rules, his expression seemed to say; he hadn't made them, but he had to abide by them.

Elena moved on. Stiff on the bench, his chin on his hand, Abe Raymond was very much aware that the jurors were darting glances in his direction to gauge his reactions to what was being said. The court officer King didn't have that kind of worry. Sprouting out of his small chair near the jury door, his dead expression hardly carried down to his legs, which were wagging back and forth like a killer plant waiting for some prey to come by. Where did he get the freedom to be so nonchalant? In a way, he radiated as much authority as Raymond did, and without the benefit of robes and an elevated seat. She couldn't tolerate the idea that King, of all people, had seen the Winters boys attack her. With his dumb machismo he had reduced everything to assault and battery.

She wandered back to her place at the table on the pretext of wanting to consult her notepad. What she really wanted was another sensation of projecting herself, of getting away from the table again under her own power. The rest, especially Manuel Torres, was abstraction. Her only remaining obligation to him was to send him back to jail every afternoon with a reminder not to discuss his case with fellow prisoners. Given his apathy, it was unlikely that he would have taken the time even to discuss it with himself, but it was still her duty to slip in the daily warning. There weren't many things more embarrassing than losing a case because of a client.

Pencil in hand, Elena checked off the nonexistent reference on her notepad and then sallied away from the table again. The jury watched her come—with more interest in her, she allowed herself to think.

7

King stood across the street from the Blue Lantern and counted up to three hundred. He should have figured on the Blue Lantern where Alvarez was concerned; like her, it was all airs. From the outside, with its blue and white shingles and blue framed windows it resembled a Dutch cottage or country inn, the kind of place where the neatness and bread aromas were never quite matched by the food; inside the place was nothing more than a luncheonette with the usual long counter, booths with plastic-covered seats, and hamburger stink. He was positive that she thought of herself as just plain folks for going to the place.

Two ninety-eight, two ninety-nine, three hundred. King stepped out in front of a bus and hurried across the street. He liked it when the douchebag bus driver honked at him. What he liked even more was seeing Alvarez in the last booth in the back with a glass of water in her hand; it was too late for her to tell him that she wanted to be alone at the counter or to change restaurants. She was swallowing some water when he stopped in front of her.

"I guess it's a small world." He smiled, but not too much.

Alvarez gave him something like a nod, put down her glass, and tugged at the cuff of her suit jacket. "Not too many other places around," she said coolly.

"Mind if I sit down?"

He hadn't planned on saying it so directly, and it surprised them both. "Actually, I really look forward to this little break. To get away and—"

"I wouldn't bother you if it wasn't important. Just a minute or two."

He took the wilting look in her eyes as consent and wedged himself into the booth across from her. It was such a tight squeeze, the edge of the table pressing into his gut and his knees bunking hers, that he was afraid she was going to change her mind. But she was satisfied to look annoyed and swing herself into the corner of her seat. She smelled like orange blossoms.

"How do you read the Torres case so far?" he asked, wishing that the waitress would hurry over with a menu so he could feel officially seated.

"I'm his counsel. I think he's not guilty."

"No, but I mean over—"

"Mr. King!"

King felt like shriveling up before her alarm. What the hell was he going on about? She was even less free to discuss the case with him than he was with Edith. "Sorry. It was just something to say. Didn't mean anything."

To his surprise, Alvarez didn't push it. She just studied her knuckles around the water glass while a waitress came over to lay out his silverware and say something to him about pea soup. "You have a legal problem?" Alvarez asked as the waitress went off to get a menu.

"Some people tell me it isn't one. I think it is." Her face showed nothing; she didn't have any way of knowing that "some people" was Edith King. "Let me just ask you this. Is there such a thing as owning your name?"

"Owning your name?"

"Yeah. Like I own John King and you own Elena Alvarez. That's an ownership of a kind, right? Like private property?"

She didn't react to having her name pronounced by him, but for the first time she looked curious. "You're born with a name, you're entitled to it, nobody can take it from you," she said. "That's why if you want a different one, you have to go to court to obtain entitlement."

"So it is like private property, then? Like a deed on a house?"

She sat back in the corner of the booth with her arms folded. He'd never understood how she could see clearly with the brown

40

flecks in the green parts of her eyes. "Suppose you tell me what you're getting at and maybe I can say something useful."

He knew that he should have expected to feel more ridiculous talking about it with a professional like Alvarez than he had with Edith, but his sudden uncertainty still disappointed him. He thought he had least persuaded himself of everything. "Well, there's this bank," he said, lining up his knife and spoon the way they should have been set. "Right around the corner."

"What about it?"

"Well, for the last week or so, they've been advertising this new cash machine card. They have this big blowup of a card in the window."

"Yes?"

"The name on the blowup card . . . it's John King."

He counted to three, then looked up. She was staring at him like she was in a trance, like she was waiting for him to say something else so she could go back to understanding. "I don't think they have a right using my name like that," he said. "I don't use that bank. I don't carry their cash machine card. But nobody who sees that blowup knows that."

He had imagined all her skepticism, all her are-you-nuts? doubts. He had rehearsed each and every one of them to himself and had come back in urgent sincerity to implore her to think about what he was saying, to consider the ramifications of banks doing whatever the hell they pleased. And, finally, he had imagined her sitting back and nodding at him—not making any promises, but at least saying that she had to think about it. Now, though, she wasn't sitting back at all; just the opposite, she sat up again to attack the tuna on toast that the waitress had returned to slide in front of her. She wasn't even impressed when he told the waitress to stop bothering him, that he hadn't made up his mind yet about her damn pea soup. "I'm really not in the mood for jokes, Mr. King," she said. "As I said, I look forward to being alone for a few minutes during lunch."

"I'm not joking."

"No?"

"It's not like I'm claiming I'm the only John King that's being screwed. It's a common enough name, I know that. And maybe most of the other John Kings don't give a damn one way or the other. But I do. I think that bank's invaded my privacy."

41

She nodded to the waitress in thanks for her coffee. "Really? How?"

"By using my name, that's how."

"What goes around comes around, I guess."

"What's that supposed to mean?"

She picked up her sandwich and bit into it mirthfully. She knew that she was making him wait while she carefully chewed and swallowed the mouthful. "It's an old Spanish adage," she said finally. "It means that since you invaded the privacy of all the John Kings born before you, the bank is evening up the scales a bit. Or maybe you can prove you're the first John King?"

"That's not the same. I'm not using my name for commercial purposes."

She pulled the tab off her half-and-half and dumped the crap into her coffee. "No? You're advertising yourself through your name sitting there right now with that ID badge on your pocket. Or maybe that's different. You're just selling King, not John King."

King recognized the hateful tone: he was every prosecution witness she had ever cross-examined. But he wasn't against her; why did she have to act like he was? "You think I'm just looking for money, don't you? You think I want you to force the bank into some kind of a settlement?"

She sipped her coffee. "It's a thought. But yours, not mine."

"For all I care, you can take this on for a lousy dollar. Some kind of associated class thing. On behalf of all the John Kings who don't want their name thrown around."

Her head came up from her cup as if he had yanked it up. "You can't truly be serious about all this."

"Why not? Because it's never been done before?"

"No. Because it's absurd."

"Other things that looked silly got into court."

She looked as if she was about to challenge him on the point, then decided to go back to her sandwich. "There have to be legal bases," she said more patiently. "A John King doesn't have one any more than a John Doe or a Jane Doe has ever had one. No intent to malign, attribute, or coerce. No objective slanderous, criminal, or exploitative association."

"That one. Exploitative."

She shook her head—finally, absolutely. It didn't bother him. In a way, he told himself, she had never gone so far with him

42

before. Aside from that momentary grip on his arm in the parking lot, she had never before used any personal gesture with him specifically. He had her attention now as he had never had it in the courthouse.

"What do you own?" he asked.

She laughed through the food in her mouth. "Not very much."

"Even less than you think, I bet."

"That's nice to hear."

"No, hear me out. Ask most people to tell you what they own and they give you a list of things. A house, a car, a TV set. But how much do they really own these things? Fire comes along, there it goes. Or maybe you'll run up a hospital bill and you have to sell off everything to pay it off. Or maybe it's the IRS or you get a divorce and she and her mother end up hauling off everything. A million ways you can lose it all. Think you own your kids or your friends? I don't have kids of my own, but my two brothers-in-law do, and they're always bitching about how they don't even know who the teenage freaks in their houses are. They say black, their kids say white. And that's when they're not smoking their minds out or getting every disease there is to get. I don't have kids of my own because my wife has a problem, but I know that just because you bring them up, you don't own them. Same thing with guys you hang around with and think you'll go to one another's funerals when you both hit ninety-five. Bullshit. I mean, crap."

She didn't seem to mind either one.

"He'll end up moving out to the end of Long Island and falling in with another crew. At most, you see each other a couple of times a year. You barely know one another after a while. You're just as glad when he says he doesn't want another beer and has to start the long drive back to the end of the Island. And I'll tell you something else, though you've probably never thought about it, and a lot of us don't like talking about it—we don't even own our own bodies! Yeah, I mean that. Oh, it's all yours when you're fifteen or sixteen. But then they all start in on you. The dentist starts putting in caps and Christ knows what. Your damn hair is falling out. Every doctor that's hung out a shingle ends up getting a piece of you. They want to change this, replace that. Even when they're not really making changes in you, they're pushing you around and fingering you this way and that like it's their body, not yours. You might as

43

well be in the lockup getting strip-searched—I don't see much of a difference, I mean that. To hell with all this crap about prisoners being humiliated. We're *all* humiliated, from day one. We don't own a goddamn thing. Except for one thing, maybe, and that's the name we're born with. That's ours; nobody can take that away. They put it on our birth certificate and they put it on our tombstone, and everybody knows who you mean. I can't be you, you can't be me. But instead of holding on to that, you're telling me I should let some goddamn bank just pick my name at random and throw it around like an old deposit slip? No, thanks."

In the wall mirror, King could see that the waitress had thought again about coming over to pester him about her pea soup. He didn't care; the only important thing was the way Alvarez was gaping at him, like someone who had never suspected that he had a brain. Suddenly, he felt stronger than she was, not just because he was a man and she was a woman, but because he had taken over her own ballpark—saying things other people had to agree with. Maybe Manuel Torres had made the wrong choice; maybe it was John King, not Elena Alvarez, who could get him off.

She bent her head to sip some coffee, swallowed it, and cleared her throat before looking at him again. The sunlight streaming through the single front window hit her directly in the eyes. "That's your life you're talking about, Mr. King," she said deliberately, "not the law."

"What's the law good for if it's got nothing to do with my life?"

She acted like she had to think about it, but he could tell she already had an answer. "Maybe less concrete things."

"Yeah?"

"Guilt. Innocence. Justice. Injustice. That kind of thing."

"That and a subway token . . ."

She ducked her head out of the glare from the street. Looking over at him from her darker place seemed to soften her; she was close to smiling. "The law is all those maddening, elusive things," she said, almost kindly. "But there's one thing that it isn't: it isn't crazy. You, Mr. King, you and your bank card, you're crazy."

King knew that he didn't have to take it. He knew that he didn't have to watch her face, as though they were two people having a civilized conversation. He knew, too, that he didn't have to shake off any other thought and lurch up on to his feet. He hadn't

44

gotten halfway into his bag of tricks, he told himself. He hadn't reminded her of the Winters kids in the parking lot, hadn't hinted a word about the suicide of Earl Winters, hadn't told her what he really thought about her—that she had the biggest broomstick up her ass of anyone he had ever seen, and he would be the one to give it a few twists. None of those things mattered now. They made no difference to the blankness he felt about her, about himself, about even being in the Blue Lantern. She wasn't even what a bitch should have been, she was just a statue of one. Hello, statue. Good-bye, statue.

The cashier started to say something, then changed his mind. King slammed into the door, but it was too heavy to reach the luncheonette's sidewalk window and bounce back. People were on their lunch hours, walking back and forth on the street. The sun wasn't at all gleaming like it had been on her face; she had used it all up.

He walked quickly back to the courthouse. He didn't like the emptiness in his stomach but didn't like caring that it was empty, either. When he was being as crazy as she had accused him of being, he shouldn't have been worrying about eating. What he should have been doing was thinking about all those "less concrete things" she had been yapping about—like getting even with her. She had left that off her list.

But he *was* hungry.

So why didn't he pick up a hot dog at the corner stand? He didn't know. He bounded up the steps of the courthouse and sailed through the main door feeling like Santa Claus carrying a sack of presents to give away. Wilke and Myers didn't want anything; they were too busy hurrying away from the metal detectors toward the elevators. Finnigan from the assembly room and Morrison from the information desk were running in the same direction. All four of them were jingling their belts and cuffs, looking self-important.

"What the hell's going on?"

Menelli, who looked annoyed to be left alone at the detectors, whirled around, ready to ream out a civilian stupid enough to bother him. He was disappointed to see another uniform. "Gunshot downstairs," he said, trying not to be overheard by stragglers in the lobby. "Hobie says it was Barbarella and Gwynn. Something about a goddamn Lotto number. Believe that, King?"

8

Hobie Morgan felt good to let go of his slash. No burn in his kidneys or anywhere else. He had to remember to thank the doctor, and to thank Barney Gallagher for having recommended the doctor. Just like both of them had promised, it had only been a question of a few pills.

More guards ran down the hall outside. Hobie figured there must have been an army surrounding the detention room by now. And for what? Barbarella was long gone by now. The only thing the reinforcements were good for was to stop Gwynn from shooting himself or the burro prisoner he was holding as a hostage. Why bother stopping him? A few suds in the right places, he thought, and they could have made it come out that the burro had been the one to start everything and that Barbarella and Gwynn had both been killed in the line of duty. Less misery all around that way.

Hobie finished pissing, rezipped his pants, flushed the urinal, and went over to the old sink. He didn't like washing his hands in the dirty basin, but he hadn't missed a single time in forty years and he wasn't going to start today just because of a few rust stains. Gwynn and Barbarella might be a couple of goofuses, but he still had the public to think about.

Somebody out in the hall shouted for Gwynn to give it up. Hobie was sure it was Morrison from the lobby information desk. He knew them all, even the new ones. If anybody had taken the trouble to ask him, he could have told them that Gwynn and Barbarella had been on a collision course for days. He had seen it coming every time they had gotten on the elevator and started talking about their goddamn Lotto numbers. Barbarella had always been something of the wise guy; Gwynn a big sorehead. No way

46

that Barbarella's usual casualness about paying off his debts wouldn't lead to trouble. Gwynn just didn't laugh like most people.

He finished washing his hands and dried them on his clean handkerchief. He had seen a lot more coming than the trouble between Barbarella and Gwynn; he had also known what the idiotic Lotto was going to lead to. It was too loose, too open. The sense of joyride luck was stronger than the sense of money—unless somebody won money; then, to hear them tell it, it had been a calculated investment all along. It hadn't been that way when he and Barney Gallagher had been handling policy. With policy, people played their numbers to get the money, not to be part of some fad advertised all over the city. He and Gallagher had never put out posters and TV commercials and screamed at their customers to play. The customers had come to them and *asked* to play. Everybody had been an adult, had known the score. If Gwynn had played with them instead of with Barbarella and Lotto, he might still have a future. But why try telling that to a goofus like Gwynn?

Hobie stepped out into the hall. It was like walking onto a battlefield. The stretch of corridor between the men's room and the detention room was covered with security men, most of them with their guns drawn, all of them either crouched down or hugging the wall.

"Get down, Hobie!"

He looked over to where Myers was waving frantically, then back at the door of the detention room. "Man shoots me," he told Myers, "he has to go aimin' at his door first to work out a three-cushion combination."

"Ever hear of a ricochet?"

"Heard of it, goofus. Also heard of takin' a bazooka to a bee. Go right to it, boys."

Hobie started back to his elevator at the other end of the hall. He had no intention of telling Myers that he didn't want to hang around on the off chance there *was* more shooting. He had seen enough already: Gwynn asking for his money in the elevator and Barbarella making fun of him; the two of them hauling the burro prisoner down the hall toward the detention room; Gwynn getting redder and redder, not at all liking the way Barbarella had even been dragging the burro Torres into the conversation. What he wished that he hadn't done was pick that moment to lock his elevator and follow them down as far as the men's room. The craziness had all

47

happened so fast—one second Barbarella was laughing and unlocking the geep prisoner's handcuffs, the next Gwynn was pulling out his gun and shooting. He hadn't seen Barbarella go down, not exactly, but he had seen Gwynn's devil eyes watching Barbarella go down. Why had that seemed more real?

Hobie shook off the thought and entered his dark elevator car. As he clicked the power back on, King hurried past to join the others. King was another one he was ready to bet on. One of these days, he was sure, the fat goofus was going to sit down and put his pistol in his mouth. No problem there, either. A lot less misery all around.

9

Manuel knew better than to look straight at Gwynn. Look a loco right in the eye, you gave him ideas he wouldn't have had otherwise. Same thing looking over at Barbarella, crumpled up against the wall unconscious. Manuel didn't want to remind Gwynn of what he had done. He had to keep floating somewhere between where he was and elsewhere, make Gwynn feel that they were just two guys waiting around in the detention room for the wagon to come.

"Come on, Mike! It's Finnigan! Give it up!"

Manuel kept his gaze on Gwynn's arm, resting on the back of his chair. The arm stayed draped over the chair, the hand with the gun pointed at the floor didn't move. What was Finnigan trying to prove by shouting? Big deal that he was outside. So were a million other pigs, from the sound of it. Outside was outside.

"Hear me, Mike?"

The hand with the gun moved. Manuel followed it carefully up to Gwynn's face. Gwynn wiped the back of his hand across his mouth, not breaking his stare at Barbarella for an instant. Gwynn looked like a mummy. It seemed like a miracle he could even raise his arm.

"Mike?"

"I hear you, Finnigan. Shut up."

Manuel was glad that Gwynn answered. Too much silence, and they would have come busting through the door. He wouldn't have had time even to crawl under the table. And even if he did, who was to say that they wouldn't have tried to take him out anyway? He needed Gwynn to talk.

"Tony's hurt, Mike! We got to get him to a doctor!"

Too late, Manuel thought: Barbarella looked like he was already off the scene. His curly hair seemed useless on his head. The collar of his uniform shirt stuck into the folds of his neck like it had choked him. Even the tiny hole under his shirt pocket seemed to have dried up. Barbarella was gone a hundred ways over.

"Want a cigarette, take a cigarette."

Gwynn had turned to him, had heard him thinking about Barbarella. "It's okay, man," Manuel said. "I don't need a smoke."

"Take a cigarette, I said."

"Yeah. Yeah, sure."

He fumbled the Merits out of his shirt pocket and got a cigarette under way with the first match. His arm and gun still hanging over the back of the chair, Gwynn watched his every move like he hadn't seen anybody light up before. He looked weirdly *interested.*

"You're going to burn your beard one of these days," Gwynn said.

Manuel laughed. He sounded nervous even to himself.

"Don't worry, Manny. I'm not going to shoot you."

"Good, man. Good."

Gwynn smiled, like a mummy. "You say so."

"For both of us, man. For you too. I mean, what's gone down so far, it may look bad, but you can always say it was an accident, nothin' serious, you know what I mean? Every day you get accidents. Nothin' weird about that."

"That what you'd tell them for me? That it was an accident?"

Manuel hadn't thought of it before, but why not, if it got him out of the detention room in one piece? "You want it, you got it."

Gwynn gave him another mummy smile, then looked back at Barbarella, immediately sagging at the shoulders again. He didn't have a clue. He was waiting for the gun in his hand to tell him what to do next, like it was the gun holding him instead of the other way

49

around. "Too late, Manny," he said. "No way I can undo it for anybody now. I just blew up my life in three goddamn seconds."

"No, you didn't, man."

"No? Think I can erase all this? Think I can just walk out of here and everybody will forget about it? Start all over again tomorrow like nothing's ever happened?"

Manuel said nothing; he didn't want to get into any debate. The more he talked to Gwynn, the more he was going to have to swear to, when they began taking statements. He didn't need that kind of bullshit interfering with his trial. No way he was going to screw up his escape plans just because he couldn't keep quiet with loco Gwynn.

"Still in there, Mike?"

"Where do you think I am?"

"Come on, Tony needs help! This isn't doing anyone any good!"

Manuel was glad that Gwynn had insisted he take a cigarette. It was better to have something to do while he worked out things. There was going to be nothing but trouble because of the shooting. Foy wouldn't want him back in the courtroom right away because the jury might start feeling sorry for a "hostage," and Miss Madrid wouldn't want him back right away so she could milk the shooting for all the publicity she could get. One way or another, they were all going to fuck him up because of Gwynn and Barbarella!

"Know what numbers they were, Manny?"

He didn't want to answer, but he didn't want to piss off Gwynn, either. "What numbers were they, man?"

"The Lotto numbers we won on. Three, four, five, seven, eight, sixteen. Only twenty-three came out instead of sixteen or we would've had the whole six million. Only won a few hundred."

"That's great, man."

"Those numbers don't mean anything to you—three, four, five, seven, eight, sixteen?"

"You mean how they're close to one another?"

"The Yankees, for Christ sake! The uniform numbers of the Yankees in the Hall of Fame. Ruth, Gehrig, Dimaggio, Mantle, Berra, Ford."

"Oh, yeah."

"No twenty-three, though. Not Mattingly, not yet anyway. The guys running the Lotto got ahead of themselves."

Manuel smiled, thinking of old Robinson at the firehouse. Eddie Robinson had been a big one for the Yankees, too. When the old man hadn't been talking about Ajax and Ulysses and all his other Greek heroes, he had been talking about Ruth and Gehrig and Casey Stengel. All of them had been gods to Eddie Robinson. And whenever the engines had been out on a call and the old man had gotten especially excited about some ancient game, he had always taken a red Spaldeen out of the desk in his entrance cubicle and insisted they have a catch. Manuel laughed to himself. It had never been much of a catch—Eddie Robinson could hardly bend and he was wild. But even after all these years he could still see the Spaldeen coming toward him with a spin, spitting off the dim sprinkler lights of the firehouse ceiling, and burning into his palms. And he also remembered sometimes reaching for the ball too soon, so that it veered down and away from his outstretched hands, bouncing and skipping on back down the treadmarks to the kitchen door in the rear. How many times had he been forced to run after the ball, down past all the hoses and axes on the walls, always feeling like he had a real good chance of doing anything he wanted and doing it the right way, but also wishing that he could have done it elsewhere?

"Mike!"

"Still here, Finnigan."

"There's an ambulance on the way for Tony! He's your partner, Mike!"

A sound like a breaking bubble came out of Barbarella's throat. Manuel was sure that he had heard the sound before, but he couldn't place it. He had never seen anyone die.

"What would you do with six million, Manny?"

"Lot of money, man."

"More than you could steal, right?"

"C'mon, man. Listen to what they're sayin'. You can still help him."

"Know what you do with six million, Manny?"

Manuel couldn't be sure, but he sensed a new kind of movement behind the paper walls in the hall. Gwynn's face showed nothing; he just kept staring over at Barbarella like he was trying to remember what it had felt like to shoot him.

"What's that?" Manuel asked.

"You make yourself another person. Nothing you've done can matter anymore. You won't look at money the same way. You won't look at your job like you always did. Even other people. You'll see everything different, like another person would."

Now Manuel *was* sure. The silence in the corridor was definitely quieter. He couldn't believe that Gwynn didn't sense it. As a cop he was a zero. If it had been Gwynn instead of Sergeant Waxman in the basement of the house, there would be no trial at all to worry about.

"Ever want to be another person, Manny?"

Manuel braced himself in his chair as much as he could without alerting Gwynn. He knew that the only move he had was to throw himself on the ground and roll over to the far wall. "Minnie Minoso. Always wanted to be Minnie."

"Chicago White Sox."

"I guess. Before my time. My old man loved him."

Gwynn didn't answer. The feel of the day itself on the other side of the barred window seemed to have disappeared. What was everybody waiting for?

"Mike!"

Finnigan's last call, Manuel told himself. When Gwynn answered, they could confirm his position, and then the pigs would come through the door.

Only Gwynn wasn't playing.

"Mike!"

First dangling it by his finger, then letting it go altogether, Gwynn let his gun fall to the floor. The metal banged around the room. But still nobody outside seemed to hear it. Manuel told himself to count to three, then shout out. But how could he do that without stirring up Gwynn again? He couldn't do anything except stare over at Barbarella, the way Gwynn was doing. He closed his eyes. He didn't want to see any of it. There was no reason he should have been more afraid of Gwynn without the gun than with it, but that was all he was—scared.

Manuel heard the shoving into the door before he saw it. When he opened his eyes, Finnigan and Morrison were already inside, pointing their guns at Gwynn like TV cops. The mummy saw nothing, not even when Finnigan kicked the gun off to the side, and blocked his line of vision to Barbarella.

"Even if he gave me the money, wouldn't have been enough," the loco mumbled.

They filled up the room like bugs, all of them carrying their pieces as if they were going to do something with them. Manuel told himself to sit without moving, not give them an inch of reason to whirl on him.

"Wouldn't have been enough for what, Mike?" Myers asked.

Gwynn said nothing, didn't even notice that they were holding his arms behind his back like some kind of compromise between cuffing and not cuffing him. A big black dude pushed his way through the others, glanced at Gwynn as if he was going to throw up his breakfast, then went over to kneel down next to Barbarella. Finnigan shook his head at the black man, who wore stripes and an ID tag that said he was MCCLOUD, and who had no eyes for any heavy news. "Get that doctor down here," he said.

"What's he talking about, Torres?"

With King standing over him and paying full attention to him, Manuel decided he could stand up without setting off any trigger fingers.

"What's Gwynn mean? Wouldn't have been enough for what?"

King looked like he really wanted to know. And he had asked so loudly that all the others, including McCloud, were now also looking at Manuel for an answer.

Manuel shrugged. He didn't owe King or any of them anything.

10

Allison knew that he should have been flattered, but the fact of the matter was that he felt mainly exasperated. Hadn't he put Margaret Brand and school behind him at Les Douceurs de Paris restaurant on a Friday night almost a year ago? Hadn't he put a seal on decisions, announcements, and good-byes, accepted toasts, kisses, and gifts, long overcome even transition problems and settled into his new and more leisurely life? Margaret Brand simply shouldn't have been sitting in his living room sipping her brandy Alexander and making job proposals to him. Twelve-year colleague or not, he had forgotten about her in that way.

"Once a week, Charles. Whatever day you wanted. Eight or nine students."

Allison sipped his wine and listened to Malcolm Arnold's First Symphony. More often than not lately, he had been reaching for English composers whenever he turned on the stereo. Nix Mozart, nix Bach, just Arnold and Elgar. Whatever the reason, he suspected it was one that didn't do him much credit.

"You could afford a couple of hours a week, couldn't you?"

"It's not just the two hours, Margaret. You know that."

She put her glass down on the end table and removed another cigarette from her bag. "I suppose I should know that," she said. "You've been talking to me all these months as though I should. But then when I was talking about this project this afternoon and your name came up, I couldn't understand what it was I was supposed to know." She clicked her lighter. "Tell me as if you've never explained it before."

"I don't want to teach anymore."

"That's it?"

"I *have* nothing more to teach."

"That's ridiculous."

"That's how I felt a year ago, that's how I feel now."

She stared at him a long moment before retrieving her glass. "Know what I think, Charles? I think Sterling High let you off too easily."

"You've said that before."

"But I wasn't really convinced until today. You came in and made your announcement, and everybody was shocked. Allison the Institution wanted out. Nobody knew how to respond, so we all did the knee-jerk thing, first trying to talk you out of it, then going through with all the good-bye parties and the rest. If any one of us had bothered to go off into a corner and think clearly, we wouldn't have let you manipulate us so easily."

"It didn't feel like manipulation, Margaret. Believe me."

"I'm not sure I do."

"Then you'll just have to take my word for it," he said, deciding he had had enough of Malcolm Arnold. "I'll admit there was a little self-pity in it all," he said, going over to the stereo, "but the basic reasons I left were my ideas about what I thought I was accomplishing, and nothing else."

"Ideas have been known to change."

"And not to."

"When you don't want them to."

Allison decided he didn't want any music at all. This wasn't a social evening; she had dropped by unannounced. Margaret was as good a friend as he had, but he preferred seeing her on weekends a couple of times a month, after they had first made plans for dinner or a concert.

"Gregory says they're a good group this year. Curious. Imaginative. A few of them have even been known to complete their assignments."

Turning to look at her, he had expected to see some sardonic disclaimer on her face. But she continued to sit erect on the lounger, holding her cigarette and drink out in front of her, as though minding them for somebody else. "My God, you really *are* trying to recruit me! Forget I know the class, Margaret? I'm not out of there that long."

"You dislike them?"

"Who said that?"

"Then what is it?"

Allison took his wine over to the credenza and set the glass down on it. He didn't mind looking restless for Margaret Brand; if not for her, for whom? In fact, he had no specific reason for his attitude at all. No matter how many venerable explanations he had given himself or muttered to friends like her—burnout, the need for a change, whatever—he had never really bought any of them himself. Had it really been anything more than an accidental coming together of small impressions and even more minute events? On that Monday morning fourteen months ago he had been routinely writing a list on the blackboard, the names of the barbarian peoples that had brought down the Roman Empire. He had pressed too hard on the chalk, cracking it and sending the broken half bouncing off the ledge and against his pants to the floor. He had stooped down to retrieve the chalk, and straightening, had discovered a white smudge on his fly. Someone—he was sure it had been Romano in the second row—had made a crack, others had giggled.

He had picked up the chalk and stood staring at it. He could have raised his eyes to the class and said one of a dozen things, he had told himself. He could have reprimanded the idiots. He could have gone along with their giddiness and thought of a fitting anecdote. He could have ignored the giggles altogether and gotten on with the lesson. He could have singled out Romano for some special mockery. There had been *so many* possibilities that none of them had any importance, none would have been less trivial than another. At that very moment, in fact, instead of writing down *Goths,* he could have written down *Lapps* or *Serbs* or *Corsicans* and proceeded for the duration of the course that way. He could have held up their texts as erroneous, could have improvised an entirely new history about everything that had ever happened. And the worst part, he had been suddenly overwhelmed to think, wasn't that his cynicism would depend on none of his students getting wise to him, but that his invented history would have been just as plausible to them as what had actually occurred! Dead dates, wars, and leaders could not have possibly contradicted him. Millions of centuries, billions of lives, but he, the man holding the chalk in the first-floor room of Sterling High on a Monday morning, this man had conceived the possibility of eradicating absolutely everything that had gone before if so moved. How could such a man have been entrusted for so long with making the decision to stick to the curriculum? Year after year, how could it have been up to him, exclusively up to him, to pass on his particular course's view of history? He was as fallible, as mortal, as anybody. There was nothing permanent, fixed about him. There was no reason for his students to believe him more readily than anyone else.

"I think we know each other a little by now, yes?"

Allison recognized Margaret's smile as the one she had once given him in a lacy Philadelphia hotel coffee shop over breakfast. She had wanted him to believe that he had truly taken possession of her, but both of them had known that he was mainly concerned with trying to block her, with not letting her go off to mingle with other people and finalize their failure. Now he again remembered what she had said that morning about people never truly knowing each other until they knew how much cream and sugar the other took with coffee. That morning he had thought it a kind, frail observation, one of her tentative attempts to persuade him that they could be good lovers another day in another place; now he wished he could remember how much cream and sugar she took with her coffee.

"I think you liked the idea of leaving the school as a gesture, as the kind of thing you do for its own sake. The kind of decision—"

"That I'd never had the courage to make before?"

She looked surprised. "If you put it that way."

"You've waited a long time to say that to me, haven't you?"

"Yes."

He wished that she would stop looking at him as though he were a delicate thing that had to be handled with great care.

"True or not?" she asked.

"Of course there's some truth to it, Margaret. I wondered about it a lot. How could I avoid it after all this time? Nobody ever confused me with one of life's great gamblers. There was a time when I wasn't just uneasy about it, I was completely miserable. I know all the alibis, rationalizations, and self-lacerations by now. Everything that goes along with the bloody terror of doing what you haven't done."

"Everyone has those fears, Charles."

"Sure. Except in my case I'm not sure I could dispute some-one who accuses me of letting the terror win. No, don't shake your

57

head. Look at me. I'm still in this living room, still turning on and off the same faucets I did the first time I could reach a sink."

"But that's no reason to defy the talent you have. To turn your back on all those years, all the good you've done."

Allison didn't like her eagerness. The only other people who had ever been so aggressive in his living room were some of his ex-students, but that had been after a boat ride or the Christmas party, and they'd been fairly drunk. "No, Margaret, that's my point exactly: one thing has nothing to do with the other. I didn't quit Sterling because of some obscure psychic whim to make up for lost opportunities. If anything, it was just the opposite. It was whim that I thought I was getting away from by quitting. Suddenly, one morning, I couldn't see any sense in staying a day longer. It might've always been there for me to see, but that morning I saw it, felt it, and knew that I had to do something about it. And if it didn't make any sense for me to be there, what the hell could I have possibly passed on of value to twenty-five teenagers? If you don't feel important, nothing you say can have any importance."

"So you think these kids are better off with a pedant like Gregory Wiley?"

"You were citing him as an authoritative source a few minutes ago."

"I'm serious, Charles."

"Then my answer is, they might be. Kids can overcome pedantry and boredom. I'm not so sure they can overcome deception as easily."

"And there's nothing I can say?"

Allison averted his eyes and shook his head, going to stand before the old Coney Island photograph of himself, his brother, and his parents in front of the Cyclone. Neither Jerry nor his mother had ever worked out who had taken it, and he had never asked his father. "I appreciate your offer, Margaret," he said, without turning. "I really do. But it's not for me." He finished his wine. "You haven't asked me about my trial yet."

"I thought you weren't supposed to talk about that. Excuse me."

Her chilly tone surprised him, and when he looked around, she was out of her chair and on the way to the bathroom. He knew that she would be leaving as soon as she came out. He couldn't remember when he had made her so mad about something personal before.

In bed that night, before drifting off, Allison tried to picture thirty years of his students in the apartment. They couldn't turn it into a reunion because they had never really been together in the first place. It would be the host's task to make sense of the evening.

The clock radio read 4:13 when he woke up with one of the throbs in his temple that Munson had told him to expect. He took a couple of aspirins, but nothing stronger. The throb was too dull to be classified as pain, he reassured himself.

The Third Day

1

As usual, it took Elena a moment to get used to the sight of her mother. Propped up in her railed bed, her arms crossed at the wrists over a neat fold of sheet and blanket, Virginia Alvarez was no longer the intense little WASP who had been so obtrusive at family gatherings. Since her stroke, what had once been a mouth warning of tartness after tartness had become a soft, withered point. The wrinkles that had once set out from all parts of her face now were so rounded and had taken over so much of her shrunken head, that she appeared undressed without a hat, like some old squaw who had lost her bowler to the wind. Even if she had been able to speak, Elena thought as she stood in the doorway of the iodine-reeking room, Virginia Alvarez looked as if she would have had nothing to say that she would have recognized as her own.

Elena went over to the bed and kissed the old woman on the cheek. She heard some kind of sound but saw no movement. Turning around to put her bag between the vase of day-old violets and the mustard-colored carafe on the cabinet against the wall, she let go of her breath. She delayed further, unzipping her bag, taking out the sour balls she had picked up across the street in the supermarket, and zipping the bag closed again. The candy struck her as no more considerate than anything else in the room. Her mother was beyond frictions and courtesies, was in some institutional state even more complete than the nursing home itself. Had the stink of the plastic seat cushions at home been so bad, after all? Elena immediately kicked away the doubt. She had been through it all before and she still wasn't a twenty-four-hour nurse. As she pulled the window chair over to the bed, she told herself to forget about the smell of urine on Virginia's dining room chairs and to think instead about the celery and lettuce aromas in the supermarket where she had bought the sour balls.

"You look all spiffy this morning. Who did it? Don't tell me it was Mrs. Feminella. She just gave me one of her great looks in the hallway. I was just waiting for it. 'Now, Ms. Alvarez, you know visiting hours don't begin until nine o'clock. We're really breaking policy letting you come in so early.' To hell with her. It's still chilly outside. I wish it would make up its mind. Took me ages in front of the closet this morning to decide what to wear. Coyote weather, is what Felipe used to call it, isn't it?" She had never understood *why* Felipe had called it that; she had always associated coyotes with warm temperatures and deserts. " 'Sleep, little one, sleep. Sleep before the coyotes come and get you.' That's still the most morbid damn lullaby I ever heard. I'm still taking you at your word that you and Father never sang that to get me to go to sleep."

Virginia Alvarez seemed to frown at a fly on the wall across from the foot of her bed. The idea of her ever having crooned any lullaby seemed absolutely foreign—not because she hadn't, but because if she had, it had been in another life, as another person. "I wonder if Cousin Felipe has piled up his second million yet. There was an article in the *Times* the other day about the fortunes being made in mobile homes. Florida and California, especially.

That's where he had all his money, isn't it? Maybe he'll talk Disneyworld into making up a character called Corey Coyote."

She seemed to hear her own silence more than her mother's. It had been a regular moment since she had started visiting the home. The pointless chatter, the non sequiturs—she seemed always to come with a supply of them that she simply had to unload, although she realized that they weren't necessary, that in fact she had more of an opportunity now than she had ever had to talk about important, personal things.

"Know what I was thinking about on my way over here this morning? I was thinking how we never seem to get the chance to do things directly. I know it isn't an original idea, but what do you expect, so early in the morning? I mean, someone does something nice for you, and in the best of cases you're grateful and you can say thank you. But how often do we really get a chance to pay back that person one on one? Most of the time, we end up doing a similar good turn for some third person, somebody who had nothing to do with the kindness we received. I know, I know—that's the way the world goes round. But sometimes I just wish I could be more direct." The fly seemed to have become frozen on the wall.

"There's this trial I started this week. Second-degree burglary. He's already been up twice on felonies. The jerk isn't even very good at being a burglar. Once he was arrested a couple of hours later, and twice he's been caught at the scene. But the thing is, Mother, I *have* to get him off. Not because I give a damn about him or want him ripping off somebody else tomorrow, but because . . . because he's entitled to what I can do for him. I don't want him to be the beneficiary of what I can do, I really don't, but he's the one there at the moment, the third person. Would you like some candy?"

Elena reached over to the cabinet for the sour balls. It was she who wanted one, she who suddenly felt thirsty and immobilized. Did she dare say the name Earl Winters? No, because a specific name would have meant something to her mother, might even have jostled her sleeping memory if she'd ever heard it on the radio or television news. She hadn't allowed Virginia to build up that kind of expectation since law school, since the afternoon she had returned home with the rumors that she was about to be named the class valedictorian. She still trembled to remember how Virginia had immediately gone to the telephone to pass along the rumor to every living Alvarez and Blake in creation, how even her father had been moved for once in his life to admit that there might have been something as important as making money. She just wasn't going to disappoint the woman a second time.

But, on the other hand, if she didn't commit herself to Virginia. . . .

"I just have to do it," she said, popping a red sour ball into her mouth. "I don't know any other way. Last night I thought about going down to Grand Central this morning to be with the Winters family when the body came down from Attica. But for what? Self-flagellation isn't what you put me through school for. I have to pay back with what I'm good at. I'm finally beginning to learn something about the law: maybe it's there because we *can't* be direct all the time. Maybe Manuel Torres just picked the winning number."

The candy was strawberry, not cherry, as she had expected. She was so surprised that she missed the head turn her mother must have made. Virginia was frowning again, but this time as though trying to identify the person at her bedside. She *did* understand, Elena thought in a panic, and in the way she always had—silently, aloof from the loudness and physical exertions of her husband and in-laws, a perpetually tense woman who kept her own counsel except when she was alone with her daughter. Then, only then, did the sharpness and the scolding take over. Virginia Blake hadn't asked for company in her solitude within the Alvarez family, but when she had to accept it, had been laden with a pregnancy at an age beyond reason, she was going to enforce her private rules. Both of them, mother and daughter, were supposed to be better than everybody else, more subtle, more sophisticated, less superstitious. So now what was all this rambling about "paying back" and "winning numbers"? That was the talk of gamblers and Catholics, of people who staged street processions and stuffed Madonnas with dollar bills for good luck. Virginia Alvarez's daughter shouldn't have been talking about such things. Virginia Alvarez's daughter would have been better off concentrating on her dignity—a genuine dignity, not to be confused with the strutting and posturing of Richard Alvarez and his family.

Elena locked the candy behind her bottom teeth and stared down the old woman's confusion. All she had to do to get back in her good graces, to put them back on an equal footing, she knew, was to talk about Santiago Torres, Señor Humildad. Then they wouldn't have been mother and daughter, but allies. They could have scoffed at the man's resolute pathos, at the virtue that he tried to make of his relentless passivity. For a second or two, she thought, she could have even put up with Virginia's turning against her, accusing her of being insolent, lecturing her that she wasn't entitled to attack the people she was attacking, which had been her mother's usual tack after such intervals.

But there had already been too many cheap shots. "I guess it's been a couple of crazy days. One man's killed himself, and another got himself shot in some harebrained fight about a couple of hundred dollars, and all I can think about is turning both things to the advantage of my client. He almost got himself killed yesterday, but I know I have to get him into the courtroom this morning, to remind those jurors that the man they see sitting at the defense table is the same one they read about in their papers over breakfast. And the funny thing is, even Foy hasn't asked for a postponement. He wants to stay on Raymond's good side. Oh, and the last straw, yesterday I'm having lunch near the courthouse, and . . ."

To mention names felt restorative, reassuring. Just to say John King and John Doe and Bernie Foy, just to go from one to the other without worrying about whether it might come back to haunt her, was to move down a path that even her mother approved of. They were People in Her Life, Elena thought, an assortment of cranks and colleagues, nuts and bores she had met on her own. They proved she was no longer dependent on the Alvarez and Blake families for human society. They were part of her personal experience, the experience she'd gained by having gone to law school, gotten a job in New York, and found her own apartment with her own rent and her own mailbox. For a moment, as she rattled on about King's bank machine card and Barbarella's lottery ticket, she could even imagine that her mother envied her, that Virginia Blake had not heard as many strangers spoken of since she had been a market research secretary for Richard Alvarez.

But then the moment passed. As soon as she said the names Alan Green and Jim Aherne, as soon as she raised the thought of working with bachelors who had daytime schedules like hers and evening schedules completely different, she knew that Virginia Alvarez envied her nothing. The only change she might still make in her life, Virginia Alvarez had already made, and had even survived. There was nothing to envy in repeating a mistake.

"Mother . . .?"

But Elena realized that the feeble woman staring at her from the bed was no longer that. It was too late now to ask Virginia to take her daughter in her arms, to tell her that all her fears were groundless, to assure her that she wasn't as mechanically calculating as she thought she was. The woman in the bed was just an old squaw who had lost her bowler to the wind and who, one day very soon, would have her hair braided in preparation for being herself blown away.

"I love you, Mother," Elena said. "I'm going to get Manuel Torres off. I swear to you."

Virginia Alvarez blinked.

2

King opened his eyes to a thought that made him feel good immediately: loonies were loose in the land, and he wasn't one of them. As he stretched out under the covers, he imagined a huge map of the U.S. swarming with thousands of gaga goons in white nightshirts, all of them wandering off in different directions, drooling and shrieking and yanking big tufts of hair out of their heads. He saw douchebag Barbarella and Gwynn and the Alvarez bitch. He saw his old friend Eddie Mannix and his mother-in-law Grace Chandler. He saw all the teachers who had always considered him a good boy and all the army instructors who hadn't liked him for being good. None of the wackos understood one another. They just roamed around like the wackos they were, while he, whenever he wanted to, could have pulled the map out from under them and sent them sliding into the oceans.

It was an hilarious picture, and King kept it in front of him through his shower, breakfast, and the drive to the courthouse. He hadn't felt so alive in ages. Even the traffic moved nimbly along the expressway. He wouldn't have minded more music and less chatter on the radio, but he supposed that a lot of people—more wackos!—

66

liked to be told that it was 8:20 and then 8:21 and then 8:22. He laughed at the thought of people listening to the station as they pulled on socks, tore socks, put on bras, got their bra hooks upside down, shaved their beards, cut their faces—all of them in a frenzy to avoid hearing the dread announcement of 8:24!

It was as he was coming up on the Hillside Avenue exit that King decided what to do. Alvarez, he realized, had been useful after all. Bitch that she was, her reaction was probably typical of what he would hear from other lawyers. Even if they didn't accuse him of being a fruitcake like she had, they weren't going to encourage him, either. As court security, he was supposed to be on the team, and the more invisibly the better. Foy, Raymond, Forte, Cunningham, all the others he had run into yesterday after Gwynn had been arrested and Barbarella taken to the hospital—it wasn't just that they had been shocked by the shooting, they had acted as if the niggers had taken over the plantation. Gwynn wasn't supposed to have pulled a gun. Barbarella wasn't supposed to have gone down. The two of them weren't supposed to have played the same Lotto ticket. Getting right down to it, the other guards shouldn't have caused so much commotion grabbing Gwynn. What was it that the bitch had said about "less concrete things?" Once you worked for the courthouse system, you were supposed to disappear inside all that justice and injustice. A security man who drew attention to himself was like an umpire who did: he was doing something wrong.

And so, King told himself as he cruised onto Hillside, he would have been wasting his time trying to interest another lawyer in his case, especially after Gwynn's explosion. The only way he was ever going to get some of that sacred justice Alvarez got orgasms over was by threatening to become as visible as the two wackos yesterday. He had to *have them come to him.* He had to have them hoping that by helping him they would also be helping themselves and protecting their precious club.

He rattled over a pothole. He didn't give a shit about Hillside Avenue's potholes or fast-food joints or Day-Glo drug centers or any of the other crap outside his window. The only thing he cared about was finding a mouth, a middleman who would drop the word in the right ear about John King's grievance. Nothing wild, just a little something that would scare the right people enough to make them come around with a friendly question or two.

He careened over another pothole; this time it felt as if he'd lost a bumper. The impact seemed to come right through the floor of the car and up into his balls. Somebody behind him shouted, and he looked in his rearview mirror. Two brothers on the sidewalk were raising their arms after him, as if to say that he was a cowboy and they liked his style. He threw a clenched fist back at them.

Turning into Sutphin Boulevard, King realized that his middleman couldn't be one of the other court officers. The best of them would just har-har everything and tell him to forget about the damn bank card, and the worst of them—a brownnoser like Morrison, for instance—would go directly to the district commander. One of the bailiffs? Most of them thought that he was a jerk-off, and he didn't trust them anyway. In fact, the only one that he could think of to pull this particular wagon was Hobie Morgan. The old spook knew everybody in the building, grunted to judges and delivery boys in the same way. The delivery boys couldn't stand him, but the judges and lawyers liked to think they were being regular guys by talking about last night's Mets game with him. To Hobie Morgan they would listen, not because he was worth listening to, but because they would have felt guilty not listening. That made the old fuck the perfect middleman.

In the locker room he found the gloomy faces he expected to find, because of the wacko Gwynn. Nobart had just heard that Barbarella was still on the critical list. Finnigan had been noticing a change in Gwynn for weeks. Morrison thought the whole thing was a disgrace. Only asshole Landers figured it was funny to ask Myers if he wanted to go halves on a Lotto ticket with him, and Myers gave him a look that said he didn't want to hear the joke a second time. King let the crap roll off his back. They didn't bother him, and he didn't join their bullshit. As he strapped on his hardware and gave his mustache a quick comb, he wondered only if any of them had picked up on what Gwynn had said in the detention room as they had been taking him into custody. There had been a moment when he could have sworn that the wacko had been talking to him personally. But he was hardly about to say that to any of them. Even the spic Torres had looked at him oddly for asking what Gwynn was talking about.

Only when he was sure that the others had already gone upstairs ahead of him did he amble over to the elevator and ring for Hobie Morgan. As soon as the black dodo opened the door, he went into his routine. "You one of the new ones? Nobody tell you about the stairs?"

King laughed loudly and stepped into the car. Why was it, he wondered, that Hobie Morgan talked like he had whiskers in his throat?

3

The first prosecution witness was a plump woman in her thirties with messy blond hair and a print shirt draped loosely over her slacks. As she made the seemingly interminable walk from the back door past the spectator seats, Allison cleared his throat deliberately. The ploy worked. For a broken second both Foy and the judge looked over at him instead of at the woman. He'd always felt a pang of anxiety for the students he had called up to the front of the classroom to read some report.

As soon as the woman reached the witness stand and the bailiff asked her to put up her right hand, Allison stopped feeling sorry for her. She was home free with the courtroom rituals; more to the point, so was he. He'd felt it as soon as he had arrived in the building. The guards at the door had acknowledged his duty card; the other jurors had nodded good morning. He had chatted with the pale nurse about American medical students in the Caribbean, gotten into line at King's order, and trooped down to the court. He had answered the bailiffs during the roll call and nodded at the judge's admonition about ignoring Manuel Torres's role in yesterday's shooting. It was an order, Allison realized, that he had depended on for most of his life, and that, only hours after he had been so firm with Margaret about not returning to Sterling, he could still accept with ease. He couldn't help wondering if he wouldn't have been more receptive to Margaret's offer if he hadn't been impaneled for the Torres trial.

The witness, a Mrs. Cicut, was relieved to see Foy, and Foy was happy to see her. She seemed to be averting her eyes from the defense table. Allison forced himself to concentrate. Mrs. Cicut had taken her dog out for an afternoon walk and had seen Manuel Torres climbing the stoop to a house and ringing the bell. Judge Raymond jotted down something. John King crossed his legs. Mrs. Cicut didn't remember the exact address of the house, but it was at the opposite end of the block from the house that had been broken into later. From his desk in the corner of the well, the bailiff glanced up at the big clock on the wall and satisfied himself that his watch was correct. Foy kept rubbing his hands together as he consulted the sheet of notes before him on the prosecution table. Mrs. Cicut had seen Manuel Torres jiggling the doorknob. Manuel Torres gazed off at the judge's bench.

"And was the house deserted at the time, Mrs. Cicut?"

"Objection."

"Sustained."

Alvarez went back to her notes. Foy smiled. "Do you know the people in the house you're referring to, Mrs. Cicut?"

"Yes, I do."

"From your acquaintance with these people—"

"They have jobs. They're not there during the day."

"Objection."

"I'll allow that. Mr. Foy?"

For a moment, Allison thought King was smiling at him. But the smile wasn't aimed at him, but at some nebulous point beyond the jury box. King looked satisfied about something.

"You say, Mrs. Cicut, you were out with your dog."

"That's right."

"What breed of dog would that be?"

"Objection. Immaterial."

Raymond hesitated, then dropped his pencil with a rueful smile. Reaching for the crutch propped next to his seat, he pulled himself up to his feet and waved curtly to Foy and Alvarez. "Approach the bench, please."

Foy quickstepped around his table to the end of the bench. As Torres threw her a curious look, Alvarez stood up, smoothing her two-tone skirt over her flanks, and walked as deliberately as she could to the same spot. Allison sensed at once that Torres's eyes wouldn't follow her, and he was right. His languor compromised by showing interest in Raymond's abrupt summons, the boy retrieved his lack of interest the only way he could—by returning Allison's stare. It was on the same plane, required not an extra centimeter of movement. Manuel Torres just happened to be looking there, and Charles Allison should have considered himself lucky to find himself at eye level.

Allison knew that his face showed nothing. After so many years of standing in front of a classroom, he was nothing if not an expert in stare-downs. But, strangely, he felt his strength suddenly rising from some deeper place as well—from all his childhood myths about hero warriors who refused to acknowledge their mortal wounds and baseball players like Joe Dimaggio who had never betrayed a jot of emotion on the playing field. And even odder, he realized with an astonishing start of energy, was that he could feel Manuel Torres on the same exact wavelength, could feel their two vibrations darting back and forth across the well of the courtroom, checking out each other's stoicism, not so much admiring it as just acknowledging it. And his sudden fancy flew even higher: even with the discovery of their common ground, neither owed anything to the other, neither would ever give anything to the other. Recognition wasn't debt, and it certainly wasn't sympathy. The juror who happened to be Charles Allison would be somewhere else, years removed, when the accused, who happened to be Manuel Torres, completed serving his sentence. *Charles Allison would be long dead.*

Allison looked away at what he hoped was exactly the same moment that the boy did. A second more and his strength would have been gone altogether. He felt suddenly weak, on the edge of nausea. His stomach heaved. He didn't remember any warnings about that from Munson. Ergo, he was making up the feeling? Munson had said so much else about high-grade astrocytomas, all of it sounding like a report on some precious diamond found in Africa, that he could not possibly have omitted simple puking. Allison scolded his stomach, tried to erase it from his thoughts.

At the far end of the bench Raymond was muttering sardonically to Alvarez while Foy stood by with a smug expression. Alvarez finally nodded, stepped off the dais, and walked back to her table. Raymond said something else to Foy, then lowered himself back into his seat. "The last question again," he said to the court reporter.

John King smiled to see Alvarez looking so discomfited by what she had heard from Raymond. Mrs. Cicut nodded at the reporter, as if to say that, yes, that was how she remembered the question, too.

"The witness may answer," Raymond said.

"It's a German shepherd."

Foy glanced at the jury. "A full-grown German shepherd, Mrs. Cicut?"

"He's seven years old, yes."

Foy looked triumphant and Alvarez depressed. Allison suddenly wished she had a brighter client.

"Would you describe what happened then, Mrs. Cicut?"

"In my own words?"

"In your own words," Foy answered, smiling benevolently.

Mrs. Cicut took a deep breath and rearranged her hands in her lap. "I was standing across the street with my dog. I saw Mr. Torres pushing the handle of the front door up and down, up and down. I called out to him and said, 'Can I help you? I don't think anyone's home.' That's when Mr. Torres turned around. When he saw me standing there—"

"Objection!"

Raymond nodded. "Just tell us what you saw, Mrs. Cicut." She looked bewildered. "I thought I was."

"No, you said, 'When Mr. Torres saw me standing there.' "

"Yes?"

Raymond sighed and Foy bowed his head. "But you don't know that he saw you there," the judge said. "He could have been looking at the house behind you or the car parked in front of you. You're not in a position to say what *he* saw."

The woman looked even more befuddled. "But I was the one who called out."

"Granted, Mrs. Cicut. But the rules are that you testify only to what you saw, not to what you assume Mr. Torres saw."

She looked over at the jury.

"Mrs. Cicut?"

Allison tried to meet her eye, but her glance went from one juror to another too frantically. Now Foy was looking worried and Alvarez interested. None of them had expected so much balking.

"A strange approach, that what you're thinking?" Raymond asked with an indulgent smile. "I grant you that. But those are the rules here. I ask you to proceed with your testimony."

She turned back to the judge; she had one last reservation. "I'm sorry. I guess I'm not used to testifying."

"We understand that."

"It's a different way of talking."

"Yes, I suppose it is."

Mrs. Cicut nodded to herself; she had run out of bewilderment. "Well, I called out to him," she said finally. "And Mr. Torres turned around. He didn't say anything . . ."

Allison felt as relieved as Raymond looked.

4

As Elena entered her office, she took a look at the seated mob in the reception room and immediately wished that she was back in court. Closing the door resignedly behind her, she didn't know whether she wanted to blame Raymond's hip for the faces she recognized or the ones she didn't. The sight of Lillian Lacy swinging her gangling black legs seemed like reason enough to call up the administrative judge and complain about Raymond's liberal use of adjournments.

"Hello there, Miss Alvarez."

Elena acknowledged Lillian Lacy with as little courtesy as she could get away with and nodded for the receptionist Glenda to follow her into the inner office. As she crossed the reception area, she figured the well-dressed man with the glasses was a tax case and the elderly married couple some kind of landlord problem. Smirking Jack Haggerty she didn't have to guess about: he was back to mooch for more investigative work to keep him in cigars, one of which was now blanketing the office in fetid smoke.

"You're not supposed to be here," Glenda said, closing the door behind them.

"Either is Lillian Lacy. She has no appointment."

"She says she's being harassed by the precinct cops."

"She always says that."

"She sounds serious."

"Give her to Alan."

"I was going to, but now that you're here . . ."

73

Elena flopped into her chair. Glenda didn't have to say it: Lillian Lacy would have swung her legs and lighted one Kent after another in the reception room for the rest of the afternoon if she thought there was a chance of taking up her complaint with "a woman who understood."

"Right," Elena said, "I'm the hooker expert."

Glenda shrugged. She wasn't responsible for the division of the sexes, the penal code, or anything else. She was just a receptionist who took her job very literally: Glenda Marciano received everybody.

"All right. What else is out there?"

Glenda began reciting from her pad. The elderly couple had indeed received a citation for overdue rent and Jack Haggerty was "just looking for a few minutes to talk some things over." The well-dressed man with the glasses, on the other hand, wanted to talk about a scofflaw summons.

"He doesn't look the type, does he?" Glenda said.

"There are only two types: the ones who sit outside because they have a problem and the ones who don't sit outside because they don't have a problem."

"Gee, that's kind of sarcastic, isn't it?"

Elena looked up at the girl. At Glenda Marciano who had changed her name from Linda Marciano because she hadn't wanted the same real name as the porno star of *Deep Throat*. At Glenda Marciano who wore contact lenses because she was afraid glasses made her unattractive and who wore a scapular atop her gold cross to feel doubly protected. "Yes, it is," she replied, wishing that she could disappear into a hole. "I'm sorry. It was just a bad morning. Foy even got me on a goddamn dog. Now we have Torres breaking into *two* houses."

"But you knew that. Alan said it was a loser from the word go."

She got over feeling bad about disappointing Glenda. "Then I guess it's a good thing Alan's not handling the case. Telephone messages?"

Glenda went back to her pad uncertainly. "Just one, Mrs. Winters."

"Winters?"

"She was very nice, but she wouldn't say what she wanted. Left her number. Asked you to call when you had a minute."

Elena had no choice but to take the pink slip. What had she been counting on, that her calls to the prison medical examiner and the prosecutor's office would have spared her personal contact?

"You know her?"

"Yeah. A client before you came here. Do me a favor, will you? Route as much of that mob to Alan as you can. I need a few minutes for myself."

"Sure thing."

Elena continued staring at the number after Glenda had gone. She realized she had to call it, and right away, but she also needed something to hold on to. For example, which Mrs. Winters? The estranged wife who hadn't shown up at the trial? If she wanted to criticize now, she didn't have a leg to stand on. Or was it the old mother who had collapsed the second day of the trial and who had to be pushing eighty? The anonymous digits didn't even make it clear whether the call had come from Brooklyn or Queens. Why had the damn phone company stopped using the letters that had once made it possible to picture a neighborhood?

She shrugged her jacket off and tried to think about the creases and wrinkles she was making in the coat as she punched out the number with her middle finger. She imagined an ancient black woman in a black dress hearing the telephone ring in an apartment filled with plastic flowers and heavy curtains. She pictured the woman walking slowly to the phone, not wanting to hear any more condolences on the loss of her son but knowing it was a custom that had to be observed.

"Hello."

"Mrs. Winters?"

"Yes." It was a middle-aged voice; somebody in her forties.

"This is Elena Alvarez. I believe you called me?"

She wanted to kick herself for sounding so officious. "Oh, yes," the voice came back, sharper, less suspicious. "You heard what happened to my husband, I know."

No, she hadn't, she wanted to say. "Yes, I did, Mrs. Winters. I'm terribly sorry. I just don't know what to say to you."

"Well, I'm not sure there is anything to say. Earl's gone, and there's no bringing him back."

"Yes, but—"

"What I was calling about, Miss Alvarez, was I heard you've

75

been asking how Earl died and everything, not even asking to be paid for your trouble."

"Well, I think we should know all—"

"Yes. But what I'd like to ask is if you'd mind not coming to the funeral tomorrow."

"Excuse me?"

"Well, I know this is going to sound cruel to you. I suppose that everybody in the city knows how and where Earl died. But we're trying to keep it a small family thing. For the sake of the boys. Try to remember the good things, if you know what I mean. I know it's not your fault you knew my husband the way you did, but it would be a reminder. For one day anyway I'd like Lawrence and Jimmy to try to remember Earl only as their father."

"Of course."

"Believe me, you don't know how hard it is for me to be asking you this. I know Lawrence and Jimmy have already hurt you once."

"Hurt *me?*"

"Well, I know what happened that day of the verdict. I guess I've been too ashamed to write you a letter of apology. Believe me, Miss Alvarez, I sat down a dozen times the last couple of years and took pen to hand, but—"

"Mrs. Winters, if anybody owes anybody an apology . . ."

"Earl was what he was, but he was still their father. They were upset, they didn't understand. If I'd known that they were near that courtroom, I would've gone over and gotten them. I thought Lawrence was at school and Jimmy down at his job at the supermarket. He's still there, by the way. Fact is, he's brought home more money in the last couple of years than Earl ever did. I know that's a terrible thing to say. Anyway, I guess what I'm saying now is just the apology I never got around to making."

"Mrs. Winters, I don't want your apology."

"I feel better giving it."

"But you weren't there. In the courtroom. You don't know."

"Oh, Lawrence told me everything. One thing those kids don't do is lie. I got it out of both of them that same night. I suppose that's when I should've called you and apologized."

"I mean the trial, Mrs. Winters. You weren't there for that."

There was a pause. Why had she said that? Hadn't Earl

Winters's suicide been enough? Why was she so intent on driving the woman deeper into misery?

The voice came back, even more matter-of-fact than it had been. "Miss Alvarez, there was no reason for me to sit in that courtroom. I knew what Earl had done because he'd told me. Why did I have to sit there and hear it coming from other people? Earl Winters was my husband. The thing he told me, I didn't like hearing it, but it was something a husband should be honest with a wife about. He was no criminal telling me what he did, he was my husband. But if I'd sat in that courtroom, what would I have been hearing? They would have all been talking about a stranger. You would have been calling him one thing and the man in the district attorney's office another thing, and that judge and jury would have been listening to it all like they were deciding about somebody who really wasn't there. I know that was your job and I really am grateful for everything you did for us, but I couldn't have sat there like that. It would have all been different, you know what I mean?"

Elena suddenly felt good, tremblingly good, to imagine that she was being observed on the telephone, that Glenda and Alan and even Jack Haggerty were in the room with her, marking her reactions to what she was hearing. It wasn't a phone conversation that was happening, she thought, it was Elena Alvarez who was happening, pressing the receiver too hard against her ear, staring at the blank page on her desk calendar. Elena Alvarez was out there as an objective person.

"But I didn't mean to get into all of that. I guess I'd just like to tell you about tomorrow and ask that you understand."

"I understand, Mrs. Winters."

There was another pause. "Well, I thank you again. Goodbye."

It wasn't Mrs. Winters who had hung up, Elena told herself at once, it was the computerized operator. A human being wouldn't have been that abrupt. How could she still know so little? She didn't know what borough she had called, she didn't know what had snapped in Earl Winters to drive him to his suicide, she didn't know what Lawrence and James Winters were thinking about her. She sat waiting, listening to the cars directly below her window start up as the light changed, wondering what could have been outrageously funny enough to make somebody at the corner guffaw so freely.

How could the woman have been so presumptuous to think

that she had intended going to the funeral? How could she herself have been so insensitive not to have considered going? Both of them had been so uselessly wrong.

"That bad?"

Alan Green closed the door quietly behind him. With his ludicrous green bow tie and brotherly smile, he looked like a messenger from a Happy Birthday service. She was grateful for his timing.

"State of Nebraska versus Melvin or Mellon or something," she answered, finally putting the receiver down. "Nineteen seventy-three, I think."

Alan shook his head. "Don't know it."

"The defendant went into some ritzy neighborhood. One of the locals was giving his pit bull his nightly walk. Mellon or whoever felt threatened by the dog, ended up trying to hide in an empty house. B and E thrown out because of reasonable threat."

"Mellon sounds like our kind of client."

"You can look it up, can't you?"

"If it's on the computer. What's so important?"

She pulled her jacket out from under her and was disappointed not to see a single wrinkle. "Foy won a battle this morning, but he may have given me an idea how to win the war."

Alan sat down on the arm of the visitor's chair. "I get a dread feeling we're talking about Manuel Torres."

"Your doubts are on the record. Do me the favor, okay?"

He hesitated, then said, "On condition you do one in return. I know they're an inferior Latin people in your eyes, but some Italians have a real knack for cooking. For instance, I know a place in Long Island City that makes the best spinach ravioli on this side of the Atlantic. An ideal place for talking about love and truth and a hundred other things you won't find in the penal code."

Elena started to say no—as automatically as she had assumed that Mrs. Winters had been estranged from her husband, she realized. "Lots of wine?" she asked.

He nodded. "Red. White. Orange. Blue."

"I thought you'd never ask."

5

Sometimes, Manuel thought, the rec room seemed like a street corner that had been moved indoors from the old neighborhood. There was the same standing around, the same mouth action, the same sizing up whatever went by, but all of it happening under a roof. The *duros* stared down everything, the *mañosos* pretended to see nothing but noticed everything, the little girls stayed by themselves to the side until they were called over. There was even noise enough to make up for the missing street traffic. The talk, the radios and the TV set, the Ping-Pong tables, the soda machines—the rec room was where it was all happening.

Which was why, Manuel thought, he hated the place as much as he did the old barrio corner outside Victor Diaz's coffeehouse. He took another toke on his fool's gold and let the noise slide off him. Glide easy, he warned himself. He still didn't know what the hell he was watching on the TV. All he could figure out was that it had to do with some ship that had sunk with a fortune in gold and jewels. The rest was mud. There were divers who hated each other, a blonde in a bathing suit who kept wiggling her ass at everybody, and a lot of bare legs running along polished decks. It was nowhere, and he was nowhere with it. He didn't even want to memorize the blonde for lights-out.

Joey Edison limped in the door, riffling the deck of cards that was never out of his hands. Manuel laughed to himself to think that the spade would be looking for somebody to play his penny-ante gin rummy long after he, Manuel, had broken out of the place. One way or another, in a box or on some Caribbean beach, he was going to be very far away by the time Joey Edison put enough treys together to win his first jailhouse ten bucks.

He would be, that was, if he remembered to call the *viejo*.

Cursing himself for forgetting the time, Manuel clipped off what remained of his smoke, stuck it into his shirt pocket, and headed back for the telephone. The old-timer in the back row had fallen asleep watching the blonde on the TV. It was another reminder that he didn't need her Hollywood ass. If he wanted to get off, he still had Miss Madrid not having a clue to what was going on behind her back. Even the white-haired guy on the jury was in on it by now. Including Santiago, that made three of them. Miss Madrid went on playing her law games on the ground floor while the upstairs was being cleaned out. By the time the place had been picked clean, everybody in the city would have known about it except her!

For a change, big Patterson had taken over only one of the phones. His goons were still parked around the other two, but they weren't using them. "You mind, man?"

The fat one named Hardy took a year to raise his eyelids; he reminded Manuel of an alligator stuck in the mud. "Give me a chance, spic, and I'll try to."

Manuel sighed and glanced over at Patterson. He had no problems with Patterson, never had. From the first day in the rec room he had gotten it across to the big spade that he didn't need much turf for himself, but he knew every inch of the turf he did need. Patterson had respected him for it—not in so many words, but by leaving him alone, by pretending he wasn't there and looking past him when they had run into each other in the corridors or in the showers. Now Patterson raised his head from the receiver, took in Hardy's stance, and nodded. The alligator moved his ass out of the way slowly, like it had been his idea after all.

Manuel dropped his quarter and punched out the number for Victor Diaz's coffeehouse. He liked the idea of putting the *viejo* on the spot with two sets of goons on either end who might have overheard—Patterson's on his end, Victor Diaz's on the old man's. Everybody but Miss Madrid was going to know, he told himself again.

"I'm still waitin', old man," he said, as soon as he heard his voice.

"You got a long wait."

"With or without you, I told you."

"I'm not goin' to help you—" The *get killed* part wouldn't

80

come out; the old man obviously had somebody's eyes on him. "You know."

"I could get it somewhere else. Don't forget that."

"Then you better get it there. I'm not bringin' it."

"It's the only thing I ever asked you."

"Go to sleep with your demons, Manuel. I don't want to hear about them anymore."

Manuel smiled quickly as the old man slammed the receiver down. At least he had upset the old man in front of Victor.

Patterson smiled, the receiver still held to his ear. "Family problems, bro?"

"Nothin' I can't handle."

"That's good. Let other people handle your problems, they get more messed up."

Manuel nodded eagerly. He liked the way Patterson was friendly and liked what the spade said. It was exactly what he had thought: the *viejo* and nobody else, not even Patterson himself, was going to slip him the razors he needed.

Going back to his seat in front of the TV, he relighted his gold. This morning he had been worried about the teacher guy guessing too much and running off to Foy or the cops. But now, he realized, he didn't have to worry about the teacher. He could tell that the guy hated Miss Madrid and her legal bullshit as much as he did. The teacher had already made up his mind about the verdict and knew what was going to come down after it. He was glad that the teacher had figured it all out.

He looked over to the picnic table where Joey Edison had found a pigeon for his card game. At least Edison *thought* the fat Latino named Amaral was a pigeon. Manuel knew better. He had seen Amaral hanging around Victor Diaz's years ago; the *gordo* had even scared him a little, because he didn't act afraid of anybody, not even Victor Diaz. He wished now that Joey Edison would do his little trick of lighting up a cigarette, then flicking the still-burning match away. The pig Amaral would probably break Edison's arm off at the elbow if the match flew too close to him.

The blonde in the movie had changed into a tank top and shorts. She was using some kind of machete to cut a loaf of bread. Manuel laughed just as somebody let out a yell at one of the Ping-Pong tables. Nobody had heard him laugh, he thought, not even the zombies sitting around the set near him.

Maybe he *would* concentrate on the blonde and save her for lights-out.

If he still had anything left by then.

6

Hobie wasn't about to admit it to Barney Gallagher, but he missed being on the lookout for the early papers. He missed the drivers like Walters and Superman on the *News* and Finkelstein on the *Mirror,* missed giving them grief over their short counts, missed beating Gallagher to the twine-cutter and the returns, missed grabbing the first pink edition of the *News* off the stack and listening to Gallagher grumble about how he was messing up the paper for a real customer. Standing in front of the stand now, his jacket collar up against the chilly night, Hobie counted only seven or eight people hanging around for the first *News,* and they were either hackies from the cab stand in front of the Long Island terminal or night-shifters from the station itself. Once upon a time there would have been a couple of dozen or more, people from the neighborhood, commuters who had worked it out how to grab their papers and then make the last car of a departing train, even young couples who had come downtown to the bars and restaurants for a special night out. But now, unless you counted a skel hole like Maloney's, there were no more bars and restaurants, and nobody with a brain took a train from the terminal after sundown. And the neighborhood? Hobie had to laugh at the idea. There hadn't been a neighborhood since Jackie Robinson had stolen his last base. Even the stripped-down cars looked better than the rubble lots they'd been abandoned in.

He looked over to where Gallagher was sorting out his change behind the counter of the stand. With his huge paws and furrowed brow, the gorilla looked like he still hadn't worked out what nickels and dimes added up to. Somebody being slowly buried alive, that's what Barney Gallagher reminded him of, standing inside his cubicle. Being buried alive by the pussy magazines that framed his window, by the stand that had lost its own sense of place since the buildings around it had begun going down, by the loose nickels and dimes that hadn't amounted to anything in thirty years. Barney Gallagher was as much of a stand-up guy as could be found, Hobie thought, but if Hobie had been the one to come home from shooting gooks in Korea and end up with a lousy newsstand, he would have sucked on a gun a long time ago. Less misery all around.

"Make your fortune yet, vet?"

Gallagher grunted, but kept on counting. Hobie had no real itch to talk to him anyway. As the clock outside the bank was there to remind him, he was going to have to deal with crazy enough talk in a few minutes when King came by. He still didn't know what the goofus wanted, and now that he was on top of the appointment he was surer than ever that it couldn't have been anything good. All his years on the elevators and the only other guard who had looked him up after work had been Billy Washington, and that had been his own fault because he had told the nigger that Dinah Washington was singing nearby. But at least with Billy Washington there had been Lady Dinah in the middle. With King he wouldn't have anybody running interference.

Two of the junkie patrol came out of the terminal and light-footed it across the street to Maloney's. They were about as under-cover as Lady Godiva, Hobie thought. Even Blind Mary in the terminal had made them the first day they had showed up with their beards and jeans.

Gallagher stopped counting to frown after the cops. "Set your watch by them."

"Goddamn farce."

Gallagher went back to his change. "You don't get it, Hobie. They're supposed to be regular as clockwork. What the army calls establishing your presence."

"Yeah. Now they're present in Maloney's and the deals are goin' down in the station."

"Where there's a third one waitin'."

"Right. And he'll grab 'em like he does every night."

Gallagher shrugged. "Strategy. Gotta have a strategy."

Hobie didn't bother answering. With the sight of King wait-ing at the corner for a green light, he had his own strategy to worry about. The guard was wearing a stocking cap and a navy jacket, looking for all the world like somebody who didn't want to be recognized.

"Here comes my friend."

Gallagher didn't look up, a sign that he had already spotted King. The vet had always had street eyes, had always known where the gooks were lurking. It was the only useful thing he had learned in Korea.

"Hey, Hobie! Found your hiding place!"

Hobie felt Gallagher's eyes on the back of his neck as King swaggered up and pulled at his hand. Hobie didn't like shaking hands and didn't like the way the guard kept his other hand in his jacket pocket. If King was holding on to a piece, he realized, the vet wouldn't have enough time to get out from behind the stand to help him.

King nodded over to Maloney's. "They sell beer over there?"

"That's what it's there for."

"Well, c'mon then. I'll buy you one."

"Want to watch those brews with those pills you're on."

King looked back at Gallagher like he had heard a joke he didn't get. The vet kept busy rolling up his quarters.

"One ain't gonna hurt, Barney."

Gallagher shrugged. "Your plumbing."

Hobie felt in charge again as he led King across the street. He didn't say anything when the goofus asked him about Gallagher. Inside Maloney's he made straight for the stools at the short arm of the bar. He didn't mind trading off the greasy stink from the food counter for being close to the door. He also liked seeing the two bearded bulls throwing shots back midway down the bar.

King finally took his hand out of his pocket and opened his jacket. "I miss places like this," he said, taking in the half-dozen skels hunched over their glasses in the old barn. "Out my way you can't get a beer without all those faggy ferns in your face."

"This place oughta be condemned."

King smiled like it was another joke he didn't get. He didn't get Maloney, either. "Guy looks like he hasn't smiled since the doctor whacked him on the ass," he said as Maloney took their order and went over to the taps.

"Maybe nothin's funny."

King glanced around. "See what you mean. Real happy times."

"You look happy enough, King. Somebody leave you money?"

"Same old Hobie. Man, you have the fuckingest disposition. Nobody ever left *you* money."

"Never asked anybody to. Never asked you to buy me a beer, either."

"Hurts, huh?"

"I'll drink it. And you'll get to the point, right?"

Maloney came back with the beers, took a ten from King, and went off to the cash register again. Hobie drank just enough to know that Gallagher had been right; would he ever again be able to sip a beer without thinking that it was running right down to his kidneys and boiling up a lot of piss?

"Truth is," King said, pulling his stool under him, "I'm a bit shaken up about this Gwynn and Barbarella thing."

"Shit happens every day."

"Yeah, yeah, I know. But it's a little close to home."

"You a friend of theirs?"

"I'm not saying that."

"Yeah?"

"I mean, I work with these guys every day. The real team."

"Real team."

"People like you and me. The guards, elevator operators, custodians. We're there in the morning before the VIPs arrive, and we're there after they've gone home to their split-levels in Westchester."

Hobie drank some more beer. Unless King was counting the once-a-month of being assigned to the court library, he couldn't remember a single time that he had gone home before the goofus.

"You like to think that at least your own guys have their heads on the right way. Christ knows we see enough of the other shit coming and going."

"Yeah. Real problem."

"No, it's more than that, Hobie. It's a problem that could've been headed off."

"Sure. Barbarella should've paid up."

"I don't mean just that."

"No?"

Maloney came back with the change. King drained his glass. "Bring it again."

85

"Not for me, King."

"You're kidding!"

"Not in the mood."

"You barely wet your lips. Two more here."

Hobie started to say no again, but something about Maloney's droopy-eyed look made him hold his tongue. The fact was, he didn't like Maloney any more than King did. He couldn't remember the last time the mick had been gracious about buying back. It served him right to keep hopping back and forth for a couple of cents of trade.

"What I'm saying is this, Hobie. Everybody in the goddamn building seemed to know Barbarella and Gwynn had their troubles. How many people you hear talking about it today? The morning after, they're all geniuses. But not one of them was clever enough to head off the trouble. They didn't want to be bothered, didn't think it was any of their business."

"It wasn't."

"Well, it's damn well affected us all!"

"You say so."

"Hey, look, the two of them might've been douchebags, but they were our people. We got to look out for one another."

Hobie finished off his first glass without feeling anything above the balls. A watery beer and he was even smelling better too, he realized: King's beer hadn't been his first drink on the night. The goofus had taken a few shots to loosen up for the old nigger.

"I'm saying we should learn from this business. When a guy has a problem, we should be ready to talk to him, see if we can help him. Think those judges and lawyers who've been depending on Gwynn all these years are going to treat him special when he goes up before them? Like hell! They'll crucify him like he's just another slimeball."

Maloney put down two more beers and grabbed more money. Hobie began to feel lighter; not dizzy, just lighter. "You got the media," he said, to say something.

"Exactly. And you know what that's good for."

Hobie was glad Gallagher wasn't there to see him picking up the second glass; he knew the vet would have been disappointed in him.

" . . . just talking to one another," King was saying.

"What's so good about that?"

"What do you mean, what's so good about that?"

"I never wanted to talk to Gwynn. You ever want to?"

King's mustache looked like it was stuck to his nose. "Well, sure. If I thought I could've helped him. You try to reach a guy like that."

"What for? To find out he's a three-dollar bill? Maybe he'll end up takin' you out instead of Barbarella."

"And maybe he'll end up taking nobody out."

Hobie couldn't help laughing. "You like those odds, King, you play them. Me, I never bet three-legged horses, English heavyweights, or the Houston Astros, and I ain't gonna start now. You go ahead, though. Free country."

Something came into the goofus's eyes—the same something that had been in them in the elevator when he had invited himself over for a drink. "That's what we like to think. But know who it's really free for, Hobie?"

"You're gonna tell me."

"For people who don't care. For the lawyers and the pimps. That's who."

"Everybody ends up payin', King."

"Sure."

"You know better, you know better."

"I care, Hobie. And I'm going to fight for what's mine."

"That's good, King."

"Starting with my name."

"Good a place as any."

The lightness in his head came back in a stronger wave, but Hobie knew it was too late to do anything about it, that even if he stopped drinking at once, he would have to pay for it tomorrow. Besides, the familiar screeching of the *News* truck outside reminded him that Gallagher didn't need him to stack the first edition anymore. He polished off his second glass while King said something about a bank. He had half a mind to give Ida Roberts a visit. He hadn't seen her in almost a year, but he knew she was still around, still fingering what was left of policy. It seemed like a million years since the night she had opened the second bottle and he had gotten his hat and walked out the door, listening to her taunts all the way down the stairs. Fucking had never been good enough for Ida. She had to drink everything but the water in the toilet bowl before going to sleep.

"Tell me the truth, Hobie. You think a name's worth getting heated up about?"

He didn't know what the goofus was talking about, but the day he began to worry about that, he'd drink out of a toilet bowl too. "Why not?"

"As good as anything else, right?"

"Better than most things."

"You agree, then? 'Cause that's what I think."

"Gotta protect what's yours."

"You got it."

Hobie's eyes went to the front of King's flannel shirt. He had never seen the goofus without his uniform and name tag before. "Least you got those little badges of yours," he said. "Nobody bothers with that for me. We're just supposed to run the elevators and sweep up the shit. We don't deserve those fancy badges."

"What're you talking about?"

Hobie went for the new round that Maloney laid down; as long as the goofus wanted to buy, he was going to be bought. "All those bullshitters you're goin' on about. The judges and the rest of them."

"Yeah?"

"Only way they even know who got shot yesterday is because your friends Gwynn and Barbarella got badges. You don't suck up to 'em, do 'em little favors with their cars and their anniversary presents, they don't have a clue. Think if one of them lawyers walked in here right now they'd recognize you? Ten to one says they wouldn't. You're just another goofus sittin' at the bar that they don't look at twice. Same thing in the buildin'. You can spend twenty years, thirty years in that buildin', and most of 'em got to look at your shirt pocket to say hello to you. I know, King. I see it every day." The geep nodded, but he wasn't sure. "But let me tell you somethin' else, too. I don't even got that. No badges for the operators or the custodians. We're not important enough. Sometimes I think about tradin' cars with Brooks, just to see if these bullshiters know who I am. They got their routines, you see. It's the same car every mornin', the same hello, the same polite bullshit. They don't see nothin'. They don't see me, and the only thing they see of you is your little badge. You ought to be thankful for small favors, King."

The goofus shook his head. "You don't believe all that."

The beards were getting ready to leave. Hobie didn't know what their hurry was; he wanted to finish his beer. "No, I don't mean shit. Just gabbin' away with you."

"Seriously."

"Seriously is what your friend Gwynn did. Now they know who he is."

King laughed. "They know Gwynn's a wacko, that's what they know."

"You say so."

"Christ sake, Hobie!"

He almost welcomed the burn in his bladder; at least it reminded him of who had given it to him. Say what you wanted about the bullshit lawyers and judges, but they weren't the ones who had to ring for the elevator instead of going up half a flight of stairs from the basement. "Look, King," he said as the beards headed for the door, "you worried you don't get enough respect, that's your problem. What I know is a geep like Barbarella comes along and tries to screw *me* out of somethin', he's gonna pay. It's Hobie Morgan he's playin' with, not some old nigger nobody knows the name of. I don't give a shit what the Mets or Knicks or your wife did yesterday. I worry about what I'm doin' today. Got that?"

"So Gwynn's a hero?"

The last swallow tasted as good as all the others. "No, he's a douchebag, just like you said," Hobie answered, getting to his feet. "But he'll never be *just* that anymore. They'll give him some number now, instead of one of those name tags, but everybody's gonna know who he is anyway. Thanks for the beer, King."

"Hey, c'mon. Hang on a few minutes."

"Nice of you, but I gotta get up early. Nobody's ever beat me to work yet, and that includes you goofus guards. Good night."

His left leg had fallen asleep. Hobie walked stiffly outside so he wouldn't have to listen to any more crap about staying for another drink. The night air seemed to be even staler than inside Maloney's. Across the street Gallagher had started packing up his porno magazines. There were no more customers hanging around. Hobie couldn't be sure from the distance, but just for a second, as he was going around to the side of the newsstand to get his lockup boards, the vet seemed to frown across the empty avenue at him, for having done something he shouldn't have.

7

Allison closed the 1970 register and set it aside. He supposed he shouldn't have been surprised that he hadn't found anyone to invite to the party; he could hardly remember the class. 1970 had been the worst of blurs; slow and tortuous days, coming and going as if waterlogged. Outside of a few glib captions in the school newspaper, not even the student demonstrations happening in every corner of the world had found an echo at Sterling High. It was as though he and everyone else at the school had made an agreement to act immune to change. It had been safer that way.

He got up from his desk and went out to the living room. He had forgotten that he'd only turned the TV's sound down before going into the study after Jerry's newscast. He took the remote control out of his bathrobe pocket, turned off the set altogether, and tossed the remote onto the couch. From atop the set Sofia watched the sudden movement in the hope that it would be the first of many; it took her two blinks to resign herself to the stillness and go back to her snooze. He went into the kitchen to warm up some milk. Sofia didn't follow him, not even after he had loudly and deliberately slammed the refrigerator door a second time. He knew it was a foolish thing after so many years, but he still always felt vaguely uneasy about entering the kitchen alone at night. The lights glared harshly, the linoleum was too bright, noises were magnified. He was too clearly by himself.

He sat down at the kitchen table to wait for the milk to heat. The wonder of it, it occurred to him with frightening abruptness, was that he could have ended it all right then and there by forgetting about the milk and the match and simply turning on the gas.

There would have been no need to go through the rest of the registers, no need to endure a single one of the serious headaches Munson had warned him about. The frailty and banality of it all was appalling: an ordinary weekday evening, an ordinary kitchen, ordinary boxes of cornflakes and Domino sugar peering out at him from the closet. The only dramatic disturbance he could forsee was the expression on the face of the landlord Heim when the police told him that he was finally free to repaint the apartment and rent it out to another tenant.

Allison tightened his fist on the table to control the quivering in his hand. He remembered Sofia and his jury duty and his party. They were his last excuse for any sense of obligation, but they were enough. He was just going to have to ignore all the fragilities until he actually started cracking.

He brought his heated milk back into the living room. He wasn't in any hurry to get onto 1971; that had been a normal academic year. It was 1970 that had been the year of Rita.

"You are going all the way to Istanbul?"

By now Allison could smile at the question without feeling his insides shrivel up. He had played it back to himself so often over the years that it had become like a once enchanting song that had lost every power except its familiarity. He could smile, too, at the thought that, wherever she was now, Rita Nardi was as old as he was, no longer the flouncing chain-smoker who had invaded his Orient Express compartment in Trieste, flopped own on a free seat, bunched her peasant skirt up over her thighs, stretched out her legs and proceeded to shoot streams of smoke at her sandaled feet. Now she probably had to eliminate the flouncing part before sprawling out and spitting smoke, he thought with a warmth that seemed to have been preserved by the separating years and ocean. If there was one benefit to Munson's sentence of doom, it was that he was fast running out of time ever to have to think about her realistically.

He drank his milk as Sofia gazed watchfully from atop the TV set. Somewhere between Yugoslavia and Rumania he had told Rita Nardi about his cat Vienna. She had listened to him as though he was crazy, and he had felt good having her think that he was. All at once he had been talking about a lot more than some pet, and he himself had been much more than a vacationing American schoolteacher with a modest line in conversation. Under her skeptical gaze and relentless puffing, he had become a fool, an eccentric, and an adventurer all rolled into one, and pushed as he had never before, he had rattled on, rhapsodizing past fact and past fiction into outrageously asinine fantasies. There had been the Siamese cat that had sung the entire score from *The King and I*, the Persian that had been able to meow only the two words *I ran*, the domesticated alley cat that had to be served its food in a garbage can. He had gone from one story to another at such a blithering pace that he'd had time only for one fear—that he would have run out of silliness before getting her to relax her wary silence. And then, just when he had about given up on her and had started to fall back on leaden thoughts about Vienna and the way his mother had probably been overfeeding the cat since he'd left, she finally looked at him with the most searching look he had ever seen, with a broad grin that knew nothing of skepticism, and pronounced him as *"Pazzo."*

Allison shook his head at Sofia; he still felt heat at the thought of the compliment. The truth was, he had always wanted to be madder than others had sometimes joked that he was. With his students and his colleagues, he had been occasionally flamboyant, occasionally drunk, and occasionally just pigheaded, but the one time that he had felt genuinely mad, genuinely *pazzo*, had been while riding through a region of Eastern Europe that he had never learned the name of in the company of a person he had ended up knowing for only two days. She had asked him for nothing. He had felt compelled to share with her what he hadn't even known he had. Not understanding a word of the chatter in the train corridor and barely able to decipher the station signs, he had never made more sense to himself or anybody else.

He started to bring the cup of milk to his mouth again but then stopped. Drinking milk was squandering time. What he really wanted was to do something mad, to feel as he had on the Orient Express with Rita Nardi in the summer of 1970. He wanted to be spontaneous again about cats that sang *The King and I* and places whose names he didn't know. By staying in the house? He had always *wanted* to be that way in the house, but in the last couple of weeks especially, the apartment seemed to have encouraged only a frightening bitterness in him. His brooding in the kitchen about the gas had been only the latest chapter. Even now he could look at the peninsula of broken plaster on the wall above the stereo and imagine himself going at it methodically with a trowel, carving away at the crack until the entire room, then the entire house, became one great fissure. Then there had been his demonic urge after leaving Munson's office to hack up one piece of furniture a day until he at least had the consolation of knowing that nothing familiar would survive him. Now again he felt his chest welling up with the terrible pointlessness of such rage. He didn't want to be so bitter, so gratuitous, and he felt demeaned even to contemplate such things. To hell with what others might or might not have expected from him, he expected a lot more from himself. He had always lived up to his responsibilities and obligations. All along he'd made his small peaces, and sure as hell was not going to fail at making the final, big peace.

Sofia glowered at him to get off the couch. Allison nodded to her and put his milk on the table. Not knowing where he was going, knowing only that if he hesitated he would lose the impulse, he got rid of his bathrobe, grabbed the first jacket he found in the hall closet, made sure he had his keys and his wallet, and went out.

The only places open on the street were two bars and the all-night supermarket. He didn't need any maudlin bar and he didn't want to go near the supermarket, because he knew that once inside he would have become practical again, buying the orange juice and butter that he was running low on. His eyes fell on the MTA worker preparing to close the gate to the subway entrance on the corner. Feeling more ambitious for the money he had in his wallet, he stood watching for a moment as the man fumbled with a large ring of keys. The man seemed to be doing everything short of pleading for one last rider to come hurrying along before it was too late.

Allison bought two tokens and hurried through the turnstile. A train rumbled into the station as soon as he stepped down on the platform. The only other passenger in the car he entered was a tall black man in a cream caftan who reeked of rose powder. The man was holding a plastic bowl in his lap that contained about a dollar in coins.

"Support the school, man?"

"What school's that?"

"Help the children."

"Do what?"

As the train rolled out of the station, the man looked at him strangely. His eyes darted around the empty car. He didn't seem to like the idea that they were on the same bench so close to one

93

another. "Keep cool, man," he sighed, sliding away. "Just keep cool."

Allison laughed and changed his mind about donating a dollar. Instead, he thought about where he was going to get off, where he knew he had to get off, now that he had taken this particular train in this particular direction. It had been ages since he had ridden this way to visit his father. Then there had been a reason to be on the train; now that he had no more real reason than he had ever had for going to Istanbul, he felt better.

8

Once past a few sips of wine, Elena had seldom resisted Alan Green. Even on the evenings that he had been at his most exasperating, diligently plying her with a big-brother cuteness or exuding the grave airs of an older colleague who had seen more swineries in the legal system than she could have imagined, she had usually ended up going home with him, trusting that there would be something familiar and something new in the way that he touched her, and that it would not take him too long to sense which she wanted.

Tonight had been no different. Throughout dinner he had spoken as the world's leading observer—on the variations in the regional Italian cuisines, on why wives did and didn't sit in court-rooms to follow their husbands' trials, on law offices that had gone out of business because of one partner's obsession with a particular case. Elena had expected it all, wondered in passing if she had even looked forward to it, and had said little to rebut him. Then, like someone who had been presuming all along that she would have been up for anything except listening to the sound of her own voice, he had driven her confidently to his East Side apartment and, barely inside the front door, had completely undressed her and laid her out on the living room rug to come into her. For once she had not minded coming before he had. She had even neared the edge a second time, as in the very instant that he had tightened his fingers on her shoulder blades, she had pulled the ballpoint in his shirt pocket from in front of her eye and listened to it land on an uncarpeted part of the floor very far away.

Now, as she made the pillow more comfortable behind her head in his bed, she was glad that she had decided to stay for the night. For a moment at least, all the worst of things seemed to have been overcome. She had overcome his lecturing at the restaurant about Mrs. Winters and Manuel Torres. He had seen that she had not lost a single pound since their last date a month ago. She had already confessed to him that she did not want to return to the file on Earl Winters that she had left strewn across her kitchen table. Enjoying her lightly glazed feeling from the wine they'd had at dinner, she told herself that the evening was still in embryo, that not even their excitement in the living room had settled them down, that there were still hours and hours ahead of them before she had to think again about guilt, judicial and otherwise.

"Brughel's woman."

"You mean I'm fat."

Alan brought the two bottles of beer around to her side of the bed. The way he held the bottles out in front of him made his prick look like a matching piece of some kind. "I mean you're a peasant," he said as patronizing as possible. "Of this earth. Not an airy thought in your head. Pure meat and potatoes. A woman of substance."

"That's very funny, Alan."

He grinned, proud of himself. "It's been my insight for some time now," he said, handing her one of the bottles and climbing over her, "that the real essence of people is what they look like, not what they think or feel or want."

"Profound."

"Easier. Got to admit that."

Elena set the beer gingerly on her stomach. She was disappointed that it wasn't colder, didn't make her start.

"You'd be surprised how little things would change if you accepted my idea. Glenda would still have the soul of an office receptionist. Jim Aherne would still be Yale 'seventy-three, eighty-fourth on the graduating list. Lillian Lacy would be the same hooker. Jack Haggerty would still be a tenth-rate gumshoe. You'd have to look at only a few people differently."

"Me, for instance."

"Absolutely."

He lifted the bottle to his lips at precisely the same moment that she raised hers. She had a vision of lying before an endless series of mirrors, being reflected smaller and smaller into some unreachable distance.

"Stereotypes," she said.

"Yup."

"I'm a stereo cut off from my type."

"Wandering in the desert."

"With a plug in my hand."

"Looking for a socket."

She reached down and grabbed his soft prick. "I think we've gotten our metaphors mixed up here."

He swigged more beer. "Nope."

She pulled back her hand. "Fuck you."

"Now there's an idea."

"Work on it."

He laughed and rolled over on his side facing her. He kept his eyes on his hand as he began to rub her stomach. "I think I owe you my latest progress report," he said. "Some progress, but not too much. Granted you're all the things you always say you are, but I still think it'd be a good idea for us to see each other more regularly."

"I'm not any of the things I said I was. I've just been trying to let you down gently."

"So you really aren't uneasy about seeing the same person morning, noon, and night?"

"Sean Connery I could manage."

"He's getting old."

"We'd agree not to point that out to each other."

"And you're really not interested only in your work?"

She cringed to remember the fervor with which she had issued that pronouncement in the past. She still believed it, she thought; she just wished she hadn't said it so often. "Pass."

He was doggedly refusing to look her in the eye. Now he followed his hand slowly down her hip, across her thigh, and down under her calf. His touch was sobering her up even faster than the beer was. "You're not in love with me?" he asked.

She swigged more beer, turning away from him to put the

96

bottle on the night table. She had hoped he would go for her cheek, and he did, bunching it between his fingers, covering it with toothless bites, then poking at it with his tongue. She wished he would stop talking about love.

"Well, which is it? Were you letting me down gently or not?"

"You don't win either way."

"I'd still like to know which way."

"I don't want a family. I don't want children."

"I never proposed it."

"It usually comes down to that."

"A thousand nights from now."

"So you don't deny it, that *is* what you want."

He finally raised his head to look up at her. He seemed to take it for granted that she would stay in her awkward position, using her body to shelter him from the glare of the lamp on the night table. "Why is it everytime I ask you a practical question, you turn the conversation into projections into the twenty-first century?" he asked.

"You're lucky, I guess."

"Seriously, Elena."

"Because I prefer it that way. Why else?"

He looked baffled. "You prefer it."

"Right."

"Well, okay, you prefer it. But you know what you're really doing, don't you?"

"What?"

"You're being evasive."

She was beginning to enjoy his bewilderment. "Yes."

"Yes! Just yes? I mean, it's weak. You see that."

She found the back of his knee with her foot. "Of course," she said trying to keep a straight face.

"And?"

There was the slightest lurch from his leg. She remembered the sensation from the last time he had grazed the back of her knees: she had hated it, had felt a shock to a dozen small bones, but had also wanted it again as soon as she had pulled away from him. "And nothing. I prefer those projections and abstractions and speculations you were talking about. Don't think that's possible?"

"I think people can talk themselves into preferring it. Settling for it because it's easier."

She stopped moving her foot; as at the restaurant, he was back to knowing more about her than she was supposed to have known about herself. "You presume an awful lot, Alan," she said, retrieving her beer and rolling over onto her back.

He tried to ignore the glare in his face. "I thought I was asking a straight question."

"And I answered you."

He thought about saying something else, then brought his own beer up to his lips. "No one's more afraid of letting go than I am, Elena," he said.

"Letting go?"

"Of everything," he shrugged. "Of what you're supposed to be. Of what you promised yourself to be. Of what others expect you to be. I know what it's all about, believe me. I had a grandfather who was shocked that my parents let me play in kindergarten instead of memorizing the Bill of Rights."

"Ha, ha."

"I'm not kidding. Ever hear of Vatslav Vorovsky?"

"No."

"Not too many people outside my family have. He was a Soviet diplomat in Switzerland in the twenties who was assassinated in the dining room of a big hotel in Lausanne. The killer was a fanatical refugee named Conradi. They caught him on the scene literally holding the smoking gun. Then the bullshit started. A dead Bolshie was a dead Bolshie. France and England started pressuring the neutral clockmakers; it was their opportunity to atone for the sin of having given refuge to Lenin before the revolution. So they have a trial under Swiss ground rules that say at least six of eleven judges have to agree on a verdict. Guess how many of them agreed that Conradi was guilty."

"Five."

"You got it. Conradi gets off. They way they put it, he was guilty *morally,* but not criminally. Moscow flips out over the whitewash; everybody else is dancing in the streets. And then a few years later the Russians get over the whole thing, too. Stalin figures it's a way of liquidating their debt to the Swiss for having sheltered Lenin, so everybody's even."

"Except your grandfather?"

98

He nodded. "Micah Green wasn't even because Vatslav Vorovsky wasn't even. My father used to say we were the only Jews in New York who observed Passover not by asking 'Why is this night different from all other nights?' but by asking 'Was Vorovsky assassinated just morally? Was he? Was he?'" He took a swig of beer. "Anyway, Micah's teaching on all this to his grandson the lawyer was very clear: 'There is no division between the moral and the legal, Alan. Remember that. If you can't defend one, you can't defend the other. Better you never win a case if you can't get *both* acquittals.'"

"Easier said."

He propped himself up on his elbow and stared at her. "No, it wasn't," he replied intently. "Micah Green was the greatest lawyer I ever knew. He *did* get both acquittals, time and time again."

"He didn't have a corrupt court like the one in Switzerland."

"He didn't have corrupt clients."

She moved her head on the pillow to see him more clearly. He smiled. "I know. Unlawyerly talk. And fortunately for the firm of Aherne and Green, I haven't always practiced what Micah told me to. But is that my failing or his? Catch me at a weak moment, like now, and I'll say that it's mine. Does that bother you?"

She started to shake her head, to give him the reassurance that she was suddenly certain he had been steeling himself to ask for from her for some time. But she couldn't manage it. There seemed to be nothing but defeat and rationalization behind such a concession. "Yes, I'm sorry, Alan. It does."

He winced. "Even just thinking it?"

"You're not just thinking it," she said, feeling surer.

"I'm not?"

"The way you describe it, your grandfather couldn't distinguish the forest from the trees. Conradi's lawyer did his job. It was the court that was corrupt, not the defense counsel."

"He was in on the whole thing!"

She reached for her beer. "You didn't say that. That's different."

He was becoming angrier. "What difference—"

"All the difference in the world. If you're going to tell me an anecdote leaving out half the facts, what am I supposed to do except shake my head or nod, or pat you on the head or something? If you're really interested in what I think, then give me all the facts.

Okay, the lawyer was corrupt too. But I didn't understand that from the way you told the story."

"It's not just a question of facts, Elena."

"What's it a question of, then? You have affectionate memories of Micah Green; fine. I envy you that, Alan, I really do. The only thing I ever heard in my house was how many pinkos were killed in the Jarama Valley. I didn't even know that Franco's fascists had *lost* that battle until three years ago! I envy you your grandfather and his Vorovsky. But God help us and anybody who ever gets a speeding ticket if we're going to relate everything to whether or not we had a good Passover when we were kids. Manuel Torres doesn't give a damn!"

"And I don't give a flying fuck about Manuel Torres!"

"We took the case, and we'll take the fee."

The words were out of her mouth before she could stop them. For a moment she felt as though she were back in front of the Earl Winters jury, just talking away until her own words came back to hang her—or him.

But Alan only smiled. He had his leverage back; his prick was deflated, but he had his leverage back. "That's right, Elena. Just one call and we stop having to worry about Manuel Torres."

She curled her toes into the ridge of the blanket, telling herself that she knew where she was stepping. "But you wouldn't."

"You said yourself he wasn't cooperating with you."

"So he's an asshole. He's not the first one."

He took another swallow of beer and leaned over to put the bottle on the table on his side of the bed. She told herself she knew what she was doing by sliding her leg over so it would be beneath him when he lay back down.

"You've sidetracked me again, haven't you?" he said, shaking his head. "The day Jim interviewed you, he came into my office grinning like some old archeologist who'd just spotted his first tomb."

"Lovely comparison."

" 'I think we've got a true believer, Alan,' he said. 'Forget affirmative action, this is affirmatissimo action.' Think you're that?"

He seemed to take it for granted that her leg would be under his haunch. He worked it out from under him and turned into her. "You know, I think we could justify a few hundred dollars of state money for Haggerty this weekend," she said.

100

"What the hell for?"

"The Cicut woman's dog, for one thing," she said, finding him already hard again. "Maybe a random of the jury. One or two people."

"They're already seated."

"So were your Swiss judges."

His fingers dug into her more purposefully. "And in the most miraculous of cases we'll get a retrial. Great. My Life With Manuel Torres."

In the most miraculous of cases, she thought, guiding his hand more gently, they got more than argument for argument's sake, remembering the way her father had once worked himself into rages about politics or religion after dinner because he had considered it a vital part of the evening. Alan brought her to easy, methodical stirrings. She didn't want to go much further a third time. She wanted to stay within those stirrings, not hearing his effort, not thinking of what she was supposed to give him. Instead, she thought about what her father had once said about a man isolated in a mountain cabin without a clock. Since the man could not have reasonably known whether it was Thursday, a fast day, or Friday, the meatless day, Richard Alvarez had said, it was all right for him to eat steak, because on the one hand, he had a sincere doubt that it was Thursday, and on the other hand, he had a sincere doubt that it was Friday. "But, Daddy," she had said, sounding so loud to herself on the couch next to her cousin Felipe, "he knew that it had to be one or the other, so there was no way he could've eaten the steak anyway if he didn't want to be guilty of sin." And Richard Alvarez had smiled at her tolerantly and had continued to smile at her that way until the Catholics changed their rules so it was possible to eat meat on both Thursdays and Fridays, even in a mountain cabin, and he had another reason to fly into a rage after meals.

When she took him into her mouth, Elena told herself that she wasn't doing it for the sake of doing it, that Alan really needed her to do it.

9

King closed the front door softly behind him, standing still for a moment. He heard nothing. Getting out of his jacket, he balled it under his arm and made his way carefully into the living room. He knew he wasn't being as light-footed as he'd hoped, but he didn't know how to be quieter. He seemed to have reached some kind of limit.

He sat down in his favorite chair and unfurled his jacket onto the rug. He liked the mess, he liked its neatness. It told Edith that he had been out late and that he had drunk too much, but it didn't make that much extra work for her. He wanted to let Edith know, not to break her back.

He opened his eyes; he must have been asleep. The green numbers ran by on the VCR. Edith was recording something. What the hell was on after three o'clock in the morning? Something Grace had told her about, probably. Grace Chandler had never missed a single program on any of the 435 channels. He had, though. He had missed a whole night of the fucking sitcoms that Edith and Grace watched like they had invested in them. And for what? For the old spook Hobie Morgan, that was what.

King brought his foot up to his knee to untie his shoe. Had he gotten anywhere spilling his guts to the spook? At least he had made him nervous. He had never made anyone nervous watching sitcoms out of the corner of his eye with Edith. They made *him* nervous.

He pulled off his shoe and sat back with it. The green lights kept running on the box. He knew what show was going on inside the set. It was about a court security man who had taken on the banking system of the U.S.A. and had won the day. The guard had beaten all the odds. His wife said he was nuts, great legal brains said he was nuts, creepy elevator operators said he was nuts, but he worked out the perfect strategy to beat them all. Just like he had worked it out back in school with history dates. Everyone was going to have to admire him, even Grace Chandler.

And Edith?

King swung his head toward the bedroom. She might be asleep, or maybe only pretending to be asleep. It didn't matter anymore. One day soon she was going to wake up to find a new person in her house. Wasn't that what the wacko Gwynn had said in the detention room? A new person. He had heard it, and the spic Torres had heard it. He had to laugh that not even a two-bit burglar like Manuel Torres had wanted him to hear it. Like everybody knew, but nobody wanted to tell him.

But he knew and he was going to tell everybody. Hobie Morgan thought a wacko like Gwynn had become a new person? He hadn't seen anything yet.

King lifted his other foot. The green lights kept flashing. He wished he had his gun—the lights were annoying.

10

Allison paused on the small incline of the parkway corner and buttoned his jacket against the wind. The avenue stretched before him for what must have been a mile, low rooftops and flat storefronts, not a single theater marquee or outsize building to break the pattern. The traffic lights seemed superfluous: the only thing still out was a bus crossing through the avenue a few blocks away, its interior fluorescence giving it the eeriness of a spaceship passing through dark, uncharted skies. Another block farther down, bright orange flames leapt up from a garbage can.

He stepped off the rise and down into the avenue. It took him only a few yards to regain his command of the familiar terrain—or, at least, of the alignment of the stoops and doorways, of the cracks in the sidewalk squares, of the ancient initials and Cupid arrows carved into the asphalt. The actual stores were another matter. After the second storefront church and head shop, he gave up looking for the groceries, dairies, delis, and cleaner franchises he had once entered so responsibly for his father every other weekend, and within which he had conspired with clerks and countermen to buy Red Robinson better things than Robinson had sent his son for. He was just as glad that the stores had been replaced.

Although Jerry had told him ages ago that the apartment house had been razed to the ground by a fire, Allison still recoiled when he turned the corner and saw nothing but rubble where the building should have been. He had never associated the six-story house with space, but now there was nothing in its place *but* space, rolling out from the bare sidewalk through what had once been an interconnecting series of back yards over to an old Chevy parked on the next street. The whole block seemed too open, out of proportion, as though the old man had taken the very physical dimensions of the neighborhood to the grave with him.

He walked over to the lot anyway. The dusty, acrid stench from the rubble couldn't possibly have been from the fire, but he liked thinking that it was, that it remained a direct link to the house he had known. Otherwise, the most weathered-looking objects around were cans and bottles, and even they belonged to Grand Union specials from only a few months ago. If there was a mythology about returning home, he thought, there definitely wasn't much of a geology for it.

After a moment he realized that he must be standing where the vestibule alcove for the mailboxes had once been. With his eyes, and then with his feet, he measured off the twelve or fifteen yards to apartment 2 on the first floor. As he gauged the distance over chalky bricks and shards of glass, Allison thought of a *Candid Camera* stunt in which unsuspecting victims had been told to deliver a package to such-and-such an address only to find that the address was merely a doorframe in the center of a lot, but they still insisted on knocking on the door rather than walking around it to the man sitting behind it in an armchair. He thought of himself now as one of *Candid Camera*'s silly messengers. Somewhere atop Mount Olympus, he was sure, Red Robinson was gazing down on him and roaring with laughter. *Look at that, Ajax. Look at that overage son of mine searching for roots that just aren't there. You'd think he'd know better by now.* It wouldn't have been the first time he had entertained his father with his naivete. Had anybody ever laughed as delightedly as Red Robinson had that Saturday afternoon when Allison had asked to be taken someday to Troy, New York, so that he could see the walls the Greek army had penetrated in the wooden horse? "The world's a bigger place than the state of New York, son," Robinson had said when he could finally speak. "You'll find that out." Allison shook his head; he wasn't sure that he had found that out.

He gravitated toward the Chevy on the next block. Halfway across the lot, his eye fell on an old cuff link glinting on the rubble. He stopped to pick it up; it was a silver rectangle with some kind of flower etched on the surface. He polished the metal on the sleeve of his jacket, decided that the flower was a gardenia beyond shining, and dropped the doodad into his shirt pocket.

As soon as he reached the next street he saw that the Chevy had been stripped of everything but its frame and windshield. Allison began to feel cumbersomely adrift. He had seen what he had traveled to see, he had no other destination, yet he still seemed to be packing a lot of unused memories. He thought of the rainy night that he had stayed on Margaret Brand's couch and had then had to cart his umbrella to school under a hot sun the following day. Sometimes portable wasn't nearly enough, he had told himself that day; sometimes only dissolvable represented progress.

It took him another moment of gaping at the car to realize what was wrong: the apartment had never been the source of his excitement when he had been sent to visit Red Robinson. It had been like a hundred other small, dimly lit apartments; the smell of stale cigars and musty bedclothes in the bedroom, of cheese and pumpernickel bread in the kitchen, of shit and aftershave lotion in the bathroom. The real excitement had been in leaving the apartment, waiting for his father to jiggle the doorknob one last time to be sure that the front door was locked, and then to feel the big hand on his shoulder as they walked the three blocks over to the firehouse. It was for the firehouse, not the apartment house, that he had always come—to see Red Robinson lead him into the Hook&Ladder and immediately undergo a transformation from a man whose words and steps meandered to somebody who slapped backs, who shouted at the men emitting pretended groans at his arrival, who on one occasion saw a rubber ball flying toward him and who grabbed a metal pick off the wall in time to blast the ball back out through the open doors into the street. That Red Robinson, Allison now thought, had always been more genuine than the one who had pussyfooted around the apartment, trying to act at ease about discussing school, what there was for supper, or what programs were on the radio. The man moving around restlessly under the low ceilings of the apartment had been constantly aware of having a son boarding with him for the weekend; the one in the firehouse had strutted around as though his son was just one more of the boys there to applaud his antics. Allison had always felt better being just one of the boys.

He knew that he had to go the rest of the way. As he went across the empty avenue, he smiled to think that not only were Achilles and Hector keeping an eye on him, but that a couple of angels were probably giving his mother a heart-to-heart, telling her not to keep cursing that the famous Robinson wiles were still at work on her children. Franklin Delano Roosevelt had been president when she had kicked the drunk out of her house, he had been president when she had given her name to her children, he had still been president when she reluctantly agreed to the periodic subway visits to Brooklyn, and yet it was still going on! So just where was eternity, after all?

Allison walked more rapidly past the garages that had once housed huge Cadillacs and Chryslers and that now seemed abandoned, with their dirty walls and broken windows. A wino was sprawled out on the stoop of an unlit house. Farther down he could see a man and a woman hanging around a phone box, but he turned off before he neared them. At once he saw the deep ruts running out from the building line into the gutter. But there was no red light on the wall of the building. He knew what he had discovered a second before he actually saw it. The silly feeling of being on *Candid Camera* came back to him. This time there wasn't even a doorframe to knock on. The green flats of the separate entrances for the Hook&Ladder and Engines had been replaced by a single gesso wall. The sign above the door said only SE REPARTE A DOMICILIO, without specifying what home delivery service.

Allison smelled the big ham and boiled potatoes on the kitchen table of the firehouse. He was surprised that the engine driver, McReynolds, could slice the meat as deftly as his mother. He was disappointed that his father took it as much for granted as she did that he would want half a plate of broccoli.

Somewhere nearby a car broke the night silence. Allison couldn't believe that he wanted to cry over such a silly disturbance. Not even Red Robinson had ever been that *pazzo,* he told himself as the Spanish sign blurred before his eyes.

The Fourth Day

1

Stanley Twitchell's house had been broken into, his possessions had been strewn around, and his rugs had been dirtied by policemen's shoes. Stanley Walter Twitchell was the quintessential victim, and there was no point trying to argue otherwise. And yet, as she watched Foy lead the man through his testimony, Elena felt the smallest twinge of satisfaction that Stanley Twitchell had been violated. Without Manuel Torres, she thought, the man with the frameless glasses and squeaky voice would have been just another head in the middle of the lynch mob; now that he himself had been ransacked, he couldn't get to the rope fast enough. If nothing else, Stanley Twitchell would never again be able to think of himself as a bystander, and that seemed worth something.

"Both your front door and vestibule door have locks, Mr. Twitchell?"

"Yes, sir."

"And both locks can be released only by a key?"

"That's correct."

"And do you recall ever giving either of those keys to the defendant Manuel Torres?"

Elena looked up from her legal pad in time to return Twitchell's glance. She had to keep going through the motions until she had instructed Jack Haggerty on the miracle she planned to have him deliver to her by Monday morning. She even felt a perverse comfort in Haggerty's sleazy presence in the seats behind her. The detective meant Monday, After the Weekend, Next Week, and Christ knew she had had enough of this week.

"And you never delegated anyone to give the keys to Mr. Torres?"

Foy continued knocking down his ducks one by one. She didn't like his self-confidence, any more than she had liked Richie Mutter's cockiness that afternoon at Rye Beach centuries ago when he had been literally knocking them down at one of the park's shooting galleries. *Oh, I'm sorry, Richie, I wasn't watching. You mean you got every one of them?* She thought again about which of the jurors were candidates for Haggerty. The tall, crew-cut man with the paunch, Benzinger, seemed like a good bet. In three days she hadn't seen him make a natural, unstudied gesture. Even for a juror he was clenched as tight as a fist, like somebody who had never gotten over some kind of shame. Would it have been too much to hope that he had once been assaulted by somebody resembling Manuel Torres and had not admitted it during jury selection? Absolutely too much—but also grounds for perjury if it turned out to be true. Benzinger was one.

"And those scratches weren't on the door when you left for work?"

"No, sir, they weren't."

King had been looking less smarmy all morning, almost content, Elena thought. He hadn't even worked up one of his usual moons when she had stood up to announce that she had no questions for Mrs. Cicut. Had King found somebody to take up his crazy case? Why not? Under some circumstances she might have imagined herself going in to Alan and Jim and arguing for it. John King wanted something for himself—maybe not something that was winnable in a courtroom, but something. Since when had an attitude like that stopped being important to her?

"And did you authorize anbody to enter your house that day? A friend or a neighbor?"

"No, I did not."

She coughed, dispelling thoughts of John King. She had never really been that much of a romantic, the "true believer" Alan had said she was. Lost causes hadn't appealed to her, not even among the law school projects she was supposed to have been enthusiastic about. Nothing, she thought now, had ever been as exciting as that first inkling of a strategy in talking with a client, of being able to relate a client's hope to her know-how and keep them together through trial, bargaining, and settlement. *That* was what she had always truly believed in, and whatever the outcome, almost all her clients had appreciated her for it. Even Earl Winters had been sincere in thanking her after the verdict.

"Your witness, Counselor."

Elena stood back up to reality; Manuel Torres didn't even move as she brushed against his leg. "No questions," she said, unable to imagine what Torres might say to her after a verdict.

Jack Haggerty couldn't wait for the guards to escort Torres away for the lunch recess. "Green said you wanted to see me," he announced loud enough for Foy to throw her a pitying smile as he hurried past.

"Sit down, Jack."

Haggerty flopped into Torres's seat, took a toothpick from his shirt pocket, and immediately began working it along his bottom teeth. She kept her head bent over her notes until she was sure from the shuffling behind her that Santiago Torres had finally gone away.

"Dog's not a problem," Haggerty said, after she had explained what she was looking for. "But it's kind of late in the game for the jury."

"You can't do it?"

"Didn't say that, sis. Just that it's short notice. I don't want you expecting weekend miracles."

"That's exactly what I do expect, Jack."

111

"Just like that?"

"Just like that."

He looked uncertainly at the jury list. "Ever know Jack Haggerty to give up before the game starts?" he asked after a moment.

"Alan told you the budget?"

"I wasn't talking about that."

"But I am, Jack."

Haggerty nodded reluctantly. "He told me. You want a thrifty miracle."

"Exactly," Elena said. "Now this Benzinger, for one. I'd bet anything there's a lie there." Haggerty's body heaved with a dry laugh. "I say something funny?" she asked.

"There's a lie everywhere, sis," he said, taking out a notebook. "But whether he raped your Torres bozo when Torres was a kid, that's something else."

"You have a great imagination, Jack."

"Learning, always learning."

Elena went back to the list. The names suddenly meant nothing to her. They were everyday citizens. They were anonymous citizens. They were such spectacularly honest citizens that she herself had already endorsed them.

"The black dame in the front row," Haggerty said. "She looks like she's honed some axes in her time."

"Weathers. She rents videos."

"Yeah? Good racket."

She looked at the list again. Weathers, Cort, Engelson, DeSilvestri. They didn't even make a good anagram.

"There's one thing you're looking for, sis. Somebody who killed the Indians."

"Somebody who killed the Indians?"

"I'm serious, sis," he said, jiggling the toothpick up and down between his teeth for her admiration. "I know what I'm talking about."

"That makes one of us. You don't even know the jurors."

"Better than you think."

"All right, I'm listening."

"You're not interested."

"I'm interested. For Christ's sake, Jack!"

"Order in this goddamn court!"

She had forgotten that Bordalato was still at the scrivener's desk. She flashed a smile over at the bailiff, who didn't even raise his head from what he was writing.

Haggerty seemed to be considering whether to exact another drop or two of blood from her, but then he leaned forward in his seat and swept her jury list into his lap. His pudgy fingers were a spectrum of brown and yellow cigar stains. "One thing you get out of your head right away," he said, pointing emphatically at his crotch, "you're not gonna find Lizzie Borden or Machine Gun Kelly hiding out under aliases here on your roster. Anybody sitting on top of a real juicy lie, the kind that could turn this trial into a house of cards, that kind never bothered answering the summons, or they gave off that little something during selection that made you or Foy drop them already. I don't say there aren't exceptions, but the kind of liar you can hope to find here is another kind altogether."

"What's that got to do with Indians?"

"A manner of speaking. What it comes down to is that some people tote things around the way you might carry around a hole in your pantyhose. The wrong move, the wrong kind of pressure, the hole gets bigger. You want to see who might qualify here."

He picked the list up off his lap and made an exaggerated show of studying it. Elena looked at the clock on the back wall. Did she still have enough time to call Mike Leong? He cost twice as much as Haggerty, and Alan wouldn't go for it, but even paying for the extra out of her own pocket suddenly seemed like the lesser of two evils.

"What you want is somebody who can be *convinced* he's a liar."

"Just that, huh?"

He let the list drop back onto his lap, seeming satisfied about something he had read. "Somebody who killed the Indians, sis. Somebody who in his heart of liberal hearts hates the dark-hued among us. The guy who went to bed with his mother, the girl who's a little too crazy about Pop. That guy who thinks he killed two hundred people because he was late for a plane that crashed. The hulk who didn't do anything while some guy was being beaten up in front of his eyes. Follow me?"

She suddenly preferred Torres in the chair. "No."

"Possibilities," he said, glancing over at Bordalato and lowering his voice. "I'm talking possibilities."

"You're talking crap," she said, for some reason whispering

113

with him. "You're talking about manipulation. Brainwashing, even."

"And you don't have enough time for it now. Yeah, I know. It's—"

"That's not what I object to, Jack."

But he wasn't listening. "Jack Haggerty isn't going to sit here promising you the world," he said blithely, "not with just a weekend to work. All I'm saying is that there's a possibility. I've seen it before. In this very building. True, it was during selection, not three days after, but you got to believe everything's possible."

Suddenly, Elena felt like smiling. It turned out to be so easy to give in to the truth. She was astonished by what a relief the feeling was. For how long had she been tormenting herself to keep the only important fact about her defense of Manuel Torres at bay—that he was guilty of committing a second-degree felony and that he was going to be found guilty of committing a second-degree felony by a jury of anonymous, honest, objective people. Now, thanks to Haggerty, she couldn't deny it anymore. Haggerty's posturing was reality. Manuel Torres was going to get seven-to-fifteen, and neither she, Earl Winters, nor promises to her mother was going to prevent that.

"You agree, sis?"

"Ever get tired of banging your head against a wall, Jack?"

"Supposed to make you feel good when you stop."

"It does. Believe me."

Haggerty gave himself a second to understand, decided it wasn't worth the effort, and shrugged. "In your place I'd probably think the same thing," he said. "No guarantees. You're liable to get your hands dirty. Could be a little messy, on your human level. And for what? For a bozo who doesn't know which end is up. I understand. Just as long as you don't let yourself turn into somebody who killed the Indians."

"Thanks for the warning, but now that I've thought about this . . ."

"Last thing you want to think is that you didn't do enough for Torres."

She reached over and snatched the list off his lap. "Good try, Jack. But I've been through it."

He nodded. "So I read the other day."

114

She didn't know why she was even talking to him. "Don't push it, all right? I'm sure Alan will find you something else."

"He's not going to find Charles Allison for me—or for you."

"The teacher?"

Haggerty stood up slowly, nodded to the paper in her hand, and buttoned his jacket. "You made the note yourself, sis. Here's a guy who's hardly popped his varicose veins and he retires. Why? To go off to the Caribbean to get a gentleman's tan? That address doesn't sound like the tropics to me."

Despite herself, she found Allison's name on the list. It seemed so much closer than the void she knew was awaiting her as soon as she got rid of Haggerty and thought about what she had been doing the last several days.

"All those years teaching, and he suddenly quits? Food for thought."

"Food for a few hundred dollars is what you mean."

"You called me, sis. I didn't call you."

The image of the silver-haired man swam in front of Elena's eyes. She had depended on him during her opening remarks. He had looked solicitous and intelligent. And also impenetrable in some basic way. He wasn't going to give her a single thing.

"Look, Alvarez, both of us know you're in a jam. If it was me in your place, I'd write this Torres bozo off as yesterday's fish. But I only got a license, and you got a degree. You got to help people despite themselves. Nobody's going to applaud you for it, but who's in your racket for a standing ovation anyway? Okay, now you have the dog. Personally, I think that's a nonstarter, but you have to give it a shot. You get Torres off on a trespass charge, I'll buy you the dinner he'll never think of buying you. But now's not the time to pull your punches. You're already on the mat, you're down by a thousand points. You got nothing to lose."

"By invading the privacy of a juror?"

"You know better than that. It's a possibility."

"Of what, Jack!"

This time Bordalato did look up, and this time she didn't bother smiling over at him. Haggerty ignored him, too. "Of whatever we turn up."

"Talk straight, Haggerty. What you're suggesting is some kind of morals incident. One, you have a sleazy mind. Two, you have a predictable mind. And three, I have no intention of going to

Raymond and challenging a juror to admit some peccadillo that, even if it happened, isn't going to influence the verdict on Manuel Torres one way or the other."

"You're widening the battlefield. The best defense is a good offense."

"Whatever that means."

"What it means, sis, is what every lawyer who ever walked into this room with a loser for a client means. You talk about winning in law what you can't win in evidence. You talk about winning over a jury. The law and the jury, they're supposed to be neutral. Well, bullshit, Ms. Alvarez. In the State of New York versus Manuel Torres, the law and the jury are as hostile to your client as the evidence is. The only one who can't see that is you, because you're too frantic trying to come up with legal ploys. It's not going to make a difference, sis. The evidence, the law, the jury—they're *all* your enemy! The only way you have a chance in hell of walking out of here with even a moral victory is to treat them for what they are and beat them to the punch."

"By taking a flier that Charles Allison is a dirty old man?"

"By taking a flier that the only difference between Manuel Torres and some members of that jury is that their skeletons are still in the closet. You drop a doubt here, you drop one there. Somebody like Allison hears it. He isn't so cocky when he goes back to the jury room. He starts to make arguments for your client that you didn't even make. After a little while you get a few more of them in there wondering. I've seen it a hundred times, sis. Get some juror to start wondering about himself, another juror, the judge, or the goddamn sweeper in the hall, know what comes out most of the time? Good old compromise. No one's quite so fast about throwing the first stone. Pebbles, yeah, but no boulders, because nobody wants to give himself away. Anybody who's killed the Indians isn't going to throw any boulders."

"Allison's a straight arrow, Jack."

"Maybe even to himself. But who's to say what dirty thoughts he might have had one afternoon twenty years ago? That's up to you to bring out, counselor. You're the one with the words."

"You really think that people are that vulnerable to suggestion?" She thought at once of King scratching his stomach.

Haggerty shrugged. "Like I said, it's only a possibility. And not even a great one, with just the weekend to work on it."

He stopped talking. Bordalato somehow managed to keep his records at the desk without making a sound. In the abrupt silence, Elena knew exactly where she was; Haggerty wasn't going to ask her directly whether he should go ahead because he didn't want to take no for an answer, and she had run out of procrastinating objections. "There's the dog," she said.

"First thing," he said, trying to keep the hope out of his voice.

She laughed, hearing her hollowness. "It's ridiculous, you have to admit it, Jack. The man probably just got tired of repeating the same subject year after year."

"We all get tired of it. But we don't all retire."

"Maybe we're not as well off as he is."

"We'll find that out. The worst thing that happens, we still have your candidate. This Benzinger."

My candidate. Elena looked over at the empty jury box. All of a sudden, John King and his problems with cash-machine-card ads seemed very wholesome.

2

The midday sun shone idly through the corroded beams of the old El and cast only the weakest of reflections on the sidewalk. As he strode along on the shadows of spars and signal lights, Allison waited for them to deepen or disappear altogether. He felt filled with influence today.

Striding along beside him, Anna DeSilvestri and Mark Benzinger managed smoothly to avoid loose words about the trial, trading cabbages for kings promptly, continuously. Allison was glad that he'd decided to spend his lunch hour on a walk rather than on a greasy hamburger, and glad too that they had had the same thought and had come along. They seemed used to him.

DeSilvestri asked a question; Benzinger replied. Their words drifted by like a neglected breeze. He trusted that other words

117

would be coming—in one life or another. At the moment the prospect was neither thrilling nor terrifying; daunting mostly, so beyond his capacities that he gazed easily up at the abandoned track overhead instead. The girders ran down the avenue as far as he could see. He thought of the El as something that had been there long before him, Anna DeSilvestri, and Mark Benzinger; he thought of the old El as world history.

He told them a story. It was a weathered story, one of his pulling-away stories, one that he had told many times before, but it sounded different to him. He himself figured in it differently—no longer as the receiver of a specific experience, but as an agent on his own, dispatched to bring back something he now had to show. It was as though the things that he had experienced, the events and incidents that he was now able to call on, had only half happened in their natural time and required his relating them on a noon walk with a couple of strangers to be complete. He knew that he had never told the story so accurately.

He knew that he was going to die.

Two blocks ahead of them, on the other side of the street, there was a commotion. A small crowd—passersby, shopkeepers, somebody who'd stopped and gotten out of an automobile—stood under the El, looking up at the tracks. They were shouting at a young black boy who was gesticulating back to them about something on the trestle.

"There's another kid up there," Anna said.

Allison saw the second boy's thin, jean-clad legs swinging wildly out over the street. The driver of the car, a portly black man in a suit and sunglasses, was tugging at the old boards that had been nailed across the steps up to the station. An elderly white man wearing a peaked cap began to pull at the boards, too.

"He shouldn't be wiggling like that." Even as he said it, Allison wasn't listening to himself. He was too startled by how effortlessly he hurried across the street—and by how much quicker Anna and Benzinger still were. She in her black boots and swinging beads, Benzinger clomping his big feet down like a horse, they were both a good twenty feet ahead when they arrived at the spot under the boy's legs. Benzinger shouted up what Allison had just said about the wiggling, but more usefully, to both the kid held at the waist by a rotten beam and to his friend. The friend repeated the

118

order, but without releasing his hold on the guardrail or taking his eyes off the sidewalk.

Allison ran directly to the staircase, where the two men seemed to have loosened a rusty nail. As soon as he gripped the top of the planking between the hands of the fat businessman and the old-timer, he felt their desperation. Loose nail or not, the board was still solidly in place. He was about to cry for Benzinger when the fat man lost his sunglasses, letting go of the board just in time to catch them against his chest. Allison waved the old man away as well, stepped back a couple feet, and, pushing what refused to be pulled, shoved his foot at the center of the board. To his astonishment, the board cracked immediately. Telling himself not to become preoccupied with how clever he was, he went at it a second and third time. Benzinger and the businessman went at it with him. DeSilvestri continued to sound calm as she shouted up at the boys. He wondered what had happened to the old man in the peaked cap.

When the board finally gave way, Allison felt his breath collected too far above his lungs to be of any use. Stepping over the lower planking and straggling up the dusty steps after Benzinger and the fat man, he thought of all the sherries he had closed off his evenings with and all the ice creams he had looked forward to on Sunday afternoons. He marveled at the speed of Benzinger: maybe not a former basketball pro as he had initially fancied, but a priest who had probably spent more than one afternoon shooting baskets in the yard of a parochial school.

He was surprised when all the huffing and puffing on the stairs above him turned out to be not from the fat man, but from Benzinger.

Allison almost caught up to them at the old wooden turnstiles. By the time they got to the top of the inside stairs and were hurrying along the platform, he was even with them. The advertising posters were for cereals and beers that looked as though they should have gone out of business but hadn't. Someone had stolen the plaque with the station's name on it. The Queens skyline, of projects and parkways and building-wide billboards, almost made him dizzy with its randomness.

The boy who had been doing all the shouting was still marooned at the guardrail and still looking down at the sidewalk. A few feet closer was the half body of the second boy, his sticklike arms planted firmly on the slat in front of him. Whatever struggling he'd been doing was now nowhere on his face: he was paralyzed, totally numb, sweat and tears running down his cheeks.

The boy at the guardrail allowed himself a peek over his shoulder to see them. "Hurry, hurry," he said, his voice a hoarse whisper.

Allison climbed down the platform ladder, stopping at the bottom rung. Benzinger and the fat man hesitated at the top of the ladder. He knew that their eyes, like his own, were searching the footing ahead of him. The walkway looked safe enough, but the chunky beams closer to the boys were at least waterlogged and probably corroded.

"Those kids are a hundred pounds lighter than us," the fat man said.

Allison laughed at the man's conservatism and stepped down onto the track. He couldn't tell whether it was his shoes or the wood beneath them that gave him the buoyancy of hard sponge as he moved out.

Seeing help approaching, the boy at the guardrail seemed on the verge of letting go of the rusty iron. The boy in the hole tried to turn his head for a better look at what his friend saw. "Just stay still," Allison said, sounding firm but wishing now that he had waited for some of the people that he now heard tramping down the platform behind him.

The walkway came to an end. The boy in the hole was about two body stretches away, the friend at the guardrail another three or four on top of that. He was close enough now to hear the trapped boy's short, abrupt inhales and exhales and to see the way tears and sweat ran over a small wart above his lip. He could also see that the broken ends of the beams supporting the kid hadn't penetrated his polo shirt, but were simply holding him like a life belt.

Allison looked for a beam that wasn't connected to those supporting the boy. He was as sure as he could be of the one he gingerly stepped on. Nothing gave. The second step felt even steadier than the first. He told himself to squat carefully. There was a tremor from the traffic in the street below. He couldn't believe that the street hadn't been closed off by now.

"Okay, now," he said, more to himself than to the boy, whose terrified eyes and slippery arms were now definitely within reach.

"See if there's room under the armpits."

Allison glanced back to see that the fat man had advanced as far as the end of the walkway. Benzinger had remained on the platform ladder to the tracks and was blocking the way of five or six other people. At least one of them, a twentyish kid in an NYU jogging suit, seemed a lot better suited for the task at hand than Allison. "Right."

He didn't know who had made him and the fat man experts on extricating trapped kids from holes, but it was too late to worry about that now. Leaning forward, he got his hands down over the back of the boy's shoulders, felt nothing protruding, and pulled back again. Going into the front the second time, he ran his fingers down the sides of the boy's chest and then down along the rib cage until he was sure there was nothing sticking into him or out of him. The boy didn't look like he would have forgiven him if he took his hands away a second time without pulling him out.

"Gotcha!"

The boy started to laugh.

"No, no, don't say anything. Is there anything sticking in you?" The boy shook his head. "Absolutely sure? Nowhere in your side?" Another quick shake of the head.

"Good, good!" the fat man called.

He was out of excuses for delaying a single second more. Before the fat man could say anything else, he meshed his fingers together behind the boy's back and, his forearms pressing into the boy's armpits, pulled back. For a second he seemed to be pulling only at himself, then in the next second he felt like he was uprooting the entire elevated structure. The boy seemed to be up in the air before he saw him, saw his own hands holding him, felt himself buckling back. For some idiotic reason one of the people back on the platform and somebody down below in the street yelled for him to keep his balance. The fat businessman was more useful: without a word of warning, he was suddenly on top of them, lifting the boy up and back. The fat man and the boy were back again on the walkway even as Allison reached behind himself to catch the edge of the beam jutting into his backbone. He sat still. He imagined he heard a crack, imagined he felt a sway. But there was nothing; only some clapping from the platform. He still had the other half of his job ahead of him.

The second boy looked across the hole and the buffer beam at him. He looked more frightened than the boy in the hole had

121

been, and he was also a good twenty pounds heavier. For a long moment he seemed mesmerized by the sight of the fat businessman carrying his friend back to the safety of the platform.

"Let go of the rail, son," Allison said.

The boy looked at him with a start; letting go of the guardrail was the last thing he was going to do.

"I can't go over there for you. You have to come to me."

The boy's hesitation was infuriating: he wasn't in half the danger his friend had been. Hadn't he gotten over to the guardrail on his own?

"Nothing to it, son. Look how I'm sitting. A day at the beach."

The kid still didn't smile, and Allison would have felt better if he hadn't chosen that moment to glimpse Anna DeSilvestri on the sidewalk below. He was too far above her to make out the color of her beads, and that seemed like sign enough that, if he fell through the rotting planks, he would be dead upon impact on the sidewalk.

"We'll take it, buddy. Come back here."

Two uniformed cops had replaced the fat businessman on the walkway. Both were young and slender; even their gear didn't look heavy on them.

"I can't go without my friend here," Allison heard himself reply. "Right?"

The boy threw another jittery look up toward the platform. "C'mon, Andy," a young voice called out. "It's easy."

Andy had to crack something like a smile at his friend's challenge. And as the boy let go of the railing and began measuring his steps over the buffer beam like an expert trackwalker, Allison had to smile too. The boy on the platform was right, he thought, readying his hands for the vault to come. It *was* easy, and much easier than taking gas in his kitchen or falling through the beams on Anna DeSilvestri. Not for Benzinger or the fat businessman or the cops or the student in the jogging outfit; but for him being a hero had been *very* easy.

Andy jumped past him.

3

Hobie knew it hadn't been *exactly* a perfect record. He had screwed that up three years ago the morning he'd been stuck on the subway for more than an hour because of some goofus with a heart attack. Then there had been last year, when on his way to the subway, he'd made the mistake of seeing a panel truck sideswipe a patrol car and had been forced to stand around forever to make a statement. Still, he told himself now as he killed the lights in his elevator car and retrieved his container of soup from behind the stool, those two times had been different, had not been completely his fault. He couldn't be responsible for geeps getting heart attacks and slamming into patrol cars; they had been pretty good excuses for showing up late. But this morning he had no excuse. This morning he just hadn't heard the goddamn alarm clock.

And he wasn't sure he would hear it right now, either. He glanced around the hall for an empty bench, his insides feeling like they were being held together by chewing gum. He would have been better off if there'd been some pain telling him what was wrong and where it was wrong. But no such luck. The goddamn beers he had downed at Maloney's were still trying to make up their mind where to punch him. They were like Mercer and Brooks: nobody had made a crack yet about him being late, but he knew it was coming. He just wished he could get it over with.

The only bench that wasn't completely occupied was at the far end of the hall. Half of it was taken by a sour-looking burro turning the pages of an *El Diario*, but as long as the geep didn't speak English, he didn't mind. Hobie camped on the bench next to the trash can. The smell of apple skins from the can reminded him of

Mercer's grumbling about how the hallways were becoming picnic areas, and he was glad again that he had never gone along with the campaign by the custodians to make the guards stricter about enforcing the ban on eating in the building. The fact was, he liked the smell of rotting apples; of old oranges and tangerines, too. They were damn nicer stinks than the sweet spices in the hair of the geep sitting next to him. A real politician, Mercer! The building was crawling with muggers, crack dealers, and killers, and all Mercer was worried about was the wrong kind of garbage in the trash cans!

He took his soup out of the bag. He wasn't really all that hungry so early in the day, but he knew he would have been worse off if he didn't eat the slop. It wasn't just Mercer and the other hens in the building he had to worry about; if he still looked like a rag after work, he was also sure to hear it from Gallagher at the stand. The last thing he wanted was for the vet to find out he'd been late for work. That would have been good for sermons right up to Christmas. Hadn't Gallagher warned him about going to Maloney's while he was on his pills? Had the stand ever missed a delivery because he, the vet, had been hung over? Suppose a regular customer had come by for his paper and found that the stand was shut because the vet hadn't gotten up yet? Scratch a customer, that's what would have happened.

And the gorilla would be right.

And for what?

As he dipped the plastic spoon into the soup and stirred around the solids laying at the bottom, Hobie knew that he would never have a good answer to that question. Twelve hours later, he still didn't know what King had been ranting about. Something about a bank that had taken his name, and so King was going to—what? Rob the bank? Blow it up? It would've even been funny, if the goofus hadn't unnerved him so much with his crazy look. A bullshitter was one thing, a nut case another. King looked like the kind who would have done something, no matter how loony, just so he wouldn't be accused of being a bullshitter. Nobody needed that kind of goofus around.

He spooned down some soup. His mother might have cooked it, all barley and celery shavings. Nobody cooked barley exactly as his mother had, but the Greek at the greasy spoon came as close as anybody.

"You mind?"

The burro was asking him permission to smoke. "No skin off my nose. I don't make the laws around here."

The geep smiled at the No Smoking sign on the wall across from the bench and then lit up. "One thing, another thing," he said. "You work here?"

He had a mouthful of soup so he figured he didn't have to answer. Besides, Hobie thought, if the goofus couldn't figure out the answer to his own question, he was as stupid as he was gloomy-looking.

"How much they pay?"

"How much you want?"

The burro smiled, rolled his shoulders around under his leather jacket, and took another drag. Hobie didn't like the guy's tone. He had to be fifty if he was a day, but he was still a wise guy from the street, an overaged punk who was probably hanging around because his son or daughter hadn't gotten away fast enough on a job their old man had been in on too.

"You work, you work," he said now. "For money, always money."

"Know somethin' else?"

The burro shook his head; he hadn't thought about it before and he wasn't going to start now. Hobie took another spoonful of barley. He had seen lots of geeps like this one. Most of them had been ten, even twenty years younger, and they'd hung around Victor Diaz's coffeehouse in Bodegaville like flies stuck to flypaper. Making a big show of escorting the runners to Diaz's table in the back. Cracking wise over what happened to runners who short-changed the bank. Deliberately shutting up while Diaz went through the slips to let a runner know that they were serious people, ready to beat up on anybody with a wrong count. Bullshitters all of them, and how Gallagher had lasted even four months working with them, Hobie had never really understood. Unless it was because he, not the vet, had been the one to make the deliveries to the coffee shop.

The door at the end of the hall opened, and Raymond, still in his robes and gimping along on a single crutch, came out of his chambers and made his way to the elevator. As soon as the burro saw him coming, he straightened up. He looked ready to jump out of his skin altogether when Raymond stopped in front of them.

125

"Guess I'm going to have to settle for a second-class ride, eh, Hobie?"

"Brooks knows the way."

Raymond smiled and nodded at his soup. "One of these days you're going to eat a real lunch."

"You make the reservation, Judge. I'll be there."

Raymond laughed like a horse and went hobbling off to the elevator. Only after he had gone down with Brooks did the burro take another puff. "He's a tough judge, yeah?"

"I don't know. What's tough?"

"Always gives the maximum."

"I don't know. You up before him?"

"Me? No, no. Just asking."

The fact was, Hobie thought, Raymond didn't have a reputation one way or the other. But he wasn't about to volunteer that information. The last time he had been stupid enough to try to reassure somebody, the day right after Henry Aaron had passed Babe Ruth, he had ended up with a screeching woman in his elevator acting like *he* had been the one to sentence her goofus son to ten years.

Wilke and Finnigan came out of the elevator, and the burro immediately got rid of his cigarette. He kept his eyes on the two goofuses until they had walked the length of the corridor and found a bench with room for both of them. Hobie wished he had seen that space.

"People ever break out of this place?"

"Out of the buildin', you mean?"

"Must've happened sometime."

"Only once I can remember. About ten years ago. A political down on the third floor. Bombin' or some damn thing."

"What happened?"

"He got away. Like I said."

"Yeah, but how?"

Hobie got tired of the soup and tossed it in the trash basket. He felt bad that it was going to screw up the apple smell. "What difference? He got away is what I'm tellin' you."

And all he was going to tell the burro. That had been a scary day. Benny Smith, who hadn't been able to ask for the time of day without sounding like one of those calypso niggers. *Mon* this, *mon* that. *Mon, you do what I say and nobody get hurt. Mon, you keep your hands*

126

where I can see them. Right out in the elevators with a teenage girl he'd taken as a hostage and the gun he'd gotten from one of the cluck guards. If he hadn't been quick enough to shut his doors, Hobie thought, it would've been him instead of Brooks who'd been forced to bring the goofus down to the lobby. Brooks had almost shit in his pants.

"All these guards," the burro said, still looking after Wilke and Finnigan at the end of the hall. "I don't see how you can escape from here."

"You don't, huh? Bring a damn bazooka in here and those two down there wouldn't see it. If they did see it, you could tell 'em it was an umbrella."

Hobie tore the cellophane off the saltines that the Greek had put in with his soup. The burro shook his head like he couldn't believe Wilke and Finnigan weren't Superman. In Bodegaville they never believed anything. They were so busy acting tough for one another that they never got around to taking a look at the bulls they were supposed to be tough about. How many times had he had all of Diaz's burros eating out of his hand after all the sums had been worked out and he had taken one of their sugary brandies? Even Victor Diaz himself had looked at him with respect when he had told them about the *real* street people, the kind who hadn't had to hide within boys clubs to be known in the neighborhood. It was what he had told the vet from the first day the bank had been passed to Diaz: burros were all talk. Any heat at all came down, they'd be out of business.

"They must know something," the geep said.

The saltines were soggy; as usual, the Greek had thrown them in the bag on top of the soup container. "Yeah, they're geniuses. Takes 'em more than a month even to remember they're two men short. Don't even know how to count their own heads." At least the saltines were still crisp in the middle. "Heads they got aren't worth countin'. One of them's in jail for shootin' his partner. Another one goes around talkin' about blowin' up a bank. Belongs in the bin. You watch those two down the hall there awhile. Give 'em an hour or so and they'll figure out how to stand up again."

The geep looked at him with a half smile: he didn't believe, he didn't doubt. Like all burros, he was looking for the hook. *"You'd break out if you had a chance?"*

"Me? What the hell you talkin' about?"

"I mean, if you were like this other one that did it ten years ago."

"Benny Smith?"

"I don't know."

"That was his name. Benny Smith. Don't you listen?"

"Whatever his name was."

"Benny Smith, that's what. You ask me, it's a miracle every goofus on trial don't just hear guilty and then cakewalk out the front door. Won't be goofuses like them two to stop him."

The burro put his head back against the wall and stared some more at Wilke and Finnigan. Hobie didn't like the way the guy seemed to be thinking a little too seriously. "You know somebody in Raymond's court?" he asked.

It seemed like a simple enough question, but the geep barely nodded.

"Just askin'. No business of mine."

"My son. Serious business."

"Yeah. I guess so."

The burro finally stopped looking at Wilke and Finnigan. "Wild kid. Always in trouble."

"Yeah, well."

"Don't like me. Liked his mother, don't like me."

"One of those things."

"Sometimes I think I don't like him, either. No . . . no nerve. Never had nerve, even when he was a kid."

Hobie could believe that: the old man didn't look like much of a daredevil, either. But he didn't need hearing about other people's troubles. He had enough of his own with the Greek and his soggy, stale saltines.

"Everyone must have nerve somewhere, no? Just one time you find enough courage to do something? Everybody must be like that."

"You say so," Hobie muttered. The burro seemed to have been drinking from the same well as King.

"That's what's more important than money, amigo," he said. He looked like he was going to cry.

"What's that?"

"Courage," the burro said, pointing at his heart and at the pen in his shirt pocket. "I think everybody should think about that

128

before money. And I think if they want to be courageous, they should be. It is what a man should be, yes?"

Hobie had had enough of both the saltines and the burro. He stood up; the Greek's crumbs would give Mercer something to do with his broom.

"You agree with me, yes, amigo?"

"Whatever you say. See you around."

Even before he turned away from the goofus, the burro went back to rolling his head against the wall, water in his eyes. Scraping over to the elevators, Hobie had the sinking feeling that he had somehow talked out of school—something he had never done at Victor Diaz's coffee shop when the burros had asked him about the Gambinos and the Gallos and some of the others who had run the bank before them. In those days he had been better at keeping his trap shut.

4

Manuel liked Joe Waxman's style. He had liked it the night he had been booked and he liked it now, in the courtroom. From the second the detective had taken the witness stand, he had been doing it by the numbers. Voice loud and clear, eyes on the jury, checking his black notebook every time Foy asked about a time or what somebody had said. There were worse things in the world than second-degree burglary, his attitude said, but he couldn't just let it ride, either. He was a pro doing his job.

Which was more than could be said for Miss Madrid. As Foy sat down and Alvarez got up, Manuel couldn't figure out how she could act so serious about so little. The most she was going to accomplish was to get it on the record that he hadn't been holding any stolen goods when Waxman had collared him in the basement of the house. Big fucking deal.

"You were called to the scene by Mrs. Cicut, Sergeant?"

"Right."

"And she told you . . .?"

Manuel scraped his chair back deliberately. He didn't like putting Waxman through such small shit, and he wanted Waxman to know it.

"There were chips and scratches around the keyhole."

"And you assumed the lock had been forced?"

"It seemed safe to assume that, yes."

"Because Mrs. Cicut told you she saw the defendant forcing the lock?"

"Because I saw it myself."

"I thought you only saw chips and scratches. Are you saying you also saw the defendant Manuel Torres forcing the lock?"

"Of course not."

"Oh."

Manuel was surprised that Waxman had left himself open for her; he'd had more on the ball in the basement and at the station house.

"You entered the house. Did you notice any disturbance on the ground floor?"

"No."

"The door leading upstairs was closed?"

"Yes."

"No sign of anyone in the living room or kitchen?"

"Right."

"What was it that made you go down to the basement?"

"Normal procedure."

"Would you explain that, please?"

Manuel glanced over at the jury box. The teacher with the white hair was a million miles away, like the engines had all gone out on a call and he didn't have a thing to do except think until they came back. But the teacher looked funnier than that, too—all puffed out, a lock of hair hanging over his forehead, even a little messy. He didn't know why he gave a shit one way or the other, but he was disappointed in the old guy. He should have been neater-looking.

"What I'm trying to understand, Sergeant, is why, if you suspected that there was an intruder behind those boxes in the basement, why didn't you just draw your gun and—?"

"It was already out."

"Oh, it was already out. Okay. Then why didn't you just call out to the person you suspected was hiding? Why did you decide to create the impression that you were leaving the premises, then sneak back down to the basement and wait all that time in the dark for the person to make the first move?"

"I wasn't sure there was only one person."

"Really? You thought there might've been more than one person squeezed into that little space between the boxes and the bookshelves?"

"I didn't want to take the chance."

"But Mrs. Cicut's call reported only one intruder, didn't it?"

"She saw one. That didn't mean there couldn't be others."

Manuel put his hand over his smile. Waxman was running circles around her. Waxman had been there, Miss Madrid hadn't. Even now he could feel the cop in the cellar with him. He crouched behind the boxes in the empty bottom shelf of the old bookcase, Waxman out in the middle of the floor. There hadn't been a single creak of wood, the sound of a single breath, but he'd known Waxman was there. He had thought of things, a thousand things, to wait the cop out. He'd thought of the lady and that dog of hers. He'd thought of her talking to the cops in the street and then going home to telephone her husband at work to tell him about all the commotion. He'd thought of being at Shea Stadium and seeing Ray Knight get his single and Mookie Wilson bounce his ground ball through Bill Buckner's legs and of wondering how so many thousands of people could go crazy over a Series that didn't have the Yankees in it. He'd looked at the hairs on his arms and counted off Alcala, Pepe, Elizabeth, Pallo, and the rest of the old barrio. He'd imagined them all swaggering into the coffeehouse to tell Victor Diaz that he was no longer running things, that a new generation was taking over. And Victor had laughed like hell, slapped Santiago on the shoulder, and told him what a macho he had for a son. And everybody had been happy and ended up drinking beer.

"And you found nothing on the person of Mr. Torres that was subsequently determined to be the property of Mr. Twitchell?"

"No."

"Nothing at all, Sergeant?"

"No, nothing."

"And nothing in the space behind the cartons? Nothing there from the upstairs or another part of the house?"

"No, nothing."

"The only thing behind the cartons in the big shelf area of the bookcase was Manuel Torres?"

"Right."

Manuel shook his head, but Waxman didn't see it. Suddenly, they weren't on the same wavelength anymore. Down in Twitchell's basement he'd thought of everything he could have, but Waxman had waited him out. The pig hadn't just wanted to collar him, he'd wanted Manuel to collar himself, to surrender, to be more of a loser than Waxman himself was a winner. Waxman had wanted to humiliate him.

"Then let me ask you this, Sergeant. The way the cartons were placed in front of the defendant, would it have been possible for me, let's say, to put my hand in the space there and reach him?"

"Without moving the cartons, you mean?"

"Without moving them. Over the top."

"No, I wouldn't say so."

"Well, granted I have relatively large hands. But what about somebody like Ms. DeSilvestri here? Do you think she'd have been able to squeeze her hand into the space?"

"Probably not. The tops of the boxes came up even with the second of the three shelves and the defendant was crouched down inside the lowest one. You would've had to push the cartons aside to touch him like you say."

"Even with small hands like Ms. DeSilvestri's?"

"I'd say so."

"So the space you're describing, Sergeant Waxman, was about equivalent to, say, what a cat's paw might fit into?"

"Not much more than that."

"A cat's paw. What about a dog's paw?"

"What kind of dog?"

"Well, for the sake of argument, let's say a German shepherd."

"Objection! Calls for speculation on the part of the witness."

"So did the question about the cat, Mr. Foy. You allowed that one, I'll allow this one. Proceed, Ms. Alvarez."

Manuel couldn't believe it: suddenly Raymond liked her and Foy looked like he had been rabbit-punched. Even King had come down from his cloud to look at Alvarez like she had said something interesting. Every one of them looked like they were ready to buy her bullshit about his hiding in the cellar to get away from the dog!

"Recall something else for us, will you, Sergeant? When you ordered the defendant to come out from behind the boxes and he did so, how would you characterize his manner? Did he look frightened, would you say?"

"I'd say so. I had my gun out."

"Of course. You had your gun out. So the defendant might've been . . . cowering? Would that be a fair description?"

"Yes."

"Frightened and cowering. Anything else?"

"Well, I guess you could say he also looked a little relieved."

"Relieved, Sergeant?"

"Well, he'd been stuck behind those boxes—"

"Let's skip that conjecture for now, Sergeant. The main thing is that, in your judgment, the defendant looked relieved. Correct?"

"I'd say so."

He had never told her that. How did she know? She hadn't been down in the cellar with him, couldn't have known what it felt like. Looking at his fucking watch every thirty seconds. The cramps above his toes and behind both knees. Afraid that even his beard might give him away by grazing one of the boxes. Knowing that he hadn't even been fast enough to grab anything worth carrying. She couldn't have had a clue to what it had felt like not to have a damn thing to show for all his moves out on the street and at the front door. He hadn't been a thief, he had been a sneak. *El solapado.* Exactly as old Robinson had once said he was in the firehouse. Who *wouldn't* have been relieved to take a deep breath and straighten his knees?

"You've testified, Sergeant Waxman, that the defendant made a statement while he was being handcuffed in the basement."

"Yes. He said I'd earned my collar."

"And?"

"And he denied he'd been trying to burglarize the premises."

"In the same breath? Somewhat contradictory, wouldn't you say?"

"Objection."

"Ms. Alvarez?"

"Your Honor, I'm simply trying to give the court the benefit of Sergeant Waxman's long experience as a police officer. I'm not asking him for his conjectures about the defendant's motives, but for his professional insights."

133

"I'll allow the question. Sergeant?"

"I'd say he was confused. He wasn't sure what he was saying exactly."

"Confused."

"Yes, confused."

"Cowering, relieved, confused."

Manuel didn't know what he was waiting for. Waxman wasn't going to help him against her. Raymond and Foy were useless. He didn't have to turn around to know how Santiago thought she was so great. "I wasn't confused!"

It seemed to take forever before they heard him. Alvarez turned around and looked over his head like it had been the *viejo* who had cried out. Raymond seemed surprised that he knew how to talk in public. Only Waxman and the typist were looking at him directly, like he was going to say something more than they wanted to hear. "That's crap! I wasn't confused!"

"That will be enough, Mr. Torres."

Fuck Raymond. But he still hadn't said enough. Behind him, Landers and Myers hadn't moved an inch to grab him. King thought he was funny. The typist just looked pissed that he'd written down something Raymond was going to tell him to erase. "All I want to say is, I wasn't confused."

"That may or may not be so, Mr. Torres. But you certainly seem confused about courtroom procedure. Please remain silent."

Foy was looking at him like he was measuring him for a new suit. The jury stared at him like it was the first time they had been allowed to look at him. Everybody except the teacher, anyway; he looked like he had known all along that Waxman was wrong, that Manuel Torres hadn't been confused.

"May I proceed, Your Honor?"

"If you think your client is sufficiently calm. The jury will ignore Mr. Torres's remarks. Go ahead, Counselor."

She lingered a second, looking over at him. She still had lemons all over her mouth, but she looked happy about something in her eyes. He had done something to please her. It was as if the bitch had planned it all!

He wished he had the razors then and there to take care of her. Even if he never made it past Landers and Myers, he would've at least gotten her.

"How long was it, Sergeant, before your backup units arrived?"

"Ten, maybe twelve, minutes."

Manuel looked around on the table for something. The plastic water pitcher was lighter than it looked. It almost flew back out of his hand before he could aim it and get rid of it. Alvarez jumped as the judge yelled and the pitcher hit the floor. She jumped so fast that she came out of her right shoe. Landers came down on him from behind, and Myers grabbed his arms around the chair. She looked funny with one shoe on and one shoe off. He didn't know why Landers and Myers were pinning him so tight against the chair. Waxman was only a few feet away and he could have told them that *el solapado* didn't carry. Not yet, anyway.

5

King refused to believe that Hobie Morgan had gone to McCloud. One of the other elevator operators, maybe some judge who'd gotten into his car at some point during the day, but the building commander? He couldn't believe it. Not even Morrison would have been so fast to score a brownie point. Frank McCloud was the last person in the world he needed on his case.

But now it was too late, and he had the headache to prove it. He'd had his grand plan to use Hobie Morgan as a middleman, and now the spook had him in McCloud's outer office waiting to be fired. What the fuck had he done? He hadn't been anything but court security for eleven years. It had been ages since the army, Morgan's garage, and the UPS. He couldn't go back to any of those things now. They had been another world. Edith had still been with her mother and father in Jackson Heights, and he had been sharing a two-room place with Eddie Mannix in Astoria. Was he totally out of his mind? Had he thrown away his job because of a lousy *bank card?*

135

"If you're going to do something disgusting, King, I wish you'd do it in the bathroom down the hall."

King gave Alice Burke the smile she seemed to expect. The bitch would have made a good assistant for the assistant principal for discipline back in school; she seemed to like nothing better than to watch people sweat as they were waiting to see McCloud. "You're funny, Alice."

She stuck another sheet of paper in the typewriter. "Well, the master isn't, today," she chirped. "He's always so charming when he has to prepare the annual budget. I hope you didn't commit any mortal sins."

"None you'd appreciate."

"Oooo! A little edge today, is it? You sound like you've been taking your vitamins."

King smiled at her again, but more confidently. His crack had come as a small surprise to him, too. Maybe she was right, he thought; maybe he *had* picked up some vitamins, taking on the bank bastards. He told himself to keep that thought in his head.

Which he did, until the intercom buzzed, Burke waved him inside, and McCloud told him what he wanted to see him about.

"A cat?"

Slumped down in his high leather chair, McCloud swung his legs over the edge of his desk and nodded. King had never seen him looking so playful. His pouchy black face—the result, according to building scuttlebutt, of a fire years ago that had killed his son and left ugly white splotches on his right cheek—was usually one sour look after another; now, though, he was practically smiling as he cleaned his nails with a letter opener.

"You know. Little furry things that go meow?"

King thought about the Torres trial. Alvarez had been talking about cats and dogs all day. But what did that have to do with him and with Hobie Morgan?

"Wait, let's be sure we're sitting in the same teepee here." McCloud interrupted his manicure to take a slip of paper from his shirt pocket. "I have a license number here. See if you can match it, Mr. King, and win our big prize. What's *your* license number?"

"My car? Four-two-seven, jay-two-four."

"Four-door Chevy? Few years on it?"

" 'Eighty-six."

McCloud put the paper back in his pocket and went back to

his manicure. "I declare you the winner, Mr. King," he said less humorously. "You're now known as John King, Killer of Cats."

"I don't get it, Captain."

"Thursday morning. Little after eight. On your way here, I suppose. A car with your plates and description ran over a cat on Hillside Avenue."

King remembered with a start: The bump he had felt as he had been going along, and the black guys who had been hollering at him from the sidewalk. And the Black Power salute he'd thrown at them.

"All coming back to you now?"

"Yeah, I think I . . ."

"Good."

"But—"

"What? Thought you only winged the thing?"

"Is this . . . this cat why you wanted to see me?"

The last of the amusement vanished from McCloud's face, but he continued picking away with the letter opener. "Not your idea of a serious problem, I guess, huh? Well, I see your point, King. Here we are with starvation, pollution, AIDS, and a thousand other things on all sides of us. The great human comedy we call life, we don't really have too much time to worry about a dead kitty. I couldn't agree with you more. Only trouble is, what you and I see clearly, some other people don't. Yesterday afternoon, for example, just as I was getting ready to call it a day and go home to some nice poached salmon, I get two stalwarts from the local neighborhood association in here. In fifteen minutes they told me everything there was to tell about the pet-keeping habits of our Hillside Avenue neighbors." He thumbed some gook off the edge of the opener. "Some real interesting stuff. Like, the cat you killed turns out to be a fixture in the neighborhood since the days of the saber-toothed tiger. Was beloved by one and all, especially by the old lady who owned him. And then you come whipping along and not only do you run over this sacred symbol, but you think it's real funny to throw off a fuck-you when some people on the street shout after you."

"That's not true, Captain. I never gave anybody the finger."

"No? What was it, then? Wouldn't have been one of those old-fashioned Black Power salutes, would it? No, of course not. You

137

wouldn't be mocking a community where we have to work every day, would you?"

"No, sir."

"I didn't hear you."

"No, sir." He had taken too many somersaults on the day to understand what was happening. It had only been a few hours ago when, sitting upstairs for the Torres farce, he had allowed himself to think that Hobie Morgan was in the building dropping the right word in the right ear. And it had only been minutes ago when, sitting outside with Alice Burke, he had been sure he was about to be fired because of the old spook. What did a goddamm cat have to do with either feeling?

" . . . Of course, you didn't realize what you'd done—that's what I managed to sell them in here yesterday afternoon. You didn't realize you'd run over their cat. You didn't realize we have a special obligation around here to blend in with the community, to make them feel that we're not here just because that's where they plopped us and we don't give them a second's thought once we go home. You didn't realize any of that shit because you were too busy doing the fucking Indianapolis Five Hundred on Hillside Avenue!"

King wondered what Burke was thinking outside the door; he could never have gotten it across to her that McCloud's shouting didn't matter, that he really did have the edge she had sensed. "I don't know what to say, Captain."

McCloud pulled his legs off the desk, sat up, and tossed aside his letter opener. "No need, King," he said, jabbing a thick black finger at him. "I'm doing all the saying. First off, I want a real sincere letter of apology to this woman you've left catless, and I want it on my desk here Monday morning. I gave Burke the name and address, so you pick it up on the way out. What I also want is you to stay the hell off Hillside Avenue. They see you just cruising along after this little episode and they might get the wrong impression about our sensitivity. You follow?"

King kept his eyes on the finger pointed at him. It still had dirt under the nail, and that suddenly seemed like reason enough to get in the last word. "You haven't talked to Hobie Morgan today, have you, Captain?"

"Who? You mean the elevator man? No. Why should I talk to him? You kill his cat too?"

"Never mind. It isn't important."

McCloud wasn't convinced. "Something bothering you, King? Something you want me to know about?"

He started to say no again; McCloud wasn't a judge and he wasn't a lawyer. Some of the others said he wasn't a good court officer, that he was just administration and public relations. But who else was there now? Even Hobie Morgan had been useless. At least McCloud had run interference for him with the local yahoos.

"Spit it out, King. Won't leave this office if it doesn't have to."

"It's kind of complicated. May sound weird to you."

"Whatever it is, I've heard worse. Believe me."

King nodded, his eyes on McCloud's ugly scar. If McCloud really had lost one of his kids in a fire, King thought, nothing he had to say could be worse. "I think you know that bank up the street? The one near the bus stop?"

"Yeah. What about it?"

"Well, they use these big cardboard blowups in the window, to sell their bank cards, you know?" McCloud picked up the letter opener again and sat back. He looked like he still hadn't decided whether or not to listen all the way to the end. "The blowup of the bank card, it's made out to a John King."

"Yeah?"

"Well, the thing is, I never gave them permission to use it. My name. They're using it like it's just theirs to take."

McCloud's eyes dropped to the back of his desk nameplate, as though stealing that would have been the same thing.

"I don't think that's right, Captain."

"You don't."

"No sir, I don't."

McCloud considered for a moment, found an idea on the side of the letter opener he was playing with, and peered up again. "What do you figure on doing about it?"

It seemed like the first time somebody had asked him that question without sneering. "That's the problem," he admitted. "I thought about starting a legal action of some kind, but lawyers tell me that won't get me very far."

"You've talked to lawyers about this?"

"Well, one. She thinks it's in the same ballpark as John Doe."

"Yeah, I can see that."

"But John Doe, Jane Doe, even John Smith—everybody

knows that they're made-up names. I don't think it's the same thing."

McCloud nodded. Grave as his expression was, he seemed to be making an effort not to look across the office to the wall where he had put all his awards and service plaques. "Despite what this lawyer told you."

"I guess so. Despite what she said."

"You know more about the law than a lawyer, that it?"

"No, sir. But I think there's a wrong here."

"So call the bank."

"Excuse me?"

"Call the bank and tell them you don't want your name used."

For a second King was sure that McCloud had gone back to being playful, that he had found his good humor again. But, in fact, he seemed absolutely serious. "And accomplish what, Captain? I'm nobody to them. With a place like that, you have to come on with some clout or you get nowhere."

McCloud took in the answer, drumming his fingers quickly on the desk. He stood up. He was so neat in his uniform that he looked overdressed. He went over to the window that faced the courtyard. "Suppose I told you to forget about it, King? Suppose I told you you were making a mountain out of a molehill?"

"You wouldn't be the first, sir."

"Including your wife?"

"Yes. Edith, too."

McCloud slapped the letter opener against his palm and nodded at something out in the courtyard. "I don't want you misinterpreting what I'm asking, King . . ."

King had to smile; he should have expected the question. "Have I lost my marbles? No, Captain, I haven't."

"What I was going to ask," McCloud said, rocking up and down and drawing out every word, "was when was the last time you had a physical."

"Same question, isn't it, sir? Last year, with everybody else."

"No problems since then? Nothing you haven't been able to take care of with a couple of aspirin?"

"No, sir."

The slap of the letter opener against his palm got louder. "And at home? No serious problems there?"

"Captain, this really only has to do with the bank card."

McCloud turned from the window. It took a moment for his friendly smile to catch up with him. "They made me a captain, King, so I could ask all these idiot questions, you follow? Now some people across the bridge might've gone to work this morning thinking that I haven't been doing a very good job asking them lately. Gwynn and Barbarella. You and your cat. I hear this afternoon we even had a prisoner throwing a water pitcher at a judge before the two slugs on Prisoner duty got to him."

"I was there, Captain. He wasn't throwing it at the judge."

"Happy to hear it," he said, coming away from the window and perching on the edge of the desk. "But it's still my responsibility to ask these questions. I have to know what my own men are going through, follow?"

"Yes, sir."

"Good. Now talk to me."

It suddenly seemed easy for him to explain. Was it because he had never been *ordered* to explain it before? Strangely, as he talked into the stale odor of some kind of fish on the man's breath, it felt like that was his edge, not McCloud's. For once, he didn't have to argue everything from scratch, get people interested in listening to him; he just had to deliver. And that made everything clearer. For the first time, for instance, he was absolutely sure in his own mind that he hadn't gotten paranoid over the whole business. It wasn't as though he had ever been afraid that the bank was going to use his name in some evil way, he now realized as he spoke. If that had been the case, he wouldn't have had a problem, because lawyers would have flocked to him to get a piece of the action. But the point had never been *how* the bank was going to exploit his name, just that it *was* being exploited. Wasn't there an indifference about that that was even worse than, say, if they'd taken his name to slander him or accuse him falsely of something? It was the arrogance of the whole thing, of people who figured they could do anything they wanted to and didn't care who was affected by it. Were the banks God? Could they make it rain one day and then make the sun shine the next? Suppose, for instance, they had advertised the name Frank McCloud instead of John King on the card?

"I might not like it," McCloud answered, nodding intently. "But then I'd probably realize I had a lot more important things to worry about. I might think that I've been working too much lately and need a few days off."

"It's more than that, sir."

"Because you're making it more than that."

"If I don't nobody else will."

McCloud waited for more, but then just nodded and got up from the edge of the desk. "Let me ask you another thing, King," he said, going around to his chair again. "Just between you and me, you think we got a morale problem around here?"

"Morale problem?"

"You know. The thing with Gwynn and Barbarella. Lot more lateness in the last few months. Maybe some people too slow reacting in certain situations."

"The Gwynn thing could've happened anytime."

"Sure. But it's still my job to see things like that coming and to cut them off at the pass. And today—again, this is between you and me—I think I took a big step in that direction. The new budget, which I'm confident will be approved for the most part, provides for four extra subs a week. That translates as much less overtime and double-time. No officer will have to extend himself beyond reason. The only good security is rested security, follow?"

King felt something sag in his chest. He had failed again. Edith, Alvarez, Hobie Morgan, and now McCloud—everybody listened, but nobody heard.

"You're on Torres now, right? Jurors duty?"

"Yes, sir."

McCloud studied the duty roster on his desk. "Should be over Monday or Tuesday?"

"I'm not tired, Captain."

"And I'm no shrink, Officer," he said without raising his eyes from the roster. "I got no idea what's in your head. Where my responsibility comes in is in giving you time to work out for yourself what's running around in there. Just thinking, off by yourself awhile. Then, when you've done that, you're back in here telling me where you think things are. Then we decide what we do next. Follow?"

Even next week was now ruined, King realized. Suddenly, Monday and Tuesday stretched before him as emptily as the weekend. "I'd like to finish the Torres case."

"You have no choice. We're shorthanded. Plus, we haven't even decided there's a problem yet, right?"

"Captain—"

"Right?"

"Right."

McCloud looked relieved. "Okay, then here's the action plan. You go home today, and over the weekend you think about all this stuff from a different perspective than you've had till now. Do it just for the sake of argument, to placate me, the big bad wolf. Take a look at the whole thing, and ask yourself whether you're overreacting, whether it's really this bank card that's bugging you or something else. No preconceived ideas. No fuck-you attitude toward the bank. No worrying about what I'll say or about your fitness sheet or any of that administrative shit. Just look for answers as honestly as you can. Then, Tuesday or Wednesday, when Torres is over, you come back in here and you tell me what you've decided. If I still don't think you're seeing the picture straight—and I've got to tell you, right now I don't—then I'll probably recommend you take another physical. Now don't get excited. I'll recommend it, we'll look at the results together, and whatever it says, I'll make sure it doesn't compromise your situation. That's my promise to you, King, right here and now. You were straight enough with me, and I'll be that way with you. If some of the others around here had come in and talked to me like you have, maybe I wouldn't have so many damn reports to write. One way or another, I'll be in your corner." He sat back, still holding the letter opener. "Now how does that sound?"

Like somebody afraid of his own fitness report, King thought. "I appreciate it, Captain. Tuesday or Wednesday, then."

"And no more talking to lawyers before then, right?"

He had been only too right about their exclusive club, he thought as he stood up. But even that didn't really matter anymore. "Okay."

"Oh, and don't forget about Monday morning. I still need that letter of apology from you."

On his way out, King picked up the cat woman's name and address from Burke. She made some crack about McCloud's shouting, but he didn't answer her. Outside, the building was practically all cleared out for the weekend. He started to take the stairs to the lockers to store his weapon for the weekend, but stopped. All week he had been making mistakes, going to the wrong people for help with his problem, and he had been on the verge of making another one. Whatever the arms rules were, he and Edith needed protection. Nobody else was going to help them.

As he walked through the front door, with his weapon on, King didn't wave good night to Menelli. He wanted the douchebag to think he was only going out only for coffee.

Once in the street, the weekend seemed less threatening.

Saturday

1

Kim Friesner still liked her cholesterol for weekend breakfasts. Two eggs sunnyside up, bacon, home fries, butter-glopping muffins—she forked them in, relishing them as if communing with the only earthly substances that she tolerated completely. Elena had to smile to think that nine years had elapsed since the first Saturday she'd sat in the same window booth of the West Side diner and questioned Kim's diet. The spidery woman's insides might not have been any better for all the fat and grease she had digested in the interval, but for someone on the threshold of sixty, Dr. Kim Friesner still seemed confident that one of medicine's most fundamental truths was going to be disproved any day by more profound findings.

"And how is throwing this pitcher out of character?" she asked, sniffling at her coffee and using her pinkie to settle her black-framed glasses back on her nose. "You know this hooligan so well you know he should never throw water pitchers?"

"I guess I am saying that, yes."

"Beware of Cnidian presumptions, Alvarez."

"Of what?"

"The Cnids. What I call them, anyway. From the ancient Greek city known to us all as Cnidus."

"You're dying to tell me, so get it out."

Kim Friesner bent her head over her plate and began forking away at the last of the white from her second egg. "The Cnids had a famous school of medicine," she said. "You went to one of their doctors, he looked at you the way old Greeks looked at people, then he ruled on what your problem was. And I do mean *ruled*. They had what they called Cnidian Sentences. Your problem fit one of these sentences, you had to follow the appropriate instructions. The patient always fit the treatment, not vice versa. Too bad for you when you went in there with a little mole on your behind and no sentence existed for it. Likely as not, they'd clobber you over the head so you *would* have some problem that fit."

"Doesn't sound like all that ancient an approach to me."

Kim grinned. "Spurious observation. Intended to deflect attention from your personal presumption."

"Throwing that carafe *was* out of character for Torres, Kim."

"And, I repeat, that assumes you know what that character is. What's odd, what's to be expected. Seriously, Alvarez, you pick up that much insight by collecting gobbledygook depositions and interviewing your average beat cop, you and I should trade practices. I still have a lot to learn, and you must be bored to death."

"Kim! All right, then. Let me try to put it another way."

Friesner stared down at her home fries as though they were only now going to reveal their worth. "Good idea. Even when they're for free, professional opinions should be solicited professionally. One of the first things we talked about many moons ago, remember?"

She had to laugh. "What I said to Alan the other night."

"Unless he threw a water pitcher too, that doesn't sound material. Get to it, girl."

Elena did, talking mainly to the top of Kim's neatly coiffed head as the woman polished off her potatoes one by one. By now she was used to the mannerism, but she also still remembered how disconcerted she had been by such apparent inattention when she had been Dr. Friesner's paying patient. She had talked and talked and talked, never to a pensive or flabbergasted expression, but to a plexus of trimmed gray hair that had kept fading in and out of her mind like a self-induced Rorschach test. A hundred times she had been on the verge of demanding more direct attention, and a hundred times she had been embarrassed to interrupt whatever the flow had been. Only on the one hundred first had she finally issued the challenge and drawn a slow, approving nod for an answer: yes, it *was* about time that Elena had gotten tired of talking to herself by proxy.

Now, with the discussion of Manuel Torres's defense back to his throwing the water pitcher, Kim Friesner speared her last potato and popped it into her mouth. "I can assume you're not exaggerating about his record?" she asked. "Arrested three times and always hours or days after the crime?"

"No exaggeration. The first time we got a suspended sentence, the second time a few months."

"And despite that record you have no doubts you could've bargained for a couple of years?"

"Three max. Foy has two murder cases on his desk."

"And you made this clear to Torres."

"Absolutely."

"So you're thinking, a client who's aching to be caught."

"Caught *and* punished. The suspended sentence didn't do it, the slap on the wrist the second time didn't. He went in looking for the whole hog this time, seven years minimum."

Kim put the dripping end of her toast into her mouth, washed it down with some coffee and sat back, wiping her lips with the napkin. "Then your water pitcher."

"He said it three times. *'I wasn't confused.'*"

"Indicating to you?"

"Something conscious. Even calculated."

"That's a big jump, girl."

"And I have absolutely nothing to substantiate it. It's just a feeling I had looking at him yesterday after he made the scene."

"What exactly?"

"Well, that he wasn't just a passive defendant ready to be

found guilty and sent off to prison. At first I let myself think that something had finally gotten through to him, that he realized what his situation was, that maybe he'd be more cooperative. But then Raymond adjourned and Torres just gave me more of his monosyllabic answers, so I thought about it again. When he fired that pitcher, he was like somebody who didn't want to be . . . misinterpreted. He prides himself on having something in his head nobody else knows about. At least till now."

"Like what?"

"I have no idea."

Kim smiled. "Come again?"

Elena retreated behind her coffee. She knew that she was going to get around to saying it, but it seemed more fatuous just blurting it out.

"I read the papers, Elena. Even Eyewitless News mentioned Earl Winters this week."

There. And immediately Elena felt better, as she had known that she would when she called Kim the night before. "I just have this creepy feeling. I don't know how else to say it."

"Has he ever mentioned suicide?" Smoothly, kindly.

"Not to me."

"To somebody else?"

"I can't imagine who. If there's a girlfriend anywhere, I haven't found her. No buddies—or even accomplices—that I know of. There's his father, I suppose, but I can't picture them talking about anything like that."

"Maybe you should make sure."

"You think it's possible?"

"I said maybe you should make sure."

Elena nodded, but the thought of talking to Santiago Torres about anything so intimate was as harrowing as it was ludicrous. Coming right down to it, she was more at ease with Manuel's indifference than with his father's searching petulance.

Friesner sat forward, abruptly, almost cheerfully. "My own quick analysis? I'd consider suicide unlikely. Your client seems to need others to put him down. Cops, prosecutors, judges. Plus, we're not at all sure that he's even half as aware of what he's been doing as you seem to think he is."

"Nobody's that dense, Kim. How can he not know by now what kind of wall he's banging his head against?"

She laughed. "You're denying the basic premise of my trade, dear."

Elena conceded the point, smiling, but then once again heard the finality and confidence of *I wasn't confused.* She still didn't believe she was wrong. She had as practiced an ear for defensiveness as Kim did, and what she had heard in the courtroom yesterday simply hadn't been that. Agreeing to hire Jack Haggerty had been defensive. Her cross-examination of Waxman had been defensive. But not Manuel Torres's outburst. Couldn't Kim see the difference?

The doctor, who seemed amused at the mention of Haggerty, nodded. "Should I touch on the contradictions now?"

It was the ritual introduction to their game, the May I? of Take a Giant Step Toward Yourself, but right now Elena could have done without it. She was already aware of a few too many contradictions without having to worry about more.

"Two I can see," Kim went on evenly, not waiting for permission. "You seem to suggest that he has some clear purpose in mind, but he commits what sounds like a perfectly gratuitous act by throwing this carafe. Clarity and gratuitousness aren't usually in the same deed."

"If the gratuitous act is meant to be diversionary, they could be."

The doctor nodded, but reluctantly and only after she seemed to recognize a new problem. "And I suppose you'd have a similar answer for what I see as the second contradiction? Your fear that your client may be suicidal and the evidence that to the contrary he seems bent on pulling out all the stops of the juridical process to help himself?"

"Yes, I guess so."

Kim nodded again, even more worriedly. The waiter came over with the check, dropped it on the table, and went away again. Elena grabbed the bill before Kim could read it. "You're willing to recompense me that much," the doctor said, smiling, "you can have a few more minutes of my time. How about walking over to the river?"

Elena had always felt awkward walking with Kim Friesner. Aside from the fact that the woman didn't even come up to her shoulder, Elena always seemed to be straining at the calves and walking out of rhythm to keep up with the doctor's peppery stride. Altogether, she felt like a goofy, gangling daughter on exhibit. But this morning, as if by explicit request, Kim kept to a deliberate pace as they headed down the hilly street toward the riverside park. Nobody passing glanced at them twice.

"I once had a patient, Elena," Kim said after a moment, "who believed that as long as she knew who she was, everything else would take care of itself. Quite an egocentric, this young lady. Capable of blathering on for weeks about every filling in her mouth, as though a therapist could possibly give a damn about her experiences with modern dental technology. A few years passed. The lady made what is clinically known as progress, progress meaning that she evolved from an egocentric, confident that the world was interested in her inlays, to an egoist who was sure that she was the greatest dentist the world had ever seen. Her new approach to achieving serenity was to believe that she just had to be handed a task and everything was going to be all right. She would take care of it. Nothing was truly impossible for her. She could make day night, black white, you name it. She could even turn guilty into not guilty."

"It's my job, Kim."

"Really? I thought your job was acting in your client's best interests."

"He wouldn't take a deal. I told you."

"Fine. One option down. But you also told me that you didn't even ask for a psychological consultancy. Even though you knew as much about who he was then as you do now."

"It wouldn't have been enough. A sentencing factor, no more."

Kim looked up at her skeptically. "Even if he has a suicidal bent? That was your insight, Elena, not mine." She faced forward again. "But we both know there is no suicidal bent, don't we? Manuel Torres is not going to be that convenient for you."

"For God's sake, Kim, you're making it sound like I'm trying to sabotage his defense! That I may as well be doing Foy's job for him!"

"Wouldn't make a difference if you were," the older woman said immediately. "Maybe the emphasis would be different, but you'd be working with the same ambivalences. The accident of the moment is that you're working for Alan Green and not the prosecutor. You're the one who enlightened me on how interchangeable those roles can be."

The park loomed up in front of them; joggers and children seemed to be everywhere. Elena suddenly wanted to go home. "This is different," she replied weakly. "I didn't mean it that way."

Kim nodded but seemed more concerned with checking out the traffic coming from both directions on Riverside Drive. "What I've been hearing for the last hour," she said, waiting for a slow caravan of cars heading south to pass, "is this. Your professional egotism is telling you that you ought to pull out all the stops to get an acquittal for this hooligan. Enter this hiring of your slimeball detective. Enter this dog business. Enter too—and I'll admit this is a shot in the dark—a lot of hurt, professional as much as personal, over Earl Winters. But something about Manuel Torres has also opened that old box of egocentrisms we spent so much of your money on a few years ago. Elena Alvarez not only wants to be the winning counsel in this case, she also wants to be the defendant. And Elena Alvarez really isn't sure she wants to get off on the strength of a lot of professional sleight of hand. She isn't even sure she wants to let the final verdict of guilty or not guilty be entrusted to anybody besides herself. C'mon. Let's not stand here all day."

Elena watched dumbly as the woman's nervous energy suddenly reasserted itself and propelled her across the street between a station wagon and a panel truck. She had come to hear just such a verdict, she thought as she remained rooted on the sidewalk, but now that she had heard it, there didn't seem to be any point in going further.

But Kim Friesner wasn't about to let go so quickly. Safely ensconced on the far sidewalk, the woman turned back to scrutinize Elena's every step across the street. Once again she seemed amused by what she saw.

"You're a case and then some, Alvarez," she chirped, grasping Elena's elbow as they proceeded down a lane toward the river. "You really are. Overall, I have the feeling that this Manuel Torres is very lucky to have you. You're not clear who you're doing this for, but you *are* doing it. You don't have the slightest idea who he is, what the hell is going on in his head, but you consult your friends about him as if he should be the most important thing in their lives, too." She peered up with a wry smile. "Guess if you really got to know him, that would spoil everything, right?"

"Look, Kim, call it sublimation, call it—"

The doctor gave her elbow a hard yank. "Now don't start

151

with that useless talk. The fact of the matter is, you *don't* know who he is, you *don't* know what's going on in his head, and the only time you get real panicky about it is when he throws a water pitcher or does something else that reminds you that he's there as more than some kind of partial reflection of Elena Alvarez. That's when we start fretting about calculations and suicides. The only person I can imagine in that courtroom who's had calculating and suicide occupying her thoughts lately is the one walking beside me right now."

"But I can't be that wrong, Kim. There *is* something."

Friesner fell silent for a moment; she hadn't expected another objection. Ahead of them, at the foot of the path, a weekend sailor came trudging up under the weight of a small outboard motor on his shoulder. The man seemed so normal: somebody, she thought, who could probably laugh without worrying about how shallow he might have appeared to others.

"Something you really think would affect your defense?" Kim asked finally.

"I guess that's what I should find out first."

The doctor nodded; she didn't seem to notice the man with the motor as he went by. "Something you can resolve this weekend?"

"I have to. There's no more time."

Kim squeezed her elbow more firmly. "Okay," she said. "What I can give you about going to the father is this. Shh, I'm in the business of reading minds, remember? The thing is, you're not defending *him*. If he knows something you think is important, pull it out of him. Be as crass as this detective of yours, if you have to be. Where your client is concerned, you're still the best dentist in the world and not the girl who has to tell everybody about her fillings. Richard Alvarez has nothing to do with this case. If the father knows anything, he doesn't sound like the kind who'll volunteer it. He'll resent you for probing. As far as he's concerned, you're a whitey up on the hill, and a woman whitey at that. That's his problem, not yours."

They came to the end of the path. In the morning sun the river seemed to glisten without ceding even a wisp of its murky grayness. "I just have to start with the father," Elena said. "He's the only one who might give me some ammunition."

Kim released Elena's elbow, shifting her bag from one shoulder to the other, and ambled over to the railing. "You still haven't answered the sixty-four-dollar question," she said. "Why Manuel Torres? God knows you've told me about sleazier clients in this wonderful profession of yours."

"I don't know. Maybe he's just one of your Cnide Sentences."

The doctor whirled on her; she wasn't amused. "Cnidian, Alvarez," she snapped. "Cnidian. And make sure he isn't. You work a little too hard for that."

2

The nightmare had been the same, but also somehow closer. Manuel had not felt the searing exhaust from the flames the first few times that he'd had it, hadn't smelled the suffocating smoke as thick as pea soup before. The fire had been advancing on him. He hadn't been safe the way Robinson had, sitting in his cubicle, he'd been about to burn or choke to death. But still Robinson hadn't noticed. The old fireman had just sat rocking back and forth near the edge of the cubicle platform, smoking an old cigar and going on about all his Greek heroes. "Think Hector didn't know Achilles was going to kill him if he took the challenge?" Robinson asked. "Of course he knew. But he had to face that terror in him. That terror was Hector's key, Manuel. We're not all big heroes like Hector, but we all got that terror key somewhere inside of us."

But Manuel hadn't known what his key was, hadn't known what to say as the flames got closer and closer. He'd just stood there, not moving and not thinking. He would've been okay even if Robinson had told him that he was going to die, but Robinson just kept talking to the callboard on the cubicle wall, as though the callboard had been his only reliable friend all along. "Know what my terror key was?" Robinson asked over and over again. "Fire! Would you believe that, Manuel? I had a terror of fire. Just hearing the engines on the street made me sweat. But then one day I realized that being

153

afraid of fire was my key, so I said to myself, 'Fight it, Robby. Focus on that terror and beat it down.' So here I am today without regrets. I found my terror key, and one of these days, Manuel, you'll find yours."

"My deal."

Manuel handed the deck to Joey Edison. The nightmare still sent cold streaking through his stomach, but at least he wasn't admitting it anymore. He didn't even flinch when Edison finished lighting his cigarette and flicked his burning match toward Flint and Morrow's double-decker. Instead, he smiled, to let Edison and everybody else on the block know that his screaming last night had been a one-time thing, that it didn't mean that he was afraid of fire or could play pork for some fire games. The dream had meant enough *mal aquero* without giving the animals around him funny ideas.

"Lost Wages style."

Manuel watched Edison fan the cards, then go through more of his one-handed shuffling. He still didn't get it. The first time he had talked to Joey Edison months ago, the spade had come on heavy about the Monte number he had once run right across the street from St. Patrick's Cathedral. A guy like that should've had his game down pat, should've played gin like an expert. Even to be cheated by him wouldn't have been the end of the world, because cards were Edison's trade, even what had left him half a cripple when a motorbike had jumped a sidewalk where he was set up and smashed into his leg. But who could count on anything? An hour into their game, it was he, not Edison, who was riding the express. On the last three hands he hadn't even had to knock, just fill out simple combinations. He had the *cojo* over a barrel by more than 350 points—enough for cigarettes *and* some fool's gold.

Edison finally finished with his bullshit and put down the deck for a cut. "I think you should talk to that lawyer of yours," he said.

"Yeah? About what?"

154

"Say you can't follow your trial too good. You got too many nightmares after that shit in the detention room the other day."

"I follow everything just fine, man."

"*They* don't know that."

Manuel cut the cards and watched Edison snatch at the piles. Last night it had seemed like a good idea to tell Edison, Morrow, and the guards that his dream had been about loco Gwynn. Even if they'd been pissed off at him for waking everybody up, they could understood that as something real. Now he was sorry that he had given them any story at all. The jailhouse lawyers like Joey Edison were going to pick up every day where Alvarez left off.

"Think about it, Manny."

"No chance."

"Try it and find out."

Manuel picked up his cards. What he needed now was advice from a *cojo* who was so smart that he'd been nabbed the first time he'd tried graduating from street scams to fencing hot jewels. The only thing Joey Edison was good at was flicking burning matches.

"What I hear, all that shit wasn't about no lottery ticket."

"What you hear."

Edison took the seven of spades and carefully repositioned his bum leg. "Off the vine. Some pussy in the middle of it all. Gwynn's old lady and Barbarella."

Manuel squeezed his cards and tuned out. He wasn't in the mood for any more bullshit. He seemed to have been listening to it forever.

"Just tellin' you what I heard on the vine."

"Thanks." He filled his third eight. He wondered what kind of a stink Joey Edison would give off in a fire.

"You don't believe it, you don't believe it."

"I was there, man. Remember?"

The *cojo* shrugged and took the nine of spades. He would be waiting the rest of the hand for the eight of spades. He suddenly seemed like more of a loser than usual. "He said he wanted to be somebody else."

"Huh?"

"The guard Gwynn. He said he wanted to win Lotto so he could be somebody else."

"Yeah? What sense that make?"

155

"None. They didn't even win the big prize. Just a coupla hundred. You can't be somebody else for that."

Manuel filled out his queens. He felt better telling Edison about the thing Gwynn had said; he didn't want to be carrying around a loco's craziness by himself.

"Who's winnin'?"

Manuel didn't like seeing Patterson or his honchos standing in front of the cell entrance. Under the low ceiling they seemed even bigger than in the rec room or the corridors. They had never bothered him before. Why now?

"Guess Manny is," Edison said, laughing nervously.

Patterson seemed to take a long time to look at Edison, but when he did, the smallest shine came into his eyes. Manuel didn't like it—or the silence that he suddenly noticed from next door and the other nearby cells. What the fuck had he done now? What difference did it make to Patterson what he had said about Gwynn?

"Hear you've been havin' bad dreams, spic."

The alligator, Hardy, was still behind Patterson's shoulder, but that didn't seem as safe as it had outside in the halls. "Didn't mean to wake you up," he remembered to say quickly.

Patterson shifted his eyes away from Edison like he was late catching up to the conversation. "How you gonna wake us up on the other side of the buildin', Manny?" He smiled. "Got powers I don't know about?"

"No, no, I just thought. . . ." It was the alligator, not Patterson, who told him. Hardy's eyes came alive the same way as Patterson's when he looked at Edison. They were after Joey Edison, not him!

"How's that bail request of yours goin', Joey?" Patterson asked.

Manuel looked down at his cards. If he memorized them before he dropped them, he told himself crazily, he could pick up the game later, after Patterson and his goons finished with Edison.

"You know lawyers," Edison said, now sounding as shaky as he looked. "I got to keep after them."

Patterson nodded, as if to cover the steps he took into the cell. But Manuel noticed him come in anyway and wished that he hadn't. "I know a way to light a fire under them," Patterson said, far enough inside so that the alligator and the thinner one with the veins popping out of his muscles could also squeeze in.

156

Edison put down his cards and grabbed another cigarette. "How's that?"

"Tell him, Hardy."

The alligator had been waiting. Not worrying about bumping Patterson on the elbow, he reached across and grabbed Edison by the shirt, swinging him up off the bed. "You play snitch."

Manuel ducked his head unnecessarily. Joey Edison's bum leg swung four or five feet away. "No, no, whaddya mean? I don't snitch to nobody."

Now it was Patterson at Hardy's shoulder, but Patterson still looked like he was in charge. "Then I guess we got a lot of coincidence lately, Joey," he said. "We got all kinds of names bein' dropped upstairs about this and that, and they're always gettin' dropped after you've had a little talk with your lawyer. Other people's business, you know what I'm sayin'? So we got a trend of thought in some quarters that you're aimin' higher than bail. You do a few months, drop some more names, and presto whammo, you're out on the street with no trial at all."

"That's crazy talk, man! Ask Manny. He knows I don't snitch. Ask him."

Manuel wanted another look at his cards, but he knew that wouldn't help at all. What did he know about Joey Edison? What the fuck did he care what Joey Edison told his lawyer? Two, three more days tops, he was gone.

"You a character witness, Manny?"

He looked at Patterson as straight as he could over Hardy's shoulder. They weren't going to listen to him whatever he said, he told himself. He had nothing to lose by telling the truth. "First I heard of this shit, man. Could be somebody else, right?"

The alligator's eyes slid away from Edison's face to Manuel. Patterson thought he was being funny. "Yeah, could be," Patterson said. "Might even be you, except we know you're not goin' anywhere. You'd even fuck up snitchin'."

Manuel told himself to keep his eyes on Patterson, to forget all the moves between Hardy and the one with the veins as they shoved into Edison and the crying started to be real, started to be about what was happening, not just about what was going to happen. He told himself to wear down Patterson, to show him that he didn't want to see what was happening to Joey Edison and that he knew that Patterson wanted to see it and would break eye contact

157

first. And he was right: Patterson did look away first, over to the back of the cell where Hardy was holding Edison by the throat as the one with the veins worked on his stomach and bum leg. Manuel closed his eyes. The curdling sound in Barbarella's throat that day with Gwynn in the detention room—he suddenly remembered where he had heard it before. It hadn't been somebody dying, it had been somebody gagging on his blood in the firehouse kitchen.

Old Robinson hadn't helped him then, either. Just like in his nightmares, old Robinson hadn't helped him then, either.

"Where you goin', spic?"

Manuel was surprised that Hardy had finished his part. The one with the veins was still kicking Joey Edison into the back wall, but the alligator had let go and was more interested in him now. "Call my old man. Okay?"

This time he didn't wait for Patterson's approval, but just kicked out his sleeping leg and walked through the door out to the safety of the corridor. He could feel the eyes on him all the way down the block. They wanted to know what was going on with Edison, they wanted to know how he had danced off like there had been nothing to it. He didn't give a fuck what they wanted to know. The *viejo* brought the razors on Monday or he'd make his break without them. He didn't have any more time.

3

The first drops of rain thudded down on the windshield as Elena killed the engine. She sat for a moment watching the slashes of water speed up until they became a wet smear. She didn't want to take her umbrella, but she had no choice. She got out of the car and locked up. Two teenage girls ran squealing along the street with what looked like library books over their heads. Elena thought of her own Saturday afternoons in the library years ago when she had felt so adult and responsible for studying on free weekend time. The squealing girls made her feel better.

Her bag heavy on her shoulder and her umbrella bucking against the driving rain, she nevertheless managed to move quickly down the avenue looking for number 783. Her search for a specific address seemed like a good excuse not to look too closely at the stores along the way. She knew plenty of stores just like them—smelled them before their acrid odors made her smell them, read their transliterated signs before their Spanish I copywriters from Madison Avenue made her read them. She still had no problem imagining such neighborhood stores being stocked with the worst brews of Miller and the oldest bars of Ivory.

Number 783 was a run-down slit of a tenement doorway between a pompous-looking coffeehouse and a Laundromat. She looked through the windows of both, seeing only two young men playing dominoes in the coffeehouse and a pregnant woman with a stroller in the Laundromat. Relieved that Santiago Torres was in neither, that she wouldn't be forced to talk to him in front of other people, she went into the peeling vestibule of the tenement. Torres's name appeared on a business card stuck in the name plate of the last mailbox. The name of the business itself was obscured by the edges of the plate. Closing her dripping umbrella over the dirty white tiles, Elena decided that business cards equaled officiousness and that officiousness equaled the top floor, not the first floor, so she pressed the highest button. The answering buzz sounded like a dispirited Bronx cheer.

The halls and narrow staircase smelled of linoleum. She could hear a fight of some kind—boxing or wrestling—on the television in one of the first-floor apartments. A baby cried from an inner room behind one of the second-floor doors. She hoped that Torres would have his door open when she reached the top floor; she didn't want to be fidgeting around in front of the wrong door. As Kim had said, it was crucial that she be on the offensive from the start.

"Mrs. Alvarez!"

The pudgy figure in the doorway of the corner apartment was dressed in bathing trunks, a flannel shirt, and sandals. It was such a hodgepodge of seasons that she was caught off guard. Had she been expecting the same drab leather jacket and polyester pants that he had been wearing to the trial? "I apologize for not calling,

Mr. Torres," she finally managed, "but I was passing by and I had a sudden thought about something. Do you have a couple of minutes?"

It was such a tinny story that even his moment of hesitation seemed to be prolonged skepticism. But then, looking more like somebody who was merely astonished to see her, Santiago Torres backed his way into the apartment. She tried not to notice how he got his sandaled feet tangled up as he waved her in after him. "Come. Please."

Elena stepped inside, glad to get out of the hall. He stared at her for another long moment in the better light of the apartment before remembering to shut the door behind her and take her umbrella. For all his surface clumsiness, he seemed more purposeful than he had in the courtroom. "I put this in the bathroom."

As he went off with the umbrella, Elena took in the apartment. It was one enormous space that had been sectioned off from front to back by a series of folding plywood dividers. She was able to see a kitchen sink at the far end, the foot of a bed in the middle section. The main room where she was standing was a conglomeration of tulip-shaped lamps, rattan chairs, and a plastic divan, all of them arranged vaguely around a long, low wooden table that seemed to have started off life as a cot support. The table was covered with several Spanish newspapers and some gas station maps. A black crucifix hung over a radiator near one of the room's two windows.

"Something important about Manuel?"

She thought about answering in Spanish but decided that she needed to keep him off balance. "I think it might be," she said, moving over to one of the chairs. "Maybe something only you can explain."

"I am making coffee. You would like some?"

"No, thank you."

"Soda? There is orange soda, and Pepsi."

The hot apartment made her say yes to the Pepsi, and he went down to the kitchen after it. She rubbed at the perspiration on her forehead. The sound of the rain gathering force outside the two shaded windows seemed to make the room even stuffier. She took off her jacket and sat down with it and her bag in her lap. The maps on the table were of Long Island. The line of the Sunrise Highway had been traced in green Magic Marker on one of them;

on another there were yellow Magic Marker dots over the exits for the Southern State Parkway.

Torres returned with a tray with his coffee and a can of Pepsi and a plastic glass on it. "How is it I can help? Tell me."

"It's about yesterday. When Manuel threw that pitcher at me."

"It was not at you, Mrs. Alvarez," he said, setting the tray down on the table. He handed her the Pepsi and the glass. "Manuel was just . . ."

"Upset?"

"Yes. Upset." He sat down on the divan.

Elena poured the soda. The bubbles felt good in her throat; she had wanted them more than the taste. "Manuel's been upset for a long time, Mr. Torres. Certainly since before yesterday."

"He is on trial now. Of course he is upset."

"Manuel couldn't care less about the trial. That's not why he fired that pitcher."

"He says he doesn't care, but—"

"Oh? So he has actually told you he doesn't care about the trial?"

He fumbled for the cigarettes in his shirt pocket. "He did not say it to me. It is what you said."

It was the fort game, Elena thought immediately. Whenever her parents had taken her to visit her cousins in Teaneck, she had spent the day in the woods behind the house where Felipe and John had built their fort. Always two of them had had the job of sneaking up on the third without being seen. Now, once again, she was in danger of being spotted and had to crawl back to try another side. "You and Manuel don't get along very well, do you, Mr. Torres?"

The protest was there, but so was the match to light his cigarette. "We have our own lives, but he is my son. You should not ask such things."

"But if something were really bothering him, you wouldn't expect him to talk to you about it, would you?"

Torres jerked the dead match into the saucer on the end table next to him; he wasn't yet as angry as he wanted her to think he was. "I do not understand these questions, Mrs. Alvarez. They have nothing to do with the trial."

"They might if I decide to put Manuel on the stand Monday."

161

"To testify? But you said you would not do that. The first time we met, you said that would not be a good idea."

"We may have to change tactics."

"But Manuel doesn't want that! He told you."

"My job is to do the best I can for Manuel. If that means putting him on the stand, that's what I'll do."

From behind his coffee and cigarette, Torres's eyes wandered over to the maps on the table, then back up to her face. "I don't understand why you are trying to excite me, Mrs. Alvarez."

"Because I need your help, and I don't know any other way of getting it. Because I can't help your son if both of you are more proud of your silence than anything else."

He smiled aloofly. "You cannot understand."

She hadn't expected it so directly. "Why? Because I'm not from this barrio?"

He nodded tentatively as he took another drag. He could get used to the idea of dangling her, his expression said.

"You're right, Mr. Torres. I'm not from this barrio. I'm from a very residential area in white, middle-class Queens. You've probably had a fantasy or two about living there, and I've certainly had a nightmare or two about living here. I'm very satisfied to remain an outsider to your barrio codes of behavior, and I wouldn't be bothering you about them now if I didn't think you could help me help Manuel. But that's my job, and you're his father."

The rain was falling more heavily, and the heat of the apartment felt near explosion.

"What is it you want to know?"

"What I asked: if he was really bothered by something, do you see Manuel coming to you to talk about it?"

Torres put the cigarette back in his mouth with an exaggerated sweep of his hand. A roll of hairless flab peeked out between the lowest buttons of his shirt. "I was always there for Manuel, Mrs. Alvarez," he said grandly. "I was here every day. Every day we saw each other. In the apartment here, down in the street, in the coffeehouse. Not every son sees his father every day, you know. They work over in Manhattan, they leave early and come home after their children are in bed. But Manuel always saw me. He knew where to come if he needed money or something."

"Aside from money, Mr. Torres."

"I am no mother, if you mean that. You could not give him

162

things like a father, I could not give him a mother's things. That is just nature. There were times when I had my business. I could not be with Manuel every second. He understood that. After his mother died, he learned to cook and sew just like a woman. For me, too."

"Until he moved out."

"He was old enough. He did not need to take care of me."

"Until he moved out and started breaking into houses and getting caught."

He lurched forward angrily, sending his coffee slopping out onto the table. "You blame me for that?"

"To be frank, Mr. Torres, there are probably some people who would blame you for the breaking in and others who would blame you for the getting caught. I haven't got time to worry about either right now. What I want to know is what's next."

"What do you mean, next?"

She wished she hadn't chosen that moment to notice the circular stain on the table next to the newspapers. It appeared to be olive oil that had never been cleaned up. Enduring bad luck, according to her father.

"There has to be something else, Mr. Torres," she said, sounding surer than she felt. "Everything points to it. There was every reason in the world for Manuel to avoid the Twitchell house after Mrs. Cicut saw him at the first house, but he broke in and got himself arrested. There was every opportunity to make a deal with the district attorney, but he insisted on a trial that's exposed him to a maximum sentence. So now he's facing a long prison term, but he's still confident about something. What?"

He understood, but he wasn't ready to admit it. "If you don't think you can help him, then he will go to jail like you say he wants. Maybe that is why he is so macho."

"Do you think that's what it is, Mr. Torres?"

He shrugged. "I understand very little of what you are saying, Mrs. Alvarez. In Manuel's place maybe I would not be too happy about having some lawyer who says she cannot help me."

She drank some soda; there were still other sides to the fort, she told herself. "And if I were in your place, Mr. Torres, maybe I would be concerned about the possibility that Manuel is thinking of killing himself."

Torres tilted his head in disbelief. The gesture was more eloquent even than Kim's skepticism, and Elena felt her own doubts

163

deepening. But it still seemed like the clearest path to an un-protected side of the fort.

"You think it's so incredible?"

"It is crazy."

"Why? Because Manuel has so much to live for? Because he has so many good friends who care about him? Because he has a father he respects and who's been there for him whenever he's needed him?"

"You have no right to say that!"

"Yes I do, Mr. Torres. You and Manuel gave me that right when you accepted me as his counsel."

"You don't know my son."

"More true than not. But I do know some things. I know that Manuel is somebody who simply isn't very good at much. He's not a good thief. He's not a good worker, or friend, he's probably not a good lover. He doesn't seem to be too great as a son, either. And what I'm saying to you now is that he realizes all that and wants to put an end to it. All the little punishments aren't enough any-more. He sees what he has to. He is *not confused!*"

She had seen hatred before, Elena reassured herself; she had seen eyes so blind in bitterness that she'd felt subhuman for pro-voking such a reaction. She was used to his look, so there was no need to cower before it.

"You understand nothing," Santiago Torres whispered. "Manuel would never do that."

She remembered the crucifix. "Because it's against his reli-gion?" Torres swallowed coffee, his eyes never leaving hers. "Or maybe because you don't think he has the nerve for it."

"Maybe," he said stonily.

Something shriveled up inside her, but she knew she was closer. He seemed to be staring at her so as not to give something away. "I wouldn't bet on it, Mr. Torres. Takes nerve to break into other people's houses. Takes nerve to wait around while policemen with guns are trying to find you. Takes even more nerve to sit quietly in a room with someone unbalanced who's already shot one person and may shoot you next. I'd say your son has quite a bit of ice water in his veins."

"So Manuel is brave. Is that what you are saying?"

"If you want to call it that."

Torres seemed on the verge of gloating. "Maybe you are so

164

busy inventing my son for yourself you don't see him in front of you."

"Then tell me where I'm wrong."

"For what?"

"So we can help him more than he's ready to help himself."

He glanced down at the maps, then sat back; he had recovered his sense of safety. "Manuel is not brave. That much I know."

"How? How do you know?"

"A father knows his son."

"That's it? A father knows his son? What exactly do you know, Mr. Torres? You know he didn't live up to your expectations? You know that he disappointed you? He didn't go off and get one of those jobs in Manhattan you never had? He didn't marry someone and give you grandchildren? What is it that you know?"

"A father knows his son."

Her heart sank. She had gotten all the way to the clearing, right to the base of the fort wall, and now Felipe was laughing at her delightedly. Once again he had caught her.

"You would not understand, Mrs. Alvarez."

He hesitated just long enough to make her understand that he had unmarried her deliberately. The wind outside picked up, blowing the rain against the windows. Elena followed Torres's eyes back to the maps. She knew why she needed a map, but why did he? "Routes, aren't they?" she asked. "Pickup or delivery, Mr. Torres?"

"They are my business," he said evenly.

"Looks like an expansion of some kind. That business card downstairs in the mailbox—what kind of business are you in?"

"It is a personal card."

"For odd jobs and things, isn't that what you once told me?"

"Yes."

"Not something you could interest Manuel in."

"What I do is what I do. Manuel cannot be good at the same things."

"Oh? Why not? Sons go into their fathers' business all the time."

He had just about finished with his coffee, his cigarette, and her. "You have to like people to do certain things," he said. "Manuel does not like people. You have seen him. He sits, he says nothing, he makes people feel uncomfortable. In business you cannot be

165

that way. I talk to the people that I see. They know me. They know I will come back. Many of them give me something to drink. They are used to seeing me. They know I don't think of them as shit. Manuel makes them feel like they are shit. Always there is some contempt on his face. He doesn't care if you or me or anybody else lives or dies. That is not the way to do business. You must face people, not always hate them or be afraid of them. And even if you don't like them, you do not let them know it. They will not want to see you again."

"You've told him this?"

Torres smiled tiredly, took a final puff and then dashed out his cigarette butt in the saucer. "When you have a son, Miss Alvarez, you will understand how you can tell them but that doesn't mean they will listen. Sometimes it takes too much courage for them to listen. They want to stay by themselves hating you. It is easier."

"So you just give up?"

He was dangling her again; she was very much on his time now. "You ask why Manuel is not confused," he said finally. "The answer is that he knows that he doesn't care if he lives or dies, and he knows that all this . . . *teatro* in your great courtroom doesn't matter either. He can be guilty, not guilty. Nothing will be different. He will always make people uncomfortable, he will not like them any better. He knows all of that already. It is a terrible thing not to be confused about, yes?"

"If it's true."

"I cannot make him a child again, a different person."

Elena had her wish: he was back to being the way he had been every day in the courtroom, all sluggish resignation and defeat. The grand stubbornness and pride had evaporated into self-pity. "Then maybe somebody else," she heard herself saying angrily, "maybe somebody else had better try shaking something into him besides your . . . wisdom of the ages."

He nodded readily. "If you think you can. Manuel is not a brave boy."

"Whatever the hell that means." She grabbed her bag and stood up. Suddenly she didn't care about the rain; maybe she even needed it to feel clean again. "But if you have any desire left at all to help him, maybe you can do him a very small favor by staying away from the trial."

166

"Stay away?"

She couldn't remember which of the two doors was the bathroom where he had put her umbrella. "Families and friends usually come to show their solidarity. I'd like to try a couple of days without your particular kind of solidarity."

Torres seemed to consider taking offense and then decided not to. "If you believe it will help."

She had to try one last time. "If what you say is even half true, Mr. Torres, you've sentenced your son to a much longer term than the court will. I think he may need a fighting chance to beat that count, too."

"And that is your job? The lawyer?"

"You seem to have given it to me."

"And you will have him testify?"

"Yes," she decided. "I will."

He looked past her. The roll of his stomach seemed to have grown; he looked like he might never get up from the divan again. "If Manuel testifies," he said after a moment, "he will have to look good, impress these people he despises. I will give you his jacket to take to him."

"I'd appreciate that."

Torres nodded as though he had expected her agreement, heaving himself up off the divan and going over to the doors near the entrance. "You will tell Manuel that you said it was better I don't come?" he asked, opening the closet door.

"Yes."

He reached into the closet and came out with a herringbone sports jacket. Elena grabbed it so he could hurry up and go back for her umbrella.

4

Dear Mrs. Thompson,

I have been informed by my superior officer that I have accidentally killed your cat. I was not at all aware of my

167

accident until I was informed of it by my superior officer on Friday. I am very sorry for this tragedy. I certainly intended no harm to you or your cat or my relations with your community.

   I have no excuse except to say that I am sorry to you and your community.

                                                    Sincerely,
                                                    John King

King still wasn't satisfied. On the first reading, the fifth version of his letter sounded a little too cold, like it had been written under McCloud's orders; on the next it sounded too groveling. He didn't want Mrs. Thompson thinking of him either way. What he wanted was for her to know that she was hearing from the genuine article, John King, that he was really sorry he had run over her cat, that he understood how people got attached to animals, but that, after all, a car accident was still a car accident and a cat was still only a cat. As for the community relations stuff, that was just a load of crap.

He crumpled up the fifth version and tried again. He figured he had a half hour yet before Edith reclaimed the kitchen table for supper. Right now, on the phone in the living room, she sounded like she was in the middle of a heavy conversation with her mother about the price of salt. Get Grace Chandler going about rip-offs, and he would have had enough time to write a book. He wouldn't have minded running over Grace Chandler's cat if she'd had one.

He told Mrs. Thompson again that he was shocked by what he had done. That much was a fact. If it hadn't actually happened, he would have thought it impossible. He had never been that kind of person. Even when he'd been a kid, he had never gone along with throwing rocks at cats or throwing water balloons on people on their way home from work. It was like a sick joke that he now had to be apologizing to Mrs. Thompson. God had decided that every other minute he had lived up to now had been unimportant compared to the few seconds that he had been driving down Hillside Avenue on one particular morning. He was now one person for himself and an entirely different one for everybody else in the world.

He read over the words on Edith's blue stationery. He was sorry about the cat, but he had sounded sorrier in the other versions. Now he was just telling the woman that he was sorry. He didn't feel it anymore. A cat was a cat. The animal had already been disposed of by the sanitation department. Mrs. Thompson had probably already started looking around for another pet. Why was he the only one spending the weekend on something nobody else gave a damn about? McCloud's only worry was getting along with the neighborhood niggers. All the niggers were worried about was flexing their block-association muscle. Nobody cared. Nobody had ever cared except him, the first few times he'd written the letter, and now even he was like the rest of them.

"Still working on that thing? I thought you finished."

He hadn't heard Edith hang up. "I have to get it right. McCloud's liable to explode if I don't."

She gave him the same saintly expression she'd given him at breakfast when he had told her about the cat and the letter. "Well, don't do it just for that, John," she said. "I'm sure the poor woman is very upset. You want to try to cheer her up."

His laugh came out as a snort. "I guess I forgot about you. *You* care."

Edith looked like she wasn't sure she wanted to know what he meant. "Mother's asking if we could have dinner at four instead of five tomorrow."

"Some show she has to get home for?"

"She just wants to get home earlier, that's all."

"Four o'clock is too early for dinner."

"But it's Sunday, John. People eat dinner earlier on Sunday. Look at any restaurant."

"That's not why we have to eat earlier. It's because she wants to."

"So I'll call her back and say no."

"That's not the point, Edith."

She looked lost. King didn't blame her. It was too late for him to take a stand against Grace Chandler's whims now. "Never mind. Four's okay."

Now it was his moods she didn't seem to understand, and he suddenly felt exhausted by her dumb expressions. He was no Mar-

169

tian. He had everyday moods. People blew hot and cold. A crisis one day was a laugh the next. Last Saturday, at exactly the same time, hadn't he been out trying to walk off his anger about the bank card ad? Now where was all that anger? In the same place as his feelings for Mrs. Thompson's cat, that was where. Nothing ever stayed the same, even how you felt about things. Why was that so hard for Edith to understand, at her age?

He got out of the kitchen before he had to answer her about whatever it was that she was going on about. He had half an idea about going over to the Keg-O'-My- Heart for a beer before supper—but what for? There was nobody to talk to there but the flat-chested donkey who acted like she had brought Greenwich Village to the neighborhood. She had nothing to say to him. Once upon a time he wouldn't have even noticed her behind the bar; she would've just been there, like some kind of moving bottle. He would've been listening to Eddie Mannix's lies about his endless uncles. The uncle who had toured the South making his money by betting on a monkey armed with a hammer against the local pit bulls. Some other uncle who had shot golf in the eighties even though he had been blind. Another one who'd flipped out while driving a city bus and gone as far as Detroit with a couple of passengers before being nabbed. Did the Irish piece down at Keg-O'-My-Heart have stories like that?

King looked over at the telephone next to the TV set. With Edith finished talking to her mother and now moving around in the kitchen, it seemed to be inviting him over to use it. But to call who? Not Mannix, so he could hear a lot more bullshit about insuring kids and getting asbestos out of the town schools. And if he called anybody else, he would have been breaking a promise to himself. They thought Edith had always been dull, that he could have done better. Fuck them all. They didn't know what she was like when she was close to him in bed. Not only did she look different, she seemed to *see* different, like her eyes had shifted in her face somehow. In bed he never thought of her as somebody who just cleaned the house, made dinner, or did the shopping. Goms like Pete Natase and Billy Ryan would never be able to understand that, so why should he look them up for a beer? He might as well have gone back for seconds with Hobie Morgan.

He sat down at the secretary and started the letter again. It was a good place to do it because he could also keep an eye on the street. Not that he really believed that McCloud would run a check on the lockers to make sure that nobody had taken his weapon out of the building, but it was good to be on the safe side. If somebody did come after him, he could head him off at the door before Edith found out and started pestering him with more of her worries.

There seemed to be no way of getting away from starting the letter by saying that he was sorry.

5

Margaret Brand raised her chin to the stage with a determination that barred Allison from her thoughts. She didn't just hear the music, he thought, she was resolved to see it. Each new front that opened up in the orchestra brought a glint of iron attention. Only after she had inspected the notes one by one did she allow them to fill the concert hall for everyone else.

Flutes, piccolos, harps. Allison smiled at the easy romance of them all. Britten's Four Sea Interludes were beside the point; the instruments had inherent powers regardless of the composer and musicians who employed them. Too much credit and too much blame went to transient factors. Temporary details didn't matter, accomplishments and failures were equally irrelevant. He had been afraid of so many things uselessly. Nobody had ever been keeping his grades; he had been keeping his own merely as a self-important distraction.

Margaret approved of the horns, and Allison approved of her perfume. He had tried to tell her how everything was different. In the cab to the concert, he had told her about the boys on the subway tracks, and about the way the other jurors had begun acting so deferentially toward him after Anna DeSilvestri and Benzinger had related their lunch-hour adventure. She had been disconcerted by his tone, as though he should have gotten more out of his experience than the dumb wonder that was what he truly felt. He felt still

171

more dumb wonder at her reaction. He could hardly blame her, since she didn't know how very little he had been risking, but still he had expected some recognition of how much less guarded he was with her, of how maybe for the first time since the Philadelphia hotel he didn't care in the least about not having been able to hold an erection for her that night. Had he been expecting too much? He wouldn't have thought so. Picking her up outside her house, he had kissed her on the cheek and taken her hand with more desire than he had felt for anyone since Rita Nardi. He had felt the difference; why hadn't she?

He listened to the music. It came and went. It didn't belong to anybody.

"You're really not hungry?" she asked afterward. "Even a sandwich?"

Allison knew that he couldn't say no to everything so abruptly, that he couldn't presume that she had become as indifferent to their routines as he had, so they sat in a restaurant for an hour. She had always looked quietly elegant in audiences and over-dressed among waiters and salt shakers, and tonight was no different. He was excited to think that even the panties and bra she was wearing had come out of some special, scented drawer.

"I guess we did all the things tourists are supposed to do when they're in Istanbul," he told her. "Shook our way across the Galata Bridge and took the boat ride down the Bosporus so we could say we'd gone to Asia. Hagia Sophia and Topkapi. But the thing I remember most is the street life. On every corner there seemed to be some big fat Turkish woman sweltering under the sun in a big overcoat. The cabs were all those Oldsmobiles or Buicks with the big fins they were selling here in the fifties. And there was this odor all the time, one part grilled meat, one part grilled corn, and one part dust. You'd get back to the hotel and you had to change your shoes and socks. Don't go if you're allergic to dust."

Margaret was listening and not listening. She had the same look of discomfort she had had in the taxi when he had been telling her about the kids on the subway tracks.

"There was one night we were in the hotel bar. The television was showing a dubbed version of *The Desperate Hours,* the Humphrey Bogart thing about these escaped convicts. It seemed funny then, hearing Bogart talking in Turkish, but later on, when I came back to New York, I found I couldn't be as enthusiastic about movies as I once had. I mean, I used to be a real moviegoer. Twice a day sometimes. But it was never the same after that dubbed version of *The Desperate Hours.*"

"Because it made you think of her?"

"I suppose. Too exotic. Too haphazard."

Allison drank some water and ate pickles. He wouldn't have been surprised if the next couple to walk in the door were Rita and her husband. He had never been able to put a face to Flavio Nardi and thought it was about time he did. Rita hadn't been carrying any snapshots with her.

"She really wanted you to run all over the continent with her? Just to keep her company till she decided to go back to her husband?"

"She hadn't made up her mind she *was* going back."

"Then why didn't you stay with her?"

"I wasn't *pazzo* enough."

She didn't blink at the word, seemed to know exactly what it meant. The desire he had felt for her when he picked her up took another leap in his chest. How had he managed to convince himself since Philadelphia that she was prim? That wasn't the case at all; never had been. At the hotel she had returned his every touch with a heat and a humor that had beckoned him into her friendship, had reassured him that for her, making love was as special and exciting as both of them wanted it to be. She had been there before and had discovered nothing solemn or sacrificial.

He was thankful for the gabby cabdriver William Wright on the way home. Neither he nor Margaret really wanted to hear any more about Turkey or boys on subway tracks. Instead, they laughed easily at William Wright's grotesque tales of taking bridges that were about to collapse and tunnels that had sprung leaks. Allison tipped the man five dollars gladly.

He had never felt so at home in her living room of small table lamps. He thought of them as dwarfs of light, as so many distinct witnesses to his return to her. She handed him his brandy and sat down beside him on the couch with her own. She smoothed her dress over her knee and appeared satisfied with her stomach.

She didn't lower the glass from her lips when he raised his arm and put it around her. He settled back, his eyes following hers to the facsimile of a Celtic family crest that hung over the fireplace. He remembered that the last time that they had allowed so much

173

quiet between them had been in the faculty room the Thursday afternoon they had agreed to go to Philadelphia for the weekend. It was an anniversary of some kind.

"Suppose you tell me what's going on," she said finally.

"Two people drinking brandy."

"Right."

"And looking at your wall furnishings."

The bewilderment in her eyes seemed anchored by her choker. "I don't recognize you tonight."

"Because I told you about Rita?"

"Partly. That only took you about fifteen years to get around to."

"I told you about her before."

"You told me about a peccadillo before. Tonight you told me you can't care anymore about something you once cared a great deal about."

"How can I?"

She didn't know; she preferred another subject anyway. "I'm not talking about Rita, or not just about her. Is there something going on, Charles? Something maybe connected to that call I got today?"

"Call?"

She seemed to be anticipating the punchline to a corny joke. "About noon or so. Somebody named Haggerty. Said he was checking out your references on an application of some kind."

Allison had no reason to doubt her, but he should have. "What kind of an application?"

"I don't know. You buying a house or something?"

He told himself to keep his arm around her shoulder, that if only he did, the nonsense would go away. "Are you serious? What did this Haggerty want to know?"

"The usual things they ask former colleagues."

"Like why I left Sterling?"

She smiled. "God knows I couldn't tell him that."

He looked back at the Celtic crest. What forms had he filled out in the world of red tape lately? Some medical insurance things for Munson and for hospital tests. The jury stuff. Some bank rollovers. "What did you tell him?"

"That we were all sorry you quit. That you had your own

174

reasons for your decision. That it was none of my business and none of his what they were."

Allison sipped his brandy to cover an absurd thought: somebody had seen his staring exchange with Manuel Torres. Somebody—Foy, the bailiff, John King—had jumped to the insane conclusion that there was some kind of complicity between him and Manuel Torres and had unleashed a policeman, Haggerty, to look into it.

"Want to let me in on it, Charles?"

"It's too crazy."

"For somebody who doesn't do crazy things, you seem to get a lot of offers."

She pulled away and turned to face him, letting him read whatever was in her face. She hadn't taken out a cigarette, had lost interest in her brandy.

"Routine jury check, I imagine."

"I'd like to know what they find out."

He hadn't thought it possible that other barriers had still been there, had still been holding him back. But now that they too were gone, that in some corner of the city an investigator named Haggerty was catching up to his astrocytomas, he felt free, purely and absolutely. He didn't have to pay any more lip service to Margaret Brand or Charles Allison. He was beyond them and all their courtesies. He was perfectly at leisure to close circles.

She locked his fingers when he put his free hand over the back of hers in her lap. Nothing was lost as he got rid of the two glasses. Her tongue felt thin, her face and neck hot. In the bedroom she laughed when he asked her to keep her choker and rings on, but then ran her fingers over his chest and shoulders so that the rings caught his skin. After she had come and a second before he did, she raised her choker and brought his mouth down to her throat. He was at the center of all her perfume.

Sunday

1

     As he entered the reception center, Manuel knew that he was going to find the *viejo* either with or without his jacket, and that it was too late for him to change whatever had been decided. What was he supposed to feel one way or another? If the jacket was there, the *viejo* might have been saying here's your chance to get away, but he might have also been saying go get yourself killed and get out of my life once and for all. If it wasn't there, he might have been saying I don't want you to get killed, but he might have also been saying go rot in a jail for seven years because I'm too much of a coward to do anything about it. It was too late for him to understand Santiago Torres—and it wouldn't have changed what had already been decided, anyway.

What he didn't expect was to see Alvarez sitting alone in Visitors. Manuel sensed that even the guard Waters was smirking as he pointed to a chair at Alvarez's table.

"Good morning, Manuel. Don't look so happy to see me."

Her bitchy stare made him feel better. She couldn't have come with any bad news; just more bullshit. "You don't take Sunday off?"

"You don't. Why should I?"

She thought she was funny. He didn't mind it, either. As he lit his cigarette, he noticed that she *had* dressed a little snazzier for Sunday. Splashy blue and red in her dress. It still covered her up to the neck, but it was nice and tight over her. She even wore dangling earrings instead of the usual buttons.

She took a pen and notebook out of her bag. From where he was standing near the door, Waters shifted his eyes like he had to be ready for something. "We get the case tomorrow morning," she said, "and I'm going to put you on the stand."

"Yeah?"

"Yeah." She looked like she was announcing the discovery of America.

"So I can say I was running away from that dog and that's how I ended up in that house?"

"If that's the truth."

He laughed. She didn't bother. "I'm not takin' any stand." It came out good and solid.

"You'll take the stand because I'm advising you to. It happens to be the only card we have."

"To say what? That I wanted to steal from Twitchell's house?"

"Your plea is that you didn't intend that. Remember?"

Whatever game she was playing, he didn't like it. "I don't testify."

"You will," she said, looking at him like it wasn't even important that he be there. "If you don't—"

What?

"You'll quit?"

"No. I'll subpoena your father."

"Him? What does he know?"

"Your character. The reasons why you do the things you do. How your mother's death affected you. What it was like, just the two of you living together all those years. What it was like to live above that coffeehouse. The friends you brought home for him to meet. All the things that won't get you off, but that might make a jury feel sorry for you."

Manuel couldn't believe how much of a *puta* she was. She was a *puta* because she was a cunt, but also because she knew that even calling her that now wouldn't have changed anything, wouldn't have gotten to her. She had already worked out all the angles. She had been around the block before he'd even been born.

"He'd never tell you any of that."

She shrugged. "Then we make the same point in a different way. An accused's father who has to be treated as a hostile witness. Speaks volumes."

"I don't want you anymore."

She nodded but kept her eyes on her notebook. "There's always that option," she said. "But you have to show cause to Judge Raymond, and I'd have to tell him why you were trying to dump me. He might go along with you and appoint a new counsel before the end of the week, he might go along with you and adjourn proceedings indefinitely, or he might not go along with you and force you to petition for a mistrial. My option at that point would be to point you out as your own best argument for a battery of psychological tests. I'm fairly sure Raymond would be sympathetic to such a motion, since most defendants in felony trials are willing to take the stand or do anything else to persuade a jury of their innocence, while you seem to be more interested in striking all these poses of yours, whatever the cost to you personally." She glanced up at him from the notebook. "But, like I say, you do have that option."

It might have been a Joey Edison shuffle, it might not have been. She knew that he wasn't sure one way or the other. "But there's nothing I can say that'll help me! What Waxman told you, what that woman with the dog said—"

"Was exactly what they saw as they recalled it," Alvarez said sharply, leaning forward. "They saw you walking down the street, climbing up a stoop, jiggling the knob of one house, hiding in the basement of another. But they didn't see you thinking and feeling while you were doing all those things. You're the only witness to all that. And that's the testimony we're going to bring out when you go on the stand."

179

Her seriousness was laughable. "And suppose what I was thinkin' was, 'I want this, I want that'? How's that supposed to help me?"

She looked at him crossly. *"Is* that what you were thinking?"

Manuel stared back at the cleft in her chin. Suddenly he didn't know if he was supposed to tell her a lie or the truth. She wasn't the same as she had been. He couldn't figure her out. She knew what the truth was, but that wasn't the same as laying it on thick with her. If he told her the wrong thing, she might just stand up and walk out on him. He was still going to need her as a hostage. Who was to say that Raymond wouldn't replace her with some bodybuilder he could never get his razor on?

"Is it, Manuel?"

"No."

She nodded like he had passed an important test. "Okay, so suppose you tell me what you were thinking inside Twitchell's house."

He laughed. "Sneaky Manny."

She gave him the same look of approval she'd given him in the courtroom after he'd thrown the water pitcher. He felt a small charge in his balls at the thought of how she'd jumped out of her shoe. He could almost feel her foot on his balls under the table.

"Because you sneaked in there even with somebody watching you?"

He told her whatever she wanted to hear. It was Sunday, it didn't matter. He would just repeat it all on the stand Monday, and that would be the end of it. By then Santiago would either have brought him the jacket or not. A final move one way or the other. It didn't make any difference what he told her now.

He told her about the whores who owned the barstools at Caballo Blanco. She was so interested she looked almost offended when the door opened behind Waters and a guard he had never seen before came in holding a shopping bag.

"Okay, Torres," the guard said, bringing the bag over and laying it on the table. "Now you can be a real clotheshorse in court."

The jacket in the bag seemed like some kind of trick. Manuel was barely aware of the guard going back across the room and out again. He had gotten it past them, that was one thing. Santiago had made a decision, that was the second thing. Okay. But how could the jacket have been delivered to him so easily? The guard he didn't even know shouldn't have given it to him, Santiago should have.

"Your father asked me to bring it."

She was looking at him like she was lying about something that she was waiting for him to work out. He didn't have a clue. She had been scrambling his head since he had sat down with her.

"I've asked him to stay away from the trial. I want you to testify and I want the jury to feel how alone you are."

Manuel took the jacket out of the bag as casually as he could. He didn't have to finger the shoulder pad more than once to feel one of the razors. "Like we pretend he's not my father?" he asked to distract her. "We pretend the jury hasn't figured that out already?"

She gave him another of her waiting looks. He could almost believe she knew about the razor blades under her nose. "The whores at the Caballo Blanco," she said finally, dropping her eyes to the notebook.

2

Hobie couldn't figure out what was supposed to be so Arab about the street fair. Leave out the high school girls giggling under their veils and the fat blowhard strutting up and down in his harem suit and Aladdin slippers, and it could've been a guinea, burro, or chiney block party. Same old come-ons to knock over the bottles and bet on the wheel. Same old beer, pizza, and shish kebab. He wouldn't have been surprised if the blowhard put on a sombrero or pigtails for other fairs on other streets and other weekends.

Tell that to Ida Roberts, though. For almost an hour now, she had been dragging him up and down the avenue to see one piece of crap after another. Hobie had seen better stuff in the backs of cars, and for less than half of what the Arabs were asking. For that matter, so had Ida. But once the hustlers had laid out their stuff on little velvet place mats and covered it all with the smell of sweet incense, they had made Ida forget her smarts. Nobody, not even some treasure hunter in Saudia Arabia, could have spent as much time inspecting chains and bracelets as she had been spending. As they meandered down the avenue, he imagined the signals going from one booth to another: A LIVE ONE, A LIVE ONE.

Still, Hobie said nothing. As long as she didn't start actually blowing money on the dyed paste, he didn't mind her acting like a kid. It was one of the few times she had been enthusiastic about something without the help of a bottle or weed. It was also part of the difference he'd noticed in her as soon as he'd stepped from the hall into her kitchen last night. She hadn't just been happy to see him after so much time, she'd been almost shy about being glad, like a little girl embarrassed to ask him for his hat. Even their fucking had been different. Instead of knowing and doing what she'd wanted, she'd held back, smiling and waiting for him to tell her what he wanted. For the first time since he'd known her, Hobie had felt like she was there to serve him.

Watching her google now over some painted shot glasses being peddled as "Islamic candle holders," he supposed her new attitude came from her sudden craziness about Jesus. He hadn't really paid all that much attention to her bullshit at the kitchen table last night, had mostly done a lot of nodding and kept the Three Feathers flowing, but once he thought about it, there really didn't seem to be any other explanation. That old-time religion hadn't just won her two numbers within six weeks and kept her rubbing him all night, it had even put some toast and tea on the breakfast table instead of the usual muscatel. He was almost sorry that she hadn't found Jesus when they had both been twenty years younger.

"They sure know how to make this shit look pretty, don't they, Hobie? You still haven't told me what you're gonna buy me."

"Whatever you want, whatever you want."

"Really?"

"No, not really."

"Even after last night?"

"Haven't seen so much gray hair since they were combin' out my mother's at the hospital."

Ida pulled on his arm. Once upon a time she had done it to remind him of how much taller she was; now she seemed to do it to tell him how much the two of them were together. "If I were you, old man," she leered at him, "I wouldn't go worryin' about the color, I'd be happy I let you see it at all."

"I'm worried, woman. Real worried."

"Oughta be." She gave him an Ida chin to peer past him at a flock of birdcages hanging in front of one of the booths. "You think Jesus meant for birds to be in cages?"

"Who says they're for birds? Maybe they're for little Arabs."

She sighed, as close as she had come to annoyance with him since they had gotten up. The only other time he'd gotten a sigh was when he had told her about his pills and had to yank the Three Feathers back from her. No harm, either, since he'd gotten up feeling as good as he ever had, certainly a lot better than after his night with the goofus guard King. She and her Jesus seemed to be ready to forgive him anything.

"Did a lot of talkin' in your sleep last night, you know."

"Yeah? Say anythin' interestin'?"

"Was all about the burros. I didn't get it all."

That reminded him. "The burros! Know what I think, Ida? I think some o' them burros are gonna pull some shit at the court-house soon."

"What kinda shit you talkin' about?"

"Break somebody out."

She seemed to have been expecting something more interesting. "What do you say that for?"

Hobie wasn't all that sure, but he had opened his eyes this morning to find the idea waiting for him. It was there again now, and this time he didn't have her big tits distracting him. "There was this geep the other day. In the hall during my break. Asked me a whole lotta questions about buildin' security, if anybody ever broke out; that kind of thing. I told him."

"What did you tell him?"

"What he asked me. If there's ever a good time to try a break, now's it."

She was ready to laugh. "You told him that? You talkin' to some burro like that?"

"Man asked me a question, I gave him an answer."

Now she did laugh—and with the shaking and wheezing she hadn't done all night. He didn't think it was that funny.

"Jesus, Hobie!"

He poked her in the side. "Wasn't in that order this mornin'."

At once she tried to look more grave, even ran her hands up to her head to make sure her pancake hat was still straight. "Well, you really think someone's gonna do that, you gotta tell 'em at the court, don't you?"

"Why? Just because I shot my mouth off to some burro don't mean what I think may happen is really gonna happen. I'd look the damn fool, wouldn't I, runnin' in to tell those guards I got this idea and they should bring in reinforcements? Let it happen, then we'll see."

"But it might be too late then, Hobie."

He had no argument to that. "Could be. But what's the worst that happens? Some burro gets himself shot? A coupla those goofus guards go down? Like I told you last night, you don't have to shake me too hard before I'll give you the name of one of those guards I wouldn't mind seein' buyin' it. The goofus even made me late for work."

Ida thought it over. He liked making her think, made him feel he was on the scoreboard, not just with her but with all the Jesuses and holy rollers inside her head. "Well, if you're not sure who it's gonna be. . . ."

"Oh, I know that. Somebody name o' Torres. Looked into it after the old burro gave me the third degree. Victor Diaz's people, ask me."

"But you're not really sure it's gonna happen."

"Didn't say that either, woman."

"No, you didn't," she agreed.

"But that ain't the same thing as actin' like it's really happened already. You ever pay off somebody who *thought* about playin' a number but just didn't get around to givin' it to you?"

"You know I haven't."

"Yeah, I know. Fact, if I know you, you ain't paid off more than a hundred dollars to anyone in years."

She made him wait a second, but then laughed and wrapped her hand even more securely around his arm. For the life of him he couldn't figure out why he'd waited so long to call her and invite himself over to her place. He certainly wasn't needed around the vet's anymore at night. All Gallagher was good for these days was moaning about his trade and lecturing him about not drinking too

184

much. Best thing all around was not to hang out at the stand until he had forgotten all about being late for work. Then he wouldn't let it slip out some day.

"There's what you're gonna buy for me, Hobie," she said, grinning. She pointed over to a big crate covered with glass figurines, mostly animals.

"What the hell you want that shit for?"

"It'd be somethin' from you."

Whatever sense that made, she let go of his arm and marched over to the crate. As he watched her go, he thought again of how he had talked too much to the goofus King and the burro in the hallway, and of how he had to stay away from the vet not to talk too much to him, too. But with Ida he'd probably said three times as much and still couldn't have cared less. He didn't give a damn, she didn't give a damn, and her Jesus didn't give a damn. That seemed like reason enough to buy her an animal. Maybe a wolf or a fox. He liked wolves and foxes.

3

"Do you ever see that friend of yours, that Mannix boy, John?"

"No."

"I thought you were so close."

"I told you a hundred times, Mother. Eddie moved out to the end of Long Island. Must be three years now, isn't it, John?"

"Yeah."

"That's right, you did say. Big job or something, wasn't it?"

"No, he just wanted to get out of the city with his family."

"How many children?"

"Two. Boy and a girl. They must be four and five now, aren't they, honey?"

"Must be."

"And you don't even talk by phone?"

"Not much."

"That's too bad."

"Why?"

"Well, I mean, you were friends for years."

"John's even the godfather to Eddie's daughter."

"Well, that's what I'm saying."

"People change, Grace."

"Have more of these, Mother."

"Yes, I suppose they do. I used to have a friend like that. Claire Milliken. You remember her, Edith."

"Sure."

"We were close for so many years. Then she took that trip out to San Francisco, and things were never really the same between us. All of a sudden I couldn't say anything to her. She knew everything about everything."

King put more salt on his roast beef. He thought about his weapon in the wooden shoeshine box in the bathroom. He still intended oiling it—while he was on the toilet, so as not to alarm Edith—but he didn't want to go in to the throne just yet. Instead of making two trips, it made more sense to eat as much as he could handle and then go in and get rid of it all.

"There's more gravy on the stove, John."

"I got enough."

"You even notice things like that on television."

"What things, Mother?"

"Well, for instance, this new kind of sign-off so many of these shows have now. They always go off saying things like 'See you next time.' They never say 'tomorrow' or 'next Thursday,' it's always this very vague 'See you next time.' Why? Because they don't really know when the next time is going to be! The program could be canceled or there might be some kind of special taking their time or maybe no one can remember what order they taped the shows. It was never that way with Arthur Godfrey. He was on every single day, and he always knew that if he was signing off on a Monday, his next show was going to be on a Tuesday. So he'd always say 'See you Tuesday,' so you could count on seeing him then. But now it's all just so . . . vague."

King was embarrassed to think of how long it had been since he had last oiled his weapon. It certainly hadn't been when the regulations demanded. Then again, who ever paid attention to the

186

regulations? So much of his training at the academy had been a waste of time. All the hours he had spent getting ahead of the other trainees by learning the name of every part of his weapon—just the thought of those squandered hours now made him tremble. Had Captain Reynolds truly singled him out for praise in front of the class just because he'd been able to remember what the army had taught him? It was hard to believe.

"Signs of getting old, Edith."

"Oh, Mother."

"I was thinking about it just yesterday. Did you see that death notice for the singer Conrad Thibault?"

"Yes, but I'd never heard of him."

"Exactly. Did you ever hear of him, John?"

"Who?"

"Conrad Thibault."

"Who's that?"

"A singer, John. Mother just said."

"Not just a singer, Edith. A very famous singer at one time. He used to be on the RCA Victor show on radio. Probably as famous in his day as some of these rock and roll people today."

"I didn't know that."

The fact was, King thought, some things just didn't need names. The hammer, the trigger, the barrel, the sight—okay, it was important to have the right word when you went into a store to ask for something specific or to complain about a feature that didn't work. But was it really necessary to have a word for things like top straps or ejector rods or cylinder latches? Giving a name to those things made them sound like they were important, but when had anybody really decided to buy a weapon because of its goddamm top strap? What a big fucking deal that he'd known what the damn thing was named and had impressed Captain Reynolds! That was useless, nothing information.

"Your grandmother adored him. Would never miss one of his broadcasts. We always knew it was the RCA Victor show when she left leftovers on the table in the dining room and went into the living room."

"That's funny."

"That's what I'm saying. It's funny to you. It was romantic to your nanny and it's funny to you, but since I seem to be the only

187

one left on earth who ever heard of the man, it just makes me feel old."

"Oh, Mother."

"Please stop saying 'Oh, Mother,' Edith. That's the way they talk to you in nursing homes while they're patting you on the hand."

"Now you're being ridiculous."

"My privilege. Right, John?"

"What's that, Grace?"

"Never mind. I didn't mean to interrupt your haze. Still thinking about getting back at that bank?"

"Oh, please, Mother. Don't bring that up again."

"Why not? I still think John could get something out of it."

"It's not important, Grace."

"Since when?"

"Since I found out there's nothing I can do about it."

"There's always something."

"Yeah? Well, you tell me what it is."

"Mother, please. I'm just as happy to forget the whole—"

"If you feel that strongly about it, sue them. I bet they'd settle with you out of court. Banks don't want bad publicity."

"You really think so, Mother?"

King forked the last piece of meat on his plate. The ejector tube was another one. There had never been any reason to give that name to the thing. Why couldn't it have been considered part of the ejector rod? Granted that the ejector rod didn't really need a name either, but at least it had more reason for a separate name than the stupid ejector tube.

"Surely you must know some lawyer at the court who could advise you."

"That might not be a bad idea, John."

"God knows people win money for far crazier things."

King nodded. It didn't make a difference anymore whether they both thought getting a lawyer had been Grace's inspiration. He was the last one to object to moving his losses around to everyone.

"Speaking of names, I heard a funny story the other day from Mrs. Goetz. Her son's out in California what—two, three years now?"

"I don't remember."

King drank the last of his beer, got rid of his napkin, and

excused himself as politely as he could. He caught Edith's look but didn't know whether she was telling him that he should have been more sociable or that she didn't want to be left alone with Grace to hear more criticism of him. Edith still didn't understand how little he cared about the way other people looked at him. He walked importantly into the bedroom; he had nothing to do there but he still had to play the scene out. It reminded him of the way he'd once acted at school dances—always on the move from one side of the gym to the other, looking like a great mixer but mainly trying to avoid having to dance with one of the girls. The unfinished letter to Mrs. Thompson on the night table didn't ask him to dance.

The glaring bathroom light relaxed him. He was on absolute display in front of the mirror, all his pores brilliant. He'd never had a great face or much of a body under his fat, but now it didn't seem to cost anything to imagine what some plastic surgeon or other specialist might have done with him. All along he had been as transformable as anybody, but he had never allowed himself to entertain the idea before. What the hell had ever been so precious about John King? He had come along on the conveyor belt exactly like everybody else. A little different here, a little different there, but otherwise the same. Like Hobie Morgan had said, the only thing that made him recognizable was his name tag. All the rest of the pieces had come out of a common trough.

He sat down on the toilet lid and placed the shoeshine box on his lap. Leaving his gun and holster in among all the waxes and polishes overnight had made them shiny and smell nice. He had to put the holster right up under his nose to sniff the leather. He didn't know if that was good or bad. He didn't much care.

There was a soft knock at the door. "You okay, John?"

"Yeah, yeah. Fine."

"Sure?"

"For Christ sake, Edith!"

"Okay, okay. Just don't forget to use the spray."

King listened to her go away. He thought about terrifying both Grace and her by walking back out to the dinner table with his weapon. But he had hardly taken the weapon home just for laughs. Once he had cleaned it and had gotten Grace out from under foot, he was going to show Edith how far he had gone to protect her. She'd probably start whining about breaking the courthouse rules, but he would put up with that to let her know how far he was willing to go.

He slid his weapon out of the holster. The quality of the hammer spur was something else he couldn't picture haggling about in a store.

4

Allison was beginning to think that the Other Holiday was, for once, going to be completely painless. The two whiskey sours before dinner had been up to Jerry's high standard. The roast lamb had been as tasty as anything that he had ever eaten from Peggy's kitchen. The strong Bardolino and easy banter had seemed like a gentle plot to get him pixilated. And he had resisted none of it. For once he hadn't even bothered to grade Jerry's performance, to thumb its edges to see if his brother was mainly interested in the sound of his own voice. Whether it was Jerry Allison, his older brother or Jerry Allison, CBS's oldest roving correspondent who had been doing the talking, Allison had just sunk into the steady wash of so much self-assurance, telling himself that the tragedies of Belfast and Beirut were to be grasped as wholly as the drug problems of one of Peggy's nephews. For the afternoon of the Other Holiday, the family Jerry and the professional Jerry had become one, and Peggy had kept looking over at Allison to be sure that he understood how natural such a state of affairs was. He hoped that he had answered her the best way possible by refilling his wineglass every time it was within a swallow of being empty.

The change came on the back deck as soon as Peggy had used Jerry's firing up his Havana as an excuse to announce that she was going to throw all the dirty dishes into the dishwasher. No sooner had she gone back inside and Jerry kindled his cigar to his satisfaction, than a familiar portentousness came into his brother's eyes. When their mother had still been alive and sitting in another room, the look had been unbearable in its mechanical suggestion of hal-

190

lowed earnestnesses, of unspeakable secrets about to be shared. If anything, it had become the ultimate invitation to share nothing. Now, without their mother in the next room, it looked mostly silly.

"So what have you been doing with your leisure time?" Jerry asked.

"I told you. Jury duty."

His brother smiled one of his best prime-time smiles. "Counting on that lasting a few years, are you?"

"Don't mock it. You have fans there. One of my fellow jurors was quite impressed when he learned I was your brother."

"I guess that's the answer to some thing I might've gotten around to asking."

"I'm not up for it today, Jer."

"For what?"

"The Sincerity Session."

Jerry looked hurt, and unsure that he should have been. "They were useful sometimes for discovering satisfactions in our angers."

"Maybe I'm just not angry right now."

Allison heard the click of Jerry shutting the door on the matter. He accepted the click. He needed locks and latches and doors and walls. He needed space and distance and simple dumbness. In fact, he hadn't thought it would have been so hard. He had never thought of himself as a particularly warm man to start with, so why hadn't he been able merely to stop trying to please, to let his detachment take over totally? But there were still damnable twinges—in his ear to hear his dismissal of Jerry, in his chest when he thought about how bloodlessly efficient he had been with Margaret, in his mind when he thought of all the people he had invited to his party. There was something unfair about it being so hard. He was dying, wasn't he? Why wasn't that enough of a price?

"Only reason I was asking," Jerry said, making a series of perfect Os with his cigar smoke as he stared at the deck rail, "is to get a couple of insights before I take the step."

"Retire? You're barely sixty."

"Which is older than you and which is all the more reason to think about it. To get more time to do what I want to do."

"Here?"

"Why not?"

"It isn't Bangkok."

191

"I'm tired of Bangkok."

"You'll get more tired of retirement."

"You don't look the worse for wear. Or are you enduring some winter of discontent beneath that hearty exterior?"

"I don't have all those memories of Bangkok."

His laugh was practically a guffaw. "Memories is right. I don't know about you, brother, but to me middle age is nothing but *paralyzing* memories. You can't look at that goddamn tree over there without remembering some other tree in another time and place. Yesterday down at the gas station, the guy's trying to be friendly so when he gives me back my key, he says, 'Nice key chain.' *Nice key chain.* Not exactly the bon mot of the month, but suddenly I was ready to crown him for reminding me of a very beautiful lady who said the same thing to me in a London pub more than twenty-five years ago."

"They're called the experiences of the international traveler."

"No, Charlie, they're called crowds. Wherever I am lately, I get to feeling like the pope wading through the multitudes. You laugh. So does Peggy. The kids who come around from journalism school to interview me, almost every one of them eventually asks if I don't get nervous thinking about the fact that I have to stand in front of millions of viewers every night."

"And you say no, you're only standing in front of a cameraman."

"Okay, so I repeat myself. But if I want to give them a straight answer, what I'd say is that I feel like I'm in the middle of millions of people and millions of memories every waking hour. Everybody reminds me of somebody else. Whatever happens seems to have happened before. Sometimes, I swear, I think I've lost my ability to come to grips with anybody or anything on its own terms. Everything seems like just a reminder of something else."

"You'd still have those memories sitting out here all day."

"For a while. But then Mother Nature's supposed to provide, right? When you grow really old, you're supposed to forget. The crowds thin out."

"I don't think senility runs in the family."

"Thanks for the encouragement."

The silence descended naturally in the twilight. The grove of stripped trees behind the pool enclosure seemed to be on familiar terms with the quiet; a fat squirrel darting along the fence was indifferent to it. Allison thought about the night Jerry had walked into the kitchen with half a tooth in his palm and announced that he had found "the easiest way to beat decay." His mother had squealed, and he too had been horrified, but by more than just the sight of the coal black filling and gray enamel. There had been a look. on Jerry's face that said he was absolutely capable of letting every one of his teeth fall out until he could get a full set of dentures. Thinking about it again now, Allison still considered it the most passive, most abject thing anyone had ever said to him. He still didn't know where he had found the strength in his fear that day to start shouting at Jerry, insisting that he make an appointment with the dentist the very next day, that his very "life was at stake." Screaming had seemed like the only alternative to covering his brother with dirt then and there.

Jerry was smiling at him. "Thinking the same thing I am?"

Allison didn't mind admitting it; it was a memory on the far side of the click. "I think you might need a dentist again."

Jerry nodded at his cigar. "You scared the bejesus out of me that night. Chased me off to Becker and his magic drill, and I don't think I've felt okay about accepting things ever since."

"You don't need me for that anymore, Jer."

"Yes, I do. In case you haven't noticed, little brother, I'm dangerously on the edge of self-pity. I feel like I've been everywhere and nowhere. About the only places I feel comfortable, outside of here, are places that don't exist anymore. The ladies over in London twenty-five years ago; the tree this one reminds me of—I just want to lay back, have it all swim over me, so that when the tide goes out again, I'll be gone. No trace except for a batch of tapes at the studio, and you can always erase them, right?"

The dishwasher cranking away in the kitchen unnerved Allison. He wandered away restlessly. "You have no right," he said, turning to face Jerry again.

"Right? What are you talking about? I'm just asking for another kick in the ass from the only brother I'd accept it from."

"You're not twenty-one anymore, and I'm not eighteen."

"True."

This time the silence wasn't so natural. The squirrel was gone, and the trees looked merely emaciated. Allison knew without looking that Jerry was puffing more perfect smoke rings over the railing.

"Peggy and I should've had kids, Charlie. We should have someone to go on after us. It's the one thing we never talk about because it's useless. I suppose I was counting on that to seem less important as we went along. Wrong, Jerome Allison. It seems to get more important."

Allison knew that he shouldn't have been angry, knew that only dessert and a cup of coffee separated him from the train and the trip home and the relief that he hadn't ruined the afternoon with his tale of woe. But the sound of the dishwasher in the kitchen was infuriating. It was going to be another half hour at least before Peggy got around to serving.

"I mean, who the hell are we going to leave our millions to?"

"To your journalism school kids," Allison snapped.

"What?"

"Who else? That's who I'd give mine to."

"Are you serious?"

"Can you think of anybody better?"

The cigar smoke drifted closer. He hadn't really thought of any other ending for his party next month. Not just a final gathering of his students, but a special prize awarded to the best of the bunch. His mother's stocks. IRAs. CDs. He still didn't know what criteria he would use for bestowing them, but he knew that one of his students would leave the party with enough money to get on with his or her study of the world. That one last grateful reaction was as far into the future as he dared to think about.

"There's one thing I never really understood, Charlie," Jerry said, suddenly blocking his view of the yard. "You, you the great gadfly, humiliated me that night in the kitchen. Got me off my duff. But you yourself never felt the need to run off."

"Or even walk off, you mean?"

He shrugged. "My first theory was that you were always somehow expecting Robinson to come home, and you didn't want to leave in case you missed him."

"What was the second theory?"

He smiled. "Didn't have one, really. But when I read somewhere that a couple of other greats, like Immanuel Kant and Thelonious Monk, never moved away from where they were born,

194

well, then, I had a cultural phenomenon to play with. Sounded awfully good after midnight in a few bars."

Allison told himself to be careful, to keep it in mind that it was just Jerry's Other Holiday talk. "So I've been a subject of conversation from London to Bangkok?"

"And all the saloons in between. There's a piano player in Rome especially. When you go over there, all you'll have to say to her is that you're Immanuel Thelonious, the philosopher-pianist. She'll buy you all night. I've got her promise on it."

"What's her name?"

"Sylvie. You'll like her. Plays all the standards."

Allison didn't know what to give him. He had to give him something in return, but what was there that wouldn't only deepen Jerry's weariness?

"You're right, Charlie," Jerry said evenly. "Thanks."

"What for?"

"We're *not* those kids in the kitchen anymore. Only one lifesaving gift to a customer, and the hell with me if I don't make it last a lifetime."

There was more, something about seeing about the coffee, about bringing his cigar into the house and annoying Peggy. Allison barely took it in. He felt the small metal square in his pants pocket, among all the coins. "What would you call a souvenir of a souvenir?"

Jerry turned at the French doors and looked at him in bewilderment. "A new racket?"

He tossed the cuff link; Jerry caught it smartly. "Went back to Robinson's house the other night. Nothing but rubble. I found that cuff link. It can't be his after all these years, but I took it anyway. Seemed like I should have."

Jerry examined the object the way Allison had when he found it in the rubble. "You took it from the house?"

"What's left of it."

Jerry nodded, looked at it again, then rubbed it against his shirt trying to see the design more clearly.

"Keep it, Jer."

"But you found it."

"I was looking for something to remind me of God knows what. That won't remind you of anything. You'll just have to take it for what it is."

Jerry looked over almost in a daze; it had always taken him a moment to appreciate being outfoxed. "You son of a bitch," he finally smiled.

"I will be one if you don't get me some coffee or wine or something."

Jerry closed his hand around the cuff link, shaking it once in his fist, and dropped it into his shirt pocket. "You got it," he said, pointing his cigar at his brother and going abruptly inside.

The squirrel was back checking the fence.

5

King felt warmed by a familiar swell. He wasn't on the phone in his living room; he was younger, looser, and back in the Waco bar across the street from the base. He and Eddie Mannix were at the end of the bar near the pool table, challenging each other to remember how many scorpions they had killed during maneuvers. He came up with easily six or seven more than Mannix.

"Admit it, Eddie. I got a lot more of the bastards than you did."

"No question, Johnny," Eddie Mannix said, again sounding like he had to whisper into the mouthpiece. "But why don't we talk about this tomorrow? I'll call you after supper. Say eight o'clock."

King sipped a little more rye, exactly as he had when the two drunken rednecks had come up to them and demanded that they apologize for killing "the official animal of Texas." "You went pussy on me that night, Mannix," he said, laughing. "You lowered your head into your beer, hoping they'd just go away. Not me."

"No, not you, Johnny," the voice said from very far away.

"Look, I'm not saying I was feeling like a hero. But I just didn't want to shake them off. I wanted them to keep pushing, you know? Okay, I guess I was feeling no pain. But I swear it was more than that, Eddie. I felt like ice, know what I'm saying? The only thing I could see was their T-shirts with those idiot things written on them. That's why I said what I said to them. Remember what I said, Eddie?"

"Yeah, Johnny. You said you were going to kill a lot more of their official state animals before the week was out."

"Right." Had he been that firm? He didn't remember actually saying that to the rednecks, but that was what he'd meant, and if Mannix wanted to credit him with the words, what was the harm? "Tell you the truth, Eddie, if the two of them had come after us, we would've been killed. But what the hell do we care now? They didn't, so we can exaggerate this story until we're a hundred."

"I got to get some sleep, Johnny. I got a hard day at the office tomorrow."

"Yeah, yeah. Guess I'm getting soft in the head before my time. But at least back then we didn't have to worry about some crummy pay envelope and all that shit."

For the first time Mannix laughed. "You got that right. I hear anybody talk about money, I get hives."

"No, I don't mean just the money. I mean everything that goes with it. You got to worry about all the things it pays for. You got to keep the little woman from getting panicky, you got—"

"Hey, tomorrow, huh, buddy? Nell's looking at me like I'm talking to another woman."

King nodded to himself. He should have guessed all along that Mannix was talking from some bedroom phone. The guy had hocked himself up to the ears, but he hadn't bothered getting an extension so he could talk in private. "Yeah, sure, tomorrow," he said. "You know my hours, right?"

"I'll get you at eight, buddy. Talk to you then."

"You got it, Eddie."

He wouldn't have minded hanging up first, but the click was so quick that he could imagine Nell grabbing the receiver out of Mannix's hand and slamming it down. He still couldn't figure out what Mannix saw in the skinny nag.

On the TV across the room a sportscaster was giving the results of the day's football games. The teams looked exactly the same, seemed to have rushed and passed and blocked exactly the same. Without the captions at the bottom of the screen, who was to say whether he was watching Atlanta or San Diego or the god-damn Jets? Everything depended on whether or not you trusted the

197

guy doing the announcing, and he didn't. He turned off the set with the remote control and counted the seconds it took for the glow from the picture to vanish. He counted almost two seconds.

Sitting in the quiet, suddenly Monday seemed too close. Why the hell had he opened his mouth to McCloud about the bank machine card? He should have just accepted the reprimand about the cat and let it go at that. But now, even if he did manage to finish the letter to Mrs. Thompson, he was still going to have to go through with a physical to convince McCloud that he wasn't a wacko. King the Psycho—he could hear it already. McCloud had probably already told Morrison about it, and that meant the whole command was going to know about it when he got there Monday morning. Whatever the physical turned up, he was finished at the court building.

King looked at the weapon in his hand, then put it down on the couch next to him. Out of his hand, it felt like a separate presence, like company. He wanted to cry, but he didn't really know why he wanted to. What he was thinking about, what he had been thinking about all afternoon, should have made him mad, not sad, so there was no sense crying. Tears would have solved nothing. Even if he lost his job at the courthouse, he would still have to go on, still have to pay the rent and put food on the table. The courthouse wasn't the world, being a court officer wasn't the be-all and end-all. Plenty of other jobs existed for somebody with his skills. He was good with his hands. He knew a lot about the insides of cars. He was certainly not the stupidest guy who had ever come down the pike. He had been at the top of his class at the academy, had been one of the brightest in his army company. He hadn't exactly been a washout at school, either. Like he'd told the juror Allison, he'd always had a head for remembering things. The odds were with him, whatever he ended up doing. It was only himself he had to be on guard against. Over and over again he had behaved like his own worst enemy. Babbling to McCloud about the bank machine card had been only his latest mistake. Nobody else would have ever given him trouble if he hadn't invited them to.

He picked up the A&S flier from the coffee table. People in the rest of the city were still having sales. He hated to think of Edith reading about the clothes and furniture and going off to bed with half a mind to go shopping tomorrow. She had fallen asleep without a clue that soon they might not have a penny. How did he dare tell

·198·

her? She had never really asked him for much, had never really made demands on him. How was he going to get up the nerve to tell her that she had to cut out her one or two afternoons in the department stores, at least until he had found another job? He wouldn't have blamed her if she took it as the last straw and moved to her mother's. She was already mortified by the business about Thompson's cat and the letter.

He put his head back against the back of the couch and thought about the best time to break the news to her. Not during their breakfast routine, that was for sure; he didn't want to ruin the day for both of them. Leaving her by herself to worry about everything while he was at work would have been cruel. Calling her from the courthouse wouldn't be much better. If he told her as soon as he came home from work, she would be too upset to make supper, and she wouldn't be able to taste her food anyway.

That left immediately after supper, when she settled down on the couch to do some knitting while she told him about the actors on the tube. He couldn't spoil that for her. It was the one chunk of the day when she seemed to open up a little, sometimes talking about people they had once thought of as close friends and every once in a while getting him to say things he hadn't known he'd thought. She with her knitting and the TV, he with his newspaper and a beer or two—they were too close to one another in the evening to ruin it with the worries he had brought down on them. That left when they went to bed, at eleven or so when they could talk after making it. But Saturday night had already passed, and the last time he had come on to her unexpectedly she'd taken his body with an alarm that something had to be bothering him, what was it? He wasn't about to confirm her suspicion that the only time he desired her was when something went wrong. There was no right time for telling her; whenever he did, he would end up hurting her.

He brought the flier up to his eyes and turned it over. The postage label read MRS. JOHN KING. Some mailroom clerk at A&S had stuck on the label without a moment's thought. Probably a clerk responsible for names beginning with *K*. No consideration had gone into it. The flier was free. MRS. JOHN KING had no reality for him, she was just somebody out there to be reeled in, someone who might spend a few bucks on a raincoat or a blender. MRS. JOHN KING was a purse or a credit card. She had made the mistake of filling out some form, so now she was going to be a target for the rest of her life.

Who she was as a person meant nothing to A&S. All she existed for as far as they were concerned was to buy. He had given Edith Chandler his name so she could turn into another shopping drudge.

He had wanted to give her so much more.

King threw the flier over the table. He knew there was no point attempting to sue a big company like A&S. Nobody would have taken his case.

He thought about another drink, then picked up his weapon instead. For some reason he thought of a kitten jumping up into his arms and then climbing up to his shoulder. He knew it wasn't Mrs. Thompson's cat. That fleabag was dead, and he'd be damned if he was going to apologize for something not his fault.

He wished Edith would get over her habit of knocking on the door of the bathroom when he was on the john to tell him to use the air freshener. Whenever she did that, she made even his stink seem small.

Everybody knew who Gwynn was now. He had embarrassed McCloud and everybody else, and he wasn't just going to go away, he was going to be in the papers and on the TV for weeks. Gwynn was going to have to be processed step by step. Nobody was going to be able to forget about that wacko soon.

He cocked his weapon. Outside of the firing range, he had never done it before when it had been loaded. It felt like a giant step away from John King. With his weapon cocked he was suddenly on new terrain. Anyone walking into the living room at that moment wouldn't have recognized him. He was on his own—no apologies, no responsibilities, no debts. One small movement of his thumb, and he was another person.

"John, are you still up?"

King thought of how gentle Finnigan and the others had been with Gwynn as they had taken him into custody. In that moment everyone had cared about Gwynn. It had been Gwynn, not the spic Torres, who had been important.

"John?" the voice called again from the bedroom.

The Fifth Day

1

King woke up with a start. He still had all his clothes on, was still on top of the covers. His weapon was where he'd left it on the night table. He reached out for it too fast, giving himself a crick in the back of his neck, then remembered that he didn't need it anyway, that he had nothing more to be worried about. He was finally alone, his fears were in the past. Even the odor of seared cork had vanished from the room while he had been dozing. He felt a surge of excitement, the kind he had once felt as a teenager waking up in the morning after a late night of beers down at the Dublin Tavern. He had scored, and the world knew it. He could hardly wait to build on it.

He looked over at Edith. The checkered blanket had slipped

down to the edge of her forehead. He assumed it must have been his fault, not hers, that he had moved an arm or a leg over the blanket during the night. Now, without even lifting his head from the pillow, he could make out the top parts of the hole. The thin breaks in the skin were like separate eyelashes, tiny streaks, not exactly red, not exactly gray. The hair above them continued to grow senselessly. It had received the message, but still it didn't give a damn. King wondered how Edith could have stood such disloyal hair for so long.

He looked away from her and up at the ceiling. The ceiling hadn't undergone any change, either. He thought about what to do now that he was by himself. The first new thing was going to be getting breakfast, and a paper to read first. Should he take over Edith's routine and go across the street to the Korean for bagels and the *News*, or should he break the routine altogether and wait till he arrived at the courthouse to get something to eat? He decided that, for one morning anyway, it would be more interesting to take over from Edith and go to the Korean's.

He got up and tramped into the bathroom. He took Edith's new underwear off the toilet tank and tossed it into the hamper. He pissed, brushed his teeth, shaved, and took a lukewarm shower. He wasn't all that sure that he was feeling anything different or wanted to feel anything different. He decided that the distinction would have been important only if he'd been able to work out what it was. He didn't try. The feel of the terry cloth towel on his back reminded him that he was now also going to be responsible for the laundry. He didn't mind that, he had done the laundry for himself before meeting Edith and getting married. There was nothing that having to do the laundry was going to teach him.

Back in the bedroom he saw that the blanket hadn't slid any farther down. He didn't want to see her wound again. He hadn't expected that much gray mush under the blood. Even contained in the hole and with only the streetlight reflecting on it, it had been a little disgusting. He hadn't expected any feeling from something dead. It had almost made him sick to his stomach. He should have covered her with the blanket without looking at it.

He dressed quickly. There was something eery about Edith's stillness under the covers while he went through the normal motions of stuffing his shirt into his pants, tying his tie, and buckling his belt. It was as if just by getting his clothes on, he was leaving her behind, sentencing her to being even more dead. He was glad when he was finally able to get his weapon from the night table and take it out to the kitchen.

He found a plastic bag in the closet under the sink and dumped his weapon into it. Back in the bathroom he retrieved his holster from the shoeshine box and put that in the bag as well. In the living room he went around turning off the lights he had left on. He was annoyed at how much going back and forth seemed to be involved in just getting out the front door. That was one thing he hadn't counted on.

He was already stepping off the stoop with the bag under his arm when it hit him how mixed up he was. Why take along his weapon if he had already decided to go to the Korean's and then have breakfast back in the house? He laughed at his goofiness as he crossed to the grocery. Kim or Kwan or whatever his name was was alone in the narrow little store. He was busy taking bran muffins and croissants out of a paper bag and laying them on a big metal tray near the front of the counter. He said hello.

"Something I get you?"

King stared at the muffins and croissants. Edith had never told him that the Korean sold the things; morning after morning, it had been the same old bagels. How many other things were there like that that she had forgotten to tell him?

"Very good," the Korean said, looking at the tray with him.

"You know who I am?"

The Korean was puzzled but smiled anyway. "Yes?"

King heard the false note. The man no more knew his name or that he was Edith King's husband than he knew how to throw a knuckleball. He had been living directly across the street from the grocery for years, but he might as well have been invisible.

"I guess we all look the same to you, huh?"

The Korean smiled because he smiled. But there was no fun in that.

"I don't want anything," he said, and made for the door before having to see the man's disappointment. He felt better back out in the weak morning sunlight. He still had his weapon, still had his car waiting for him across the street. It wasn't like he had actually promised anybody that he'd eat breakfast back in the house.

His gauge was pushing empty. He could have hit the gas

203

station just before getting on the expressway or he could have nerved it through and gone to the station near Hillside Avenue. He laughed at such an obvious choice. Now that he was invisible, he had no reason not to go to Hillside Avenue.

The radio came on as soon as he turned the ignition key. Just in time to learn that it was 7:25. Dum-da-dum-dum. It was the earliest that he had ever pulled away from the house.

2

Elena watched Jack Haggerty through her windshield. The detective came plodding across the boulevard so mindlessly, not even acknowledging the traffic that he was holding up in both directions, that she had an impulse to switch on her wipers and swat him away. She suddenly had reservations about sitting together in the front seat with him.

Reaching the sidewalk in front of the parking lot, Haggerty hesitated only a second before spotting her and ambling over to the car. She felt better seeing him reach into his pocket for a match as he opened the passenger door: he needed his crutches with her more than she needed any with him.

"Why is it, sis, I get the idea you think a parking lot is the right place for meeting Jack Haggerty?"

The smell of his talcum powder was overwhelming in the front seat. "I just want to get this over with before I go in there. I have a busy morning."

Haggerty considered it as if trying to detect an insult, shrugged, then reached into his jacket pocket for his notebook. He didn't notice John King swaggering past the last line of cars and heading for the side entrance of the court building. "Like I figured," he said, maneuvering the match between his teeth. "I got zilch on the dog. No neighborhood kids attacked. A regular Rin Tin Tin."

"It was worth looking into."

He didn't believe her any more than she believed herself, but he kept his eyes on his notebook. "The juror Benzinger's another zero," he said matter-of-factly. "Guy was a priest until two years ago. Now every once in a while that offers possibilities—"

"What you found out, Jack."

"Right. Well, seems he just quit to get married. Mary Lawrence from the Borough of Churches. They have a nine-month-old named—"

"I'm not interested."

Haggerty nodded promptly and turned to another page. She had expected it all weekend, but now she knew for certain that she had nothing in front of her except Manuel Torres on the witness stand.

"Now here's where we have some food for thought. Charles Allison."

"What about him?"

Haggerty put the notebook on his lap and started working his match more seriously between his teeth. "Called up a few people at the school Friday and Saturday. A regular Mr. Chips for years, but then suddenly he quits last year for reasons nobody understands or wants to talk about. No better job, no romance, no inheritance. This gets me to brooding. I call an old friend over at the county Blue Cross. Seems Sterling High has the usual medical policy that runs out after you're gone three months. Most people either keep up the policy for a heftier rate or switch to Blue Cross. Allison switched."

"So?"

He looked at her expectantly. "Bingo. Three months ago Allison went over to Long Island Jewish for a series of tests. Guess for what?" She didn't even want to shake her head; she didn't want to know anything at all that he was telling her. "Brain tumor. Something called an astrocytoma, and that doesn't mean some kind of indoor stadium. The man is dying. Probably has only a few months."

Elena tried to keep the words from reaching her. The silver-haired man with the attentive expression rose up in front of her, then was driven away again. It was not possible that she had asked for such crass information; Haggerty's hateful nonchalance couldn't have been hers.

"So now we're back to possibilities. Here's a juror who's got problems on his mind. Literally. A juror who can't concentrate. Maybe too much pressure physically—"

"What in God's name made you call Blue Cross?"

He was taken aback by her anger. "A hunch," he said, peering at her as though she owed him better behavior. "Lots of people hate the idea of playing out the string on familiar ground. Like the elephants."

"And you just happen to know somebody at Blue Cross."

"No happen about it, sis," he said, more annoyed. "It's my profession. You make contacts where they're useful. That reminds me . . ."

Elena looked back out at the boulevard. She thought of the sign in the window of the grocery store near Santiago Torres's place. BLACK FLAG. MATA INSECTOS. IA CIENCIA CIERTA. Pressing a spray would have been an even better way of getting rid of Haggerty than turning on her windshield wipers.

". . . Sunday's not exactly a working day. He did me a favor."

"What're you talking about?"

"My friend at Blue Cross. I have to budget a few bucks for him."

"You do that, Jack."

"Hey, look, sis, I'm just telling you what I found out."

She knew he was right, of course. She was the one who had sent him off. And what difference did any of it make anyway? She still had her new strategy of putting Manuel on the stand. Allison's tumor was irrelevant.

"You know this guy?" Haggerty asked.

"Who?"

"Allison."

Elena gripped the steering wheel and pulled herself into the idea. Instead of answering no, she tried to imagine what knowing Allison might be like. She found it oddly easy to imagine herself sitting at his bedside and holding his hand as he lapsed into a final coma. She wouldn't have a lot of trouble persuading him that she truly cared, she thought.

"I didn't mean to lay it on you this way."

She released the wheel and smiled. Haggerty could be absolutely hilarious in his crudity. "Sorry, Jack. No personal angle for you to sell somewhere else. I appreciate how fast you worked. Send me the bill."

She was grateful that he didn't push it, that he just returned her smile, replaced his notebook in his pocket, and reached for the door handle. "You know where to find me, sis."

She did. And looking away from him back out at the boulevard and watching a group of pedestrians coming across with the light, she was surprised to see that she also knew where to find Alan Green. As far as she remembered, he was supposed to have taken his bow tie over to Manhattan this morning.

3

Hobie stood with one foot in and one foot out of his elevator car, watching the morning parade pass through the metal detectors at the entrance. He liked the way the clucks dragged their bags off the inspection desks and then gaped around for a lobby directory. It was their sucker moment between the self-importance they'd felt hurrying up the stairs outside and the self-importance they would recover as soon as they discovered where their courtroom was. Sometimes he felt like taking a picture of them as they gazed around from one wall to another, first looking surprised, then annoyed, before finally seeing the information desk tucked away in the corner. What he would've done with the pictures he had no idea, which was why he had never bothered taking them.

He recognized the mick with the broomstick up his ass coming toward him. One of the jurors from Rubin's court. The mick walked like a bishop and had some of crazy Gwynn's cement for a face. Being the goofus that he was, he took only a glance at Brooks's car, counted the burros and blacks already packed to the door, and kept on coming. One old brownie was the lesser of evils.

"Morning," the mick said stiffly.

Hobie nodded to be polite but made the goofus go around his elbow to get inside. He wasn't running any hotel.

The buzzer rang from the basement. He knew that the red

light on the panel was King again. King had too much nerve. Would it be too good to be true that the burros would take King out with a perfect shot while they were making their escape? He supposed it would be, but he could still think about it. Lot less misery all around.

The mick coughed like he was in a hurry to get upstairs. Hobie watched the juror from Raymond's courtroom make it through the detectors and come toward him. A big one for talking about the weather. He didn't mind though: man even had some style, with his gray hair and charcoal suit.

"How are you this morning?" gray hair asked.

"I'm here, I'm here," Hobie said, moving his elbow out of the way so the guy could step into the car.

The guineas from the second floor were his, too. Squat Mama and squat Papa and two sons fatter than both of them. Whatever their troubles were, it wasn't getting a fork into their mouth. He had to step out of the car altogether to let them in.

The buzzer from the basement came again. Hobie had to laugh at the goofus King. Take the bolt out of the screwball's head and all the pieces would come tumbling out. One more passenger, he decided, and the car was going upstairs, not downstairs.

He would have preferred somebody besides Alvarez, though. As she came marching toward him with her big shoulder bag and bulging attaché case, Hobie thought about what Ida had said yesterday about warning somebody about the burros. Alvarez was the Torres punk's lawyer, which meant that she was either in on the escape or was close enough to it to get herself killed if the geeps went into action. Problem was, he didn't know which.

"Good morning, Hobie."

He nodded to her and followed her back into the car. For a second he felt like a cop who'd stumbled across a crap game. From one rear corner of the car to the other, above the heads of the guineas, Raymond's juror was staring over at the mick nervously. And no sooner did Alvarez spot Raymond's juror than, all white in the face, she turned around quickly to the front of the car.

"Be a good idea if you told me where you're goin'," he said.

They all said their piece while he closed the gate. He didn't need them to tell him where to stop since he was going to stop at every floor anyway, but he didn't want them getting the idea he was a mind reader. The light was still on in the basement panel. He was sorry they'd never installed one of those old-fashioned indicators above the door in the basement; he would've liked to imagine King's face as the arrow went upward.

He stopped at two. Nobody wanted to get off, nobody got on. He didn't care what they thought. The fact was, he needed a few extra seconds to make up his mind about Alvarez. Burros were burros, they stuck together. But if the Diaz mob considered her a different kind of burro, she could get hurt. He had no particular reason to want to see that. Alvarez might have been a geep, but at least she was no screwy guard talking about blowing up a bank and demanding private car service from the basement. If only he could figure out what side of the coin she was on, he could park for a minute or so upstairs and tell her what he knew.

He got rid of the mick and the guineas on three. Through his mirror he watched Raymond's juror track the mick's every step out of the elevator. In the corner of his eye he saw Alvarez pulling in her big chest and making an extra effort to forget the guy behind her. Whatever was in the air this morning seemed to be making everybody edgy. It was like the last day with Gwynn and Barbarella in the elevator.

Raymond's juror walked his worries off at four. Alvarez sighed as soon as he was gone.

"Long mornin' already?"

"Something like that," she said.

Hobie tried to think of something in the middle, something that might have told her that he knew what he knew without telling her that he did. "Can't be worse than that business the other day with the guards," he said. "You got two people shootin' at one another. You got two less guards for stoppin' any breakouts. You got all kinds of security problems."

She nodded, looking at the door like she couldn't wait for it to open again. He didn't care. He had to try again.

"Thing I can't figure out," he said, holding the lever down as far as he could without stopping the car altogether, "is why there ain't been more people tryin' to break out around here. Not since Benny Smith years ago. You got to figure with all these goofus guards and all these characters showin' up to see their friends bein' put away, somethin's gonna happen somewhere along the line."

"I guess you're right. We're lucky. Look, is there something wrong with the elevator? We're really crawling."

Fuck her. Now he was being criticized for not knowing how to run his own car! He nudged the lever just far enough to give her a little jolt when they reached the top floor. "No sweat, lady. Here we are."

She glared at him as she marched out. Too bad for her, Hobie thought. But at least he could tell Ida that he'd tried.

4

Allison knew that he was squandering his fellow jurors' goodwill. As he stood at the window of the jury room, staring out at the real estate office across the street, he knew that he still had time to turn around and accept the invitation to join one of the conversations at the table, to squelch the impression that he was cold-shouldering everyone. He couldn't do it, though. He had lost an important mooring for himself and now felt miserably adrift. Markings, personal markings, had somehow fallen away back in the elevator at the sight of James Conboy, his racist friend from the first day of the jury assembly.

Once again, he tried to think it through rationally, step by step: there was the trial that morning; there was going to be the trial the next morning; a day or two after, there would be the verdict and the dismissal of the jury; three days after that there would be two weeks until his party—a last valley of time for him to get a grip on things.

But now James Conboy, whom Alvarez had rejected out of hand for the Torres trial, was still somewhere in the building. The redneck had evidently returned to the assembly room, been selected for another courtroom, and been accepted for a case. Was the defendant a Puerto Rican? A black? Somebody else in James Conboy's black book of unacceptable races? How was it possible for the man to still be around? Allison hadn't planned on having to worry about such practical things one way or the other anymore.

John King stuck his large head inside to announce another

210

five minutes of waiting. The guard smiled benevolently at a jibe from Mrs. Everett and ducked back out again. Allison couldn't believe that less than a week ago he had been so caught up in his impression of King as some kind of evil incarnate. Obviously, he had been wafting along lately on more than one fantasy.

Anna DeSilvestri came over and peered up at him coyly. "Bad weekend?"

He said the first thing that came into his head. "Know how you say *weekend* in Serbo-Croatian?"

She shook her head brightly. "No, Professor. How do you say it?"

He turned halfway around to include Engelson and Cort in his answer. "I have no idea, but not for lack of trying. As I recall, the dictionaries I consulted didn't have a separate entry for 'weekend.' They had words for 'week' and for 'end,' but not together. So I think it has to be something like *kraj nedelja.*"

"Why would anyone want to say 'weekend' in Serbo-Croatian?"

"Many reasons," he said, bowing to Mrs. Everett and willing himself out of his funk. "If you're talking to a Serb on a Tuesday, you might want to make some appointment for Saturday. Or maybe you fell in love in Yugoslavia and want to write to your lover saying how much your time together meant."

Benzinger laughed. "Especially that *kraj nedelja.*"

"Exactly."

"Was that your situation, Mr. Allison?"

Allison smiled at the absurdity of Mrs. Weathers's prim expression. It wasn't possible that she was Dr. Munson's secret agent in the room, but he could hardly deny the sudden sensation. It didn't seem like pain at all. It was so massive, gripped him so suddenly and completely, that he imagined frantically that it was something that had descended on the entire building. There were no familiar throbs, no easy rise from something dull to something slightly less dull. He wasn't on it, it was on him. Even when his eyes began to tear, he was sure he was warning everybody else about it, telling them to get under the table, to close their eyes, cover their ears until it passed by. But in fact he couldn't utter a word. His mouth was useless. Mrs. Weathers, the Port Authority man, Benzinger—everybody recognized him for who he was. It didn't make the slightest difference when he finally relented and closed his eyes;

it was already too late. Everyone had already seen how he had gotten chalk on his fly.

He couldn't believe he was sitting. The stabbing pain shouldn't have permitted him to be so free, to be able to move his body at will. Space was everywhere around him, air was everywhere around him. He hadn't asked for space and air. He ought to have been allowed to faint.

"Migraine?"

Anna looked so fearful that he nodded to reassure her. He wanted her to stop looking like his personal nurse and go back to being everybody's nurse, wanted her to be absolutely detached as she talked about the neighborhood hospitals or something else that had nothing to do with him.

"You have something for it?" She was searching his jacket pockets before he could stop her. Cort and Mrs. Everett looked scandalized by her forwardness. "These?" She came out with the vial that Munson had given him. He could feel a bottoming out somewhere above his ears, but the cloud above felt thicker, angrier at being localized. And then she made it still worse: one glance at the label and she peered back at him as though he had betrayed her in some way.

She knew everything at once.

"Get some water, somebody."

Allison closed his eyes; he was already everybody's patient, and the concessions no longer mattered. He could hear water running in one of the bathrooms. A hand gripped his shoulder, and for some reason the pain rebelled against it—jumping up, then subsiding. It knew it was running out of strength.

"Maybe you should go home."

"The hell with that," he said quickly, opening his eyes. Benzinger put a paper cup in his hand and Anna gave him the pill she had extracted from the vial. He threw it down before he had to think too long about the excuses he was going to have to make to everyone.

"They're terrible," somebody at the table said. "My wife gets them, and there's really nothing you can do about them."

"I thought they had a treatment," somebody else said.

Allison drank his water slowly. He welcomed the dull throb; he was back to running familiar scales.

"You sure you're okay?" Anna asked, low enough for the others not to go back to hectoring him.

" 'Okay.' There's another word I looked up in the Serbo-Croatian dictionary."

She nodded sardonically. "And they say 'okay' too, right?"

"Right."

By the time John King returned to line them up for the walk downstairs, the jurors had moved on to other topics. His earlier moodiness, the spectacle he had made of himself—Allison told himself they were dead issues. The others were back to expecting only the best from him.

As he was back to expecting only the best from himself. At the very least he had to find out what kind of trial James Conboy was sitting on.

5

"Would you please state your full name to the jury."

"Manuel Torres."

"And how old are you, Mr. Torres?"

She hadn't warned him that she was going to start off with idiot questions, but Manuel didn't mind. He kind of liked shooting his answers out over her and at the pasty-faced dude with the bow tie sitting where Santiago usually sat. The bow tie couldn't have given a shit about how old he was, where he had been living, and how much school he had done, and that made it funnier to tell him.

"How many times have you been arrested, Mr. Torres?"

He seemed to have said something wrong even before he said it. The DA eyed Alvarez like she had dropped an ice cube on his balls. The crippled judge started coughing. The bow tie let go with a loud sigh, crossed his legs, and stared at the ceiling. Only Miss Madrid looked satisfied.

"Tell me, Mr. Torres: if you had to put a monetary value on

every item you took on those occasions, how much do you think it would be?"

"Objection!"

The judge cleared his throat. "Sustained. I think I know where you're headed, Ms. Alvarez, but find another way to put the question."

She nodded coolly. "The first time you got caught with stolen property, Mr. Torres, what exactly was it?"

Manuel told her what she wanted to hear. He'd figured she would have pretended to be more surprised, like she was hearing it for the first time, but she gave away nothing. Back and forth from the defense table to the jury box, from the jury box back over to the defense table, she was in her own flow, not giving a damn if everybody in the courtroom knew they had worked out their answers in Visitors yesterday.

"And how much would you say that ring was worth?"

In Visitors he had told her a hundred dollars, and she had kept staring at him with the pencil eraser against her chin until he had changed it to fifty. Now, when he told her thirty dollars, she didn't look at all grateful to him, just paced another couple steps back to the jury and asked about the old Greek cups he had grabbed from that insurance company guy's house two years ago. It was the tennis game she had said it would be—boom, boom, boom, back and forth. And he was okay at it. He was like an actor or somebody who made speeches. She had worked out so many angles that he even remembered little things that had never come to him when he was shooting the shit with Edison back in his cell or in the rec room.

Foy objected again—exactly as she had predicted—and the *cojo* Raymond told her to stop asking questions about the cost of everything he had ever grabbed. She gave Raymond her promise, but then right away she was through the back door again with the Caballo Blanco whores, and Foy looked like he wanted to go back to the thirty-dollar rings. He told her again about Santiago paying for the first couple of times with Mara and Sylvia, and this time she peeked out of the corner of her eye to see the reaction of the jurors. They were all looking at him like he had two heads. So was Foy. He tried to imagine Foy going into the Caballo Blanco. Mara would've taken him to a back table and pulled at his pecker until she had his money folded away—then she'd get up with one of her horse laughs and go back to the bar, leaving him sitting with his hard-on. If he tried to go after her, Armando would've come out from behind the bar and cracked open his skull.

"How old were you at this point, Mr. Torres?"

"The first time with Sylvia? Twelve, thirteen. I don't remember."

King looked around at him like he didn't believe shit. King was right: Manuel remembered exactly that he had been two weeks older than his twelfth birthday.

"So there was your apartment, the coffeehouse, and the Caballo Blanco. What about school? Church?"

"Yeah, sure. Some of that too."

"Some of that. Anyplace else you spent much time in that period?"

"The firehouse, I guess."

"That was nearby?"

"Coupla blocks away."

"What did you do in this firehouse?"

"Nothin' much. Just hung around. Sometimes they'd ask me to get sandwiches and things."

"And how long would you usually 'hang around'?"

"Coupla hours."

"How often? Every day?"

"Yeah."

"For how long? Couple of months? A year?"

Manuel hadn't really counted it up until she had asked him in Visitors, and even now three years seemed longer than it had been. But three years was what it had been.

Foy jumped up again. "I'm sure Mr. Torres had an interesting childhood, Your Honor. But the point here would seem to be his adult activities, specifically regarding the very adult charges that have occasioned the present trial."

She gave the judge her big back and high ass as she walked down the jury box to the well rail. "The court's patience is not infinite, Mr. Foy," the *cojo* said. "But I would suggest that to take a few more minutes approaching Ms. Alvarez's presumed destination is a small price for the prosecution to pay in exchange for the invitation the defense has extended you to enter certain legal waters."

The bow tie behind the rail blew out more air and recrossed

his legs. "Did they have a nickname for you around the firehouse, Mr. Torres?"

"Yeah. Sneaky Manny."

"And how did you get that nickname?"

"I think it was because one day I went into the kitchen to grab a few crackers. They saw me and thought it was real funny."

"Did you think it was funny?"

"Didn't bother me none."

"You never got the idea they were making fun of your Latin background in some indirect way?"

"Don't have to be Latino to be sneaky." Landers thought that was funny; so did the spade woman in the front row of the jury. "But no, they weren't that way."

"What way, Mr. Torres?"

"Racist and stuff. One of them especially, he'd get all over you when you started usin' words like nigger. Spades is okay, he'd say, but don't go usin' the word nigger because you hurt people's feelin's."

The spade juror couldn't straighten out her dress fast enough; the teacher nodded at something in his head. Alvarez looked pleased with herself. "And when did you stop hanging around the firehouse?"

She liked hearing about the night Cookie Alomar had gotten beaten up. He still didn't know why he had told her about it in Visitors, but as soon as he had opened his mouth yesterday, she hadn't wanted to hear anything else.

"And the night of this incident with Mr. Alomar, you were in the firehouse playing catch with one of the firemen, is that correct?"

"Right."

"And then what happened?"

Manuel told himself to ignore the bow tie, who was now slumped down in his seat as far as he could get, his hand on his face. "Yeah, we were playin' catch, and there was this honk from a car outside the door. Robby ran over to slide open the door. It was Conklin's car. He was the chief. Soon as Conklin drove in, he jumped out and told Robby to close up again. The old man did like he was told."

"Was this unexpected, the return of Chief Conklin?"

"Sure. It was a three-alarmer. Big factory on Classon. Conklin was supposed to be on the scene."

"Anything else unusual about the chief's return that night?"

"Yeah. Brinkman and Lemon were in the car with Cookie Alomar. They were hook-and-ladder. They shouldn't have been with the chief."

"And how did the chief explain all this?"

"I think Lemon and Brinkman—"

"Your Honor, I must object!"

The Judge thought Foy was funny. "On which of your several grounds do you base this objection, counselor?"

"Hearsay, irrelevance, speculation—"

"That'll do, that'll do," the judge said, reaching over for his crutch and getting up with a groan. "Please approach the bench, counsel."

Alvarez moved off her spot against the railing and clomped on her big legs over to the far end of the platform behind Foy. She had predicted it all, Manuel thought—everything except how close to the end they really were. He was running out of time. He had to do more than think about grabbing her and using her to get out of the building, he had to actually do it. Even Santiago expected that from him now. Where had all the time gone? Waiting for the trial, picking the jurors, listening to Waxman and the other witnesses—it had all gone by too fast. It was up to him now to slow things down. Nobody else was going to.

The judge broke up all the bullshit, and everybody went back to the starting gate. Miss Madrid looked happy, and Foy looked like he had been asked to give more favors than he wanted.

"The witness is cautioned to confine his account to what he actually saw or heard said."

Whatever the hell that meant.

"Okay, Mr. Torres, then what?"

"They dragged Cookie to the kitchen in the back."

"Without saying anything to you or to this fireman you were playing catch with?"

"Conklin said Cookie might have started the fire. Then he gave me this look. He didn't like seein' me there."

"Ob—"

"Sustained. Cut that last remark."

"Did Chief Conklin say anything else to the other fireman?"

217

"Yeah, he told Robby to call the precinct."

"And did Robby?"

"No, he just went over to his cubicle and picked up this book he had. It was like Conklin hadn't said anythin' to him."

"What did you do?"

She walked over to the bow tie and stood in front of him. He didn't know why, but she didn't want him seeing how uptight the guy was acting. "I told him what Conklin had said about callin' the precinct. Robby kind of laughed and said the cops would get there soon enough. I said, not unless you call them, Robby. He said not to worry about it, what I didn't know wouldn't hurt me. I told him Conklin was goin' to be pissed at him, and he said. . . ."

"He said what, Manuel?"

It seemed funny now that he'd once been so bothered by it. But nobody else he'd ever met had ever thought of him as a Joey Edison. "He said bein' Sneaky Manny was okay as a joke, but it was another thing if I was goin' to be some kind of snitch."

"By 'snitch' you mean an informer?"

Like she suddenly didn't know. "Yeah."

"Then what happened, Manuel?"

Why was she calling him that? What'd happened to "Mr. Torres"? "I bugged him some more. He started gettin' mad, but he picked up the phone."

"To call the precinct?"

"Yeah. He kinda turned into the wall and started talkin' to somebody. I figured it was a desk sergeant. Started sayin' all this funny crap."

"Like what?"

"Well, stuff that wasn't important. The fire. How many alarms. How he was lucky not to go out on calls anymore."

"In other words, it took Robby some time to get around to the purpose of the call?"

"Right. Like he was tryin' to drag it all out."

"And while Robby was on the phone, what did you do?"

He didn't care about embarrassing her; she was putting him through hoops, so why couldn't he put her through some? "Like I told you already."

She smiled tightly. "Tell everybody, Manuel."

He'd gained nothing. "He wasn't watchin'. He had his back

218

to me. I wanted to see what Conklin and the others were doin' in the back."

"So you . . . sneaked back there?"

She thought she was being funny. So did the guard Landers. But none of them had been there. He'd felt as naked as one of the poles as he had edged toward the back of the firehouse. He could've suffocated on the smell of gasoline and minted water in the air. The picks and axes on the wall had seemed like weapons to be used against him. The light shining under the kitchen door had made it seem like the door was going to fly off its hinges at him. "Yeah."

"Because you wanted to help Cookie Alomar?"

"How could I help him? There were three of them, not countin' Robby."

"Just to see what was going on, then."

"I guess."

"Was the kitchen door closed?"

"Yeah, but there was only one place you could put Cookie and have room to swing at him. I figured I had about two seconds to throw open the door, see what was goin' on, and then get out."

"Is that how it worked out?"

"Mostly." He'd turned the doorknob and thrown open the door—and frozen. Lemon and Brinkman had been standing over Cookie like they really *had* been beating on him. And the other funny thing was that Lemon had taken a swing at Cookie's chest, not at his stomach, like he didn't care if he hurt his hand on Cookie's bones or didn't know where he was supposed to aim. He hadn't figured on exactly those things as he had been edging his way to the back; maybe something like them, but not exactly what he saw.

"You saw them punching Mr. Alomar. Then what?"

"I got out."

"Back down the length of the firehouse?"

"It was the only way." King didn't think that was funny.

"And did they come after you?"

"Sure."

"Running? Shouting? How?"

"Conklin was shoutin'. They didn't have time to run. He was shoutin' for Robby in the cubicle."

"Did Robby try to intercept you?"

Try was right. "Yeah. He acted like the Cyclops."

219

"Like what, Manuel?"

He had almost lost them. He liked the worry in her face. Even the teacher guy on the jury looked like he was going to have a heart attack. "Like he was hung over. Came staggerin' out of the cubicle. He couldn't move on those old legs, but he came close."

"Close enough to make contact?"

"Yeah. I gave him a shove in the stomach." And had almost stopped running right there. He could still feel Robinson's big hard sponge of a stomach. But Manuel hadn't stopped. He'd cut his fingernail on the latch of the peep door, but he'd made it to the street. Even as he'd kept running, he'd taken the ball out of his pocket so it would stop pressing on his leg, stop slowing him down. There'd been those big sidewalk squares with new cement. He'd jumped the squares at the same second that he'd fired the ball out into the gutter. He'd cleared the squares and then some before the ball bounced.

"And after you got out of the firehouse, Manuel, where did you go?"

Manuel glanced at the clock on the back wall. At the rate he was going, he wasn't going to have to answer Foy's questions until after lunch at the earliest. He was eating up more time than he'd hoped. "The coffeehouse. I told them what was happenin'."

"You mean you told your father, who was in the coffeehouse?"

"Him and Victor Diaz. Everybody knew Cookie Alomar. He wasn't some guy who went around startin' fires, like Conklin said."

"And what did your father and Victor Diaz say?"

"Victor said it was none of my business. He said Cookie was always into things he shouldn't have been. He said everythin' would work out."

"Did you agree?"

"Everybody thought Victor knew the score."

"I asked whether you agreed, Manuel."

How the hell was he ever going to get his blade out and get behind her? Did he really think that Landers and Myers would just sit there while he ripped apart his jacket?

"Did you agree, Manuel?"

"No. Cookie was in trouble. He needed help."

"Did your father agree?"

"No."

220

"So what did you do?"

"Nothin'."

She finally stepped away from the bow tie. Now the dude seemed to be as interested in what he was saying as she was. "Nothing, Manuel? Didn't the coffeehouse have a phone?"

"Yeah, I guess."

"So did you think about using it?"

"I guess."

"What happened?"

He didn't know why everybody was looking so conned by her. Even the DA seemed to have run out of objections. "I didn't have any change."

"Not even a dime? That's how much it cost then, wasn't it?"

"I didn't have any change."

"So then?"

"So nothin'. I didn't have any change."

"Did you ask your father for a dime, Manuel?" She wasn't really looking at him anymore; she seemed to be looking right through him. "You asked your father for a dime, and he didn't give it to you, isn't that the way it happened, Manuel?"

He still had two or three days to go, Manuel thought. He still had a lot of time to work it all out. The guards in the van hadn't frisked him at all that morning. What was to stop him from removing the razors in his cell tonight and slipping them under his belt?

"Why did your father refuse to give you the dime, Manuel?"

"He said Cookie Alomar was none of my business."

"Anything else?"

He had nothing to lose by telling her; the *viejo* wasn't in the courtroom to hear it. "He said Victor knew best and I didn't want to get a reputation."

The bow tie rolled his eyes behind Alvarez's back; he looked like he suddenly had the hots for her. "A reputation for being somebody who went around blowing a whistle on other people? A reputation as a snitch?"

"Yeah."

She liked his answer so much she didn't say anything for a second, just took her time going over to the defense table and looking at one of the boxes she was always doodling on her notepad. All the jurors except the gray-haired teacher were watching

221

her. He wouldn't have minded the teacher looking at her too—the guy's stare made him nervous.

"One more thing, Manuel," she said finally, looking up at him like she was surprised to find him still sitting there. "When your father refused to give you the dime, why didn't you make the call anyway?"

"I told you. I had no change."

"What about the operator, or nine-one-one? You don't need money to call them."

"I didn't think of it."

She nodded. "Normal enough."

"Yeah." She was fishing again. He'd never told her about wanting to kick himself that night for not remembering that he could've made the call free. But it hadn't made any difference then and didn't make any now. A few days later Cookie Alomar had been back on the street like nothing had happened. They'd even started kidding Manuel in front of Cookie about what a baby he'd been.

"Normal enough because I guess you were pretty upset that day."

"I guess."

"You'd just seen somebody you knew beaten up. You'd just shoved somebody you considered a friend. You'd just run all the way from the firehouse to the coffeehouse afraid that maybe you'd end up like Cookie Alomar. You'd just heard Victor Diaz, a man that everybody in your neighborhood said knew the score, you'd just heard him tell you to forget everything. You'd just had your own father refuse to give you a dime and warn you about being a snitch. Normal enough in those circumstances to forget something like calling an operator for free. You were upset, weren't you?"

"I guess."

She came closer, twirling her goddamm pencil like it was a baton. "But it wasn't a total loss, either, was it?"

"Your Honor!"

"I'm with you, Mr. Foy. Miss Alvarez, we agreed on a certain latitude. I think we're just about in the Atlantic Ocean right now."

She smiled, but nobody else did. "Two more minutes, if it please the court." She was so close to him that her boobs were practically in his face. "When I say it wasn't a total loss, Manuel, I mean you accomplished a couple of things that day. You sneaked all the way to the back of the firehouse as you wanted to. You opened the kitchen door and saw what was going on as you wanted to. You ran the length of the firehouse again and escaped into the street as you wanted to. You'd set all those goals for yourself successfully, am I right?"

He didn't know why Foy and the judge just sat there. None of her shit had anything to do with breaking into Twitchell's house.

"And of course you didn't snitch either, did you? You came close, yes. You might've done it if Victor Diaz and your father hadn't stopped you in time. But the bottom line is that you didn't snitch. Nothing to regret there, either. Am I right?"

He could smell the squeeze coming. It was like she had worked it all out from the start, had brought his jacket to him just to show him up, to rub his nose in it that he didn't have a prayer of using her to get away.

"I submit that you're a very lucky man, Manuel."

"Yeah?"

"Well, look at it. Most kids growing up like you did—no mother, no supervised schooling, not much of a home life—most kids would have been left to drift along by themselves, to get into even heavier trouble to do even worse things than you're charged with doing today. But you've always had a lot of people looking out for you in the barrio. Your father. Victor Diaz. Robby down at the firehouse. A whole network of people. You've always known where to run if you were in a jam."

"You say so."

"No risk, really. Whatever the problem, you've always felt safe somehow. Am I right?"

He could've fucked her in front of every one of them—in the mouth, until she was gagging. In her ass. Wherever she didn't like it.

"Back and forth, back and forth. One day the coffeehouse, the next day in that building where all those men with the blue uniforms and fire engines work. You really liked them all."

He didn't care what her big plan was. "That's crap. They were all bullshitters."

"Badgering her own witness, Your Honor!"

"Mr. Foy will do the cross-examining, Ms. Alvarez. Last warning."

She nodded, only to get Raymond to shut up. "Of course,

223

that's what I meant, Manuel," she said. "You couldn't stand any of them. Those who weren't hypocrites or liars were cowards or goons. But you also knew if you kept traveling back and forth between them, you might be okay. They wouldn't be able to pin you down, wouldn't be able to trap you into going through life the way they did. You could even use them, one against the other, until you got around to doing what you really wanted to do, the only thing you've ever wanted to do. And what's that, Manuel?"

He'd been sitting on his chair too long. His leg had fallen asleep. The clock said it was almost lunchtime. Why didn't the *cojo* judge bang his gavel and send everybody away? "You tell me, you're so smart."

She whirled her face away to Raymond like she had been slapped. But she was still happy about something. "Your Honor?"

Raymond looked doubtful. "Even *I'm* getting hostile to you, Ms. Alvarez, and I'm not your client."

"Two more minutes, Your Honor."

"I'm counting them."

She came back to him. "Go ahead, Manuel. The only thing you ever *really* wanted to do."

"I told you, you're so smart, you tell me."

"What else? Escape!"

"Es— . . . ?"

"The only thing you've ever wanted to do. The only thing you could ever look at and say, yes, *that's* what's next for me."

Manuel felt no strength against the laugh in his throat. He might as well have been on the gold. He'd never met anyone cleverer than she was. Even Waxman hadn't sneaked up on him like she had. She was the biggest goddamm sneak he'd ever known.

"All the little escapes so far. It hasn't really been too important what you've taken, has it? A thirty-dollar ring to make it look good. A Kodak camera that you could've had for free if you'd taken out a magazine subscription. Some token has always been necessary, right? Only somebody really loco breaks in somewhere and comes away with absolutely nothing. You've still got to live. You still have be macho, to make it look good. You have to impress yourself and you have to impress everybody back at Victor's coffeehouse."

"I don't impress nobody!"

She glanced over at King. She had more games behind her

eyes than Joey Edison had ever dreamed of. "I know that, Manuel," she said, sounding almost sad. "Everyone in this court knows it. For example, if Officer King here were to hand you his gun right now, I don't think you'd know what to do with it, would you?"

King recoiled like she was going to jump in his lap. But this time Manuel could laugh to himself, she didn't know what she was talking about. He'd seen plenty of guns. Mario Joaquin had let him fire a .38 out behind a garage near the Flatlands. It was what he'd decided not to do, not what he didn't know how to do. "They're not smart."

She was happy with him again. "Right. Guns aren't smart. But what about knives, Manuel? Ever carry one of those into a house you were breaking into?"

"They never got me for possession."

"Right. That's on the record too. But the main thing, Manuel, is that you've never carried a weapon because you wouldn't know what to do with one anyway."

"I didn't say that."

"No, but the record says it, Manuel. The record that Mr. Foy's about to jump up and say isn't at issue here."

"I'll administer in here, Ms. Alvarez."

"Sorry, Your Honor. But it's the record, Manuel, that says you're too smart to carry a weapon."

"I'd know what to do."

"Really? Then prove it."

"What?"

She stood back like some old actress and threw out her big arms. "The jury doesn't care about some tough-guy image that you might have, Manuel. The jury can judge you only on the basis of facts. Give us one fact that will convince the jury that you're adept at using a lethal weapon, that you're one very dangerous hombre."

He knew that she wasn't going to stop—that nobody was going to stop her. She was going to go on and on until he took his jacket off and got the razor. Foy was yelling for her to cut it out, but she wasn't listening. Raymond was banging his gavel, but it was too late for him to be doing that. They didn't count. She didn't give a damn about their legal shit anymore. She was too much into mocking him with her waving arms, like he was some kind of fucking bull that was supposed to knock her down with his horns. He'd never wanted to hurt her that way. He wouldn't have even hurt her with the razor. Used her to get out of the building, but never hurt her. He'd never hurt anybody deliberately. He'd always had his head on straight about that. Hadn't he been against Patterson beating up on Joey Edison? Victor Diaz might have broken a few arms over the years, but not even Santiago had ever gone for that part of the business. Where was the percentage? Why did she think he was a crazy man?

"You're not gonna get me to do that!"

Foy was back in his seat. The judge was almost yelling at her. The bow tie was looking at her like she was the Virgin Mary. The teacher and the spade woman looked like they were on his side, like they were going to acquit him. He hadn't asked them to do that. They were going to fuck up everything!

"I know I'm not, Manuel." She was back in his face, smelling of a lot of sweet things that she had rubbed all over herself in her bathroom. Why did everybody else have to be looking at them? They should have been off by themselves in some quiet place.

"Back and forth, back and forth," she said. "From the coffeehouse to the firehouse. Little escapes, right? Not a real big one, just little ones, so you can have something to look forward to without risking everything. A few months in jail, some time outside. Back and forth, back and forth as you've always done. About that you've never been confused at all, have you?"

Manuel shook his head. It seemed like the only way to keep his balance and keep from falling off the platform, the only way to shut her and everybody else up so he could get back to his cell.

6

King stood close enough to the phone booth so that the woman understood that he was waiting his turn, but far enough away so that he didn't appear to be eavesdropping. It was the kind of balance he thought he'd always been good at, one of the reasons he was in the court building as a security guard instead of a felon. Somewhere along the line he had mastered important things.

The woman finally hung up, grabbed her newspaper off the little shelf, and took off down the lobby. She wasn't the kind of cheapo who waited to make sure her quarter didn't come back. Liking her for that, King went into the booth and punched in his number. He knew that he was probably wasting his time, that it had been little more than five minutes since he had last tried, but there was always the outside chance that Edith had been in the bathroom and not out shopping. He listened for the click, then the familiar purr. Their phone had always purred, never beeped or jangled like some others. He figured that was one of the benefits of living in the suburbs.

There was still no answer. He hung up on the tenth purr, got his quarter back, and punched out Grace's number. Her ring was more of a shrill beep.

"Hello."

"Hi, Grace. How are you?"

"Oh, John. I was just trying to call Edith. Do you know if she went to that A and S sale?"

King hoped she hadn't; he still had to drop the bomb on her about the new money problems. "I don't know. I've been trying to get her all morning. Thought she might be with you."

Morrison came out of Administration looking like he'd just been fired. Finnigan passed him, Morrison mumbled something, and Finnigan stopped dead in his tracks as Morrison kept walking. Finnigan looked like he had been pink-slipped, too.

"I really hope she didn't. I told her I would go with her."

Finnigan noticed him on the phone and gave him a thumbs-down, whatever the hell that was supposed to mean. "Don't get your tit in a wringer, Grace."

"What did you say?"

Down near the main entrance Morrison was talking to Wilke and Menelli. Whatever news he was carrying around to everybody seemed to be about as welcome as the plague. "Don't worry about Edith, Grace. She'll check in with you. She always does, right? Talk to you soon."

King slammed down the receiver before she could say anything else. There was no need for him to hurry, though: Finnigan stood waiting for him in the middle of the hall. "It's Tony," he announced. "Just died."

It took him a second to connect the name *Tony* to Barbarella. He didn't know why, since he couldn't think of any other Tony he knew.

"Gwynn's got a murder rap now."

King nodded because Finnigan seemed to expect it of him. He was glad that Finnigan didn't say anything else but just went on into Administration. He stood for a second in honor of Barbarella. Since he was probably going to be fired soon, he wouldn't have to show up for the douche's funeral, so now was the moment for a little respect. He couldn't imagine Barbarella doing more for him if their positions had been reversed.

"Oh, there you are, King. McCloud's about to send out a general alarm for you."

Alice Burke looked shorter and less imposing when she was out from behind her desk. He didn't even owe her the respect he owed Barbarella. "He'll get his letter. Tell him not to have a stroke."

The usual raised eyebrow. "Oh? In those exact words?"

He didn't want to get into a fight with her. "Look, I just heard the news about Barbarella. I'm a little on edge."

She accepted that. "I know. It's terrible. But please don't forget to give me that letter before you go home."

Burke marched off like a little colonel. He wondered how cocky she was going to be around five when she found out he'd gone without giving her the damn letter. Maybe by then she would have something more important to worry about than Barbarella and Gwynn.

7

Elena smiled to see the streetlights come on along the avenue. It had been ages since she had been watching at exactly the right moment, had felt part of some small municipal sense of order, and she considered it part of the fullness of the day.

What had she done?

She had done her job.

Sitting in her desk chair, she toe-and-heeled her pumps off and put her feet on the radiator cabinet below the windowsill. She had not so much won, she thought, as accounted for something. She had filled in the blanks, found the missing earring. Her satisfaction—the twinges of it that she allowed to peek from under her thoughts—was at having reestablished the ordinary. She had been a little more thorough at it than Bernie Foy, period. Now she had to count on twelve people recognizing the difference. It didn't seem like too much to ask.

And if they didn't give her the right answer, she would turn into the Angel of Vengeance and haunt their lives to the gates of hell!

Ho, ho.

She looked down at the run that was beginning to announce itself in her stocking above her left knee. She'd haunt eleven of them anyway. She wished Allison wouldn't die of his tumor. Who said it was a rule that people always had to die of deadly things? That seemed like submitting to some arbitrary tautology. She expected more from Allison with his amused, intelligent eyes. He had not struck her as a quitter.

There was a short, sharp rap on the door. She stopped herself from replying automatically. Alan had waited this long to come in and talk to her, she thought, trying to interest herself in the traffic below, he could stand another few seconds of *her* evasiveness.

Another knock. "Yes?"

"Interrupting?" Alan asked, putting his head in the door.

"Absolutely. You'd be surprised how many commuters from Oklahoma and Alaska drive home along Queens Boulevard at this hour."

The door clicked closed behind him. "You aged me today."

"That why you sat in? Because you wanted to be aged?"

"No. It was because I talked to Haggerty last night."

She should have guessed it, of course. She should have guessed it, been angry about it, and then let it all go. Because now it didn't matter.

"I was this close to taking the case away from you," he said, hovering over the visitor's chair. "Tell you the truth, Elena, I thought you'd gone around the bend. That you were so obsessed with this guy that you were deliberately undermining your own defense."

"Agreed. It was a gamble."

"Oh, it was a lot more than that."

Her ankles couldn't stand touching one another. She had expected the lecture, but she had also expected it to sound more academic, even embarrassed. "Well, then let's just say we were lucky," she conceded. "I've seen Bernie Foy a lot better than he was this afternoon."

"He was good enough."

Elena took her feet off the radiator box and turned her chair to face him. She hadn't expected the Nobel Prize, but she deserved more than the mournful look Green gave her as he unwrapped a stick of gum and put it in his mouth. "When Torres stepped down from that witness stand, Alan, he was a trespasser to that jury, not a burglar. I'm not saying it's in the bag, but they have a lot more doubts than they had on Friday. Foy simply didn't do enough."

He rolled up the silver gum wrapper and dropped it in her clean ashtray. She had the sinking feeling that he had already anticipated her answer. "Yeah," he nodded. "And I think Foy has the same doubts. Not big ones, but maybe just enough to give us a tiny bit of room. That much you accomplished today. It was really a bravura performance, Elena."

Now she *was* lost. She hadn't heard such a cold, condescending compliment since Matthews had singled her out in front of the classroom in Contract II. Had it been only a few minutes ago that she had entertained the idea of going through Alan's obligatory lecture over a bottle of wine? "You've talked to Foy?"

"Half hour ago. He didn't come right out and say it, but I think he'll go back to dealing. B and E. Torres does eighteen months."

"You're joking."

He finally tried a smile. "To your credit, lady. You spooked him. He's not going to win many points with Raymond or his office by folding his tent at this stage, but that's his worry, not ours."

"Alan, do you know what you're saying? Summations are tomorrow."

"I know."

"The jury will have the case before noon."

He shrugged. "And you accepted a jury before you hired Haggerty to dig into a couple of them. What I'm saying, you've taught Foy a few wrinkles."

Elena sat back and tried to blink him into clearer focus, tried to fit herself into the monotonous rhythms of his jaw as it worked the gum up and down, up and down. She knew she was missing some vital piece of what he was saying, and she knew she wasn't going to identify it by talking.

"Maybe the jury comes back with less than burglary," he said. "This way we're absolutely sure."

She had no answer to that—if that was the question.

"And it's not exactly as if we're back at square one. The Manuel Torres who spat a deal a few months ago isn't the same one we have today. You softened him up pretty good. He'll go along. Bet on it."

It was the one argument too many, she thought: he wasn't reprimanding or advising her, he was making a pitch. "What did Foy want, Alan?"

He thought about going at it for another round but then smiled, slapping at the back of the chair he was leaning on. "He's got more to offer because he wants more. Hear about that guard Barbarella? A building security man assaulting his partner is bad enough. Killing him is a red alarm."

"They're closing ranks."

"What do you expect?"

"A straight answer."

He had rehearsed enough to look at her squarely. "Torres was there. Saw it all, heard it all. He's the key witness."

"And he's already made his statement to the police."

"He's made *a* statement. All that Lotto stuff."

"That's what he heard Gwynn and Barbarella arguing about, Alan."

"Premeditated motive. If they wanted to, they could tag Gwynn with murder one. Murder two at the least."

"But they don't want to go after that either?"

He walked away from the chair restlessly. From the side his billowing yellow shirt made him look paunchy. "Gwynn was out of his skull. Diminished capacity. He may have landed on Lotto, but

231

it could've been anything. He was stretched tighter than your average rubber band. Anything at all, and snap."

"But it wasn't 'anything at all.' He had a specific grievance against Barbarella. A specific cause-and-effect motive."

"Sure. And know what that would sound like if some halfway competent defense counsel got ahold of it?"

"Like the truth. With a flourish here and there."

"Right. And it's the flourishes nobody in that building wants."

She knew what the answer was, but she had to ask anyway. "Not even a prosecutor with a can't-lose case?"

He looked back at her from inside his rationalizations. She was surprised at how familiar his self-disdain seemed to her. "From what I read between the lines, this isn't Foy's call. Someone somewhere in the building has decided it isn't in anyone's interests to mount a big show. Doesn't do anything for the security force, for relations in the building, et cetera, et cetera. Gwynn cops to a diminished capacity, the prosecutor doesn't push, away it goes."

"Just like Barbarella."

He couldn't believe her stubbornness. "Excuse me, but have I walked into somebody else's office? Or are you on Foy's staff now? They want to throw a big game, why's it any skin off our nose?"

"Because, in case you've forgotten, Manuel Torres is still our client. What are they after, Alan? A retraction of his statement? Torres has this sudden illumination that Gwynn was incoherent, made no sense at all? And in exchange for that, Foy buys out on the Twitchell house? That it?"

"With the residue."

"Residue?"

He pretended to be interested in her framed degrees on the wall. "There isn't a judge in the building who won't breathe easier for not getting the Gwynn case," he said. "Foy himself may hate what he's been asked to do, but those people who got him to call me won't forget. And that's not even counting the security people." He turned back to her. "That's a lot of residue, Elena. Raymond will remember it every time one of those guards opens a door for him instead of watching him struggle with his crutch. Restoring the atmosphere so everybody can get back to work."

"And this office needs the work."

"Well, hard as you may find it to believe, Manuel Torres won't be the last case you'll have in that building, either."

Elena wanted to do so many things at once she felt powerless to do anything. She wanted to throw the ashtray at Green, she wanted to telephone Bernie Foy and tell him to have some balls, she wanted to look at her degrees herself and see what they actually said. In fact, she couldn't even find her goddamm shoes.

"I said eighteen months. Who's to say we can't get it down to a year? And if it's the cops you're worried about, don't."

"Oh, not for a second, Alan. One statement, two statements. Who's counting?"

He suddenly seemed to think she was funny scrambling around under her desk after her shoes. He even dared smiling at her like a friend. "And great as you were today, don't forget we've also got to think of Torres. Leave those jurors by themselves a couple of days and they're going to start getting some distance from your little torch song that some people break into homes because that's all they know how to do."

"I guess you *have* been talking to Haggerty. He's got a lot of theories about jury room behavior, too."

He seemed to regard her more seriously for finding her left pump. "Okay, Elena," he said evenly. "Know why I almost took Torres away from you? Not only because you'd risked your own defense. Wouldn't be the first time you did that. You were risking everything you ever learned. You deliberately introduced Torres's past record. You practically spat in Raymond's face despite half a dozen procedural warnings. You got that jury to think of your client as some kind of boob who's going to keep stumbling through life until some cop with a trigger finger itchier than Waxman's ends his misery once and for all. You weren't asking that jury to acquit him or return with a lesser verdict, you were asking them to judge Manuel Torres's life and pronounce him guilty or not guilty for living it. Because that's the one verdict you haven't made up your own mind about."

"I defended Torres on the basis of who he is and what he did!"

"No, Elena! You didn't defend Manuel Torres at all, you prosecuted the son of a bitch!"

The abyss seemed to have opened beside her chair. She merely had to shift one more thought in that direction, Elena told herself, and she would fall into it. He had done this to her before, lots of Alan Greens had done this to her before, and she had always bought it. So why not buy it again now and remove that suddenly heavy weight from between her eyes?

"Do you see what I'm saying?" Earnestness now; the sympathetic voice of the man who wanted to be her friend as much as her lover. "Like it or not, as imperfect as everybody knows it is, we've got this process for helping people like Torres. Some of the rules suck. We know that. But we have an obligation to work within them. Our personal problems—well, they're just that, personal. God help clients if we let those problems dictate what we do in a courtroom."

She felt near tears but knew with a certainty that she wasn't going to let them come. She remembered now where she had seen his look of self-contempt before. "Know what, Alan?" she heard herself saying. "I defended Manuel Torres on the basis of my conviction that he was absolutely innocent of anything more than breaking and entering. I grant that Micah Green would not consider that the perfect match between the moral and the legal, but it's what I have to work with."

"Sounds like we're back to being the true believer."

"I've never been that, Alan. You, *you're* the true believer. If you can't get everything, it doesn't really matter to you after awhile how much of what you do get is sold off or given away. The usual term is rationalization. But I thank you for telling me about Foy's call. Manuel Torres is still my client, and I'll put it to him tomorrow morning. I'll make a recommendation, but it's his decision. Just as long as he doesn't choose on the basis of any head games I play with him—or anybody tries to play with me."

It seemed to take forever for him to turn away and walk out. As she reached down to the bottom drawer for the pack of Marlboros she had stored there for an emergency more than a year ago, Elena thought of how she had once waited for the light in her parents' bedroom to go off at night before sneaking her cigarettes out of her closet.

8

King sat up in his uniform. He
hadn't liked the idea of being in bed in his underwear when the cops
came; just thinking about it had made him feel exposed. But now,
with the VCR clock reading twenty-three minutes after midnight
and even the Johnny Carson rerun winding to an end, he knew it
was likely that no one at all would be coming tonight, that all the
care he had taken to snack only on what was in the refrigerator and
not to budge beyond the living room, kitchen, and bathroom had
been wasted. Grace hadn't followed up her hourly calls with a call
to the cops. McCloud hadn't sent anybody after him to get the letter
about the nigger's cat. None of the neighbors had come by to pry
into why they hadn't seen Edith all day. For all that anybody
noticed, they might as well have been living in a black hole.

Or in a city where douchebag Mike Gwynn was now a
famous murderer.

King drained the last of his beer and set the can down on the
table alongside the other three empties. He had promised himself
not to drink too much, to be completely sober when the cops came,
and now that too had been a wasted effort. He could have polished
off every Bud in the refrigerator with no harm done.

He decided to give it until twelve thirty, until the old Carson
program went off. He was a little sorry Grace wasn't with him, to
hear Carson announce his guests for "Thursday," even though the
show wasn't necessarily going to be rerun on a Wednesday. Grace
never knew what the hell she was talking about.

At least he hadn't had to tape the show for Edith. She had
seen it when it had been on the first time.

There had been changes, of course. He should've expected

235

them. The flier from A&S was where he had dropped it on the rug last night; the Sunday edition of the *News* was still strewn over the table; Sunday dinner scraps were still in the kitchen trashcan. Because he hadn't taken care of business, no one had.

But who was going to notice, except the cops who eventually came after him?

He watched Carson thank his guests and then stand up and come out from behind his desk to shake their hands. He waited until the last second, until the NBC peacock was flashed to end the show officially, and then switched off the set. As he clicked off the two table lamps and walked into the bedroom, he felt good about the perfection of his timing with the television. A second more either way and he would've had to see either more than he'd wanted or not as much as he'd wanted. Somewhere along the line he had learned something about timing.

The air in the bedroom smelled thicker and more sour than it had when he had opened the window after coming home. He took off his holster and put it on the night table. Kicking off his shoes, he decided against undressing altogether. He had no intention of getting under the covers, but he had no intention of freezing next to the open window, either.

Lying down, he held his nose against the odor. It wasn't any harder than holding it against sperm or fart or belch smells. He and Edith had slept with them all from the beginning of their marriage. The truth of it was that he had never been as turned off by the stinks as by Edith's coyness about them—her great pronouncements about how "romance starts to die the first time you fart in your lover's face" or about how "comes never seems to go." She hadn't meant it critically, she'd been trying to be cute, but she'd still ended up making both of them more self-conscious, more hesitant toward one another. He could still feel the relief he'd felt when he had been forced to stay in bed with the flu three years ago: then he'd been sick, and not even Edith could criticize his sweat and staleness. Both Connors the doctor and Gould the pharmacist had told him he was entitled to his odors.

He wished he had a flu again.

"They're still not paying attention, Edith."

King listened to his voice travel around the bedroom. It sounded like the voice he had always had, even as a kid. He knew he couldn't sound to others now like he had then, but to his own ear he sounded the same, as though all his acne and pubic hair and middle-aged fat had left something basic in him untouched. It wasn't true, of course. If Mrs. Kaplan walked in at that very moment and played his voice on the tapes that she had made in seventh grade history class, he probably wouldn't have heard any similarity at all. Still, on some other level, deep inside somewhere where other people had tin ears and tape recorders weren't accurate, wasn't it possible that he had held on to something that he'd been born with?

"Once they decide to get rid of you, Edith, you don't exist. Unless you rub their noses in it, they don't have to be bothered."

But how much of it was his own fault?

"I don't know. You never hurt anybody. You always took the dumbest douches, like Eddie Mannix, like you were happy to see them. Shouldn't that alone have entitled you to more attention than Tony Barbarella or a damn alley cat? Maybe you just married the wrong guy. You married a loser, Edith."

It didn't hurt to say it, to hear it filling the room and lying in all the corners and rising to the ceiling. He *was* a loser. He'd always been a loser. The best he'd ever gotten from people was a lot of tut-tutting and condescending smiles. McCloud must have thought he was a bag of shit for talking about the goddamn bank card. Hobie Morgan had almost pissed in his pants in that greasy saloon. Even the teacher Allison had looked at him weird when he had told him about memorizing those history dates. Why had it taken him so long to see what other people thought of him?

He wanted to do it, so he did it—not admitting the second of doubt that sneaked into him as he pulled back the blanket. The hole over her nose was uglier than he had thought, like some kind of wild sunset gone colorless and crusty. He didn't look any longer than he had to. Her chest and chin felt hard under his cheek, but also familiar. He knew that he wasn't trespassing on her, that wherever she was watching him from at that moment, she would've understood. That was why she had left so much of herself behind for him, he thought.

"They want to push it this far, okay. You got my promise, Edith. It's Tuesday tomorrow? Okay, see you Tuesday, McCloud. See you Tuesday, old Gracie. See everybody Tuesday."

King smiled and closed his eyes. He was going to be hurt very soon, but he wasn't hurt yet.

The Last Day

1

The ball sailed up and bounced against the dark ceiling. Manuel snatched at it awkwardly and shot it back on a hop. Robinson wound up like a pitcher on the mound and fired the ball past him. He chased it to the back of the firehouse, swiped at it, and without a second's hesitation whirled and fired at Robinson's belly. It was the greatest throw that he had ever made. Roberto Clemente couldn't have done better. He tried to be cool about all the clapping from the other firemen.

He was surprised at all the blackness. Nobody had ever told him flames were like that. He had never heard of black flames. They were supposed to be sort of orange. Robinson laughed and threw the ball again. He really didn't want to stick around to catch it, but he had to because it was up in the air already. Robinson didn't care about the blackness, so he couldn't care either. He caught the ball like a major leaguer.

Robinson sat in his cubicle laughing. Manuel had the ball and didn't know where to throw it now that Robinson wasn't there anymore. Nobody ever got stuck with a ball. Throw it, catch it, throw it back. He cried out for Robinson to come back out of the cubicle. Robinson read his book. He shouted again, but Robinson just laughed and said he had the key now, the key to his terror that he had always been looking for. Robinson said good-bye, said there was nothing else to say to him now that he knew that his key was the escaping that Alvarez had talked about.

Manuel didn't want his key. He didn't want the ball in his hand. He just wanted to play catch. Was that so much? Robinson pointed to the blackness and laughed again. Was he such an idiot that he couldn't smell it by now? Pea soup coming out of all the walls and into the firehouse. Soak it all up, Robinson said, laughing. Hector and Achilles had soaked it up in their time, now it was Manuel's turn to soak it up. Forget the catch. There were a lot more important things than playing catch.

Manuel threw the ball. He coughed. The ball went nowhere. It went out of his hand, then just stayed up in the air somewhere. He couldn't see it. It was somewhere inside all the blackness. He watched for it to come back down to him. He coughed louder so it would know where to find him. The ball laughed at him like Robinson laughed at him. He got mad. He knew the ball couldn't stay lost in the air forever. It was just a ball. He shouted for it to come back down. He coughed without wanting to. The smoke smelled like acid in his nose.

He asked Robinson to send the ball down. Robinson kept reading his book like he didn't hear a word. Manuel took a step toward the cubicle. It was the only sneaky step he could manage before the blackness and the smoke realized what he was trying to do and moved quickly to block him. He stood still, trying to figure out his next move. He heard the ball bounce behind him, on the spot he had just left. He knew better than to look around; then he would have lost even the step he had taken forward. He kept looking at the cubicle and at the front door. Forward, not backward, was the direction he had to move in. He let the ball bounce and bounce and bounce behind him. The other firemen weren't there

240

anymore, so nobody stopped the ball bouncing. The only fireman left was Robinson.

"Robby!"

Robinson finally laid his book on the desk and looked out at him with a shake of his head. There were babies and there were babies, he said. Like it or not, finding the key was the only important thing, and Manuel had found his, so what else did he want? Why was he still complaining? A little fire, a little smoke? Everybody lived, everybody died. What was so special about that? Time to grow up and be a man, to stop whining about things he couldn't do anything about anyway.

"Robby!"

Robinson laughed and opened his shirt collar. He pointed to the smoke swirling around the entrance to the cubicle. A little smoke never hurt anybody. Manuel had to roll with the punches. Everybody had to roll with them. Think anybody lived just to throw and catch a ball? The only people who did that were ballplayers, who got millions for doing it.

Manuel took another step forward. He didn't care how mad the blackness got, he was going to break through it, move it back. He was hot, awfully hot. He was sweating. He lowered his face into an oven. He could hardly breathe. He could smell heavy shit in his throat. But then he was through one oven, and he knew he could go through the others behind it. The ovens were lined up for him. He closed his eyes so they wouldn't burn. He didn't care all that much about his nose. People could get along without noses. He didn't need his nose as much as he needed his eyes. He breathed through his mouth. It was the wrong thing to do. There was smoke in his throat—so much smoke he couldn't even get out a good cough.

"Robby!"

Robinson hadn't moved, but the cubicle had. It was still as far away from him as it had been before he'd stepped forward. The ball was still bouncing up and down behind him. That didn't make sense. No ball had that many bounces in it. He told himself to stand still. The ball was behind him and the cubicle in front of him; he had to reach one of them but didn't know which one to go to first. The smoke and the blackness came around him again. He had given away what he'd gained. There was something wooden crackling into flame above his head. He remembered what Robinson had told him about staying close to the ground in a fire. He got down on the floor. Robinson was right—it *was* cooler. He felt a couple of drops of water from the hose. He should've gotten down sooner. He could feel the water already turning into steam. His eyes started tearing. He knew his tears were about to turn to steam, too. He didn't want steam coming out of his face. As long as he held on to his face, there was sure to be somebody who could pick him out of the blackness. Maybe even Patterson. Yeah, why not Patterson? Patterson was even bigger than Robinson, and much younger. And what Patterson was, the alligator Hardy was twice as much. He just had to keep his eyes closed and his face on the floor until Patterson and Hardy came.

But he opened his eyes anyway. There was a smaller blackness inside the bigger one. The bars seemed to measure off the small blackness from the big blackness. Joey Edison was crying over at the sink. Flint was leaning down from his bunk and puking all over Morrow's shoulder. Morrow was asleep. Manuel was glad that he could see the big blackness outside the small one. He didn't have to worry about whatever people were screaming about outside in the big blackness. It was bad enough having to hear all their running and shouting. Joey Edison had turned on the sink full blast and was crying into towels, like he didn't understand that he was smothering himself. He didn't know why the snitch didn't do something about all the flickering lights on his legs. The lights were ruining the *cojo*'s neat chinos and white woolen socks. Joey Edison was so busy covering his face with towels that he didn't see why he was being hurt!

His head felt cut away, its heaviness somewhere apart from him. He didn't know how he could still smell, but he could. Flint's puke made the smoke smell almost sweet. He'd never smelled that mix before. Someone outside in the big blackness was screaming about a hose. He didn't want any hose ruining Flint's puke. He started to shout, to make them stop, but he had lost his voice. It didn't make any difference anyway. The four of them were protected forever. There wasn't a chance in hell the outsiders would break in and spoil it all.

"Jesus, Jesus!" Joey Edison kept screeching. The *viejo* had once mumbled the same thing at Rosario's Funeral Home. Had his mother felt the same dull tickle on her ankles as he felt now? Manuel hoped that she had. It made everything seem all right. All the heavy shit inside his neck and chest couldn't compete with the tickling. He wasn't with his trapped breath, he was with his legs. They were outside him. They were friends. When he asked them to move, they moved.

"Jesus!" Joey Edison cried again.

Manuel coughed. He got all wet over his mouth and shirt. It was like he'd vomited on himself from a great height. His *head* had vomited on the rest of him. Somebody was going to bring a mop and a pail soon, but how long was it going to take? He wanted to sleep, to be where Morrow was. Let the others get all excited. He could be as cool as Morrow. He had always been cool, even with the pea soup he hated. That was why it was trying to hurt him now. He understood that. He had always hated pea soup. He had no complaints.

But he had to be sure.

"Robby!"

Robinson laughed. Robinson told him about Hector and Achilles. There hadn't been any sneaks in Troy. Everything had been out in the open.

Manuel hated Robinson. He wanted to kill Robinson. But Robinson wasn't sitting in the cubicle anymore. Robinson had passed the word and gotten out. He hated Robinson for doing that. He hadn't told anybody, so why had Robinson?

An arm came up outside him. It was his own arm, very far away. A face that resembled Flint's was staring at him from over the edge of the bunk. But then he couldn't make out Flint anymore. The small blackness now had an even smaller blackness inside it. Flint was gone. Joey Edison was gone. Something was sizzling.

"Robby!"

Robinson wasn't there. He had passed the word and given his seat in the cubicle to the white-haired teacher on the jury. It was the teacher who was laughing at him. . . .

243

2

Allison laughed with her. Margaret raised herself just high enough to pull his face down into her hands and kiss him. She lay back again, stretching her slender neck. He had never expected to see such bright drops of light in her eyes. He had never expected anything that was happening to him.

"I love you, Charles."

Allison made sure to look at her, not past her to where she had stored all the schedules and deadlines he had given her before dinner. He found it easy to lean down and return her kiss. What he should have done, he thought, was to bring her with him to Munson's office and the hospital; then the results would have been different.

She tossed her arm up over her head and sighed, gazing out the window. "Am I truly the first one in this bed?"

"Absolutely."

"Waste of a good bed."

"Late bloomer. It took a long time to grow up."

She abandoned the light from the lamppost to look back at him. "The two of us are pretty pathetic for this day and age, you know. I bet there are cartoon animals on television who've had a more active sex life than we've had."

"I said you were the first in *this* bed."

"Vanitas vanitatum."

"Another absolute."

"Want to hear about all my secret affairs?" she asked.

"No."

"Not even one? I let you tell me about one."

"One, then."

"The duke of Aragon."

"Who the hell's that?"

"The duke of Aragon. Very tall, had a pointed beard on his chin."

"Good place to have a beard."

"Dashing mustache, too. Always swept me in and out of drawing rooms with big chandeliers. Bows whenever he greeted me. Plume on his hat. Sword in his scabbard. Took my hand and blew ever so slightly on my fingertips. You know, of course, you're not actually supposed to kiss the woman's hand."

"I'll remember."

"Anyway, the duke had no name. He was just the duke of Aragon. Did I mention his black boots? He always wore black boots. And he was always lifting me up and sweeping me into a luxurious four-poster."

"Was he a good lover?"

"I guess so. I never really knew. He was always with me up to the moment that he took off all my shifts and straddled me. But the moment he came into me, he went back to sweeping into the drawing room and bowing again. At the last second it was always somebody else. And then afterward the duke returned, covering me with a blanket and promising that he would come back to me the following evening. The duke of Aragon."

"Dare I ask?"

She smiled and tightened her wrists around his neck. "Do you think I'd be telling you this story if the answer wasn't yes? Sometimes history teachers can be much worthier than gallant nobles, Mr. Allison."

"I thank you."

"I always meant it, Charles."

He had no answer to the new certainty in her eyes. And she had no question she didn't already have the answer to. They shouldn't have been talking about time to begin with, he thought, as the silence that had been waiting for them all along slipped under the covers. He tried to distinguish some kind of shape in the light from the streetlamp reflecting on the ceiling, but he came up with nothing.

"I don't know what to say, Charles."

The glibnesses rushed up at him and then went away again. Even last week, sitting in the kitchen waiting for his milk to heat

245

up and thinking about never having to get up from the table again—
now it seemed so simplistic and banal. That hadn't been Charles
Allison at the table, he thought, only some notion of himself that
he had almost believed in. The best and the worst hadn't even
begun then.

"The other night," he said.

"The other night you fucked me," she said, snuggling deeper
into his arms. "It wasn't you there with me, it was some . . . thing."
He nodded. "So I guess I've been to bed with two men in the last
three days."

The silence seemed suddenly forgiving.

"I'm scared, Margaret."

The silence was just silence.

He almost said it again, to hear it for himself a second and
official time. But he didn't.

"Anything," she whispered after a moment.

Allison closed his eyes. He thought of the Chinese teenager
that he'd seen on the bus coming home from the court building the
previous evening. The boy had been wearing an Eisenhower jacket
with a patch that said JE MAINTIENDRAI—PRINS MAURITS. "That's
Mauritius, right?"

"I think so," she said.

"Not Mauritania, but Mauritius."

"I'm pretty sure."

"Why should anyone be walking around with a patch like
that?"

"French Foreign Legion?"

"Oh, right," he said. "I forgot about that."

"Glamorous adventure."

"In Mauritius? Poorest country in the world, isn't it? Next
to Togo?"

She rolled over onto him, stretching herself against him.
"Another anything," she commanded.

He remembered the way Manuel Torres had gone out of his
way to embarrass Mrs. Weathers with his racial innuendos. "Colors," he said. "I never understood them."

"You mean race?"

"Race. Umbrellas."

She shifted on his stomach with a giggle. "Umbrellas?"

246

"You know, how men are supposed to carry only black ones."

"Oh."

"Chuckles, too. I always liked all the colors."

"Flavors."

"You call them flavors. We called them colors."

"And you liked them all."

"Right."

"Very pragmatic of you."

"Red Robinson taught me those things."

"About colors."

"About colors. About never use the word nigger, like Torres said. How to be respectful even when you don't agree with somebody. Never call the cops if you don't have to."

She inched up, bringing her face close to his. He could smell the onion she'd eaten with her steak, and the honey-colored shampoo he had seen in her bathroom Saturday night. What he really wanted was for her to use her thighs to scissor his cock back to life, but she was only interested in hovering over him, waiting for something that he hadn't given her yet.

"It just caught me so much by surprise," he said. She nodded. "I don't mean just Torres and Robinson. It was more than that, Margaret. It was like there was a whole continent suddenly in front of me, so much that I'd . . . overlooked. About everything, Margaret! I'm just not ready!"

He knew that he had no right to say it, no right to cause her to be stymied between trying to act normal and trying to treat him with a special concern. But she wasn't the one who was going to die, he was.

"What Manuel Torres was telling me was that I was passing through my so-called life without a clue as to what it'd been about. Close to sixty years, and I was like some seasick passenger who'd spent the entire crossing of the Atlantic cooped up in my cabin. He even knew my father."

"Not better than you did."

"No, not better. Differently. He knew Red Robinson in another way. Things I would've never guessed at."

"Things you didn't want to know?"

No, Allison told himself, he was clear on that. "I never thought of the man as an angel. He was a goddamn alcoholic who

247

walked out on his family, for Christ's sake. Sure, it was unpleasant hearing Torres's story. But I'm not talking about Uncovering Dirty Secrets. The son discovers that Willy Loman had somebody on the side. No, it was more that I realized I hadn't given myself even the opportunity to decide what I wanted to know about him and what I wanted to block out, shove into the background. Nobody told me what the choices were. *I never let myself find out what they were.* He helped beat up a Puerto Rican kid? Great, that was at least something that got through. Sorry, Manuel Torres. Sorry, Cookie whatever-the-hell-your-name-was. I got at least that much out of your pain. But how many other things are there like that I'll never know? What the streets of Paris look like. What it might've been like to live in another apartment. And even those things are only a fraction of it. My mother. My brother. You. That student in the back row who was always being a cutup. Things I don't even realize right now, here with you, and that all the earnest intentions in the world are not going to give me a chance to learn. Suddenly, there's just . . . no more time."

He didn't want her to do it. He thought he would suffocate. But as soon as she put her tongue in his mouth he felt all right again, felt something to hold on to. He didn't ever want to let go of her tongue.

"I'm sorry, Margaret," he said when she finally took her mouth from his.

"Shhh."

"No, no shhh. Anything but shhh." He felt his hands, *his own hands,* on her small, hard cheeks, felt himself moving her onto him. "What's it like to not have to think about things? I should know better than anybody what that feels like, but I don't." She moved slowly, purposefully. There was a clear line to it, like the elevated track he had gazed at during his lunchtime walk with Anna DeSilvestri and Benzinger. "Everything is allowed, right?"

"Everything," she whispered.

"Not just because—"

"Because we're making love, that's why."

Yes, they were making love. They seemed to have been making love for hours. It was almost daylight. And he was also making sadness. If there was no other reason for him not to die, there was always the reason that he did not want her feeling lonely in some cemetery, did not want to open up feelings in her that were

248

only going to be shut down again within a short time. She had to know that as much as he did, had to know that there was the faintest glimmer of perversity in what she called her love. She had to have that knowledge in her teeth, in her nipples, in her vagina, in her knees, in her toes. She had to have it for him to suck out of her, like some lethal snake poison that must not be allowed to flow through her blood.

And then there was the other thing: the thing that he had not accepted since the first night he had thought about destroying his living room piece by piece.

"Bite," she said.

And he did. Easily, but still a bite. And he bit and bit. His anger was of the gods, he thought crazily; of Achilles and Ulysses and all the great warriors. That part of him would never die. He would simply bite and lick his way through her salt and sweat until he woke up to hear that all of it had been a deception, that Munson and the hospital staff and Margaret and everybody in the courtroom had been only leading him on so that he would be caught completely off guard when they jumped out at him and told him that it was a surprise party.

He would only pretend to be angry with them, Allison thought, when they did that to him.

3

Elena concentrated on the vending machine in the waiting room. Every button represented a possibility, she told herself. Black coffee meant the pure accident that Dr. Wagner and the head guard Delaney had told her about. Black coffee with sugar meant that one of the inmates had deliberately set the fire to even some score against one of Manuel's cellmates. Milk and sugar was the plot to kill Manuel before he could testify against Gwynn. Just milk was the colossal joke that somebody had played on her and all her self-righteousness yesterday with Alan.

She turned away from the machine: it simply wasn't natural for her to be sitting there contemplating so many lurid possibilities so calmly.

She looked over at the door where Santiago Torres was still staring out into the hospital corridor. His leather jacket ran up over his shoulder blades as if it were about to leap off his back altogether. She wished that he would stop flicking cigarette ashes at his feet. He was going to get in trouble with some nurse.

Bernie Foy nodded at the coffee machine. She shook her head. Foy looked down at the paper cup that he had just emptied. Tieless and unshaven, he looked as cheated as she felt. She had no sympathy for him and his sixty cents of generosity. Gestures were not their own reward.

Santiago stiffened at the sound of someone approaching, relaxing again when a young intern passed by. She wished he would stop being so goddamn anxious to see the unseeable. He would be repelled soon enough; there was no need for him to rush it. Charred bodies were charred bodies.

"Rye bread does it sometimes."

She looked back at Foy. He kept his eyes on his empty cup until Santiago lost interest in him and went back to staring out into the hall.

"Rye bread?"

"Ergotism," he nodded. "I read about it once. Seems that one of the most common symptoms is nightmares about fires."

Elena understood. As soon as they left the hospital, she and Foy were going to investigate the jail kitchen together. Maybe they would discover that Manuel had been on a diet of poisoned bread, and that had been the main reason for the nightmares Delaney had told them about. Finding a culprit lurking in the breadbox would have been even better than blaming Joey Edison's habit of pitching lighted matches everywhere.

"May be worth a look."

She nodded. Two empty gestures seemed better than one.

"Mr. Torres?"

Wagner was standing in the door of the waiting room. The doctor was trying to look sympathetic and trying to keep his eyes off Torres's cigarette at the same time. Elena grabbed Foy's cup out of his hand and quickly took it over to Torres at the door. She was

250

relieved that neither the doctor nor Santiago looked at her as she snatched the cigarette and sizzled it in the coffee residue.

As they walked down the hall, she stayed behind Wagner and Torres and ahead of Foy. She was grateful for the click of her heels. Everyone else seemed to be walking too quietly, as if nothing extraordinary were happening, the faster and smoother everything was over with, the better. The hanging signs on the doors they passed reminded her of the Stations of the Cross her father had once insisted she accompany him on for Good Friday: then, too, they had advanced from the unpleasant to the end. What was the hospital's equivalent of Easter?

Wagner went through a door without a sign. Santiago stopped abruptly to hold the door open for her, and she almost walked up his heels. The anteroom inside was dark and reeking of what she knew was some kind of formaldehyde. A young black woman wearing a hospital gown and a mask down under her chin looked at them from a lab table and then quickly lowered her eyes again. Ignoring her, Santiago Torres continued blindly after Wagner.

The doctor stopped in front of an inner door and cleared his throat. He was so much taller than Santiago that even when he was talking directly to him, he seemed to be looking over his head, ignoring him to address her and Foy. She resented the man's height: neither she nor Foy was any more of an expert on what was inside than Santiago Torres was.

There was a viewing glass immediately inside the door. An elderly bald-headed man with a wart on his chin was waiting next to a gurney on the other side of the glass. Santiago scraped up to the glass without any nudging from Wagner. The bald-headed man was practiced enough to keep his eyes only on Wagner, and when the doctor nodded, he pulled back the sheet as though he had already practiced drawing it aside.

Elena swallowed hard and ordered herself to take it piece by evidentiary piece. No hair left on the scalp, so it might or might not have been Manuel Torres. Big, crepe-paper swellings of gray where the eyes and nose and mouth had been, so that might or might not have been Manuel Torres. Swatches around the chin, suggesting a beard or goatee, so that could have been Manuel Torres. Four even front teeth on top, so that could have been Manuel Torres. The height looked right under the sheet. The skin color couldn't have been *that* affected by the smoke and fire, so that too looked right. There was the teardrop mark of a melted chain below the cup of the throat; she vaguely recalled that Manuel Torres wore a chain, so that was another indication. It was pretty conclusive, she decided.

But, the ends of the sheet in his hands, the attendant still waited. She wasn't the one who had to be convinced, Santiago was. And the old man's face reflected in the glass showed nothing. He just stared and stared. Her surmises were those of an outsider, she reminded herself, and weren't necessarily correct.

Santiago Torres finally nodded. For a long second the attendant refused to be satisfied. He just kept holding up the sheet.

"Okay," Foy suddenly said. Wagner came awake with the order. He nodded, and the attendant replaced the sheet. There was nothing else for any of them to do about Manuel Torres. Ever.

She hurried back out through the lab and into the corridor before she had to hear Foy ask Santiago Torres one more time, officially. The blue paint on the corridor walls seemed obscene. Sickness was life, so the clot in her sternum was life. How could anyone be satisfied with so little?

At the sound of the door being opened, she took a deep breath and turned around. Santiago was standing there unsteadily. Neither Foy nor Wagner had offered him a hand. The most they were going to do was to catch him if he fell.

"I'm very sorry, Mr. Torres," she said.

The man started to nod. She hadn't been the first to say it to him; both Wagner and Delaney had said it to him when he had arrived at the hospital, and Foy had muttered something like it. But now he seemed to think about it, as if maybe it was something that shouldn't have been said to him. "You are?"

"Yes."

There was no center in the way he was looking at her. "Then you tell me. Why Manuel?"

Foy started talking. She didn't listen any more than Santiago did. *Why Manuel?* It wasn't the same question that Kim Friesner had asked her in the park nearby the river Saturday morning, couldn't have been the same question, but it suddenly felt the same.

"Why, Mrs. Alvarez?"

"It was an accident, Mr. Torres," Foy insisted. "One of the men sharing Manuel's cell . . ." He trailed off as Santiago stared at him, seeming to recognize Foy for the first time.

"Manuel would have been able to go home. He would have been free," Santiago said. Foy clamped his mouth shut; Wagner looked fidgety. "Isn't that right, Mrs. Alvarez? He was going to be free because you were going to help him more than I could help him or he could do anythin' for himself. Isn't that right?"

"That's right."

Foy and Wagner seemed as astonished as the old man. But she was thought out and guilted out. She had pleaded her last case before the unseated juries of prosecutors, doctors, numbers runners, and bosses who had always waited for her to square impossible circles. Now, she told herself, before a grief that hadn't even become grief yet, she had to recite the facts and only the facts.

"Half right, anyway. Manuel would've had to do some time, because I would've advised him to accept a deal." Foy got over his astonishment. "But the other thing, helping him more than . . . than he had been helped before, yes, I think I did."

She watched him come without flinching. It seemed like such a predictable attack that she didn't understand why it took him so long, why he was letting the fury in his puffy face slow him down, stop him from grabbing her by the neck. Even when he finally succeeded in getting his hands around her windpipe and she felt the shock of her head hitting the wall, even as she struggled to breathe, she knew he was botching up everything, giving himself away in exactly the way she hadn't by specifically not accusing him of failing Manuel. Didn't the *viejo* know that he had only a second or two before Foy and Wagner took him off her or she kneed him in the balls? Didn't he know that if he throttled her, she was never going to be able to tell him about how the olive oil on his table had brought him and his family bad luck?

"Stop it, Torres!"

She felt ridiculous as she slid to the floor, bumping the base of her spine on the woodwork. Grown men were wrestling around above her, and now sneakered feet were thumping down the corridor toward them. Dignity was definitely not her strong suit so early in the morning.

"Why Manuel? Why Manuel? You tell me, Lawyer!"

Elena thought it must have been somebody above her who said it: "Because he was so afraid," the voice like hers said. "Afraid and too late to do a damn thing about it. Everything else is superstition."

253

4

Hobie knew something was up as soon as Morrison caught the john door with a smile and walked in after him. The last time Morrison had smiled at him had been two years ago when he'd been handing out cigars for some goofus son or daughter. He acted proud of something now too.

"Got a second, Hobe?"

"Just for you, Morrison." Hobie parked in front of the urinal and unzipped. Since he'd started drinking Ida's celery juice, he didn't mind pissing. He knew it was an exam his kidneys were going to pass.

"Guess you heard about Manuel Torres."

He had, and he'd felt better for the news. Now there was going to be no escape attempt by the burro, and no need for Hobie to worry about the Alvarez woman. He had heard the last of Ida's crap, too.

"Terrible thing," Morrison said. "But not so bad for Mike Gwynn."

"No? How's that?"

"Well, you know. The crazy story he told the cops about the Lotto thing with Barbarella. Thing like that could've made Mike's situation tricky."

Hobie smiled to himself. Morrison wouldn't have noticed his reaction in any case, he was so busy trying to act nonchalant about gazing off at the window and not catching sight of somebody else's pecker.

"Guess so. Too bad everybody else in the buildin' heard it, too."

Morrison shifted his feet and leaned against the sink. He was making a lot of moves short of reaching into his pocket and coming out with a few dollars. "Well, that's the thing, Hobe. Nobody in the building seems to know how all that stuff got started. Wilke thinks he heard it first from Landers, but Landers says he was only repeating what he'd heard in the locker room. Nobody seems to have heard it directly from Gwynn."

"Except me, you mean?"

The goofus shrugged. "If you really heard it."

He dried off and zipped up; he still didn't see Morrison going into his pocket for some money. "Oh, I heard it all right. Clear as day. Gwynn wanted his Lotto money and Barbarella thought he was bein' funny."

"Well, sure, that's what you told the cops. Not too many people were thinking clearly that day. But now that you've had time . . ."

Hobie liked the way the goofus got out of his way at the sink without being asked. "I didn't tell no cops nothin'," he said, turning on the faucet. "I'm just saying' what I *could* tell them."

"You mean you haven't given them a statement? Nobody's been around to get your story?"

He shook his head. The truth was, he hadn't thought about it one way or the other. But seeing Morrison's expression in the grime-encrusted mirror now, he realized that he should have thought about it. Why *hadn't* he been asked what he knew? "Guess because I wandered away from all you sharpshooters that day, nobody remembered I was on the elevator with those two goofuses."

Morrison was looking happier and happier. "That's right."

"You mean the cops collected statements from everybody else?"

Morrison nodded brightly. "Torres. Security. Alice Burke."

Hobie could sense Morrison refolding the bills in his pocket without even showing them. "Well, like they say, better late than never. They don't have that geep Torres, I guess I'm their best witness now. Better get down to the station house after work today. Which one's handlin' it, you know?"

The guard's sigh was almost a laugh. "Two-oh-seven," he said, putting his hands in his back pockets and heading for the door. "Come upstairs, I'll give you directions."

"That supposed to be funny?"

255

Morrison pulled open the heavy door. "You're not in it by now, Hobie, you're not stupid enough to make extra trouble for yourself. See you."

"Morrison!"

But the goofus just threw a lazy wave and went out, like somebody who knew a sure thing when he saw one.

5

King liked the way they were scattered around the hall like little lost sheep. They looked glad to see him coming, like he was their shepherd. He collected them together, counted heads, and set off through the fire exit to jury room A. They had a million questions about Manuel Torres and the jail fire. He told them nothing. It wasn't his responsibility.

He closed the jury room door on their stupid expressions and went back down the stairs to the courtroom. Foy and Alvarez were sitting at their usual places. Foy glanced at him, then went back to staring off at the window above the bailiff's desk. Alvarez wore a big green scarf around her neck and seemed to be kneading a headache. Landers and Myers were standing in the back gabbing. Bordalato came out of the judge's chambers, looked at the clock on the back wall, and flashed five fingers. Five minutes before Raymond was ready.

King closed the jury exit door behind him and stood listening for the sound of anybody on the stairs. Nobody seemed to be using B, C, or D. Nobody seemed to be doing much of anything this morning. They were all waiting for him to get the ball rolling.

He walked back up the stairs slowly. Two minutes up, a minute to line up everybody in the jury room, then two minutes back down. Five minutes exactly. He knocked on the jury room door and walked in. They were surprised to see him back so fast. He smiled off their questions about the spic Torres and told them to make the usual line against the wall. Most of them did it quickly,

256

but Allison looked at him oddly. He didn't need the teacher looking at him at all.

"Eyes forward!"

The writer and the video lady laughed. He smiled with them. Only Allison didn't seem to think he was funny. He was going to have to include Allison in his aim when the time came.

"All right now, listen up! We want double time down the stairs. Anybody falls, you keep on moving. Don't stop to pick up stragglers. Those scorpions out there don't play favorites. Ready? Let's move it!"

As they went down the first staircase he stayed ahead of Allison and the Port Authority man. He didn't bother reminding them to watch their step; if they didn't know how to do that by now, he couldn't help them. The trick, he had learned a long time ago, was not to think about what he was doing, not to let his doubts climb all over his head. Constant movement was the secret. He couldn't be swallowed up by a place that he'd already left.

He waited at the first landing for a few of them to pass him. The sickly-looking nurse with the beads wasn't going to make it. The writer wouldn't, either. He smiled at them anyway. Just because he was better than they were didn't mean that he had to lord it over them.

He wedged his way past the ones who had gotten ahead of him. The two alternates tried to make their complaints sound like a joke, but he knew that they were really annoyed with him. He considered the muttering behind his back a good sign. In the end, he knew, they would gang together against him, show some real solidarity as a unit.

He caught up to Allison and the Port Authority man before they got to the door of the courtroom. "All right now, I want to count again!"

He counted fifteen heads, and Allison was looking at him again weirdly. "I think you counted yourself," the teacher said, so quietly he sounded sad.

He knew Allison was right, but he had to start all over again anyway. So what if he hadn't been a great counter in school? He'd always been good at history. Besides, their number didn't matter anymore anyway. Once they went into the courtroom, they were going to be dismissed by Raymond, break up, and disappear into individuals again. By noon they would have all forgotten whether he had been a good counter or a bad counter. They wouldn't remember him at all.

Or at least that's what they thought right now.

6

"Ladies and Gentlemen, I know I am also speaking for Mr. Foy and Ms. Alvarez in commending you for acquitting yourselves so alertly and responsibly. As tragic as the circumstances are that have abbreviated your service to this court, they cannot annul the example of civic duty that you have exhibited so clearly here for the last several days. As you know full well, a criminal hearing such as we have had here over the last week is not a contest for determining a winner and a loser. It is a test of principles that we are called upon to strengthen or weaken every time we are summoned to consult for a verdict in the context of the facts presented and the law demonstrated by the two sides. The lack of a verdict in this specific hearing regarding Manuel Torres should not suggest less of an examination of these principles. What it should remind us of are the enormous human complexities that were taken into account in the drafting of our legal system. Nobody is perfect. The system is not perfect. We need go no further back than this morning's tragedy to recall that we are always dealing with human fallibility, the unpredictable, and the ferociously mortal. But, if I may speak personally, I take great comfort in knowing that it was your very awareness of this human reality that led you to deliberate so rigorously, if not as a group within the normal course of procedural events, within your own consciences these past few days. This cannot come as any consolation to the friends and relatives of Manuel Torres and the other victims of the catastrophe this morning, but it should always stand as an encouragement to those who for one reason or another find themselves directly called to account by our system of laws and rights. For this I commend you, I congratulate you, I thank you.

258

"Now, unless you have any questions I can answer, I will declare this jury dismissed and this proceeding at an end."

Whatever the cost to Raymond, who stood awkwardly with his crutch, Allison was glad for the silly questions. He was in no hurry to stand up and walk out of the courtroom. He wanted to postpone for as long as possible the feeling of dispersal that was already gathering around him. And so he tried to savor every word of Benzinger's question about whether they had to report back to the assembly room and Raymond's answer that they did not, Mrs. Everett's request for more information about the prison fire and the judge's practiced reply. They were like the last highway signs before he had to turn off to James Conboy, his party, and the short valley of time in between. He had passed all the alternate routes.

When Raymond finally did hobble off his platform and go into his chambers for the last time, he was surprised at how casual the actual dispersal was. Good-byes like see-you-tomorrows, the most fleeting of smiles from Foy before he marched out, hardly an acknowledgment from Alvarez. The guards who had been escorting Torres had slipped out without being noticed. Even his farewell dinner at Les Douceurs de Paris had seemed more definitive.

"You must call me if there's anything I can help you with."

Allison was flustered by Anna DeSilvestri's sincerity—and grateful for it. But even as he tried to tell her that he was, that he knew that she knew what neither of them had any reason to talk about explicitly, he caught another glimpse of John King. The guard had remained slumped in his seat near the jury door, not even standing for Raymond's exit. Coming down to the courtroom, he had been acting like a drunk determined to prove that he had more of a sense of humor than anybody else; now he looked like a drunk itching for a brawl. His glower was for everybody and nobody.

"You will, won't you?"

He told himself that he was Anna's champion for taking her arm and walking her down the aisle to the back door. He had forgotten his original, fearful impression of KING his first day in the courtroom, but now, as the feeling came back so suddenly and strongly, it was as though it had been up to him all along to protect other people from the guard.

His bravado faded as soon as he was safely out in the hall. After a long handshake, he excused himself from Anna's pregnant invitation to have a coffee with her, kissed her, and dashed for the elevator, which barely had enough room for him. The crusty old operator named Hobie grunted when he asked to go only one floor down. The fact was, he knew, James Conboy could be sitting in on a white-collar case involving defendants named O'Brien and Riordan.

Allison found the man in the third courtroom he peered into. James Conboy was sitting erect in the front row of the jury box, listening to a lanky, dark-skinned man saying something about stocks and bonds. There were almost two solid rows of spectators, and the contrast with the Manuel Torres trial made them seem even more numerous. Two men were sitting at the defense table, with the third chair belonging to the attorney now questioning the witness. Like the witness, the two defendants could have been Arabs.

Allison took a seat in the last row, near the door, already beginning to feel ridiculous. He hadn't factored in Arabs. They were a wild card. To somebody like Conboy they were probably as bad as Hispanics, but suppose they had been indicted for swindling a Jew? He felt more ridiculous. Coming right down to it, he was sitting where he was only because of a passing crack. Suppose Conboy had only been trying to get a rise out of him? Suppose the man had a home filled with foster children of all races and colors? Suppose what Conboy had said had been some form of humor that Allison had been too narrow to understand? He felt like a presumptuous fool.

But he didn't leave. The defense counsel, a husky man with an incongruous twang, went through a lot of stocks-and-bonds questions. Allison began to feel safer. It was apparently some kind of fraud case. Conboy showed nothing. The crime was a paper abstraction, and the lawyer seemed bent on confining it to that. Nobody had touched or assaulted anybody else with dark hands. Numbers, dates, and amounts were the only issue. Allison couldn't imagine Conboy caring.

He was wrong. At first, he thought he had willed the snicker, had jumped automatically from the lawyer's reference to a "Mr. Rabinowitz" to what he had dedicated himself to seeing in the jury box. But then there was no mistaking the way that Conboy rippled his fingers in front of his mouth to half cover a smile. Whoever Rabinowitz was, he was clearly someone who had gotten what Conboy would have been delighted to give him. Did that make the defendants more or less guilty in Conboy's eyes? It depended on whether they had acted with or against Rabinowitz.

Allison didn't know what to do. He had his impressions, his predispositions, but nothing else. A snicker, a smile of satisfaction, and some week-old passing remark. If somebody accused him of something on the basis of such factors, he would have felt slandered. When had it become his job to make an issue of what two competent lawyers had been unfazed by? He needed more proof.

He slid down in his seat and watched for it. Guilty until proven innocent or innocent until proven guilty seemed irrelevant. Time, the time he had until the noon recess, when he could go home telling himself that he'd done everything possible, only that mattered. Within the confines of a clock and growling stomachs, he realized, he could be absolutely open to anyone's persuasiveness. He was able to entertain the thought of any number of Conboys—from the redneck to the decent man with all those foster children of various races and colors waiting for him around the table at home. All James Conboys were equal before Charles Allison. Presumptuousness was only a necessary starting point.

His own stomach was beginning to growl when Conboy decided the issue. The prosecutor read a statement attributed to somebody named Sadler. Sadler had joked to somebody about Rabinowitz "threatening to call the cops." Conboy remembered it vividly. His smirk said that he had heard it a hundred times before, his glance at the woman juror next to him said that Rabinowitz had always been an idiot. So Rabinowitz had made good on his threat. So what? Here was where the threat had led him. The circle was being closed in the jury box.

Allison sat up in his seat. He had reached his verdict, and now he had to do something about it. Let others decide if he was right or wrong. He wasn't *that* presumptuous. He would say what he had to say and leave his name and address.

But with whom?

He must have looked as consternated as he felt. He could feel the sudden attention he was getting from the woman who had slipped into the courtroom a few minutes ago and taken a seat at the far end of the row. He had been so caught up with Conboy that he had seen her only out of the corner of his eye. Now he was enormously relieved to see that it was Elena Alvarez and that she was looking at him in total recognition.

261

7

Elena didn't know why she had been so quick to volunteer as a messenger for Allison. It had taken her a watery cup of coffee at the luncheonette up the street for her to decide to come back to the courthouse and talk to Jim Aherne, but now that she was back she was letting herself be sidetracked again. Was it because of the teacher's earnestness, or because of her own cold feet about telling Aherne that she wanted to be considered as having given thirty days' notice?

"Like I say, I really can't prove anything," Allison repeated as they sat together on the bench outside the courtroom. Balancing her notebook on his knee, he jotted down his telephone number. "But I think it's something somebody should know."

Elena thought about what Alan had once said about Aherne's slapdash way of interviewing prospective jurors, and about her own hiring of Haggerty to investigate the man seated next to her. It seemed to add up to one vindication and one embarrassment, but she wasn't sure which fact went with which feeling.

"I'll make a point of telling Jim."

"He's the one with the twang?"

"Right. It's his jury. He'll be interested."

Allison handed her back the notebook; he had an elegant handwriting. "I don't think you know how much of a load you're taking off my mind."

No, she didn't, she thought; in fact, she was still toying with the initial suspicion she'd felt when he'd come up to her at the recess before she could get to Aherne. In his place she wouldn't have given a damn about some juror, racist or otherwise. Had Allison's tumor unbalanced him?

He smiled. "You're supposed to thank me for my civic sense of duty."

"I thank you. The system thanks you."

He nodded reflectively. "It wasn't much to walk away with today after all your work, was it?"

She folded her notebook back into her bag. She shouldn't have been talking so much. She had had a sore throat ever since Santiago Torres had throttled her, as though his fingers had somehow gotten inside her larynx. "Raymond said what he had to say. He didn't have too much of a choice, either."

"I suppose."

She wanted to know and, throat or no throat, she saw no reason not to ask. "Mind a question, Mr. Allison?"

"Manuel Torres?"

"Yes."

He threaded his fingers together and leaned forward, his eyes on the floor. She felt furtive about seeing the neat waves of silver hair over his scalp. "Guilty," he said quietly.

"Of attempted burglary or breaking and entering?"

"Well, as I understand the way the law was explained to us, the more serious charge. The attempted burglary."

She had never had a chance. "I see."

He seemed to stare at the floor between his legs forever. When he at last looked up at her, he smiled like somebody who had just passed through a tunnel. "But I think I would have resisted the rigid logic of it."

"How?"

"By holding out for the lesser charge."

"But you couldn't. If you accepted the logic of the law as you understood it, you had no choice."

"Why not?"

"You know why not. I'm not asking you to tell me what I want to hear."

"I'm not. I'm telling you what I think I would've done."

She was lingering too long. Instead of soliciting the man's sympathy, she should have been tracking down Aherne. "I appreciate what you're saying, Mr. Allison. But I just don't believe you."

"I believed you," he said evenly. "The things you brought out yesterday when Torres was on the witness stand. And to me they were more important than the letter of the law. Does that make me a lousy juror?"

"Frankly, yes."

"Then so be it. If the logic of the law can't provide for Charles Allison's aberrations, it can't be a very comprehensive logic."

"Just like that?"

He gazed past her. "No, not just like that. With lots of on-the-one-hands and on-the-other-hands. With lots of personal ghosts flitting about. With a lot of coincidences, memories, and feelings involved. With prejudices pulling this way and some very strange fantasies pulling that way. With my utter dedication to the theatrical and my deep appreciation of somebody with a dramatic flair like yours." He grinned at her. "Is it imperative that the republic always be defended through the art of syllogism?"

"You took an oath to defend it."

He nodded.

"Well?"

"Well what? I suppose I would've had to break my oath."

"To the point of hanging the jury?"

"Yes, I guess it could have come to that."

There had to be more, Elena thought, and of course there was. There was what Haggerty had told her in the front seat of her car. How could Allison have possibly felt bound by his oath with so little time left? She was the irresponsible one for insisting on winning an academic argument. "I think I understand."

He was amused. "You do?"

She looked away from him to gather up her files from the bench. Why was she even carrying her half written summation for Manuel Torres's trial?

"Maybe I was right about you, after all." He was looking at her with a still deeper delight. "Well, you see, one of the first days in court I looked at you and I decided that you were a very dangerous woman. Forgive me for being so forward, but I saw a lot of knowhow and a lot of the cold-bloodedness that seems to come with knowhow, but not really much else. Then yesterday as you were questioning Torres I had the same impression that you were dangerous—to anyone who wasn't on your side. And now again."

It hurt her throat to laugh, but she didn't care. "What have I done now?"

"You say you understand something I've only really understood for a few hours. I still seem to be underrating you."

"I don't think you are, Mr. Allison," she said, once again sorry she had ever allowed Jack Haggerty to sit in her car.

"Oh, I think so," he said.

"No. It's just that . . . . I know something about you I have no business knowing."

"That sounds enticing."

"Just intrusive."

He kept his smile, but there was the faintest paling under his cheeks. "A Mr. Haggerty?"

"He's a private detective I hired."

"I see. And a very thorough one, I suppose."

"Thorough enough."

He thought about it a moment, then spotted another delight. "And what was it you suspected me of?"

"I was just grasping at straws. Sometimes it comes with the territory."

He nodded. "Well, you don't have to be grasping at them now."

"Now?"

"You still seem to be suspecting me of something. Like for example, because I'm probably not going to be the poster child for the World Health Organization next year, you don't have to treat too seriously what we were just talking about." She prayed that she didn't look as embarrassed as she felt. "I would like to think you were wrong, for me as much as for you. I'd like to think I would've done what I said I would, whatever the circumstances. And I'd like to think that you wouldn't need my illness to win over a juror."

She started. For a second she didn't know whether it was because of the earnest way he was staring at her or because of the two sharp cracks from the fire stairs.

8

King knew that his nerve was going. It had started going on him the second Raymond had dismissed the jury and the jurors, Foy, Alvarez, Landers, and Myers had drifted out of the courtroom. For what now seemed like hours he had been frittering away his chances by staying where he was, daring Bordalato to do more than ask him if he was all right or sneak worried looks over at him from behind his desk. Fat chance that Bordalato cared about anything but clearing the courtroom for the next trial! And now even the bailiff had finished whatever he had been doing and had gone off maybe to lunch, maybe to tell McCloud that one of the court officers was acting screwy. Everybody seemed to be going away from him instead of coming to him. It was the same old story: he had to be the one to start something or nothing was going to happen. Everybody else was too busy trying to protect douchebag Gwynn or pretending to be sad about the spic Torres.

He couldn't sit anymore. His clothes stank like he had been living in them for a week. He got up and started for the jury door, then stopped. If he went through the jury door, he wouldn't have run into anybody. It was already lunch hour, and nobody used the back stairs during lunch hour. The rest of his nerve would have been gone before he hit the lobby. His only chance was to go out the main door and see who was still hanging around the halls. *Somebody* was sure to make a mistake.

He didn't know the people in the hall. A woman and a small boy were on the farthest bench. Two lawyers were arguing about something while they waited for the elevator. There was no guard at the reception desk, meaning that he was either gabbing with somebody in the library or copping a smoke in the john. King considered the library: there were sure to be pricks in there to challenge him. He could have gotten five or six of them before they realized what was happening. But how did he break the silence of everything to begin with? Just thinking about barging in and having to make the first noise gave him a chill. Maybe after he had broken the ice somewhere else he could go into the library. But not to start with.

If only it could already be happening!

He looked over to where the lawyers were trying to be sly about watching him as they talked. Two guineas. There were too many guineas for it to make a difference if he took two of them out. He seemed to have thought about everything except the practical matter of ammunition. Maybe he would've been better off taking the stairs down to the lobby and going home, after all. Tomorrow was another day. He could come back with more ammunition.

But it was too late. Even before the elevator door opened and he saw Brooks, he knew it was too late. McCloud, Morrison, and Bordalato came tumbling out so fast they were almost comical. McCloud was so busy being the energetic commander of the situation that he'd already taken several giant steps out into the hall before he stopped in his tracks, like Morrison and Bordalato behind him. "Oh, there you are, John," McCloud said, like everybody was supposed to believe that he'd come on the run for a casual conversation. "Bordalato was saying you were up here, and that reminded me of that little matter we never got around to tying up. You follow?"

It took him a second to realize why McCloud looked so strange standing in front of him. The captain didn't belong in an upstairs corridor. He should've been back down in his office, with his desk. He had looked weird that day down in the basement with Gwynn and he looked weird now.

"Hear what I'm saying, John?"

Morrison took a step forward. "Captain—"

He didn't wait for Morrison to finish his ass-kissing warning. He palmed his weapon before he had to watch McCloud's ugly black face admit that something was out of his control. The weapon felt like his now, just as much as it had felt like his back in his bathroom. It had come to work with him. It knew how to point and seize and crack when he called on it: they had practiced together.

The flash seemed so much higher than the sudden pull. He was taken aback to see McCloud reach for the pens in his shirt pocket before he staggered, looking mad at himself for staggering. King had been aiming higher. He was so out of weapons practice that he didn't know what he was doing anymore. The hall was making a booming noise, and the woman with the boy was screaming and Brooks was slamming his door closed like there was a wild man around who couldn't control where he was shooting. McCloud took forever to go down. Bordalato and ass-kisser Morrison looked terrified that McCloud would never hit the ground. *But it was happening.*

He snapped out of it. Morrison was worse than he was. The ass-kisser was so fast to worry about taking McCloud's job that he kept looking to make sure the captain was hurt on the ground. King was more accurate with Morrison—right into the beef through his hand above his holster. Morrison recoiled, going into the wall and then sliding down to the floor like runny butter. Blood started out of his side and down his pants like it wanted to make a pool with McCloud's, but it couldn't get past his hipbone. There was no way he was ever even going to leak together with McCloud, let alone take his job.

King remembered just in time that he'd been standing in one place far too long. His reflexes were still slow. He heard the yelling and the loud click of a door from down at the other end of the hall, but he didn't look around until he'd hurried over to get Morrison's weapon. Morrison gaped at him like a dead fish. The douche smelled of tuna, just like McCloud always did. The brownie had even eaten a breakfast like McCloud's to score points!

Bordalato was somewhere over near the window sobbing. Now that he had more ammunition, he should've plugged the fucker for being a tattletale and going downstairs after McCloud. Or did he owe Bordalato one for getting everything over with? Whichever, he had a more immediate problem with whoever was running down the hall toward him. He turned, switching his weapon to his left hand. He had never fired it before with his left hand, but it seemed appropriate now: one enemy showing from around the corner on his left, one shot fired from his left hand.

He scored a bull's-eye. Landers still hadn't seen what he'd hurried to see as he grabbed for his jaw and went spinning back against one of the wall benches. Landers's weapon, already drawn and cocked, banged on the floor and slid away without discharging.

There was no way the hammer couldn't have been screwed up, King thought, but Landers was past worrying about it. He was probably very sorry that he'd ever joked with Myers about going in on a Lotto ticket together.

He surveyed his terrain. There wasn't enough quiet, but there wasn't enough noise, either. Bordalato kept praying to himself under the window and the practical joker Landers kept gargling something. Down the hall the woman with the boy and somebody else were sounding excited behind a door. He didn't want anything from them. They had nothing to give him. He forgot about them as he put Morrison's weapon in his belt and went over to the fire exit. It was only when the heavy fire door slammed behind him that he remembered the library, and the court officer who must've been hiding inside with the lawyers. Should he go back? There had already been enough noise so that he wouldn't exactly be starting anything. But fuck them. They might get him as he went through the door. He wasn't going to be that easy a target. Just because McCloud, Morrison, and Landers had acted like shooting-gallery pigeons didn't mean they were all going to be that easy.

He started down the metal fire stairs. Someone was coming up in a rush. He hoped it wasn't Myers. He wanted Myers to find Landers first and be grateful to him for taking out the asshole. He was glad to see that it was Wilke and not Myers.

"King! What the hell is going—"

He shivered to hear Wilke's innocence. Morrison's weapon in his belt gave him away. But then Wilke's eyes gave *him* away. King was two squeezes to the good before Wilke got his hand to obey his brain. Hawk and thunder and spit, Wilke went head over heels down the staircase, his big ears not helping the dumbo fly at all. It felt better than cutting down Landers with his left hand. Push, fall. Fall, tumble. Kill, die. He would've never figured Wilke for the best one, for rolling over so fast that he managed to keep his blood to himself. The only thing he'd ever done with Wilke had been sharing the runs pool in the World Series the year the Cardinals had taken the Brewers. There were still going to be surprises.

He almost lost his footing climbing over the contorted heap that Wilke had made of himself on the next-to-last step. He stopped in front of the door on the landing just long enough to take out Morrison's weapon and holster his own. He shook away the thought that he might've been propositioning bad luck by switching. The important thing was that Morrison's weapon was loaded and his was down to one cartridge. He yanked open the fire door before he had to think about it too long.

He took in three people in the hall: one standing near the elevators, the other two on one of the benches about halfway down. Runty Rubin stared at him as if to say that he had no right being where he was if there was real trouble upstairs. King detested the stupidity on the judge's fart face. He tightened his hand on Morrison's weapon. Had Morrison really bitched to him about its being off slightly to the right, or had that been Finnigan's gun? He couldn't remember. He had to take the chance that it'd been Morrison and that Morrison had been right. Rubin didn't move even after being hit: he just stood still as a rock, ignoring the smear on his vest and squinting like somebody trying to read a sign with small letters. King fired again, lower and to the left. Morrison had been right about the flaw. Rubin dropped down so hard that the floor must've cracked his kneecap; then he just toppled forward onto his face and glasses.

He commandoed his weapon over to where the two on the bench were getting an idea about running away like the woman and the kid upstairs. It was too good to be true. He began to feel giddy. Alvarez started to yell or cry or just open her mouth; the teacher Allison stopped her and took a step forward. She was already wincing like she knew what it was going to feel like to be shot. Allison was standing partway in front of her like he could have chewed up anything thrown his way. She knew nothing. Allison knew nothing. The two of them were ridiculous.

"Mr. King . . ."

"That's right, Allison."

"Whatever . . . the problem is, there must be some way—"

"None."

His laugh finally got away from him. Allison didn't know what to say to him. The teacher, the professional talker, had run out of words. His polished shoes and neat suit were useless. He was going to fall down in a heap, and so was Alvarez. "I'm crazy. Ask her."

He shouldn't have said it. Even as he aimed at her, she was taking in what he'd said and straightening up behind Allison. He had been an imbecile to remind her of what he'd said back in the luncheonette, and now she was agreeing with herself all over again.

She was slipping away from him, even faster than Allison was. They didn't look like they were waiting to be killed anymore. Why the fuck had he opened his mouth?

And why didn't *they* say something?

He jumped at the tinkle as the red light went on over the first elevator. A herd of elephants seemed to be tramping up the fire stairs behind him. He had figured on a pincer move, but not so fast. But why think of Allison and Alvarez as part of the maneuver? They weren't. They were his way out of the trap. For now at least, they were more useful to him alive than dead.

"Over here, the two of you."

They didn't move. He'd given them an order, but he might as well have said nothing.

"I said over here!"

Allison finally nudged her, and the two of them started toward him.

The elevator was whining to a stop. "Faster!"

Allison led, she followed. She wouldn't have taken a step if the teacher hadn't insisted. But there would be time to puncture her airs later. He didn't mind making up the last few feet between them himself. The important thing was to have all their perfume and cologne in front of him when the elevator door finally opened.

Hobie Morgan stared out at Rubin on the floor. The giddiness started to rise in King's throat again. He'd drawn to an inside straight. "Right where you are, spook."

Morgan's blank eyes took in nothing. Only his twitching mouth gave him away. But one, two, three, it was too late for him to try to close the elevator door again. He hated admitting it. "Whatever you say, brother."

The elephants had stopped their stampede. He could smell them standing outside together on the landing, checking their weapons and giving each other the count before pulling open the fire door. He figured on Nobart and Finnigan for sure, maybe even Menelli off the main entrance. He still hoped that Myers would have a chance to get upstairs to see Landers before getting his feet wet.

The door came slamming open so hard that it seemed to boom off its hinges. Nobart and Finnigan, sure enough, scrambled in, guns drawn, like they were a circus act.

"John!" Finnigan earned a point for finding him first.

271

"We're all walking, Finn. The four of us."

"Walking where?"

He hadn't worked that out but was hardly going to say so. "First to Hobie's car," he heard himself decide. "We're going down to the lobby slowly, and you're going to clear out everybody down there."

"No way, John."

King didn't like the way Nobart was looking at his legs, like he was thinking a disabling shot might've been a better bet than a head kill. "You have eyes, Finn? I've got three of them. You need a show of my good intentions, I'll give you one and still have two left. You follow?"

Finnigan didn't get the joke about McCloud's favorite expression. "You can't get anywhere with this, John. We both know that."

King couldn't help laughing. "That's what you told Gwynn too, wasn't it?" Finnigan said nothing. "We're moving into the elevator now. We'll wait a few seconds so you'll have time to get downstairs and clear the lobby, then we're going down. Try playing with the power or anything like that, and these three are your responsibility. Understand?"

Finnigan nodded.

"Out loud, Finn! I want you and Nobart and everybody else on the same wavelength here."

"Yes."

"A-one."

He almost moved out too fast from behind Allison. Nobart was still realizing it as King yanked the teacher back in front of him. He liked the way that Alvarez came along automatically as part of the pair. She and Allison hadn't stopped holding hands since Finnigan and Nobart had crashed into the corridor.

"What now, brother?"

Hobie Morgan was another story. The statues of the three monkeys he had once had on his dresser as a kid had been swifter than the old nigger. They hadn't looked so ratty, either. "I just said what. Back up in there, and keep your hand away from the lever until I tell you to move it."

It couldn't have gone more smoothly if he had planned it for months. Hobie went back into the elevator, King kept Allison and Alvarez in front of him as he brought them over to the car, and

Finnigan and Nobart did nothing but keep their crouches. As Hobie reached over to pull the door closed, King felt like he had started something almost natural.

"We'll give them a minute to clear the lobby, then we go down. But only when I say so. Got that, Happy?"

Hobie nodded but didn't turn around. "You're the judge, brother."

Allison and Alvarez had stopped holding hands. The teacher stood in a corner of the car with his arms spread out over the railings on either side of him, looking down at his shoes like he was searching for some new ploy. Alvarez didn't look quite as superior. There were small beads of sweat on her forehead, and her mascara was smudged. He wondered if he smelled as bad to them as he did to himself. It really hadn't been too bright, closing himself into a small space with them.

"Look at the good side." Allison and Alvarez looked at him as if under orders. "If McCloud was still alive, he'd have one helluva time trying to explain two shooting incidents in one week. Now he doesn't have to worry."

Allison didn't know who McCloud was, but Alvarez did. She seemed to think it entitled her to something. "The thing we were discussing last week. In the luncheonette."

"That bank card business? Yeah, I was really off the deep end that afternoon. You were right. I was wacko. I've forgotten all about it."

If she'd volunteered to take his case that day, she couldn't have made him feel as warm as she did now by looking so helpless.

Allison cleared his throat. "Whatever they tell you they're going to do, pulling back or giving in to your demands, you know they never really do it. There's always a bad ending."

"For you too, then, teach."

"I'll take that chance. But you should let these two people go once we reach the lobby." He ignored Alvarez's look. "You're not thinking very clearly, King. There's no way you can reach the street with three hostages. It's too unwieldy. One hostage maybe, but not three."

Morgan seemed tempted to turn around and second the motion. Alvarez just stared at Allison like he was pulling a fast one on her. "You've got a point, Allison. One is enough—so I'll take her. Okay?"

Allison didn't have any more sense of humor than Finnigan had. He should have never told him about how he'd memorized dates in school.

"Okay, Hobe. Down we go. Nice and slow."

Morgan nudged the lever with his left hand and kept his right hand up on the bar of the door. The car gave off a small lurch, then started down.

"Think, King. With one hostage you might get out."

He laughed. Get out to where? It was almost worth telling Allison he hadn't planned that far ahead to see the expression on his face.

"Nobody ever got out this way."

"Benny Smith did."

He looked back at Morgan. The old fuck was looking down like he'd said nothing. "Say something, Hobe?"

Morgan kept looking at the door. "Benny Smith got out," he mumbled the same way. "Shot up a few in the buildin', but not the ones he took out with him. He let 'em go safe and sound coupla blocks away. Oughta keep that in mind, King."

He remembered Benny Smith. Years ago. He'd been in the Poconos on vacation with Edith. Hadn't been his fault that he hadn't been on the scene to help out against Smith. He'd been sitting next to the motel pool watching the Mannixes and Edith splashing water at the shallow end.

Allison, now mad at Hobie Morgan, started to say something else, but Alvarez cut him off. "Never mind. It doesn't matter. I don't think Officer King has thought things through beyond where we are right now. Have you?"

She knew that he hadn't. He hadn't even planned on all their jabber. He wished everything would just get itself over with.

"Here's the lobby."

He still had a few seconds before he told Hobie to open the door. He could've gotten them all, reloaded, and waited for Finnigan to blast through the door. He hadn't planned anything more than that. He didn't want some big goddamn scene. All he wanted was to be noticed as much as some punk like Manuel Torres.

"I open it up?"

Now even the spook was mocking him. But shooting the old bastard in the back would have been as satisfying as shooting a stone or a piece of the elevator wall.

"Where to, Officer King?"

She insisted on taunting him, on taking it right to him. She *wanted* him to go after her instead of after someone else. Who? Allison? Why was she so interested in protecting Allison? At least the teacher had the excuse of being a man.

"The administration offices," he said, returning her stare. "We're all going to walk over to McCloud's office and set up there for a while. You, over here."

She stepped over to the door like she was doing him a favor. She seemed to be getting bored with him and the big bag on her shoulder. The sweats on her forehead hadn't run down her face; they were still small beads.

"Okay, Hobie. Open up."

Morgan pulled back the door deliberately; he didn't want to see what was outside. The two elevators across the hall were sealed tight, or seemed to be. There was some scuffling off to the right. Court officers moving into better position, he was sure.

"You're the flower girl, Hobie. Just stay right in front of the lovely couple and go left."

Morgan stepped out. He started to glance right, didn't like whatever he caught sight of, and jerked his head back. "Sure about this, brother?"

He waited until Allison lifted his foot, then grabbed Alvarez under the left armpit and shoved the nozzle of his weapon under her left ear. They were a threesome now, none of them a clear target. "Just go slow," he said to Allison, who was apparently having second thoughts about moving.

It was easier to move than he would've thought. He caught Finnigan and Menelli out of the corner of his eye: They were with another uniform behind the entrance desks, looking like pioneers ready to defend their wagon train against the Indians. How many more of them were up ahead crouching near the offices?

None!

He couldn't believe their stupidity. They had packed all the visitors to the building inside the offices with the secretaries. The geese didn't know whether to stand frozen or dive under the desks. A big woman with a pink hat seemed to decide for everybody: she stood frozen, so everyone else was petrified. They were barely able to open up a passage for them. One of the secretaries in the back had collapsed at her desk. Nobody seemed to notice her. He had never been so close to so much fear in his life. They were like a gauntlet. They were fascinated. They watched him come, they watched him pass, they blocked off Finnigan's aim at his back by watching him go. A stupid telephone rang on one of the desks. An electric typewriter hummed. Morgan stepped over one of the typewriter wires like he was afraid of being electrocuted. The blond secretary named Cindy hadn't even bothered to stand; she just sat on her aisle stool staring at him with a new respect. He almost said something to her but then decided not to. He didn't want to make trouble for her once everything was over. He could tell from the commotion behind him that Finnigan had come out from behind his covered wagon and dashed over to the door to the offices. King could feel their weapons on his back, knew that the visitors he'd already passed were being hustled back out into the hall. Finnigan was improvising as much as he was. Without McCloud and Morrison around to tell him what to do, the douche was just trying to keep things together until the precinct sent reinforcements.

Morgan reached Alice Burke's desk and hesitated. There was no Burke in sight. King hoped she wasn't hiding in McCloud's office. He had nothing special against her, but he didn't need her around reminding him of the letter to Mrs. Thompson, either. "Keep going, Hobie."

Morgan started to move faster toward McCloud's door. Allison and Alvarez didn't follow his lead; they knew the pace King wanted.

"John!"

He almost went for it, almost took his weapon out of Alvarez's ear and turned back so he could see why everybody was scrambling again. "Nice try, Finn," he said, but so low that only Alvarez and Allison heard him.

He kicked McCloud's door closed behind him. They all looked like they felt safer to be on McCloud's carpet. Alvarez didn't even wait for him to tell her that it was okay to go over to the couch; she just pulled away and flopped down. Morgan gazed around like he was disappointed he had no more walking to do. He looked even smaller standing there in the office in his crummy work shirt than he had in the halls and the elevator.

Allison looked around at the wall plaques and framed photographs. He was unimpressed. "Now what?"

"You sit. We all sit."

He edged over to the window. Downstairs there were two squad cars and a crowd of about twenty or thirty people. Most of the bystanders looked like they had come from the unemployment office across the street. He drew the curtain and flopped down in McCloud's chair. Allison had taken a seat on the couch alongside Alvarez. Morgan lowered himself into the chair in front of the desk; he looked like somebody about to ask for a raise.

"Some work problem I can help you with, Officer Morgan?"

The spook grunted. Nobody thought anything was funny today.

"You better ask for something," Allison said, hitching up the legs of his pants so he wouldn't spoil the creases. "They're waiting."

He laughed and took his weapon from his holster. "Suppose I don't want anything?"

"Then I guess you have what you want."

He didn't know what that meant, but then teachers like Allison had always said a lot of shit they didn't want understood. The only time they got mad was when somebody called them on it. "Since we've all got lots of time, why don't you tell us what that's supposed to mean."

He didn't like watching Allison squirm. Instead, he concentrated on opening his cartridge snap and reloading his own weapon; he had gone as far as he dared with Morrison's weapon. It was a wonder he'd gotten through the lobby with the damn thing, if those squad cars outside meant that cops had already been out there with douchebag Finnigan.

"What about the bank card? Still want help on that?" Alvarez asked.

She was amazing, he thought. Once she clamped her big teeth around something, she didn't let go. "I told you. That's yesterday's news."

"Why? Because you want to give up without a fight?"

He almost fell for it, almost reminded her of why she was sitting on the couch in the first place. "No. Matter of fact, Alvarez, I passed that bank on the way to work this morning. They have a new card there now. Says Elena Alvarez. What do you figure to do about that?"

"Sue them, maybe."

"Nah, don't bother. Won't get you anywhere." He felt better with his own weapon reloaded. "Soon as you file your suit, some genius at the bank will get rid of the Elena Alvarez card and replace it with another one. Maybe one that says Hobie Morgan or something. What's your real name, Hobie?"

"Hubert."

"There you go. A Hubert Morgan card. That's how the changers work."

"Changers?"

For a teacher Allison understood nothing. "People who don't ever bother telling you what they're going to do. They figure you'll go along with whatever they decide. Like all we are is fucking house pets. Here, kitty, here's a new brand of cat food for you. Eat this or starve. Changers." Allison nodded like he finally understood; it was about time. "Your problem if you think you can get the best of them."

Allison stopped nodding. Alvarez didn't want to hear it. "Got something there, brother," Morgan said.

Just what he needed, having the spook agree with him. He would've been better off having Grace Chandler on his side. But why think about any shit like that now? He laid Morrison's weapon on the desk blotter and put his own on his lap where he could get to it faster than Finnigan or anyone else could open the door and zero in on him. It seemed to be taking them forever to remember that they could've reached him through McCloud's phone.

"C'mon, Allison. How about a game?"

"Game?"

"What we always used to do when there was a bunch of us and we had some time to kill. You know, like the state capitals. Something like that."

Alvarez was back to watching Allison for her lead; the teacher knew it too. "I guess we could do that," he said after a moment. "What stakes?"

"Stakes? What're you talking about?"

Allison sat back and crossed his legs. "Make it more interesting."

"I never bet on something like that. It was just for fun."

Now Morgan was watching Allison, too; it was like they had cooked up something together. "As long as you got them right, it was fun," the teacher said. "But when I was going to school, geography always stumped me. Particularly things like state capitals. I always forgot a few."

278

King knew which ones, too: South Dakota, South Carolina, and Vermont, for sure. "I never had that problem."

"You're lucky."

He recognized the tone: Finnigan trying to sweet-talk Gwynn down in the basement. But it was worth playing dumb to see how far Allison could take it. "Yeah. Bet against me, you'll lose for sure."

Allison nodded again. "Probably. Pierre, that's one I remember."

Morgan looked disgusted: he had been hoping for some action, and now Allison was giving away the hardest capitals for free.

"What stakes you have in mind?" King asked. Allison started to go into another number. "Cut the bullshit. Just say it."

He'd expected a little more bullshit; instead, Allison looked over at him defiantly. "Two capitals. You get the first one right, Ms. Alvarez stays. The second one right, Hobie stays. Get both wrong, they both walk out."

"That's it?"

"That's it."

Morgan's look across the desk was so hungry it was pathetic.

"You got to be kidding, teacher," King said. "If I lose, I lose. If I win, I get to keep what I've already got. You should buy yourself a casino."

"Either way, you'll still have me, which will make it easier for you to maneuver. And there's no one better than Ms. Alvarez to present your case to the public while we're both sitting in here."

"What case?"

"The reasons for all this, what else?"

"Who said there were reasons?"

Allison hesitated only a second. "If you prefer it that way, she can say that too. One way or another, people will know who you are and how you see things. You know Elena can do that."

He was treading water, and he wasn't the only one; Alvarez's expression said that she didn't know what the hell Allison was talking about either. "It's not because of some goddamn Lotto ticket, I'll tell you that much."

Allison nodded. "Exactly what Elena can say to them. There's bound to be television and newspaper people out there by now, King. She can tell them whatever you want."

He liked the way she was looking more and more uncomfortable at the idea of being his mouthpiece. He would've liked it a lot more if there was any real chance of it happening. But there wasn't. Even if he agreed to play Allison's game, he would win it, and she would never leave the office. There was as much chance of her being his lawyer as there was of her asking him to fuck her.

"But you won't mention any of that bank card stuff. That was a lot of crap, right, Alvarez?"

"Whatever you say."

Allison edged forward on the sofa. "Are we agreed?"

He could imagine her standing behind a battery of microphones and making a fool of herself trying to explain why there were so many bodies lying around the building. Not because of Lotto. Not because of a bank card. Not because Court Officer John King made less money than Morrison. Not because of some cat on Hillside Avenue or Edith or Grace Chandler or Eddie Mannix or a thousand other things. It would've been hilarious, he thought. Even dead, he would have the last laugh on everybody. She'd be defending him by defending nothing!

"What do you say, King?"

The intercom light on McCloud's phone finally came on. What Finnigan didn't know was that McCloud had cut the buzzer. "Go ahead. The first one for Alvarez."

"State capitals?"

"State capitals."

Allison sat back again, trying not to show how satisfied he was with himself. "Washington," he said.

He used to know that. Washington hadn't been one of the hard ones, like South Carolina or South Dakota. It had never been on his special memorization list. The capital had to be a well-known city. But was it Seattle or Tacoma?

"Do we have to go through with this?"

Allison waved Alvarez quiet without even looking at her. She fell back into the corner of the couch and covered her mouth in distaste. Morgan, on the other hand, was waiting for his answer like a railbird watching the horses cross the finish line.

"Washington," Allison said again.

"Seattle."

Allison shook his head. Morgan smiled, seeing Allison's response. Alvarez just continued looking disgusted. "It's Olympia."

He didn't remembered that. Had he ever known it? Where the fuck was a city named Olympia?

"Now mine," Hobie said to Allison. "Give him another good one."

The changers, he thought. When he'd been going to school, the capital had been Seattle. But now the changers had moved it to goddamn Olympia. Why hadn't he seen that trick coming?

"Ready, King?" He nodded for the hell of it; he couldn't win *or* lose. "Alaska."

That one he should've known, but he didn't. "I give up."

Allison was surprised by such a quick surrender. But he didn't offer him another chance. "Okay, then. They walk."

Hobie was already poised to get up; even Alvarez now looked interested despite herself.

He laughed. "Like hell they do."

"The answer is Juneau."

"That's nice. I'll remember the next time."

Allison moved up to the edge of the couch again, leaning forward like he was blaming himself for not being clear. "We made an agreement."

"No, we made a bet. And I guess I'm welching on it."

Allison didn't know where to look. His eyes seemed to get bigger in his drawn face. "You agreed."

He thought about answering the intercom; if he did, he wouldn't have to listen anymore to Allison. "It was a bet, a game. You won. Congratulations."

"It was no game!"

He didn't like the sudden redness in Allison's face; the guy looked like he was about to burst a blood vessel. Even the spook seemed afraid of something more than not getting out the door.

"For Christ's sake, King, you have to let them go! Those guards will be crashing through that door any second!"

He had to keep calm. "They will if you keep shouting. Shut up."

Alvarez leaned toward Allison, and the movement was enough to calm him down. But his face was still red, and his white hands were trembling. "You're right, of course. I'm sorry. But you have to let them go."

King put his hand on the receiver. He had to stall Finnigan and the cops. "And if I don't?"

"You can't mean that. Have the decency to live up to your bargain."

"No." He picked up the receiver. He felt better at the sound of Finnigan's voice asking if it was him. "That's right, Finn. I'm at McCloud's desk. Think that will help you any barging in? Don't bet on it. Talk to you later."

He put the receiver back. He had bought time. But for what? There was something petrifying in the way Allison was glaring at him. There was not a trace of forgiveness in his face, not even a pretense of understanding. He had crossed some line with Allison. He hadn't meant to, not to the point of exciting him like this.

"Listen to me, King. You let them out now or I'll come over there and take that gun away from you."

He answered—said something cool and daring. But he didn't believe his own words. The only thing to do was to shoot Allison and bring on the finish. All he had to do was take his weapon off his lap and aim. It would have even been a kind of self-defense.

"Now, King. Right now."

He was confused. He didn't know why Allison was insisting so meanly. Morgan and Alvarez could've stood up and walked out. He didn't own any of them. They were free to do what they wanted. He hadn't counted on taking hostages anyway. Why were they looking at him like it was up to him?

"Mr. Allison—" Alvarez was too late. The teacher stood up and took a step toward the desk. He seemed so much taller, so much broader, under the low ceiling. If only he had a weapon, he wouldn't have had to watch Allison's rage advancing toward him. He could've cut it down. There hadn't been any reason to bring matters to this point. He had never seen Allison so mad at him.

"Please, King," Alvarez called out from somewhere behind Allison. "He's serious."

"I'm asking you for the last time, King."

Allison was standing over him. He had never seen so much certainty. The man *was* going to take his weapon away from him. Would he even mind that? "If I let them go, I'm dead. You know that."

Allison didn't care; he didn't know what sympathy was. "I don't give a damn. Elena, Hobie, get out."

"You don't know what you're doing. I'll get you first."

"Now, Elena!"

282

Allison heard the shot and winced. He hadn't been the one to plan the sound. The electric fuzz in King's chest was like an alarm that had gone off too late.

Allison stopped looking at him across the desk and peered back at Hobie sitting below his elbow. Hobie was holding Morrison's weapon. The weapon had been fired recently. King could smell the cordite, even see it, across the desk. The spook looked paralyzed with shock. What had Hobie expected? You press the trigger of a loaded weapon, it almost always goes off.

His own weapon fell off his lap. He looked down at his shirt. It seemed to be on somebody else. It was billowing out over his stomach like it was trying to get off his body. His chest agreed: it was pulling from the other direction. There was going to be no more middle to him. He was stuck in between. He didn't even have enough left to recover his weapon from the rug.

Allison looked so sad, like he was going to cry. But at least he wasn't mad anymore.

Alvarez was standing in front of the couch, covering her mouth again. Hobie didn't know what to look like.

The door flew open. He recognized Finnigan and Myers. They had come looking for John King. He wanted to point to the window and tell them that John King had already left. They were too late. John King was already another person. . . .

9

Elena swallowed the two tablets before she drank the water, then swallowed a little water anyway. She handed the paper cup back to the paramedic. She couldn't remember having been in a judge's chambers before without the judge present. Was it even allowed?

"I'll drive you home," Jim Aherne said.

She shook her head. She didn't hear anything rattling around.

"You're in no condition to drive, Elena."

"Man's right, lady. You got to take it easy."

She agreed with whatever the paramedic wanted her to agree with. She was relieved when he finally packed up his satchel and walked out past the policeman posted in front of the door. She didn't want to talk about medical things. "What about Conboy?"

Aherne shrugged. "I know what your friend means. The guy's a neon sign. No way you can miss it."

Even with her nerves reduced to sawdust, she heard all the flaws in his reply. "A, he isn't my friend; B, he's making a serious accusation; C, if the accusation has any validity, you could be compromising your case; and D, Allison would never have gotten mixed up in this other business if he hadn't decided to stick around the building and help you do your job."

She thought at first he'd decided to humor her, but he just frowned. "You'll at least concede the possibility that I may know a little more about my jury than you or Mr. Allison? Call it a calculated risk."

"I call it shit, Jim."

Aherne nodded; he had expected the reaction. "And that's where we'll leave it until tomorrow," he said, putting a hand under her elbow and an arm around her shoulders and raising her from the chair. "But now let's get you home to bed."

She told herself that she was resisting him by not resisting him. She was *making* him stand her up, *making* him work her arms through the sleeves of her jacket, *making* him pick up and carry her bag for her. She had given him all these tasks, and that was the way he had to accept her.

He held her against him. She felt accepted.

At the door the policeman saluted her like she was somebody who should be saluted. She didn't have to acknowledge him, she had her lawyer to do all her talking for her. She wanted to laugh at the mess she had been reduced to. She had accumulated so many petty dysfunctions, she thought, that she didn't have time for any single one of them. The aching throat that she had felt since Santiago Torres's attack would simply have to make another appointment for hurting her in a special way. And not too soon, either, because she wasn't about to confuse her bruises with the bloodbath upstairs or the holocaust over at the jail. Her mess was still of small, random irritations.

Aherne steered her past the elevators and around to the side entrance. Down the hall a mob of television and newspaper people still had Hobie Morgan in a tight circle of silver-blue glare. Before today she had never seen one man kill another—she still hadn't. She had seen John King die, but she hadn't exactly seen Hobie Morgan kill him. She was thankful for small favors. Whenever she looked at the elevator operator again, she was going to see his scrawny shoulders and the palomino skin of his old hand around the gun, but never his face.

Whenever?

She stopped as soon as they stepped outside into the parking lot. She still had to make a decision, she remembered. Whenever she saw Hobie Morgan again, or *if* she ever saw him again?

Aherne was looking at her worriedly. "What is it?"

"The only reason I came back to the courthouse was to tell you I'm giving a month's notice."

He shook his head. "Tell me tomorrow."

"I'm telling you now."

"Okay, you've told me."

She resisted him. "Don't you want to know why?"

"Because you don't want to do it anymore," he said, talking more to the cars than to her. "Because you're fed up with the clerical work and the politics and that goddamm feeling you wake up to every morning that you ought to be a better lawyer than you are."

"Try better *person.*"

Aherne sighed; she was heavy, leaning on his arm. "Well, in your particular case, the better person is a better lawyer. Unless you want to start selling real estate."

She had been stupid to open her mouth, she thought; suddenly, everything was opening up inside her. He hadn't volunteered to carry her tears on top of everything else. She'd already put too much weight on him.

"It's okay," he said.

But she knew that it wasn't. She was even spoiling the effect of whatever pills the paramedic had given her. The numbness seemed to run right down her face to her chest and stomach. Her head was clearing too fast. She was going to be left with her headache again, and this time she couldn't take any pills for it. What she really needed was a whack with a rolled-up newspaper.

285

"I'm going to call the Winters boys," she said, looking over at the fins of an old Cadillac.

"For what?"

Elena shook her head, but the fins didn't disappear. "They're already getting used to the absence of their father," she told herself to say. "Even while we're standing here, they're getting used to it. His death is just prison time forever. I want them to know I understand that, that I would like to help them if I can. John King won't be able to interfere anymore."

Aherne seemed to understand. He didn't try to talk her out of anything as he led her over to his car. He did all the right things, even putting her in the front seat without making her feel that he was letting go of her, that she was on her own again. He strapped the seat belt across her chest. She was in no danger of flying through the windshield if he had to brake abruptly, she thought.

10

Hobie was disappointed. He'd figured at least one of the goofuses back at the building would've offered him a ride home. Stupid him. As soon as he'd finished answering all their questions, he'd been thrown right back into the pond. They all had jobs to get back to, they said. Had to get back to their papers and write their stories. Had to rush their tapes back to the TV stations so they wouldn't be late for the six o'clock news. Like he didn't know what having a job meant! Right now, making his way to the subway, he was still only twenty minutes ahead of the schedule he'd been on since before most of them had even known what a job was. That ought to have added up at least to a lousy lift in one of their TV trucks.

He shot a perfect gob into the trash basket on the corner. He'd saved at least two lives besides his own, and all he'd gotten out of it was a twenty-minute jump on tomorrow, which was probably going to run him into even more of those high school hooligans on the train.

Almost the only thing he had gotten out of it. For sure he was better off than the goofus King, with those pansy worries of his about not having more than an ID badge and about wanting to blow up some goddamn bank. And what about Morrison? Now let that goofus try to tell the other stiffs in the morgue how Hobie Morgan didn't count as much as a burro like Manuel Torres. Would have been talking out of the side of his mouth if he was still saying things like that.

The Indian was still taking it in hand over fist in the candy store. No denying that the shooting had been good for the geep's business, and if he knew his potatoes, the Indian would be collecting even more tomorrow before the building opened, with customers hanging around to talk those extra couple of minutes and buying gum and candy they wouldn't have bought normally. A few of them, he thought, might even go in for a Lotto ticket. The numbers were certainly obvious enough.

One for the shot that had brought down King.

Two for Allison and Alvarez being saved.

Three for the DOAs King had piled up in the building.

Four for the stiffs, counting King's wife.

Five for the date.

Six for tomorrow's date.

Hobie had to shake his head at their stupidity. Even if the numbers did come out 123456 by some miracle, the combination would've been spread around the city so thin, nobody would've won more than a few thousand. Policy was still the only numbers game worth getting into. Even a geep like Victor Diaz was a better bet than goddamn Lotto.

He came to the subway stairs and fished out his token. The old goofus coming up the stairs looked at him like he was a mugger or something. Thing was, he'd promised to give Ida a call after supper. But he really wasn't in the mood to tell her about everything and then have to listen to how it had all been the will of Jesus that he'd done what he'd done. It had taken more balls than Jesus had ever shown for him to grab the gun off the desk and plug King. He hadn't even been sure that all the safety gadgets had been off.

No, Hobie decided, he was going to give Ida a rain check for now. Let her hear about everything on the TV. What he wanted to do first was to see the expression on the vet's face. *Now* let Gallagher keep bullshitting him about all his military tactics and planning ahead. The only thing the vet had ever planned ahead for was having the old nigger around to cut the twine from the papers for him. Well, no more papers, and maybe the old nigger turned out to know more about tactics than Gallagher had ever dreamed of.

He went down the subway stairs and through the turnstile. The goddamn train was already leaving the station.

Later

1

On Margaret's advice, Allison had let the party develop without excessive ministrations by the host. She had been right. The guests nearest each other in graduation years had huddled together in small blocs around the living room and kitchen for less than an hour. As soon as they had exhausted real and invented memories, they had begun sounding out the younger or older blocs in other parts of the house, using a common profession, Sofia's skittish retreats under the furniture, or Allison himself to make the crossing. Now, more than two hours and two cheese-dish refills later, the years had merged almost completely. Nineteen sixty-five compared the cost of her wedding reception to what 1981 had just finished paying. Nineteen

289

eighty-three couldn't believe that 1968 had three children. Nineteen seventy-four had once worked for the same magazine publisher where 1984 had just started. Time, age, and interests had gone into the blender and come out as an antidote to awkwardness. Even the husbands, wives, lovers, and dates who had come along as bodyguards no longer were residue. Allison recognized them all as his party.

"I think we're over the lonely-hearts-club phase," Margaret said, emptying another bag of pretzels into a bowl on the kitchen counter.

Allison took a sip of wine and shared his smile with Lanny. In 1975, he recalled, Lanny had told him that she was making her boyfriend take her to a different ethnic restaurant whenever either of them could afford it. At one point she had reported twenty-seven national or regional cuisines accounted for. He was still fond of her. "And how old is Melissa?"

"Four next week," Lanny said promptly. "It gets messy sometimes, but my sister and parents have been a big help. The other day I read that David got a part in a new television series and I even felt happy for him. Maturity, Mr. Allison."

"Charles."

She shook her head, swallowing a mouthful of wine. "Chuck or Chuckie, okay," she declared. "But not Charles. I think I'll stick to Mr. Allison."

"Chuck or Chuckie! Do you hear that, Margaret?"

"Come to think of it . . ."

"To hell with both of you."

"Mr. Allison, then?"

Allison nodded. It wasn't a concession to distance, he thought, but only a confirmation of memory. He had no wish to change the memories now; they were what they were. Reinvention would have to come from Lanny's four-year-old daughter; she didn't know who he was.

Back in the living room he heard names that he hadn't heard since he'd retired. Arnold of Brescia. Cola di Rienzo. Anne of Cleves. Zinovyev. Zachary Taylor and Zachary Scott. He wondered who had invited them, then realized that he had. He counted another billion or so guests in the house. Fortunately, none of them had worn coats or were thirsty.

Paul Harper composed music. Elizabeth Geis and George

Martinez worked alongside one another for the city housing authority. Veronese was "into clothes" and Williams was just into her junior year of college. He took it all in until it was time to get down to work and tell them why he had invited them.

"You should've known you weren't going to get away without at least a few minutes of speechmaking." He let the mock groans subside. He wasn't used to behaving so formally in the middle of his own living room, but it also seemed appropriate. For the moment, they were the hosts and he was their guest. "What I have to say is this. Thanks to my unswerving dedication to a miserly way of life, the wonders of a rent-controlled apartment, and some astute investments made by my mother ages ago, I now have what is called a little nestegg. What I've decided I'd like to do with a part of that money is to establish an annual scholarship in world history at our favorite high school. That way, maybe all those dour administrative types you remember in your nightmares won't lose interest in the subject the moment Margaret decides that she'd rather go yachting in the Mediterranean than continue badgering them for a box of chalk."

He had counted on almost everything—the laughs, the surprise, the looks of approval—everything except Margaret slipping out of the room and into the kitchen before any eyes found her.

"Anyway, I'm mentioning this to you tonight because I would like the scholarship to bear not my name, but the names of all your classes. I think we have enough Rockefellers, Fords, and Carnegies to play the grand old humanitarian without adding the venerable name of Allison to the list. Besides, it'll make me seem generous *and* modest, and how many of us can claim to be both?" He was all right, he told himself, so Margaret had to be, too. "So what I'm trying to say here is that I want your permission to use your names and those of your classmates as the benefactors of this scholarship."

"Helluva long graduation ceremony."

Allison was glad he had invited Harper; he needed to laugh, too. "I suspect we can find some way of condensing the name. What I'd just like to know now is whether you're agreed and we can go forward."

Margaret appeared again in the entrance to the kitchen, a fresh glass of wine in her hand.

"Was that your intention from the beginning?" she asked

later as they sat in the window seat in the study looking out over the silent back yards.

"Hardly. If I had any intention at all, it was 'let's honor what's left of the old wreck while there's still time because nobody else will.' So maybe Elena Alvarez was wrong, after all."

"About what?"

"When she was warning King that I had nothing to lose. I did—an opportunity to change my mind about tonight."

Margaret rubbed her slender arms against the night chill and stared out at the sheets hanging on Mrs. Ellenman's line. She didn't like talking about the guard John King.

"Now there's something dryers have ruined," he said. "By the time she hauls in those sheets tomorrow morning, they'll be stiff as boards. I loved it when my mother gave me the job of folding them when they were like that. I imagined that they were linen soldiers. You had to give them the old one-two to get them down."

"Did you really believe King was going to let them go? Or didn't you care?"

Allison didn't recognize the brassy music coming from the living room. He knew it had to be his tape, but when had he bought it? "Oh, I cared plenty." She wanted more. "No, Margaret, I wasn't trying to get myself shot."

"Really?"

"Really."

He felt her relax. "Sorry. I just wondered."

"So did I. But only afterward. The damnedest ignorances end up getting called heroics or masochism or just suicide."

He started even more than Margaret did when Sofia suddenly leapt into her lap. The cat couldn't believe her luck to find the window wide open. "You never let her out?" Margaret asked, holding the animal by the scruff of the neck.

"She got out a couple of times as a kitten. Should have seen me trying to get over those two fences there after her. I suppose that made me afraid she'd get lost and I'd never see her again. Now she'd just get hurt if I let her out."

She smiled at Sofia, who stared intently into the night. "See these beautiful legs of mine, Mr. Allison?"

"Mmmm."

"They used to be quite good at climbing fences and trees."

"Not on your life."

292

"Okay," she smiled. "Not at night. But what about tomorrow, during the day?"

Sofia seemed to be awaiting his agreement as much as Margaret. "You'll change your mind when you sober up."

"Bet I don't."

"They're your legs."

"It's your cat."

"In the daylight."

"Only in the daylight."

She carried Sofia back out to the living room. Allison gave the cigarette smoke five more seconds to find the window and get out of the house, then he shut the window. Now somebody had put on one of his old Bud Powell in Paris albums. He hadn't listened to Powell's piano in years, maybe not since he had come home from Europe and, as part of his lingering grasp on Rita Nardi, had wanted to think about Americans on the other side of the Atlantic. There were a whole lot of things in the house he had forgotten about, it seemed lately. Maybe he still had enough time to get around to rediscovering them.

"You know who that is, don't you?" Paul Harper said, pointing to the stereo.

"Of course I know, it's my record." Allison laughed. "It's a woman in a Rome nightclub. Her name is Sylvie, and she knows all about me."

2

Elena came awake in the chair. The room was too dark, the light out in the hall too bright. She shouldn't have noticed either thing, she realized, she should have been sent home hours ago.

But now, focusing on the slight figure in the high bed, she knew that it was too late to go home. She had committed herself with her mother and the floor nurse as much as she had ever committed herself with Felipe and John when she had agreed to try to sneak up on their fort. If she stood up now and left the room, she would have been seen, and that would have wasted even the time she had already put in on everything. She had to stick it out.

She could tell that her mother was still breathing underneath the oxygen mask. She could also tell that the steady ralings belonged to her mother's lungs, not to some echo from the oxygen tubes. The distinction seemed important, seemed to emphasize that Virginia Alvarez was still very much among the living.

Elena shifted in her chair carefully, to see how many aches she had brought on her body by nodding off. She felt only a dull throb above her tailbone and a first pass by Mister Fuzz at her tongue. She attended to Mister Fuzz by reaching for a sour ball from the box on the table next to her. In bringing the candy up to her mouth, she wondered if there was something profound in the notion that it was easier to recognize the dark grape color in the darkness than it had been to recognize a light lemon or cherry piece before her catnap. She decided that there was nothing profound involved.

The doctor had said twenty-four hours at most, and Elena figured that about half of that was already gone. Did that mean everything would be finally over by noon tomorrow? Charles Allison, the juror on the Manuel Torres case, would have disapproved of the stringency of her logic, she thought; Allison would have insisted that she be less rigid and more rational. With her attitude, her mother would have until noon, not a second more or less; with Allison's, Virginia would last far beyond the doctor's prognosis or maybe not even another hour. Which was better?

She looked over at the bed again. Her mother would decide which was better, she told herself.

And in the meantime?

Elena thought about Richard Amos. There was no question that the cops had given him a going-over at the station house after the arrest. But had they also planted those two vials of crack in his car, as Amos claimed? She was going to have to take a closer look at Amos's relations with the precinct cops.

The grape taste of the candy was surprisingly strong. Her mother's raling under the oxygen was so consistent that it seemed almost natural.